THE LEGEND OF THE IMMORTAL KINGDOM

CALEB AND KATIE GARRAWAY

BOOK TWO

SEEKERS

CACVMEN PETRARVM ID EST

VBI TERRAM ATTINGIT SOLEM USQVE AD.

Iuvenci Caput

Sola Apicem

Castracta
Secretorum

Magna Fractionis

STAT ANIMA EIVS MONSTRABIT TIBI VIAM. SI NON

AVDIERIS DEIICIES VIAM I

The Legend of the Immortal Kingdom

Remnant Publishing
Copyright 2022 Caleb & Katie Garraway
ISBN: 978-0-9998795-8-0

REMNANT MINISTRIES
215 S. Marion Avenue
Washington, IA 52353

Remnant Ministries is a ministry sent out of the Marion Avenue Baptist Church. It is our passion that God would use our ministry to reignite a sacred fire in the hearts of His people to do their part in standing for Bible truth, reaching the lost, and pursuing national revival. We believe that from the youngest to the oldest, it is our time to do our part in reaching our generation. God has not called us to be comfortable or complacent, but to be courageous and committed. **Remnant Ministries** is God-and-Country in nature with a strong three-fold thrust: Redemption to the lost, Revival to the church, and Restoration to the country.

www.remnantministriesonline.com
calebgarraway@gmail.com
917.412.0059

Scripture quotations are from the Authorized King James Version.
Edited by Terri Sawyer.

PROLOGUE

Off the Eastern Coast
of South America
1574 A.D.

The night burst to life as cannon fire blazed on the horizon and rolled like thunder across the rough waves of the sea. Carlos Mendina grabbed hold of the railing and peered into the darkness as he heard the artillery shells whizz high overhead, narrowly missing the main mast.

"Pirates!" he shouted furiously.

Men instinctively scurried about the deck, preparing the ship for defense. Others below began to ready their offensive positions under the barking orders of their first officer. Mendina felt the ship come alive as multiple cannons roared, blindly piercing the darkness and violently shaking the flooring of the deck. One of their shots found its mark as it struck the front end of the pirate's vessel. The men cheered, but after a few moments of thick silence, another enemy salvo illuminated the horizon again to reveal not one pirate vessel present but seven. Like enraged hornets, volleys came erratically and relentlessly from their entire fleet.

A giant plume of salt water splashed into Mendina's weathered face as cannon fire decimated the ocean before them. He gritted his teeth and rubbed his eyes clean. Peering over his shoulder through the flapping sails, he found the other two ships in his convoy falling behind as five of the pirate vessels broke away from their attack formation and began to run them down.

Suddenly, like an unexpected punch to the gut, the wind was knocked out of him and he was thrown back across the deck as two cannon balls slammed into the side of the Spanish galleon. Bits of timber and debris showered him as he quickly stumbled to his feet and gripped the railing once again. His eyes began to search for the coast. They were close, so close, but he feared they wouldn't make it, not in time, and not after the intensity of this sort of attack.

In spite of the crew's best efforts to put distance between them and the pirates chasing them down, the enemy vessels loomed larger and larger. Absently, he reached up to clutch the gold medallion hanging from his neck. Shutting his eyes, he bowed his head. The sounds of the battle swirling about him fell away and a moment later, he opened his eyes with resolve and knew what he must do.

"Aapo!" he shouted over the yells and cries of the crew, "Aapo, where are you?"

Mendina squinted, straining to find the young man, his adopted son, amidst the chaos, debris and smoke. His mind drifted back to the first moment he saw the boy in the wilds of the Amazon, whimpering up in the nook of a tree, alone and afraid. Someone had been foraging in their makeshift camp at night and Mendina wanted to put an end to it. But when his eyes set upon the starving form of the child, his heart melted. He discovered that the boy's tribe had abandoned him when both of his parents died in an accident. They superstitiously believed that he was a bad omen and left him on the banks of a far-away tributary for the gods to deal with in their own way. Aapo struggled to survive for the next month until his salvation finally came. Carlos Mendina, Spanish explorer commissioned by King Philip II to discover what secrets the Incan jungle held, came across the frightened, malnourished lad and lovingly took him in as his own. That was a decade ago. Now Aapo was a resourceful eighteen-year-old who brought humor and morale to Mendina's men as they traversed the unknown.

Rushing across the main deck, Mendina spotted him hunkered down low, trying to help the crew by handing out their weapons and reloading their flintlock pistols and rifles as quickly as his hands could move.

"Master Mendina!" Aapo exclaimed with wide eyes when the explorer took hold of his arm.

"Son, you must do something for me," Mendina told him urgently. "One last thing?"

"What?" Aapo asked, confused. "What do you mean?"

It crushed Mendina to see such fear in the young man's eyes, but there was no time for fear, not with the enemy closing in around them.

Mendina opened his mouth to explain when the ship lurched forward and an explosion made his ears ring. He glanced toward the stern as black smoke billowed into the night sky, blocking out the bright light of the stars.

"Captain! The rudder's out! We're dead in the water!" a sailor bellowed as he climbed up out of the hatchway. By now, the pirates' vessel was closing in fast. Several pirates hung from the rigging, poised for attack, whistling and jeering. Some were even singing menacingly as they paced back and forth on deck with sword in hand. Their eyes gleamed fiendishly in the flicker of the blazing torchlight.

"All men to stations," Captain Barto ordered. "Prepare to be boarded! Fight for your lives!"

"Aapo, listen to me," Mendina said, grabbing hold of the young man's shoulders. "The pirates cannot get hold of the medallion. Do you understand me?"

Aapo bobbed his head. "Yes, of course."

The ship jolted as the pirate vessel brushed up close to their own. Mendina removed the medallion from around his neck, grabbing his dagger and a wooden mallet lying on the floor near an ammunition barrel. He laid the gold piece atop the barrel, placed his dagger in the center, and with a grunt, struck the dagger handle with the mallet. A crack in the medallion appeared, and after a couple more strokes of the mallet, it split in half. He quickly handed one piece to Aapo. "Guard this with your life. No matter what happens to me, you *must* keep it safe!"

Musket fire sporadically cracked back and forth between each vessel as the pirates flung over grappling hooks to bind the two ships together.

"Here they come!" a sailor shouted fearfully as vicious enemies swung over the railing to engage in hand-to-hand combat.

"Fight, men! I'll not lose my ship this day!" Barto roared as a second pirate ship came along their other side and bound itself to them. "Fight!"

Mendina pulled Aapo into a desperate embrace.

"Whatever happens, know that I love you, my son! Now, go quickly and hide," he whispered to the boy, then drew the cutlass at his hip, and rushed into the fray.

The fighting was fierce, and there seemed to be no end in sight. One by one, the crew fell until only a handful of men, including Mendina and Captain Barto, remained.

"Lay down yer arms!" a deep voice ordered. He paced authoritatively across the quarterdeck, glaring down at his captors with bloodshot menacing eyes. "Surrender and I'll spare yer lives!"

Barto lifted his chin into the air but dropped his sword. His men and Mendina followed his lead. "What do you want, pirate?" the captain snarled. "We have no gold or goods aboard this vessel! We are the king's men! Your attack on us is a direct violation of the Crown! Do you seek to make war with King Philip himself?"

"Your king be not here to save ye now," a man behind them ruthlessly remarked in a low-tone.

Mendina turned his attention to the pirate standing on the deck above them, his hand resting casually on the helm. A wicked grin spread across his face as he laid his cutlass on his shoulder. A dark brown messy beard hung from a face that was weathered by the sun and scarred by his days at sea. His shirt and breeches were stained with blood as he stomped down the steps to the main deck. His blue eyes narrowed, not on Captain Barto who stood defiantly, but on Mendina.

"Ye may not have treasure, I'll grant ye that, but I do have on good word that ye possess something the best bullion in the world could not offer," the pirate said as he approached Mendina. Their eyes locked in a steely gaze. The pirate's lips formed a cruel half smile revealing a few remaining yellowed rotten teeth. He raised his cutlass to the explorer's neck. "Ye do have somethin' of value, don't ye?" he spoke softly.

Mendina stiffened. "I am not frightened of you, pirate."

"Oh no?" he cackled, turning to his shipmates. "That is a shame, now isn't it, lads?" His companions joined with him in belting out obnoxious laughs.

"Me hears things on the water," the pirate went on, keeping his blade pointed at Mendina's throat. "Ye found something, didn't ye? Because I know who ye are, Carlos Mendina, famed explorer."

Barto and the other surviving crewmen exchanged uneasy glances at this remark. The pirate slithered closer, whispering, his foul breath making it hard for Mendina not to gag. "Ye know the whereabouts of the city of gold."

His men cheered as he shouted, "And why sweat and bleed for just a few chests of it when we can live in rooms made out of it?"

Mendina opened his mouth to deny it when the pirate's blade shifted and pulled up the gold chain hanging around the man's neck. He grabbed for the medallion, eyeing it greedily.

"In the name of the king," Mendina uttered, "our lips will forever remain sealed."

"Will they now?" the pirate said with a leer. "We'll see about that." He yanked the chain free and Mendina tried to grab for it. The pirate stared at the dangling half medallion, then thrust his arm over his head for the rest of his crew to see.

Captain Barto suddenly lunged forward, a dagger in his hands Mendina hadn't seen, and attacked. The rest of the crew shouted and the fighting started once again. More of the crew who had kept themselves hidden below charged the deck and Mendina rolled to the planks, picked up his sword, and went after the pirate captain who was quickly escaping with the medallion. Not caring for his own safety, he threw himself at the man's legs, tackling him to the deck and punching him in the face. They rolled and came up to their feet. The pirate captain clutched the medallion in his fist, glaring Mendina down.

"Ye won't win this fight," he warned.

Mendina took a step closer. "And you won't find what you seek without all the pieces."

The pirate held up the medallion again, as if just realizing it was incomplete, and let out a furious roar. He charged Mendina, swinging his sword wildly and yelling at him to hand over the rest of it. The explorer said nothing but dodged the attacks, his sole purpose now to retrieve the medallion. But a familiar yell distracted him and he whipped around to find Aapo near the railing on the other side of the vessel, wrestling with a pirate. The man barred a toothless grin as he struggled to pry out the glint of gold that was in the young man's hand.

"Leave him alone!" Mendina blasted, surging forward, but he stumbled to his knees as he was clobbered on the back of the head by his adversary's sword handle. His own sword clattered to the deck and was kicked far from him by his enemy's bloody boot.

"This laddie means something to ye now, does he?" the bearded pirate jeered, walking past Mendina, the tip of his sword scraping into the wooden deck. "Bring him to me and I will run him through with my own blade!" Three other pirates grabbed hold of the young man, and began to drag him forward. Aapo's fist still tightly clutched what was within.

"What be causin' yer knuckles to turn white, boy?"

A burst of desperation pushed Mendina back to his feet. With a yell, he latched onto the pirate's back and brought a small knife up to the man's throat.

"Leave him be!" Mendina warned. "Right now! Leave him be!"

The pirate captain carelessly laughed as he felt the blade nicking his skin, but the other men quickly released the boy from their grasp out of respect for their leader.

Mendina's gaze locked with Aapo's.

"Go!" he shouted to the boy. "You must go *now!*"

An explosion ripped the ship apart sending crew and pirates sailing through the air. Mendina spun wildly and landed hard on his back, staring up into nothingness. Fire crackled around him as it consumed the ship. Boots and bare feet stomped past his head, but no one stopped to see if he was alive. Slowly and grunting in pain, he tried to sit up and found the part of the ship where Aapo had been standing was gone, devoured in the explosion.

"No," he whispered. "Oh God, please, no! Let him live..."

The pirate captain staggered over Mendina, his face bloodied and twisted in fury.

"At least you'll never find the city now," the explorer softly chuckled as he looked up into the man's wild eyes.

The pirate's lip twitched, his sword hovering over Mendina's chest. "I will, I promise ye that. And ye won't be alive te stop me."

CHAPTER I

Dominica
1995

Adrian Fitzgerald breathed in the salty ocean air as he eagerly watched a pod of striped dolphins playfully swim alongside the research vessel. The clear Caribbean water sparkled with various shades of blue and green. He grinned, not believing he was finally out in the real world and on a real-life treasure hunt. For years he'd been dying to get out of the classrooms and library and make a name for himself. He smirked a little as he scratched at the scruff on his face and mulled over the endless possibilities. The wind whipped through his curly black hair. It felt exhilarating to be on his first adventure fresh out of college.

A hand clapped him on the shoulder and he turned to find his friend James Alexander staring out over the ocean with a bright smile on his face. "Beautiful, aren't they?" he asked, pointing to the aquatic creatures that whistled and squeaked as they jumped in cadence out of the water. Adrian nodded. "God's diverse design has always fascinated me," James remarked, almost lost in a trance as he observed the playful mammals.

The lush island of Dominica jutted out of the blue water in the distance. "Well, we've made it, Jim!" Adrian said with a laugh, changing the subject. "We actually made it."

"I'm thankful the board approved this expedition," James' smile broadened as he glanced over his shoulder at the rest of the team sent by the university. "This is going to be great for our dissertations."

"Just think about it. We could make a discovery that'll change history!"

James laughed, "How about we first find something worthwhile to study?"

Adrian shook his head absently. Ever since they'd met in the registration line of Cambridge University as freshmen, the two had become fast friends; but they were almost polar opposites. Besides having different native homelands, James being from Great Britain and Adrian growing up in Scotland, their personalities and life goals were quite different. In Adrian's mind, his best friend had never been overly ambitious — being content to explore simply for the sake of exploring and learning. But not Adrian. He was determined to leave his mark on the world one way or another. Great discovery always meant great legacy, he believed, and why waste your life just working in the shadows?

Their expedition to Dominica was born from the rumors of a Spanish galleon convoy that was fiercely attacked at sea during the late 1500's somewhere off the coast of South America. But these were not just any ships; according to legend, they carried King Philip's personal exploration team who had traveled deep into the heart of the Amazon during the fall of the Incan Empire. It was believed that they had come across something big. But before they could share their findings with the world, they were allegedly tracked down and destroyed by Captain Isidro "Bloodfist" Torres.

There was only one problem — this notorious pirate was a myth, like Davy Jones. There was no documentation of his existence. Supposedly, his small fleet of ships would slither out of the mist under the cover of night and blanket their prey with cannon fire. Within a matter of minutes, they looted, slaughtered, and sank treasure-laden vessels. Most believed it was a fabricated story to keep crews frightened away from the islands surrounding Dominica close to

South America. It was discovered years later that many questionable characters sought refuge here and wished to remain undisturbed from snooping ships or government-employed galleons. However, whenever a lone vessel or straying convoy entered these unfamiliar waters, they were never seen or heard from again. It was said to be the work of Captain Torres.

According to legend, Bloodfist, as most referred to him, possessed a vast treasure trove and an even greater secret — but most scholars believed this to be nothing more than the result of intoxicated pirate talk. Adrian Fitzgerald, however, did not. Over the years, Adrian's fascination with this pirate and his treasure grew, eventually causing him to choose to study it for his doctoral thesis.

His painstaking research led him to tirelessly traverse back and forth from the British Library in London — the largest library in the world — and Biblioteca Nacional de España in Madrid, Spain. After carefully cross-referencing countless letters, original documents, and seamen diaries from the 16th and 17th centuries, he started to believe that the rumors of Captain Bloodfist were true.

All his findings pointed to Dominica as the pirate's base of operations. Could it be that Bloodfist himself was the one who originated the rumors to keep prying eyes away from his hideout along the coast? The chain of islands around Dominica had been used over the centuries as safe havens for pirates and other ships passing through. They'd been explored countless times before, but Adrian adamantly believed that Dominica still held something that had yet to be discovered. Something vital about Captain Bloodfist himself. All the signs seemed to point to it, and he felt it deep down within his soul.

His final discovery was three months ago, when he found an obscure ledger on a dusty old library shelf in Madrid. It was a thick, heavy book with an animal skin cover and two metal latches that kept it fastened shut. No key could be found to unlock them, so Adrian gently pried them open with his pocketknife when no one was looking. Within, he found a catalogue of the names and last words of men who were hung in Barcelona, Spain, for crimes they had committed at sea.

It did not take long to find the name that he had been looking for: Bartolomeu Santos, a Portuguese pirate captain that was captured by the Spanish in 1632. In a state of frenzy to avoid hanging, he spewed forth news that he knew of a treasure trove worth millions. As the noose was being slipped around his neck, sporadic words were recorded in Portuguese about a field of rocks in the north, broken holes, along with something about fists and blood. The writer must have thought these were incoherent babblings, but Adrian understood that this had to do with Bloodfist himself. He already knew that Santos boasted of being a member of Captain Torres's crew when he was a young man. And Dominica was the only island in all his research that had an uninhabitable rocky region in the northern-most tip of the island. How coincidental, he thought, that Agoucha Bay was even close by — a small inlet perfectly surrounded by tall cliff ridges that could easily hide a couple of vessels. This had to be it; all the evidence seemed to point to this location.

Through his gathered material, Adrian was able to convince the archeological panel at his university that the rumors of Bloodfist's existence were potentially true. The men on the board smiled at his youthful enthusiasm. They gave him their blessing with a limited three-week budget and the ability to choose up to eight fellow graduate students to go with him during their summer break.

Adrian walked out of that meeting with his head held high. He knew that spearheading such an expedition from such an elite school would make an impressive line item at the top of his resumé.

Of course, when it came time to recruit, his best friend James Alexander was all in, and together they were able to persuade seven other members to join their team. Over the last couple of months, James often gave Adrian a hard time about how intense he was in his work — that this research was consuming him. But Adrian let him. He knew that James enjoyed ribbing him, and the fun banter back and forth sustained him as he endured many sleepless nights poring over old documents. Adrian always quipped that he would be the one laughing at his chum when it turned out the rumors of Captain Isidro

"Bloodfist" Torres were true.

What truly motivated Adrian Fitzgerald was his secret desire to ultimately uncover what King Philip's men had found deep in the Amazon. Could it be this was the 'great secret' that Bloodfist's legend spoke of? Did he ever record what it was? Adrian had so many questions racing through his mind and heart, but no one — not even his friend James Alexander — knew that this was his endgame. He was willing to go to the ends of the earth to figure it out. *One step at a time, one clue at a time. It will be the discovery of the century,* he convinced himself. But the first step would be finding Bloodfist's treasure trove. If there were any answers, they would be safely stowed away in the man's most precious belongings.

Adrian grinned again as he looked with wide eyes at Dominica; he believed destiny awaited him on the mountainous island. "You got this, old boy," he whispered to himself, then turned to help his team gather their equipment to make landfall.

Once most of the crates had been organized on deck, he stood atop one of them and gave a few last-minute instructions to the crew. They scattered into small teams and began completing their checklists. Hopping down, he strolled over to where Alexander was double-checking the scuba gear they would possibly use.

"You're a natural born leader," James grinned. "That was quite the rousing pep talk."

"What can I say," Adrian sniffed, laying on his natural-born accent a little thicker. "It's in my Scottish blood."

"Yeah, yeah, royal blood and all that… descending from Robert the Bruce. Well, I hope we find what you're looking for," he nodded toward Dominica. "You've spent a lot of time getting us to where we're at today."

"Yes," Adrian sighed, with a far-off look. "I know this is the place. It *has* to be."

"Your findings are pretty convincing, but it's still just a hunch… uh, an educated guess," his friend teased him.

Adrian laughed, "Come on, Jim, it's more than that!" He gave a sly smile. "Besides, when have I ever been wrong?"

"Our finals last semester," James answered without hesitation and his friend punched him lightly on the arm. "I'll follow you, Adrian, you know that. If nothing else, *someone* has to keep you out of trouble."

"And that is exactly why I specifically asked for *you* to be on this expedition. But one of these days, you might want to get out of my shadow."

James looked up at him, "Is that what you think I've been doing all this time?"

"I'm just saying, as your friend, don't you want some great discovery to be under *your* name one day? Have people talk about *your* adventures?" Adrian winked, "Not how you merely tagged along with your handsome, smart, charming friend?"

James sighed, shaking his head. "Maybe one of these days you'll learn not to be so full of yourself."

"Oh, come on. Why else have we been studying for the last five years, eh? Why are we bothering to get our PhD's if we don't want to be the first to discover something legendary lost in the annals of time?"

"For the sake of the lore and the history," James replied, becoming a little more serious. "To keep it alive for generations to come. To learn from our past. To glean from ancient cultures. Come on, Adrian, we've had this discussion many times."

Adrian shrugged to lighten the direction of the conversation and said, "I think I'm just excited to finally be digging in the dirt, you know? That's it." He glanced up to find James watching him worriedly. "Look, if we don't find anything here, I'll be okay." Adrian smiled broadly. "Promise! I'll shift my focus and move on to something else. But I truly think something is out there."

"That's what bothers me," James said in a lower tone, eying to see if anyone else from the rest of the team on deck had been listening. "It could simply be *something*. What happens when you find only one thing? One clue? One piece to a much larger puzzle? It always leads to another. And another. And another."

"Then the game will be afoot!" Adrian laughed, slapping his friend on the back. "That's the glory of exploration. Besides, we have our whole lives ahead of us!"

"True, but there have been many people just like us who have spent their whole life following clues that ultimately led to a dead end. Is a pirate's treasure really worth your whole lifetime?" James paused for a moment, then shook his head. "Adrian, forgive me. I shouldn't have let this conversation go so far. I know how much this means to you, but before we step off this vessel, I just wanted to make sure you've asked yourself if this is the journey you wish to take with your career? If we find something, I just don't want you to lose your way," his voice trailed off.

Adrian burst into a heart-warming laugh again, "Lose my way on something that has no meaning?" His eyes glinted. "I genuinely appreciate your concern, old chum. I know you always have my back! You're a good man."

James gave him a kind smile, and then mentioned that he needed to speak with the some of their team.

After watching his friend go, Adrian hurried to his cabin below deck. He closed his door and, using the key hanging around his neck, unlocked his footlocker. *If Jim only knew the things I have uncovered. If they all knew,* he thought to himself.

"I will be the next Percy Harrison Fawcett," he whispered, smiling to himself. "Only I will come back alive." He pulled out his stacks of notes on Captain Isidro Torres and tossed them aside. Beneath them was a metal lockbox. Using a second key, he unlocked it and gingerly picked out several very old and brittle documents to look at again. He never grew tired of smelling their pages and running his hands over their handwritten words. He was drawn to them. *Addicted to them, Jim would say,* he chuckled. He had lied to James, lied to everyone, about his true purpose. But if he found what he sought, it would be worth it in the end.

⊗ ⊗ ⊗

James Alexander rolled back off the small motorboat and fell into the water. He checked his oxygen levels as he moved slowly, watching as Adrian followed him down. The afternoon golden sun illuminated much of the seabed far below. Schools of bright colored fish swam in and out around the kelp and coral rocks that rose up from the sandy floor. James gave his friend a thumbs up and they headed forward together.

According to the information Adrian had gathered, they were looking for a network of caves on the rocky, far northern side of the island. The locals were greatly skeptical of the existence of such a place, however. Many of those Adrian and James interacted with just smiled — none of them had heard of the name Captain Isidro "Bloodfist" Torres before and none of them had ever heard of such an 'outlandish legend of buried treasure,' as they called it.

"There is much conspiracy about sunken pirate vessels in the waters around Dominica," one notable local guide mentioned. "But they are just good stories at best," he finished with a toothy grin. People looked at the two young men and their team as naïve thrill-seekers, which inwardly infuriated Adrian. Whenever his face would grow red, James would lay a knowing hand on his shoulder and that always seemed to defuse him.

The entire northern region was rarely traversed on foot since it was useless to those who lived there. The landscape was littered with massive algae-covered rocks and thick with trees and jungle vegetation. The coast was lined with jagged cliffs and jutting, slick outcroppings. Through the generations, children were told to stay away from this dangerous territory because of the natural hazards. Numerous times Adrian and his team discovered precarious places where one could easily slip and fall to their death — either being dashed on sharp rocks or drowned in the rough, foamy waters below. Nevertheless, they pushed on carefully. Because the vast area was avoided by locals, it gave Adrian all the more reason to thoroughly explore it. Yet after two weeks of searching, nothing had been found.

This made Adrian furious and discouraged. Late one evening, James knocked on the door of his friend's room at the Rejens Hotel in Portsmouth and gave him a brilliant idea that made him restless with excitement. What if they had been looking in the wrong place? He reasoned that it *was* over 400 years ago when the treasure was supposedly hidden. A lot can change in nature's landscape over that period of time, especially when there's the constant erosion and shifting of rough seas. What if they could find an entrance to the caves *under* the surface of the water? Adrian decided to give the team a day off to enjoy the island while he and his friend followed their hunch.

Earlier this morning as they loaded their gear into a rented motorboat, some of the local fishermen on the pier gave warnings of caution. Very few ever swam or fished in those rocky waters. Sharks were known to swarm there at various times throughout the year and the currents could be unpredictable at best. But the two young men, feeling desperate after coming this far, were willing to make that risk.

The swim through the water at the island's northern tip wasn't smooth. The current was much stronger than they had anticipated; and, at times, they were helplessly thrust against rock outcroppings or flatly pressed against the submerged cliff face they were carefully searching. They moved slowly and methodically along the two-mile stretch for hours. James quietly prayed they'd survive in one piece as he followed his friend's flippered feet. Adrian dove deeper and James stayed right behind him. Aside from the dangers close at hand, they enjoyed their work. Tropical fish darted around them and giant kelp rising from the sandy ocean floor made for a surreal environment beneath the waves.

Adrian suddenly slowed, then righted himself, gesturing ahead to murkier waters. James squinted through his goggles and then nodded. There, barely visible in the rocks, was a jagged opening. Adrian's mind flashed to the words of the Portuguese prisoner — 'broken holes.' *Could it be?* He pushed himself farther down and switched on the flashlight attached to his scuba suit. He felt James's hand moments later and his friend pointed to another opening some twenty meters to the right. *Yes!* Adrian's heart was racing. *This had to be it!*

There turned out to be a half-dozen caves total. All of them appeared to be small inlets but one; the opening of the largest cave was big enough for both men to go in, side-by-side, floating upright. Adrian signaled that he wanted to save that one for last. They took turns exploring the smaller inlets, discovering that the caves only went in about five to ten meters and simply nestled sea cucumbers, urchins, and starfish that wished to remain undisturbed.

Adrian waited for James with anticipation at the mouth of the largest cave. He shook his head as his friend finally slipped out of the small inlet he had been exploring. Of course nothing was going to be found in there, but James always enjoyed taking his time to "observe God's beautiful creation" as he would say.

They floated together for a moment, staring up at the wide, dark, jagged mouth. A soft current gently sucked them forward. As they surrendered to its pull, their lights scanned the coral-studded walls. Adrian suddenly grabbed James' arm and the men froze as a large shark swam between them, not paying attention to them at all. Thankfully, it looked like a nurse shark and didn't seem to care about the two men. Once the creature was gone, Adrian slowly led the way. The tunnel narrowed at times but continued to work its way deeper and deeper into the cliff, while it was also working its way upward. Adrian abruptly stopped, causing James to nearly bump into him. The roof above the angled tunnel rose up into what appeared to be a dark underground pool.

They carefully swam up and through and found themselves breaking the surface of the water in a large cavern. They moved toward a stone ledge and hauled themselves out of the water.

"This is incredible!" James blurted out as he removed his tank and mask.

Adrian gazed with wide eyes. "Indeed! I think we're somewhere inside the cliff and below the very rocks we've been exploring these last couple of weeks!" He turned around, taking in the cavern as his friend stood and did the same. "Look at the ledges surrounding this pool," he remarked, tracing his flashlight along the rim, "These stones, they were *carved* to look like this."

James nodded, running his hand appreciatively along the smooth, hewn stone. "This took time to do."

"Look over there!" Adrian exclaimed. Off to the far end was a small landing area crudely dug out of the rock. Old gin bottles lay sprawled on the ground, a few wooden crates stood loosely stacked around each other with a bronze candelabrum on top, and two hammocks stretched out on hooks protruding from the rough stone wall. Adrian let out an elated laugh, "This is it, old chum!"

From the small landing, a narrower set of ledges had been carved, leading up like stairs along the side of the rock. He pointed them out to James and they set off swimming across the pool toward them. Taking their time feeling for the best finger holds so they didn't slip, they reached the end of the narrow steps to find a shallow alcove toward the top of the cavern. It too had been roughly carved out of the rock.

"Help me out, Jim!" Adrian shouted back to his friend. Before him was a hewn entrance, but earth and large stones the size of basketballs had filled the doorway.

"Be careful," James warned as he surveyed the damage. "We don't want to cause another cave-in!"

"The earth is not fresh; this has been here for a while, so we should be fine." Adrian was already rolling the big rocks away to make his way through.

"Adrian, you don't know how far this is going to —"

"I didn't come all this way to let a few stones keep me out!" he gasped, cutting off his friend as he hurled more rocks into the pool far below. "Come on, man! Don't just stand there!"

James knew there was no stopping him, so he cautiously proceeded to help.

After ten minutes of digging, they both collapsed to the floor to catch their breath. James squeezed his friend's slumped shoulder.

"Maybe we could come back with the rest of the team."

Adrian pulled his shoulder away, quickly leaping to his feet and snarling, "Not a chance, Jim! I want to be the first one to —" His foot slipped and he spun backwards into the rocks. Instead of stopping, the stones groaned and gave way, cascading down into a deep chasm. Adrian's momentum plunged his body through the doorway. He frantically grasped the sides of the opening, before his body was flung through the hole and followed the rocks that had gone before him. James rushed forward to grab his friend, clutching Adrian's scuba suit and bracing himself in the entryway to support both of their weight. Adrian let out a wild expression of relief as he regained his balance, safely suspended with his feet still on the ledge. He slowly turned around to see another very large cavern.

Light spilled down through slits in the rock ceiling above. This one was far from empty.

"Jim," Adrian gasped.

"I see it," James replied with a whisper, his eyes widening. "You…were right!"

Adrian shouted with excitement as James pulled him back up. As quickly as caution would let them, they descended the narrow steps lining the cavern wall to the wide floor below. Many more ledges had been carved here, stacked with numerous chests, trunks, and crates. Several gold coins littered the ground and James picked one up slowly. "This is Spanish bullion," he whispered in awe.

Adrian ran his hands over all the trunks but paused at one in particular. "Jim, look at this."

James rushed over to see two crossed fists carved into the wooden lid. "Do you think…?"

Adrian held his breath and lifted the lid. It creaked as bits of wood splintered and fell to the ground. Inside were various trinkets, rolled up maps, and an old worn coat. A flintlock pistol and sheathed cutlass were also among the items, but on top was a small leather-bound book. Gingerly, Adrian opened it and gasped.

His hands trembled with excitement as he pointed to the

flowery signature on the inside cover of the book. "The log book of Captain Isidro Torres." he whispered. "He was real, Jim! He was real!"

He carefully turned the first few pages, and a slow smile crept over his face. "This is incredible! There's so much that we can learn from this." After a few moments of silence, he looked at James who was reading over his shoulder. "It looks like he documents everything... dates, ship names, locations as best as he could describe. Think of all the treasure yet to be discovered!" Adrian exclaimed with a laugh.

James clenched his jaw as Adrian passed him the ledger. He was growing more and more concerned with his brilliant friend. He had such a bright future in archeology — not amateur treasure seeking. Sure, all of this was thrilling, but he was afraid that it would consume Adrian. Why would he want to throw his career away chasing ghosts and vague wreck sites?

"What are you looking for?" he asked as his friend took things out of the chest and frantically dug further into it.

"Something's got to be here."

James was bewildered. "What are you talking about? This is what you wanted. Proof of Bloodfist's existence. It's all right here!"

Adrian suddenly let out a triumphant yell, "Hello! What's this?"

He gently removed a folded bit of parchment from the trunk. Slowly, he opened it to find a handwritten letter and something gold attached to a chain resting inside. His eyes widened as they quickly scanned the document, "The greater secret...I believe I've found it!"

"What? You lost me," James frowned.

Adrian looked up in glee, "*This*, my friend, is what all of the research has been for. I knew that if we could find Bloodfist's trove, a clue would be left behind. Listen carefully: '*On ye pendant bears the symbol of the coveted city, Paititi. I sought its riches years on end. Alas, no man ever split his lips, no matter how much blood lost. The answer resides with the rest of the pendant, it must. My body weakens and I fear I'll never lay eyes upon it.*'"

"Paititi?" James asked in disbelief. "Adrian, is this what you've been after this whole time?"

Adrian's eyes held a lustful glint as he held up the chain. The gold pendant glimmered in the glow from their flashlights. "Famed city of gold, Jim. Can't you just see it? We could be the first ones to actually find it. This pendant right here, this is the key!"

James shook his head. "Do you hear yourself right now? That place is a myth, nothing more."

"Just like Bloodfist was a myth?" Adrian demanded sarcastically. "No, it's real and this is the proof. We can find it now. We'll be famous! Our legacies would be immortalized!"

"I don't believe this!" James stepped back. "What happened to the guy who simply loved history and lore? Since when did you become so keen on fame and glory? And wealth?"

"Since I realized what was out there for the taking." Adrian declared with an unsettling coldness. He then began to rehearse to his friend the entire legend. The Spanish galleons. The king's exploration team. Something big in the heart of the Amazon.

James sat down, his mind spinning, "This is crazy."

"But this is where it all begins. Come on, old chum. No one has ever been able to find it; but you and me — we could do it! We're brilliant. You know that we make a good team." Adrian leaned forward, dangling the pendant into the light cascading from above. "And this is the first clue that's going to lead us to it."

James hesitated for a moment, but then he shook his head. "I'm sorry, my friend. But I can't do it. I won't." He stood up and tossed the ledger back in the trunk. "I'm pursuing my passion for linguistics and archeological studies. Not treasure hunting."

"You're going to waste your time in old books?"

"And you're going to waste your life on a fool's errand?" he argued, feeling like his friend was turning into a stranger right before his eyes. "This has been sitting here for hundreds of years. That second half of the pendant he claims to exist could be at the bottom of the ocean. You'll never find it. And even if you do, who's to say it'll lead you to anything at all?"

Adrian's eyes darkened. "Say what you want, but this would be the greatest discovery of modern times. Paititi has been the most coveted lost city in human history."

"And how many people have died trying to find it?"

Adrian chuckled menacingly, "With great risk comes great reward, my friend. We're *already* one step closer than everyone else."

James sighed. "Look at where you're standing. We're in Bloodfist's cave! He's real. Your research paid off. Can't you just be happy with what we've found here? It'll take months to catalogue all of this stuff —"

"It's not enough!" Adrian shouted, his voice reverberating off the walls.

James flinched at his harsh tone. Adrian's eyes softened as he realized that he had hurt his friend. "I-I'm sorry, old chum. I didn't mean to yell at you like that. I'm just... so excited that something far greater could come of this, you know?"

"I understand," James nodded. "And I forgive you. Just keep your head in the game, you hear?" He smiled to try to lighten the mood. "I don't want your ambition to get you killed!"

Adrian sniffed and then slapped his friend heartily on the back, "I wonder what those old birds on the university panel are going to think of what we've discovered!" They both laughed together.

"Speaking of which," James turned to make his way back up the narrow ledges, thinking that Adrian was right behind him. "We need to inform our team of what we've found down here. Knowing them, they'll be impatient to see it! We should also contact the local authorities right away; I'm sure they'll be more than thrilled to lend a hand. I wonder if there's a way we could excavate through the ceiling and remove everything that way? Wouldn't it be a whole lot easier if we could haul these heavy chests up with a crane? Of course, it might take us a couple of days to pinpoint the location from above, but hey, at least we've found it!" By now he had reached the top of the cavern. He looked back over his shoulder to find Adrian sitting Indian-style on the stone floor under the light flipping through Bloodfist's logbook.

"You coming?" James shouted down to him.

Adrian snapped his head up from deep concentration and stirred to his feet. "Yes, I'll just be a few seconds behind you."

James hesitated, then made his way down the short entryway they had dug their way through. As he carefully climbed down the second set of narrow ledges, he debated whether or not he should leave Adrian alone with the pendant, but he wouldn't steal it, would he? No. James believed his friend to be better than that.

Still sitting on the cavern floor, Adrian studied the intricate markings on the half of the pendant he held in his hand. One way or another, he'd track down the missing piece. There had to be a clue in the journal. He had made sure that James never looked through the entire chest. Beneath where the parchment and pendent lay on the bottom was another small leather-bound book — Bloodfist's own writings. No one deserved to read that but him. And if it was filled with Captain Torres' personal quest to discover Paititi, this was information the rest of the world did not need to know about until he had discovered the city of gold himself.

He took the parchment, folded it into pieces, and shoved it into the front of the diary while he made a quick plan of action. If James said anything about the diary or the pendant to the team, Adrian would consistently claim he was mistaken. There was no photographed evidence, and their conversation had not been recorded. Though his deceit would forever remain between the two men, Adrian was willing to live with that. *With great sacrifice comes great reward,* he thought to himself. After securing the pendant and journal in a watertight pouch at his thigh, he quickly put his gear back on, gave the cavern one last smile, and ascended the narrow steps.

CHAPTER II

Present Day

G
o Drew!" Kaci shouted, beaming from ear to ear as she jumped to her feet in the stands. Her mom was right beside her, and together they cheered as he caught the football and charged twenty yards down the field before being tackled. He flashed them a smile as he tossed the ball to the ref, then hustled back to be with his team before the next snap.

It had been just a few months since their adventure with Uncle James during Spring break. Some days she still didn't believe what they had accomplished together — a hair-raising adventure following clues left by the early Church to find 1st century Bible scrolls before the Demeons could destroy them. Every once in a while, she still woke up in the middle of the night from a scary dream of Kadir and his hooded acolytes.

Their mom was stunned at all the danger they had so boldly faced. As the two teenagers spared no detail, Kaci lost count of how many times their mother had put her hands up to her mouth. Even though she voiced her disapproval at all the risks they took, she couldn't help but beam at the character and courage of her two children. "You're walking in your father's footsteps," Mrs. Howard said. "He would be so proud of you, as am I. God used you both in a wonderful way. But please — don't put yourselves in harm's way like that ever again!"

Since then, Drew and Kaci's lives had pretty much returned to normal. They jumped back in and finished the rest of their school semester with admirable grades. Now, they were thoroughly enjoying summer. Though Mrs. Howard was still fairly busy at her law firm, she dedicated much more time to spend with her children after their harrowing adventure. This thrilled 15-year-old Kaci. She loved hanging out with her mom, who lately felt more like a best friend. Together they keenly watched as Drew hurried to take his position on the field as running back and waited for the ball to be snapped. Kaci tucked her long golden brown hair behind her ears and continued to clap, her green eyes sparkling with excitement.

That summer, an NFL team in the region had sponsored ten different football camps across Minnesota, Iowa and Nebraska for a few hundred of the most talented high school players. Drew was lucky enough to be selected to attend the one held in their rural Iowa town. He had held out little hope of being chosen, figuring there were many more qualified guys than himself out there. But Kaci never doubted her brother. He was just a year older than she was and all their lives they'd been close, especially since their dad's death. Kaci couldn't believe how much Drew had improved his game since starting football camp. He pushed himself hard that week in the drills, learning as much as he could from the former college and professional athletes investing in their training. They formed the young men into teams, creating an intermural league, and each afternoon and evening they played against each other. This was now the final game determining which of the two remaining teams would be champions.

"This is intense. I don't know if I can watch!" her mom laughed, sitting down and shaking her head. Things were down to the wire for Drew's team. They were still 40 yards from the endzone with less than a minute remaining on the clock. They were behind by four points, so a field goal was out of the question. What they needed was one final touchdown. The ball was snapped and Kaci held her breath, watching the clock wind down.

The quarterback stepped back then launched the ball into the air. Drew sprinted down the field, eyes completely focused on the ball. Kaci's mom was on her feet again. They clutched each other's hands, holding their breath as the ball flew through the air. Just as it looked like it was going to go too far, Drew leaped up, thrust his hand out, and caught it nimbly with his fingertips. He dodged a tackle and landed right in the endzone. The stands exploded, but Kaci and her mom cheered the loudest as the ref blew his whistle and signaled upright with his hands. Touchdown!

In a matter of moments, the game was over, and Drew was surrounded by his teammates. They hoisted him up into the air, shouting his name as he removed his helmet. His short brown hair was wet and plastered to his head, but he didn't care. He laughed, his blue eyes bright with joy. He did it! He won the game for his team. His sister had been right. He should have more faith in himself. His smile faltered, wishing his dad and Uncle James had been there to see it all. The guys set him down on his feet a few moments later and buzzed excitedly as their coach called them toward the locker room.

"That was quite a bit of talent you showed out there, young man," a voice said and Drew turned to see four men standing near the locker room door with clipboards under their arms. Drew noticed the college insignias on their polos, and he respectfully stopped to greet them. They shook his hand in turn, beaming at him.

"Thanks. Lots of practice," Drew told them, his heart racing. These had to be the college scouts who were rumored to come to the championship games of the summer camps.

"Well, rest assured we've got our eyes on you, son," a man with a black beard and white baseball cap said. "All of us do. If you keep going down this road, there is a good chance you'll have a successful career with the pros."

Drew felt his face grow hot. "Wow, that would be awesome!"

The four men chuckled. "That it would." The scout in the white cap slapped Drew on the shoulder. "Now go on, celebrate with your team. We'll be in touch."

Drew turned and raced into the locker room to be bombarded by his team all over again. He had met most of them here at camp and had become fast friends with them all. They goofed around with each other, tossing dirty jerseys and cackling until their coach walked in. He clapped his hands and the boys settled down.

"That was one *awesome* game!" he declared, and the boys cheered and whooped some more. "Alex," he pointed at the team's quarterback, "good throw! Drew, good catch, son." The room erupted again. "And team!" coach interjected. "It would not have been possible if everyone didn't work together. You guys on the offensive line and those of you who blocked for Drew... That's what it's all about! Because —" he let his voice trail off while he cupped his hand to his ear.

"Teamwork makes the dream work!" the players shouted in unison.

"That's right! All of you young men have a promising future in football. Think of it — you are the *winning* team in one of the most premier football camps in America! Did you see all of the scouts up in the bleachers?" The players nodded as they looked at each other knowingly. "Pursue your dreams. Don't let anything stand in your way. Plow through any obstacle just like I've trained you to plow through the defensive line."

Drew and a few of the other boys smirked at the coach's metaphors. He always liked to go a bit overboard.

"Most importantly, follow your heart. Anything is possible if you put your mind to it. But you need to know what you want to do. Is it football? Is so, run toward that endzone and never look back. I believe in you, boys, all of you." The coach held out his hand and the whole team closed in, covering his hand with theirs. "1, 2, 3 —"

"To victory!" they all shouted.

"Now hurry up; you've got something waitin' for you that you've all earned!"

Drew and the rest of the team cleaned themselves up and exited the locker room in a herd with their duffle bags. The band played a victory march as they walked out. The announcers box welcomed them theatrically, stirring the crowd to their feet as they roared with a sweet cheer. Drew's heart raced as he felt exhilaration rush over him. Their coach led them to the center of the field as they basked in the glow of victory. Each player was warmly greeted by the team rep from the Vikings and given a small shiny football trophy. *How cool!* Drew thought. *I'm going to put this on my bookshelf. Whenever I see it, it'll remind me of how amazing it felt to make that winning catch!*

Afterward, the team took a few moments to say goodbye to each other.

When Drew spotted Kaci chatting with some friends from their church's youth group and his mom talking to their youth pastor, Mark, he rushed over to join them. He picked Kaci up in a hug, then did the same for his mom, making her squeal. He turned and held out his hand to Pastor Mark who gave it a hearty shake.

"What a game, Drew!" he smiled.

"You were great out there," his mom said proudly.

"Yeah, you were amazing!" Kaci chimed in. "I saw you talking with some scouts. What did they tell you?"

"That… they were impressed," Drew said hesitantly.

"They should be! That last catch at the end?" Kaci stretched her hand up as high as she could, "I was worried you weren't going to make it!"

He playfully rolled his eyes. "Thanks for the vote of confidence."

"What? Just being honest," she joked.

"Uh-huh." Drew waved to his last few teammates heading off with their families. He turned to his friends in the youth group. "Thank you guys for being here! Means an awful lot to me that you'd come all this way."

"We wouldn't miss it!" Pastor Mark said, and the teenagers nodded in agreement. "Stuck in the church van with this crew?" he winked. "That was the only down side about it." The young people laughed.

"Seriously though, you did awesome out there, man. Way to

hustle and give it all you've got." His friends nodded their agreement and began clapping again.

"Thanks, Pastor Mark! And thank you, guys!" Drew remarked, a little bashful with all the attention. "Pastor Mark? Can I, uh, can I talk to you for a minute?"

"Sure, Drew," Mark said, putting his arm around him and pulling him off to the side. "You guys can head to the van with my wife; I'll be there in a minute."

The youth group waved goodbye and sauntered toward the gravel parking lot. Kaci was in the thick of them, chatting excitedly with all the girls.

"I'll be in the car when you're ready to go," his mom told him, hugging him once more. "You take your time."

When they were by themselves walking along the field in silence, Pastor Mark started by saying, "You really were good out there. You should be proud of yourself. All your hard work and practice is serving you well. You're a great testimony of Ecclesiastics 9:10 — 'Whatsoever thy hand findeth to do, do it with thy might;'"

Drew rubbed the back of his neck, his cheeks growing hot. "Thank you."

"You don't like all the compliments," Mark said with a quiet laugh.

"It's just a lot to take in, you know? I worry sometimes that I'm going to get wrapped up in all of this," he said, spreading his arms wide.

Mark nodded. "I'm glad you're being careful about this stuff going to your head. Because it can. And fast. Remember what I've told you since day one?"

"Yeah. That football is fun, but it shouldn't be my life," Drew replied.

"Yes. Enjoy it; this is a part of the season you're in. But there's so much more to life than this game. You've told me a few times before that you feel like God is calling you to go into full-time ministry. Remember last year at youth conference? Tell me honestly, do you think football fits into that?"

Drew puffed out his cheeks. "Honestly? No. But then when I talk to the scouts and hear coach and my teammates — I wonder sometimes. I wonder if *that's* what I should be pursuing."

"I want you to succeed," Mark told him sincerely. "But I really believe that you'll only reach your full potential by finding and doing God's will."

Drew exhaled, thankful he was able to open up to his youth pastor. "I know what you're saying is true. But it's just so hard sometimes. Like, I can't see the will of God. I'm not sure what the next step is that I'm supposed to take. I'm a 'go-getter,' you know? I like to have a plan and accomplish stuff. Honestly, part of me wants to go all in on football because… why not? I could go so far and have a great life. College and then the pros maybe. It'd be amazing. The scouts tonight singled me out and talked to me. You know how incredible that is? As a pro player, I could make a lot of money and then give a lot of it to God. I can see things laid out for me this way…." His voice trailed off.

Pastor Mark waited for Drew to finish before he shared with the young man some truths God had been impressing upon his heart all evening.

"Deep down though," Drew continued in a more thoughtful tone, "like at night when I'm just lying in bed and I can't fall asleep, it's just me and God. And I feel like He wants me to live for Him — like there is a burning in my chest. I just don't know how." He sighed again and Pastor Mark patted him on the shoulder.

"It's okay to wonder about the future. God wants us to be completely dependent on Him. We are to walk by faith and not by sight. What does Proverbs 3:5 and 6 say?"

"'*Trust in the Lord with all thine heart; and lean not unto thine own understanding. In all thy ways acknowledge him, and he shall direct thy paths,*'" Drew easily quoted from memory.

"Do you believe that to be true?"

"Yes sir, I really do."

"God's got this; He *will* lead you. Sometimes it's difficult to wait, but waiting for God's will is never wasted time. It's *part* of God's will. The next verse in Proverbs 3 is overlooked many times. You know what it says?" Drew shook his head. Pastor Mark continued, "'*Be not wise in thine own eyes: fear the Lord, and depart from evil.*' Be careful not to make big decisions based on what *you* think is best. Instead, stand in awe of who God is and follow after Him, running far from sin. Remember, the Bible warns that if we ignore God's leading and go our own way, '*the end thereof are the ways of death.*'"

Pastor Mark laughed as he thought about what he was saying. "I'm not saying that playing football is going to kill you. It's just that if we choose to go our own way without God's stamp of approval, we're going to be absolutely miserable. I'm not saying it'll be easy, choosing God over fame and popularity. But I can promise you that living a life for God will never bring regrets." Pastor Mark smiled as he said, "I've always been happiest when I was in the center of God's will. I'll pray for you, Drew, that God will show you His will, that His calling in your life will be evident, and that you'll be willing to choose His way over your will when the time comes."

He paused for a moment looking out over the field as the evening sun spilled forth its golden rays. "Honestly, Drew, the will of God is the most adventurous thing that life could ever bring."

Drew couldn't help but smile as he thought back to his recent escapades with Uncle James and Kaci. "Yeah," he said with a soft chuckle, "I guess you're right."

"Just keep your eyes on the Lord and remember He has a wonderful future ahead of you. Focus on obeying Him every day in the little things, and eventually He'll show you His will for the big things."

Drew nodded, but he couldn't help thinking back over the game he'd just played, the golden trophy he'd held in his hand, and how amazing it felt to be cheered on by his team and the people in the stands. It wasn't hard for him to imagine that times 100 if he made it in the pros. He could be a star. Everyone would know his name. Those scouts were pretty positive he'd make it big.

"Any chance I could do both?" he asked Pastor Mark with a grin.

"Be in the ministry and play pro football? That would be a sight," the youth pastor smiled. "Just pray about what I've shared with you. Ultimately, no man can tell you what the will of God is for your life. That's something you will only be able to know from the Lord as you daily walk and talk with Him." He suddenly changed the subject, knowing the hour was growing late. "Tell you what, why don't you and your sister join us for ice cream at Marty's? I'll even buy you a double cheeseburger if you're really hungry. You deserve it!"

After they found Kaci and Mrs. Howard and got permission to ride with the youth group, their mom said she'd see them at home. Their rural town was small enough for everything to be in a safe walking distance, which Drew and Kaci loved. It would be nice to enjoy the cooler night air together on their short walk home after a hot summer day.

They squeezed into the church van and headed from the school toward Marty's Burgers and Custard, one of their favorite hangout places in town. As talk of the exciting game swirled around him, Drew did his best to remember his conversation with Pastor Mark. He was thankful for the chance to get some of his worries off his chest and appreciated the solid Biblical counsel from his youth pastor. *My future can wait,* he thought as he gazed out the van window. Right now, he just wanted to enjoy his friends, a juicy burger, and the lingering thrill of the big win.

James Alexander shuffled the pages together and set them gently inside the leather binder. A lop-sided grin slowly spread across his face as he remembered the adventure he had with his niece and nephew just a few months earlier. Greece would certainly never be the same without them around. They were two of the brightest teenagers he knew. He sighed, standing to place the binder on the bookshelf in his study.

He circled back around his ornate L-shaped executive desk and settled down into the plush leather office chair. He took off his glasses, gently holding the gold and brown tortoise frame as he cleaned them. Ever since the monsters went home, his house had been quiet. He didn't realize how large, empty and lonely his stately mansion was until Drew and Kaci had come and filled it with laughter and life. Now, the silence echoed off the ornately carved wooden walls and sloped ceilings. He hoped they would've been able to visit him in London again this summer, but Drew had been invited to that football camp. That, and he didn't think his sister would let them come back too soon after he let them join him on his quest throughout Europe and Egypt. Of course, in his defense, he had no idea that it would get as dangerous as it did. It all started out as an innocent trip to France... Alexander shook his head with a chuckle and put his glasses back on.

At least his sister was spending more time with her children. She sounded happy the last time he spoke to her on the phone, and it eased some of his worry. Things had not been easy since her husband died.

As the antique grandfather clock in the corner of his office chimed 1 am, Alexander stretched and yawned. He considered turning in for the night, but his mind was moving too quickly to fall asleep yet. *Just a bit more studying, a mug of warm milk, and then I'll head to bed,* he decided.

He leaned forward and dug into his notes on the lecture coming up. Things had not slowed down for the professor as he entered the summer months. Students and interns from around the world flooded in for the summer semester, keeping him busy giving lectures and teaching several courses at Cambridge. There hadn't been much time to catch his breath, but he liked it that way. Idle time did not suit him, and nothing was more frustrating than wandering aimlessly around his home.

A phone rang down the hall and a moment later, Simmons, his butler, appeared in the doorway. "Call for you, sir. It's the monsters," he said with a grin.

Even Simmons missed the teenagers running around the mansion.

Alexander thanked him and took out the cordless phone. "And what trouble are you two up to today?" he asked.

"Hey Uncle James," Kaci and Drew said together making him laugh. "Sorry to call you so late," Drew continued. "But we figured you'd still be up."

"Drew's game was today," Kaci glowed. "You should've seen it!"

"I take it you won?"

"Oh, he did. He scored the winning touchdown and the scouts were there. It was the best game he's played ever."

Alexander laughed as Drew tried to shush his sister. "Sounds like I missed a great time."

"It's okay," Drew assured him. "We know how busy you are."

"That is sadly the case. But I want to hear all about it!"

"After you tell us all about these lectures you've been giving," Drew told him with an edge of excitement in his voice. "We hear you've been talking about our adventure. I wish we could be there and listen sometime. Maybe even help fill in some of the epic details about the train ride and the Demeons and all that."

"I'm sure they would love to hear from you and watch your sister's rendition of certain events, too. She would be highly entertaining." They all laughed together. Alexander then proceeded to share with them the lectures he'd been giving and how much more research was being done thanks to the discoveries they'd made. Drew and Kaci in turn gave him a play by play of the game. His nephew didn't sound as happy about all of it as Kaci did. Alexander worried for him sometimes; he could tell something was weighing down on him. Drew was a talented young man, but his future would be wasted if he spent his life playing football instead of pursuing the will of God. As he listened, he prayed that somehow he would get an opportunity to be more of a spiritual influence on the boy.

"Well, Uncle James, we're on our way home right now from

eating ice cream with our youth group," Kaci concluded.

"Thanks for taking our call!" Drew interjected.

"Anytime, my little monsters. I love you both very much; you're never a bother to me. Be safe!" Alexander warmly replied.

"Okay! Bye!" the teenagers said in unison.

Alexander hung up and sighed. Maybe a trip to the States wouldn't be such a bad idea after all. He ran his fingers through his gently combed back brown-gray hair.

"Simmons," he called and his faithful friend appeared in the study doorway. "I think I'm going to plan a trip soon."

"Ah! Going to squeeze in a vacation between all your lectures and classes?" the tuxedoed butler smiled.

"Why not?" Alexander grinned, as he fondly pondered the idea.

"Several rather important people might not be too thrilled about it, but I think you need a bit of time away from this stuffy old place. Cambridge will survive without the great James Alexander for a little while." He winked and said he would start working to clear Alexander's schedule. James was thankful for his family's butler; Simmons had worked for the Alexanders since James was young. He wasn't sure where he'd be without the man.

Alexander paced around his study. The bookshelves lining the walls were filled with texts, scrolls, artifacts, and various other souvenirs he'd collected over the years. Every bit of wall space was covered with maps, framed photographs, and postcards. Knickknacks from his visits to countries around world lined more shelves, each one with a story behind it. His gaze lingered on a map tacked to the wall, a map he hadn't looked at in a very long time. For the last few years, it had been covered with various other projects and archaeological finds. Seeing it uncovered startled him and piqued his curiosity. He must've removed what had hung in front of the map absentmindedly and never noticed what had been hidden underneath. He slowly walked over and ran his fingers along the strings leading to several pins dotting the vast interior of the Amazon jungle. His hand lingered on the word he'd written off to the side.

"Fools' errand," he muttered sadly, though it had been of some fascination to him ever since his first adventure fresh out of college. He patted the map as he snapped out of his reverie. "Right, definitely need some time away." He hurried out of his study, shutting off the light on his way and plunging the map with the word *Paititi* into darkness.

☻ ☻ ☻

"You think Mom would be up for us visiting Uncle James?" Kaci asked her brother as they walked along the sidewalk toward home enjoying the cooler breeze and the final moments of sunset. Tiredness was setting in after the big game and hanging out with friends for the past hour filling up on greasy burgers, fries and custard blizzards. Their call to Uncle James had gotten them thinking again of how much they loved spending time with him. It was no secret both longed to go on another crazy adventure.

Drew smiled, "I don't know why not. Maybe we can convince her to come with us next time."

"Yeah, I think she'd like that. She hasn't been back to her 'homeland across the pond' in a long time." Kaci giggled at her attempt at a British accent. "Besides, we can swim all day in the pool and enjoy first-class room service from Simmons and his kitchen staff." Kaci sighed, linking her arm around her brother's, smirking when he rolled his eyes.

Her heart swelled as she glanced around at their small town and deeply breathed in the cool night air. *Life is so wonderful*, she thought to herself, smiling. *Drew won his game, Mom's happy again, and we have all of summer break ahead of us with maybe a trip to visit Uncle James in store.* She and Drew were so busy discussing exactly how they should broach the subject of a London vacation to their mom that they didn't notice the black cargo van parked a few shops down. As they walked past it, the vehicle inconspicuously started its engine, keeping its headlights off.

CHAPTER III

T hough the tomb of Timothy was discovered near the ruins of Diana's temple, that was not where the scrolls were found," Alexander said to the full lecture hall. He glanced at his watch and stepped around the podium. "Alas, that is where today's adventure must end."

There was a chorus of groans from the students, and he laughed, his hand stroking his gray stubbled beard.

"I'll see you all again in a week and we'll pick it up from there. Be sure to read your assignments and get your reports to me by our next class period. Good day to you all."

Alexander watched the students pack up, talking excitedly to each other about the day's discourse. He glanced at the image up on the screen, one of the many photos of Timothy's tomb, and sighed. It'd probably be a very long time until he had another grand adventure such as that one.

"Professor!"

Alexander turned in time to see Maxwell Blaine, the department's administrative assistant rushing toward him waiving a folder. "Ah, Max, you look as flushed and flummoxed as always. What can I do for you?"

The short, pudgy man doubled over in an attempt to catch his breath. "Big news is what."

"About...?" Some of the students close by perked up, trying to quietly pack their things so they could overhear the conversation.

Maxwell straightened and handed over the folder. "Everything you need to know is in this folder, including tickets."

"Tickets? Maxwell, I was making ready to take a few days off so I could plan a trip."

"Your trip is going to have to put on hold. Sorry, Professor, but this comes from the top. It is of the highest importance."

Alexander took the folder, shaking his head. "It always is," responding dryly. "You're sure it can't wait?"

"I'm afraid it's an anonymous donor who gave a substantial amount of money to the University. You know how that goes. But the discovery you will be researching is a game-changer." Some of the students quietly cheered. More adventures meant more epic stories for their class periods. Maxwell sniffed, "Now then, wheels up in four hours. If all goes well, perhaps you can fly from Peru to the States."

"Peru?" Alexander repeated. "We have a team on the ground in Peru?"

This was news to him, but then again, he had been quite busy and wasn't aware of every dig going on at the moment.

"It's not technically one of our own," Maxwell clarified. "But an extension of the University of Lima that collaborates with Cambridge on occasion. You will find the information there," nodding at the dossier Alexander was flipping through.

There was no arguing with Maxwell when a big-time donor was involved, and Alexander assured him he'd make it to the airport in time. He tucked the folder in his leather satchel, slung it across his body, and hurried to his office to grab his go bag, his leather Bible belt, and head to the airport. He would inform Simmons of his altered plans on the way.

⊗ ⊗ ⊗

The plane landed in Lima and Alexander was more than ready to stretch his legs. He followed the crowd of passengers from the plane, through the airport, and out to the main lobby. He loved South

American culture and enjoyed hearing the melodic cadence of the Spanish language. The instructions in the folder said a limousine would be waiting for him. Before he could head to the dig site, he was to meet with a leading Incan professor on the project. The man's dossier revealed some fascinating details. Something to do with recently unearthed stone tablets that signified the burial location of Pachacuti Inca Yupanqui. This would be a huge breakthrough for Incan history.

Yupanqui was the 9th Incan ruler (1438-1471) who founded their empire with conquests in the Cuzco Valley and beyond. He is also credited with founding Machu Picchu, a city built into the Peruvian mountains, whose ruins have become a famous tourist attraction today.

His title *Pachacuti*, which he gave himself on his accession, means 'Reverser of the World' or 'Earth-shaker.' An appropriate title, according to Incan historians, for a ruler who set his people on the road to prosperity and built an empire which would eventually be the largest ever seen in the Americas.

The Incan ruler died in 1471 and, according to his wishes, his empire mourned for one whole year. They then held a month-long celebration of their great leader during which his personal items were paraded around the corners of the empire.

Yupanqui was mummified and believed to be buried in a shrine known as Patallacta at Kenko on the heights above Cuzco. Even after death, the ruler continued to be venerated and his mummy was regularly brought outside the shrine where it was ritually fed and even, on occasion, 'consulted' in times of political strife.

In 1559 the Spanish discovered Pachacuti's mummy, which had been secretly hidden by the Incas after their empire was overthrown in 1533. It was sent to Lima by Conquistador Juan Polo de Ondegardo but was lost in transit or perhaps simply destroyed like so many other symbols of Incan culture. So everyone thought. Until now.

James Alexander was Cambridge's leading archeological linguist. He knew multiple languages and dialects, had vast experience in numerous cultures, and knew his way around an archeological dig.

One of the difficulties at being so good at your job is being the one always tapped on the shoulder to get the job done, he frowned. He wished at the moment that he were walking through a terminal in United States about to be greeted by his little monsters.

He stepped out into the humid air and spotted a man near a luxurious black limo holding a sign with Alexander's name on it. The man with the sign smiled politely as Alexander approached. "Professor, I presume?" he said with an accent Alexander couldn't quite place.

"Yes. I take it you're my ride?"

"That I am, good sir. I will take bags and then we be on our way."

Alexander handed over his duffle but kept his leather satchel as he climbed into the back of the shiny black car. As the driver pulled away from the curb, Alexander took in the city streets and the people going about their day. So many people. So many lost souls. He rubbed his weary eyes from the long flight and thought of the missionaries he financially supported in South America.

The driver opened the small tinted window that separated him from the plush back area of the vehicle. "I will stop your hotel for you get refreshed and drop off things before your appointment with Dr. Edwardo Sanchez at University of Lima." Alexander nodded, soaking up the architecture that moved past them. The old buildings mixed in with the new were a sight to see. He wondered if there'd be time for some sight-seeing. He had been to Peru only once before and had several places he would still love to take the time to explore while he was here.

The limo pulled up outside a fancy hotel, the front lined with white shutters over the windows and metal balconies for the guest rooms. The driver handed Alexander his duffle before he entered the lobby to get checked in. As he walked to his room on the third floor, he took his time admiring the paintings that decorated the lobby and the wall-papered halls, all of them scenic landscapes of the countryside. Once he reached his room, he used an antique-looking brass key to unlock the door before stepping inside.

The room was massive and he whistled. Marble floors, silk curtains, crystal light fixtures, and plush leather furniture. Alexander didn't yet know who was funding the expedition and research; but whoever they were, they certainly wanted him to be comfortable. The fact that the notes were vague at best as to whom this donor was did not surprise him. Many times, multi-millionaire CEO's enjoyed anonymously financing research; once something of significance was discovered, they would step forward and bask in the limelight of their own generosity.

He dropped his duffle to the floor and flipped on the light. Four lamps popped on in the room and Alexander stiffened to find he was not alone.

"James Alexander. Been a long time, my friend. How's Cambridge treating you these days?"

Alexander clutched his leather satchel, his jaw clenching. Years ago, he heard rumors that Adrian Fitzgerald had been killed in some terrible accident. Deep down, Alexander doubted the hearsay, knowing how sly and sinister his college friend had become. Now he knew he'd been right.

It had been years since he'd seen the man, but he'd know those eyes anywhere... their quick, glossy brightness that offered a piercing gaze like that of a madman's. The greed he saw on their first and only expedition together had only grown more defined on his face.

"Death suits you well," Alexander managed to reply, and Fitzgerald smirked. "And Cambridge treats me just fine. They would've done the same for you if you had found a way to get over your greed. You were far more gifted than I."

Fitzgerald waved him off and let out a sardonic laugh. "Greed? That's what you think this is about?"

"That's what it's always been about for you."

"I wasn't banned from the Archaeological Society because of greed," Fitzgerald argued, his lip twitching in annoyance. "I was banned because they never liked my methods. You were always their favorite anyway and too soft on your crew."

Alexander could sense bitterness in the man's tone. He'd heard of the several expeditions Fitzgerald led over the years. It seemed that he always pushed his team a little too hard and allowed little sleep. Though they made record time discovering select artifacts on dig sites, it caused exhausted people to work clumsily and recklessly. On a handful of occasions, members of his team were severely wounded and the final straw was when a young intern accidentally died. When investigations were conducted, everyone quickly accused Adrian Fitzgerald of creating hostile working environments. At times, he even lashed out in unprovoked anger and was difficult to please, making his subordinates fearful and uneasy when they worked around him.

As he stood before the board and heard their unanimous decision, he flew into such a rage that he had to be escorted out of the building by two armed guards. The Archaeological Society banned Fitzgerald with no mercy for reapplication. After being stripped of his credentials for life, he took off across the globe. A few years later, news came that he died in a terrible accident. Yet here he sat wearing a dark navy tuxedo vest over a white shirt with rolled up sleeves and the top button undone. His navy suit slacks appeared freshly pressed, and his polished light blue shoes matched his loosened silk tie. The Scotchman's high and tight haircut seemed more chopped than faded as it progressed up to the curly black and silver hair on top of this head. Alexander shuddered as he noticed identical red tattoos running up both of the man's forearms — a large, flying, tattered flag bearing two crossed fists. The last place he had seen *that* symbol was carved on the wooden lid of Captain Bloodfist's personal trunk.

Adrian Fitzgerald's appearance, along with the hard, wrinkled look of his eyes and the stubble on his face, made him look more like a mercenary than an archaeologist. He smiled broadly and gestured to the armchair directly across from him. "Why don't you join me, old chum?"

"I'm guessing there's no meeting with Dr. Edwardo Sanchez?"

Alexander remarked as he carefully sat down and set his satchel on the floor beside him.

"No. Amazing the things blackmail can do," Fitzgerald laughed. "He still owed me a favor from something that I quietly took care of."

"Look at you," Alexander said coldly. "Turned into a bottom feeder. You're dabbling in extortion and intimidation now?"

"Without hesitation," Fitzgerald calmly replied. He leaned forward in his chair, arm muscles bulging beneath his crisp white shirt. "And that's not the beginning of it. I've earned quite the reputation in the underworld. My organization is known for getting the job done *and* getting what it wants on the black market."

"Organization?" Alexander tried to hide his concern. "The black market?"

"Oh, don't you judge me, James Alexander," Fitzgerald interjected, waving his hand. His words turned cruel as he sat back. "I didn't have everything handed to me on a silver platter. You were *born* into a luxurious inherited estate. I came from nothing, had to make a name for myself — only to be kicked to the curb by a board of starchy aristocrats."

"But we were given the same opportunities, and you made your own choices. You let greed and the lust for power consume you."

Fitzgerald laughed again and crossed his arms. "It's no matter. I'm glad they kicked me out. I'm far better off without them and your precious Cambridge. *My* mansion," he flashed a smile, "is stocked full of priceless artifacts that I would have never been able to enjoy otherwise."

Alexander shook his head and sighed. "They belong in a museum for the world to enjoy, Adrian." He looked around the room. "So why am I here?" He pulled out a cellphone; he only carried one when he went overseas. He didn't have one when he was home so he could remain focused on his studies and work. If anyone wanted to contact him, they could easily leave a message with his secretary at the University or with Simmons at the estate. He began to dial Maxwell's number. "I'm about to book passage back to England."

"Stop being so difficult, Jim." Fitzgerald spoke softly, sounding more like a psychopath than someone trying to be friendly. "Okay, so I developed an elaborate ruse to get you here." He leaned forward again. "But I've found the next piece to our puzzle." He pulled out something metallic hanging from a cord around his neck. The light glinted off it, and Alexander tensed at the sight of the golden pendant — one he hadn't seen in over twenty years.

But he noticed that it was much different; it wasn't the rugged half-moon shape that he'd seen before. Fitzgerald somehow had both halves now, and they were expertly soldered together with delicate precision. *This is going to be interesting,* he thought. Sighing, he asked aloud, "Are you still chasing ghosts?"

Within a week of Fiztgerald's dismissal from the Archaeological Society, the logbook of Captain Isidro Torres went missing. Alexander knew that there was only one person who would do such a thing. Over the years, other artifacts related to Bloodfist went missing as well.

Fitzgerald read his mind. "I have searched the wreck sites described in that logbook for two decades."

Alexander sat up straighter. "All these years, the stories I've heard about a crazed treasure hunter and his crew scouring the Caribbean — that was you! You're a wanted criminal in many countries."

"A wanted man? Captain Bloodfist made me a *wealthy* man. I'm a multi-millionaire." He paused for a moment to savor the reaction on Alexander's face, and then taunted, "You should've been by my side. The adventures we could've had together. The spoils we could've shared."

"I'm glad I passed on the 'opportunity,'" Alexander sarcastically responded using air quotes.

"Your loss was my gain," Fitzgerald chuckled. "In recent years, I've expanded my enterprise by offering the distinctive services my team and I can provide to clients all over the world. We call ourselves the *Bloodfists.*"

"How original," Alexander responded drily. "I'm guessing that prestigious list includes drug cartels, arms deals, traffickers, and dictators in third-world countries."

Fitzgerald whistled. "My, my — here I am, thrilled to see my friend again, and you've done nothing but condemn me." He rested his hand over his heart. "And I thought this would be a great chance for us to catch up and smooth things over... be friends again."

"I haven't seen you in twenty-five years."

"I was a bit busy." He held up the pendant again. "But in my travels as a respected entrepreneur, I finally found the piece to our next move."

"Our? Whatever *you're* after, I'm not helping you." Alexander bent to pick up his satchel, but Fitzgerald shifted his vest and the butt of a large shiny revolver appeared.

"Not until you've heard me out, old chum."

Alexander stilled as Fitzgerald rested his hand on the butt of the gun, but kept it holstered at his side. "I'll admit, it's taken me a lot longer than I would've liked to get some answers, but I've finally found them. I came across something quite interesting while on a heist in the Vatican."

Alexander started to stand, ready to lecture the man, but Fitzgerald's warning glare had him sitting back down.

"While removing some rather expensive artifacts for a client, I came across a calves-skin bound package. Imagine my surprise when I realized the gold seal over it matches this pendant, the same one you and I found together in that cavern." He stared at the necklace fondly. "And you know what I found inside that package? The other half I'd been searching for, thinking all this time that it had sunk to the bottom of the sea. But no, the Vatican had it in their possession the entire time. Hoarding it."

"Keeping it safe from people like you," Alexander corrected.

Fitzgerald sighed, letting the pendant fall to rest on his shirt. "Inside the package was a detailed letter to the Pope. The man who wrote it claimed he knew the location of Paititi, and he believed the Vicar was the only person worthy of such knowledge. How preposterous!" Adrian slapped his knee as he humored only himself. "Once I safely removed this parcel from the Vatican, I cancelled any further personal obligations I had to remaining clients and dedicated my time to solely study the other half of this pendant and the letter itself. Interested yet?"

Alexander shrugged.

"The man's name was Aapo, an Incan native. He shared his story of how he became the adopted son of Explorer Carlos Mendina when he was a boy. The man loved him as his own. Taught him to read and write Latin. Blah blah blah. As conquistadors methodically seized the Incan Empire, they heard word among the natives about a fortress that was impenetrable. A city of gold that contained immortality at its core. We already knew all of this from myth and legend — but there was never any proof until now."

Alexander raised an eyebrow. *Immortality?* He thought to himself. *What fiction has he been reading?* He chose his words carefully. "Have you gone mad, Adrian? The place is a myth. No one has *ever* been able to find it. Every clue always leads to a dead end."

"True, but no one has ever had what I now possess. Let me finish. Mendina and his men had been personally appointed by King Phillip II to discover this secret within the jungle — *and they found it.* On their way back to Spain, they were attacked by a fleet of pirate vessels."

"Your beloved Captain Bloodfist."

"Yes," the man broadly smiled. "Aapo wrote extensively of the attack and how he was blown off of the ship with the other half of this pendant in hand. All of the details corroborate with the account that Bloodfist himself gave in his own diary."

Alexander sat up straighter. "What diary?"

"Oh!" Fitzgerald burst into laughter. "I forgot to tell you. It was in his trunk we discovered together, but I purposely hid it from you and kept it for myself."

"Along with the pendent that I knew you stole."

"Touché." Adrian sarcastically engaged in a slow clap, then

continued. "Aapo floated along with the current that night on a piece of debris from the wooden hull of his galleon. By dawn, he was able to get ashore on the northern coast of South America. It became his life's mission to hide the location of Paititi with his people. In his letter, he skipped to the end of his life's story. Unfortunate really, because we don't know any more about him — but I think he was keeping details hidden on purpose. Now as an old man, he found his way to Rome to hand-deliver his half of the pendent and this letter to the Pope himself...." His voice trailed off for a moment. "At the very end of his tale, he describes the location, not of where the city is — it would never be *that* easy of course — but the location of a map to it." He looked up to make direct eye contact with Alexander. "He stated that only those worthy enough could find it."

Alexander's heart sunk, not liking where this was going at all. He glanced toward the door, but the chances of him making it there without Fitzgerald pulling a gun on him were slim.

"Sadly, the map is not in my possession. Yet."

"Perhaps it's for the best. And you have blood on your hands anyway. You're not worthy."

Fitzgerald burst out laughing. "Always the jokester, aren't you? I don't believe in that sort of nonsense. For you see, Aapo ended his letter with a riddle — words that I've memorized. Words that have led me here. *'Where the sun gives the earth life, and the sacrifice is made, the key to the heart of the sun can be found. Inside one must venture to the heart of the god from the rising to the setting, lest they become locked within the earth forever.'* Sounds much better in Latin of course. Everything rhymed and what-not."

Alexander said nothing, crossing his arms, and arching his brow. Waiting.

"You can try to hide your curiosity all you want, but I know you too well. I mediated upon those words, and I finally realized what they must mean. It could only refer to Torreón, Temple of the Sun."

As much as Alexander didn't want to be, he was indeed becoming more intrigued and found himself wanting Fitzgerald to get on with it so he could figure out what else the man knew.

"That of course led to Machu Picchu. There's a rock slab inside that temple, one that served as an altar. During the June Solstice, the rising sun shines directly through one of the windows and creates a perfect alignment between the sun, the window, and the rock. Only on the June solstice. I believe something at that exact spot is key."

It was Alexander's turn to clap. "Bravo. You've figured out the next piece to the puzzle. The solstice is soon. You should get a move on if you want to be there in time for the alignment."

Fitzgerald tapped his temple. "Now, you see, that's my issue. As brilliant as I am, I never was as good at linguistics as you are. Sadly, you're the only man I know who will be able to accurately translate whatever we may come across."

"You're seriously asking *me* to help you?" Alexander barked a laugh. "You're a thief and a crook and you should be in jail. You're supposed to be dead, Adrian. I told you years ago that this was a fool's errand."

Fitzgerald's eyes flickered, thinking back to their time together in Bloodfist's cave. "You said that my ambition was going to get me killed — but I assure you that is not going to happen, because you're going to be there to help me!"

"I won't help you."

Fitzgerald merely smiled. "You can't tell me you haven't wondered where this city has been hiding all these centuries? You can't honestly say you never once thought about where it might be located? That it could be somewhere in Peru? I know you, Jim. It's like an itch and it won't go away until you have all the answers."

Alexander opened his mouth to argue, but he recalled the map hanging in his study back home. No, he hadn't been obsessed with it, but he did dabble in his spare time with studying any leads he picked up from explorers that passed through Cambridge over the years.

His hesitation had Fitzgerald cackling. "My point exactly."

"I might have done some research over the years," Alexander admitted, "but I never let it consume me as you did. I found my calling, found what I wanted to do and spent my years studying events and artifacts that pointed to Biblical history and verification of the Scripture. Not some mythical city of gold," he muttered.

"Still as pious and holy as ever." Fitzgerald jeered. "Glad to see some things never change."

"Adrian, I'm *not* going help you," Alexander stated, feeling a little bolder. "I'm glad to see you're alive, but I won't be brought down to your level. I won't let you turn me into a criminal, and I certainly won't help you continue your obsession with this worthless expedition."

Fitzgerald reached into his pants pocket and pulled out his cell phone. "I knew you'd be too much of a good man to come along on the adventure."

"Right, because whatever you're planning on doing isn't illegal at all."

Fitzgerald smirked. "I never said anything about it being legal, but since you brought it up, I'm afraid my actions lately are hardly ever in the realm of the law. Thankfully, I thought of a way to remedy this situation. Call it collateral if you will. You come along and do as I say and everything will be just fine."

Alexander was about to tell Fitzgerald whatever he had wouldn't be enough to make him give in, until the man turned his phone around. Alexander jumped out of his chair and grabbed it, staring horrified at the video on the screen.

"They're safe for the moment," Fitzgerald assured him. "And this feed is live. Your niece and nephew are quite the rascally bunch. Gave my men a run for their money," he chuckled, shaking his head.

Alexander wanted it to be fake, but the longer he stared, watching Kaci and Drew tied to chairs and obviously scared as they talked to one another and to whoever was holding the phone, he realized he had no choice. Then another worry hit him: Susan!

As if he'd read his mind, Fitzgerald said, "We warned your sister not to contact you."

"I-I've got to call her. She must be beside herself wondering where the children are!"

"All in good time," Fitzgerald yanked his phone back and shoved it in his pocket. "It's simple really. You help me and the kids go free," he promised. "We have a deal, Jim?" he asked, stretching out his hand.

Alexander took it and squeezed. Hard. "If any harm comes to those kids, you'll regret ever seeking me out," he warned.

Fitzgerald clapped him on the shoulder. "Perhaps *you* shouldn't be making any threats, old chum. Come along now. Let's get started!"

CHAPTER IV

Drew glowered at the guards watching him and Kaci from across the room. The warehouse they were being held in was dimly lit by the few scattered lights that worked. For the past couple of hours, he'd been scanning the ceiling and the walls for any sign of how they could get out of there, but their chance of escape seemed hopeless. Kaci stirred beside him and he squeezed her hand, hoping she'd sleep a bit longer. They agreed to take shifts, but Drew wasn't about to close his eyes until he knew exactly what was going on. They had been there long enough.

He wasn't sure how many days had passed since he and his sister were yanked off the street. The black cargo van had come out of nowhere as it swerved up onto the sidewalk and he'd told Kaci to run. Men dressed in black with ski masks jumped out chasing after her. Two men violently grabbed him and he fought with everything he had; but they were twice his size and, after a few moments, were able to drag him into the vehicle. Kaci's muffled screams sounded a few seconds later as she was thrown in next to him. As the van pulled away, they were roughly handcuffed and black hoods were placed over their heads. It still gave him chills as he remembered his sister crying uncontrollably. He tried to calm her by telling her over and over again that it was going to be okay — in between which he shouted threateningly at the men not to touch her.

One of them smacked him across the face. It came unexpectedly, and his nose smarted, causing his eyes to tear up. He shook it off and calmly stated to Kaci, "Just pray." The man who hit him gruffly snarled, "Shut up!" Drew knew these men meant business, so the two young people sat in silence, praying to God as their bodies shivered in fright. It had been a traumatic experience.

Drew felt slightly relieved, however, when he overheard some of the men talking to each other up front — something about not hurting the kids and that they were a sort of "insurance policy." The ruffians snickered as they thought about how pleased their boss would be.

They rode along in silence for about 45 minutes; Kaci sat as close as she could to her brother. Suddenly, they both felt a searing prick in their shoulders as something was injected into them. The next thing they knew, they were waking up on a dank, cold floor — here in this place.

Roaches skittered along the shadows around the stacks of crates and boxes that were strewn about. The only windows in the building were too high up for Drew to make out any details of where they were. The dingy glass made it nearly impossible for any sunlight to filter through. He shifted, his body protesting from sitting on a hard surface for so long.

A few other guards sat at a nearby table playing poker. They muttered quietly to each other, hardly paying any attention to their captives. If he knew there was a sure way out of this place, he'd wait for the cover of night and try to escape with his sister. But it wasn't the men sitting a few yards away that had him worried. Nor was it the ones flanking the door with AK-47s. It was the one in charge of them. She looked only a few years older than Drew, but these burly men with their rugged countenances and forearms covered with red cross-fisted tattoos were terrified of her.

A door creaked open loudly, metal grating on metal, and Kaci jerked awake, bolting upright. She shifted closer to her brother as he squeezed her hand, doing his best to keep her calm.

"Drew," she whispered, voice shaking.

"We'll be fine," he told her quietly. "Don't be afraid."

"Hard not to be."

"Just remember, God is with us," he whispered. "He will *always* be with us."

She nodded and some of the fear slipped from her eyes.

Boots stomped across the hard, concrete floor and the young woman appeared from around the tall-stacked crates followed by four men. She carried a set of ninja throwing knives at her side and was dressed in dark greens and browns, her clothing tactical in appearance. Her straight shoulder-length blonde hair was parted down the middle and appeared razor sharp. The guards hadn't noticed her yet and were still going about their game. Her eyes narrowed and she bit the toothpick in half she'd been chewing on and spit it aside. She planted her hands on her hips, glaring.

"Give me one reason why I shouldn't drag you outside right now," she snapped.

The guards shot to their feet, knocking over their chairs in the process. They averted their eyes as the woman walked slowly around them, turning her back on Drew and Kaci.

"Pathetic," she said, shaking her head. "I thought we hired the best."

"You did," one of the men said and, in a blink, she had a knife in her hand pressed to the man's throat.

Drew and Kaci gasped, clinging to each other at the dark glint in her eyes. "What was that?" she whispered in his ear.

The man sputtered, and the attention of everyone in the room was no longer on their prisoners. Even the guards who stood by the front door had sauntered up with smirks to watch the confrontation. If they were ever going to sneak out of this warehouse and get back home, Drew realized that *now* was their only chance. If they stayed low, they could use the large wooden crates as cover and make it to the door. Drew expected there to be more guards outside, but if they could run and find help, they'd have a chance.

He nudged Kaci, nodding toward his right. She frowned, but he mimicked them walking with his hands and after a few seconds' hesitation, she nodded. He had just made it quietly to his knees, ready to crawl to the stack nearby, when a knife whizzed past him and embedded in the wooden crate inches from his face.

"You don't get to leave yet, I'm afraid," the young woman said as Drew slowly turned to find her watching him. "You or your sister."

Drew gulped and stood, dragging Kaci to her feet beside him. "We're not afraid of you."

"Yeah?" She stalked closer like a predator about to pounce. She stood as tall as Drew, her cold eyes boring into his. She wrenched the knife free and sheathed it at her hip. "You should be."

"Please, just let us go," Kaci softly pleaded. "What have we done to deserve this? We don't even know why you're holding us here!"

"Sorry, but I've got orders."

"Orders from who?" Drew asked. "Why are we here, huh? Why?"

The woman pulled another toothpick from her pocket and chewed on it slowly, her brow furrowing. "You've got spirit, I'll give you that. Next time you try to escape, well, let's just say we won't be having such a pleasant conversation. I'll have the men bring you some dinner." She clapped him on the shoulder and Drew took a daring step toward her. Her brow arched like she was waiting for him to do something. If he had been alone, he would risk it, but not with Kaci next to him. He couldn't let anything happen to his sister. He moved back and the young woman sighed. "Shame. I was hoping for some entertainment tonight." She smiled coldly and marched away, yelling at the men to get rid of their poker game. They hastily responded, murmuring among themselves, and scurried to their posts.

Drew and Kaci sank back to the floor, the guards now stared at them intently. Kaci's hand shook as Drew held it, trying to keep her calm. He shut his eyes and did the only thing he could think of. He prayed. They would get through this together. They just had to hold onto hope that someone would find them.

❀ ❀ ❀

Alexander climbed out of the van, Fitzgerald doing the same. The Cambridge professor was dressed in his normal archeological attire — a thin-striped shirt with the sleeves rolled up, suspenders, and brown slacks. He normally wore a bowtie, but in this heat and with the hike ahead of them, he decided to stow it in his suitcase and unbutton his top button. Fitzgerald wore a dark cargo vest over his tan short-sleeve shirt. His cargo pants and dark brown boots caked with dried mud made him look like the hardened mercenary that he was.

The men escorting them looked nothing like tourists no matter how hard they tried. One of them, a man with piercing blue eyes, returned Alexander's glare. His skin was pale and his white blonde hair and thin form made him appear sickly in nature. His brow rose slightly when Alexander continued to stare at him, the hair on the back of his neck beginning to stand on end. The man took a step back and Alexander finally broke eye contact. *I'll call him Blondie,* Alexander thought to himself.

The other men were much stockier in build; all of them were sweating profusely, not being used to such a humid climate. The one to Blondie's right had a shining bald head dotted with beads of sweat. *Baldy.* Another man walked around the front of the vehicle with a backpack in hand. He was a massively strong man, and his long, scraggly hair was pulled back into a rubber-banded ponytail. *Girly,* Alexander smiled. And another stood off to the side, scratching at his goatee as he spit sunflower seed shells out of the corner of his mouth. *Goatee.* The last man speaking quietly with Adrian had a chiseled chin and dark, unblinking features. Alexander shook his head. *Well, I thought I could get them all to rhyme, but this one is too much. That piercing gaze. I'll just have to settle for Beady Eyes.*

Alexander was by no means a small man; he stood over 6 feet with broad shoulders. Though he had a concentrated dash of gray in his temples, he was still fit for his age. But any of these guys would give him a run for his money. Not to mention all of them were heavily armed beneath their clothes.

The drive to the Andes had been long and filled with Fitzgerald talking about all he'd done to get to this point. Alexander hadn't paid any attention, his mind too occupied with worry for Drew and Kaci. He pleaded with Fitzgerald to let him call his niece and nephew or their mother who must be sick with worry, but his friend didn't budge.

"I hope you're ready for a hike," the Scot chuckled, handing Alexander a canteen. "Three hours, old chum."

Alexander said nothing and slipped the canteen over his shoulder. He fixed the brown leather pouch on his belt toward his back right hip. It carried his small worn Bible. It was a special design of his own making. On the right column of every page was the perfectly translated King James Version. Each left column of the Old Testament contained the corresponding Ben Chayyim Masoretic Hebrew text. The same pattern had been used for the New Testament of his Bible with the paralleled columns of the *Textus Receptus* from the Traditional Text family in Koine Greek. He had designed it this way not to correct the translation of the King James Version, but for quick referencing access while working with Bible manuscripts in the field. Alexander knew beyond a shadow of a doubt that the Masoretic Text and the *Textus Receptus* were the correct, uncorrupted sources of the Hebrew and Greek.

Alexander absolutely loved his Bible; not a day went by that he didn't read it. It was a lamp unto his feet and light unto his path. Without fail, there were verses in his devotions that spoke to his heart, bringing him daily encouragement and wisdom. The Bible meant everything to him, because it was the living Word of God. His heart was constantly warmed by the wonderful fact that the King James Version was accurately and beautifully translated into the English language from the Hebrew and Greek.

"You always carry around that thing?" Blondie scoffed.

"Always. It never leaves my side."

Girly chuckled sarcastically, "You gonna try to convert us? 'Cause we're all going to Hell."

"Yes, you are," Alexander calmed replied, "if you die without

Jesus Christ as your personal Saviour." The men didn't know how to respond to such a bold statement, and Fitzgerald quickly ended the conversation by snatching Alexander's arm.

"What?"

"You're going to make this trip less than enjoyable if you talk about your Bible trash."

"Don't you *dare* speak about God's Word like that." Alexander yanked his arm free, glowering at the man he once called his friend. He pointed his finger directly into Fitzgerald's chest. "Let's get a couple of things straight. I'm coming along to translate for you, and you're going to release my niece and nephew unharmed when I'm done. I expect you to respect my positions and my beliefs. If I want to talk about them, I will. You will not harm me or my little monsters because you *need* me."

"Oh, how sweet. Your 'little monsters'," Fitzgerald laughed, making fun of him; then his personality snapped into something sinister. "Just keep your opinions to yourself, because we didn't ask."

"They brought it up. I was just making conversation —"

"We have a long walk ahead of us," the mercenary interrupted. "And none of us want to be tortured by you boring us with your religious fairy tales." He then coldly smiled with wide unblinking eyes. "Come along now. We have no time to waste. The Solstice is upon us."

Fitzgerald turned on his feet and headed down the path that would take them through the jungle to Machu Picchu. After taking a moment to silently pray for strength, Alexander followed him into the dense overgrowth with the other men trailing behind.

Three hours later, drenched in sweat and legs burning from the strenuous hike, Alexander stepped through the last line of vines and trees to finally see what they came here for. Despite his current predicament, he couldn't help but be taken aback by what towered above them in the distance.

He was struck by the sight of Machu Picchu, situated on the eastern slope of the Andes. The tiered structure of what had once been a flourishing center for the Incan culture was a marvel to behold, built into the very rock of the mountains. The view in all directions was breathtaking and Alexander breathed in, the air being crisp nearly eight thousand feet above sea level. Far below them ran the Urubamba River, its waters rushing along in a swift current. Colorful flora and fauna of the jungle crept up the slopes making it a true paradise on earth.

Too bad I'm not here for sightseeing. What a splendid place! Alexander sighed, dragging his gaze away from the views to the number of tourists there also visiting this great ancient wonder. For a fleeting second, he considered darting into the crowd and disappearing, but he had no idea where Drew and Kaci were being held. Fitzgerald had already warned him a few times on their trek that if he tried to escape — if he tried anything — the kids would pay the price. The man only needed to place one call on his satellite phone, and they would be killed. Alexander hated working with criminals, but at this point, he had no choice.

"Going to be hard to do anything with so many people around," he commented as Fitzgerald approached.

"Always so worried about everyone else when you should be worrying about yourself."

"You need me alive."

"That I do. But shooting you in the kneecap wouldn't damage your brain," the man leered, his eyes narrowing. "Get moving. We're on a schedule."

Alexander didn't move at first; he didn't like being threatened. But Blondie shoved him hard in the back. Reluctantly, he gave in and followed Fitzgerald into the crowd of tourists excited for the June Solstice. The attraction was only open to those who purchased tickets for the day's grand event. Alexander watched Fitzgerald personally hand over theirs to a park receptionist. He smiled sweetly at the young lady and spoke softly with her in Spanish. Seeing his former colleague pretending to be friendly gave him chills under the bright hot sun. He noticed that while Fitzgerald chatted with her, Girly discreetly stepped passed them both with his backpack down toward the ground. *What are you planning, Adrian Fitzgerald?* Alexander frowned.

There was a limited amount of people who could witness the event, but the crowd was still larger than made Alexander comfortable, considering he was being escorted by armed mercenaries. There were even more people outside, among the ruins of Machu Picchu, just to be on location when the event happened. Once they had entered the ancient edifice, Alexander noticed rooms on either side of the walkway, with Incan artifacts on display. Ethnic music softly played through a hidden speaker system, and tourists milled around, taking in the sights of each room. Fitzgerald and his men walked past these terraced sections, however, and headed straight for the Temple of the Sun.

"You know, this city was considered a sacred place by the people," Fitzgerald commented to his men as they took in the magnificent sites and stone archways of the architectural design. "It served as a royal retreat and a religious sanctuary solely used by Emperor Pachacuti and Incan aristocracy."

He led them forward to the temple entrance and pointed, "Up ahead is Torreón." He flashed a smile, "We will discover its secrets soon. But first, follow me." Where most of the tourists headed up the sloping stone floor that led to the main room, Fitzgerald veered to the left and descended a set of steps that were roughly hewn into a sharply angled corridor. The winding stairs were difficult to navigate, which was probably why most tourists avoided the space. They led to a large cavern directly underneath the temple lit by several floor LED lights scattered around the perimeter.

"Machu Picchu was discovered back in 1911 by Hiram Bingham, an American archeologist from Yale," Fitzgerald informed his group as they entered. Slowly Alexander turned, taking in the space. He moved along the outer wall, reaching out to run his hand over the stone. Several carvings of various images depicted the Incan gods; a few remained visible while most had faded over time.

He wasn't entirely sure what they were doing down here, but Alexander kept quiet. There were two other tourists down there with them who nodded politely as they passed and made their way to the makeshift stairs. The second they were gone, Fitzgerald nodded, and his men removed their shirts to reveal ones matching those worn by the park rangers, each also bearing an official badge. They put on matching ball caps they had hidden in their cargo pants and geared up with comm earpieces out of the backpack Girly was carrying.

"Check one-two," Blondie muttered with his soft German accent. The other men gave him a thumbs up. He turned to Fitzgerald. "We are ready at your command."

"Go."

All but Beady Eyes headed upstairs. He remained down below with Fitzgerald and Alexander and fixed a steely gaze on the professor, as if daring him to try something foolish.

"We're going to stay down here for a bit, old chum," Fitzgerald said with a sly smile. "Just so we can stay out of sight while the fun begins."

Concern was etched all over Alexander's face. "What are you planning?"

"Nothing to get all wound tight about," Fitzgerald replied with a laugh. "Just a little, let's say — 'distraction' — to let us go about our work."

He spun around and moved toward what appeared to be a set of random etchings at the far end of the cavern on either side of a rather flat section of stone. It was narrow and smooth with no markings on it at all. Curiously, Alexander watched the man pick up a small rock from the ground and lean against the abnormally smooth patch of wall.

"Bingham assumed that where we're now standing served as a sort of royal mausoleum," Fitzgerald lectured, his voice echoing in the cavern. "But there is no proof that it was a burial chamber; mummified corpses were never found. No one *really* knows what its purpose is, but I think it serves as a foyer to something larger, deeper within the mountain. I've studied photographs of this cavern. There is something very obvious here that everyone has overlooked." He grinned.

"Something right in front of their faces, so simple they just couldn't see it. They were not looking as I do — in light of Paititi."

He turned, and Alexander peered closer. In his mind, he traced the incomplete symbols on either side of the smooth section of the wall. Meanwhile, Fitzgerald scratched lines into the stone with the rock. To the unassuming eye, the markings on the wall appeared to be random lines, but with Paititi specifically in mind, it was clear how he could easily "connect the dots" to match the same symbol on the pendant hanging around his neck.

"Remember the riddle? *'Where the sun gives the earth life, and the sacrifice is made,"* Fitzgerald quoted. *"The key to the heart of the sun can be found. Inside one must venture to the heart of the god from the rising to the setting, lest they become locked within the earth forever.'* I believe behind this very wall is the map that will lead us to Paititi! We are standing at the precipice to *'the heart of the god.'"*

"What if you're wrong?" Alexander questioned. "It's just a wild guess."

"No, I am absolutely certain. This can be the only place. I *have* to be right!"

Suddenly, the cavern shook and small pebbles, and dirt vibrated from the ceiling above. The cavern's lights fell askew. Distant screams could be heard.

"What was that?" Alexander sharply asked as he steadied himself.

Fitzgerald smirked, "It's the sound of history about to be made."

"What have you done?"

"Nothing devastating. Just a few small charges strategically placed by my men to simulate an earthquake." He chuckled with a sinister grin. "A gentle nudge to clear the premises for our work."

Alexander strode to the bottom of the stairs — as close as he dared get to Beady Eyes — and listened as Fitzgerald's men directed panicked tourists to evacuate safely in an orderly fashion.

"It will be over soon," Fitzgerald calmly assured him. Alexander looked at him incredulously, trying to process what was happening.

He heard the nervous cries of women and children. *I can't believe they just planted bombs and committed an act of terror on foreign soil,* he thought to himself, gritting his teeth.

"Don't worry, Jim. We made sure that no one would be hurt. I'm not as inhumane as you think I might be." Fitzgerald slapped him on the back and escorted him back to the smooth section of wall with his arm around his old friend's shoulder.

"Machu Picchu has always been very fascinating to me. And now I believe I know why I have always felt drawn to it," the man rambled. "In 1450, the Incans started building this place, and they finished it somewhere toward the beginning of the 1490's. Spanish explorer Francisco Pizarro invaded the Incan Empire in 1532."

He now paced back and forth looking down at the ground with a distant look in his eyes as if talking to himself. Alexander remained still, silently listening with his arms crossed. "The Spanish conquered all the Incan lands within 40 years, taking vast quantities of gold, destroying the cities, and nearly erasing this entire civilization." He looked up at Alexander. "But Machu Picchu, located here, high in the Andes Mountains, was hidden from the Spanish and left intact. Because they viewed this place as a sacred site, Incans would die first before revealing its location, and many of them did. The rest of the outside world would never know this place existed, until Bingham discovered it in 1911 of course. Once Aapo returned to his people with the knowledge of Paititi's location, he must have covertly united the remaining factions of the Empire to build a sanctuary here to guard their culture's most precious secret — the city of gold. But I believe they painstakingly hid its location because it contains *more* than just that. Something even more priceless..."

His voice trailed off, and Alexander frowned. *There he goes again,* he thought to himself. *What's he getting at?* "Anyway," Fitzgerald interrupted Alexander's train of thought, "with Machu Picchu off the map, they had plenty of time to leave clues for only the worthy to find."

Alexander gave the man a sharp look. Fitzgerald sarcastically laughed and slapped his former friend again on the back. "Good thing I have you with me, old chum! Your immeasurable virtue will counterbalance all of us 'bad guys' combined!"

The last of the distressed voices fell away and one of Fitzgerald's men yelled it was clear.

"After you," he said, motioning Alexander to move on ahead.

With Beady Eyes standing right there, Alexander didn't have much choice but to return up the rough staircase to the temple. The room was empty, and Goatee now stood at the temple entrance, still occasionally spitting out sunflower shells. The rest had most likely gone to keep shepherding the confused tourists out of the way and then stand watch. Alexander sighed, thankful at least Fitzgerald had been true to his word and seemed to not want to hurt any innocent people.

Torreón, the temple of the Sun, was of unique design, especially for 13th century architecture. The entryway opened into a large circular tower with a peculiar trapezoid-shaped window high above. The walls were made up of smooth bricks, clearly hand-made with reverence and care. The temple was built up on the top of a big granite rock that was part of the mountain, taking advantage of its natural outline. In the middle of the room, a rock slab stood elevated, serving as an altar toward the open ceiling.

"Human sacrifices were conducted *right here*, Jim, when the annual solstice sun would strike." Fitzgerald commented with a glint in his eye, his hand running along the smooth stone.

"Ghastly." Alexander replied with disgust, aware of the history of this heathen practice. "They thought it would appease Inti, the sun god, and guarantee heaven's blessing upon the Empire until the next solstice. So sad."

"Where the sun gives the earth life, and the sacrifice is made," Fitzgerald quoted Aapo's riddle from memory as he slowly walked about the curved wall. *"The key to the heart of the sun can be found."*

The clouds above broke and the sun began to brightly shine. The height of the temple's tower-like walls kept the sun from directly shining within the room, but a beam of sunlight hit the far end the altar through a corner of the trapezoid window. Alexander checked his watch, Fitzgerald doing the same.

"It is happening now!" Fitzgerald whispered. "Perfect."

With each passing moment, the ray of light slowly moved down the very center of the stone slab. After an hour of the men patiently waiting, the beam drifted off of the altar to the floor and finally onto the far wall. Once it reached eye-level, it suddenly stood still and began to fade away as the sun's rays passed beyond the opening of the trapezoid window.

"Yes!" Fitzgerald exclaimed, rubbing his hands together. "This is our moment!"

He drew a large knife from under his vest and rapidly approached the spot marked by the vanishing beam. With a firm grip, he smashed the hilt of his knife hard into the bricks. After three strikes, the mortar cracked. He carefully scraped and dug it out from around the bricks with his blade. Once he realized the blocks still wouldn't budge, he viciously smashed them over and over again, sending out sprays of stone chips. Finally, he was able to tug the broken chunks free, and the daylight glinted off something polished and gold. He began to laugh, wildly looking over his shoulder at the others and pointing at what was there.

It was a small section of golden bricks. In the middle was a square image depicting Inti, the sun god, and the deeply etched lines in the blocks surrounding him stretched out like rays emanating from his face. "I told you, Jim! Today, we make history!"

Without hesitation, he slammed his fist into the golden face of the sun god. It gave way and fell back into the wall, leaving an ominous dark hole. The temple shook and Alexander struggled to stay on his feet as the tremors worsened. Dust and mortar fell from the high walls and Fitzgerald yelled in excitement as a loud grinding sound echoed up from the direction of the cavern beneath them.

Just when Alexander started to wonder if the entire mountain was about to collapse, the noise and shaking stopped. There was no waiting this time and Fitzgerald yelled at him to hurry. Beady Eyes shoved Alexander back to the stairs and the men ran back into the cavern with Goatee bringing up the rear. As the dust cleared, Alexander's eyes widened in shock.

"Just as I expected, Jim!" Fitzgerald gloated. "Let's move."

The narrow smooth section of wall where he had scratched in the rest of Paititi's symbol was now gone — either slid to the side or sunk into the floor. Fitzgerald and his two men ran down the sloped path beyond the doorway, pulling out flashlights as Beady Eyes shoved Alexander again in the back to get him moving. Just as he was passing through the opening, he spotted an emerald and pyrite studded symbol of Paititi in the rock ceiling above. The path curved around jagged stone outcroppings and the floor was slick with moisture running down the walls the deeper they went. Alexander was trying to figure out how far beneath the temple they were, when he noticed Fitzgerald's light catch something shiny barely protruding from the right wall. The mercenary and his men missed it. Instinctively, Alexander lunged forward and grabbed the man by his vest. Fitzgerald yelled as Alexander yanked him off his feet. A second later, four spears shot across the stone passageway, embedding themselves into the left wall. Fitzgerald sat up in a hurry, jaw dropping.

"The floor," Alexander pointed. "Look at the floor."

"A pressure plate!" Fitzgerald exclaimed quietly. "How did you even see that?"

"I didn't. I saw the spear jutting out of the wall." He pushed to his feet and to his surprise, Fitzgerald handed him a flashlight.

"Keep your eyes open, old chum." He turned to the others and barked, "Step lightly."

The remainder of the walk was slow going, each man testing the floor and checking the walls and ceiling for traps. The tunnel opened wide at one point and all of them stilled. Alexander aimed his flashlight up to find a metal grid covered in spikes hanging precariously overhead. There had to be a trigger for it somewhere and after a few moments, Fitzgerald found it. A thin tripwire stretched across the tunnel leading to a lever on their right. All four men carefully stepped over the wire, Beady Eyes keeping his light trained on it to ensure no one triggered the trap. Once they passed it, the tunnel sloped upward and they climbed until the tunnel opened up into another cavern easily ten times the size of the one before.

"Still think it's a fool's errand?" Fitzgerald asked, switching off his flashlight.

There was no need for the extra light now. High above them was a large jagged opening. Birds flew overhead and vines and flowers hung down, the jungle slowly encroaching on what had remained undisturbed for centuries. How no one had found this room baffled Alexander, but then again, he had no way to know where they were in relation to the main temple. The region surrounding Machu Picchu was treacherous and overgrown with rugged terrain.

The opening high above them appeared to have grown larger over time from the crumbling rock littering the back portion of the cavern floor. Sitting atop a raised stone platform was a massive statue of the sun god. Streaks of jade and gold ran through his arms and rays of sunlight were carved around him, catching the light coming in. A cobblestone floor stretched out before him reaching the entryway where they stood. It contained various shaped stones that appeared to have markings etched on each of them.

"This is another trap." Alexander mused, and the men stood there in silence for a moment.

"Who would like to go first?" Fitzgerald asked, eyeing Alexander. Then he burst out laughing. "Nothing to worry about, Jim. Just follow my lead!" He stepped up to the stone path and gingerly stepped forward.

Alexander held his breath, but as Fitzgerald moved across the stones, he figured out how the man knew which ones to step on. Each one had the Paititi symbol on it in one way or another. Sometimes it was turned on its side or twisted upside down. A few of Fitzgerald's steps had to practically be jumps as the distance between the marked stones was over five feet.

As he reached the edge of the wide path, he stopped dead in his tracks. "Well, hello there!" he blurted out. He looked back over his shoulder and shouted, "There's a surprise here that you can't see from back there!" He gestured, arching out his arms. "A sort of chasm surrounds the statue. It's not terribly wide —" he jumped mid-sentence and easily reached the wide ledge at the base of the platform. "But just be careful! Come on, Jim!"

Beady Eyes slightly nudged Alexander to ensure he went next.

Taking a deep breath, he moved for the first stone, throwing out his arms as the floor seemed to shift beneath his weight. Fitzgerald snickered, "Don't die on me!"

"I'll try not to. But the mud from your boots you smeared on these stones isn't making things any easier," he muttered.

He took another step then another. As he jumped toward the next, his foot accidentally slid off and tapped another cobblestone. It crumbled, revealing a spike sticking out of the ground ten feet below ready to meet him. He steadied himself then continued, trying not to overthink what he was walking on. Only the *'Paititi'* marked stones were supported by centuries old wooden beams — the rest were tightly wedged together to form a suspended pathway above a wide dug-out spike pit. One misstep, and down you go. Alexander prayed that the old beams would support him the rest of the way there and back.

Finally, he reached the other end, jumped across the open chasm, then allowed himself to breath. Fitzgerald motioned for his men to stay at the cavern's entryway. "No need for you to come! The professor and I will handle things from here!"

He turned to Alexander and teased, "You should smile more. We're about to make a discovery that will change history!"

"Honestly? I'll smile when my family is back home safe and I never see you again."

Fitzgerald sighed. He stepped up to the statue, leaned back, and smirked. *"'Inside one must venture to the heart of the god from the rising to the setting, lest they become locked within the earth forever,'"* he quoted. "Look up there. See?"

Alexander followed Fitzgerald's pointed finger and noticed a small circular opening in the chest of the sun god. "I believe Aapo built this in such a way that if the two pieces of the medallion were reunited, it would fit perfectly into that slot." He burst out laughing again. "Destiny is in our favor, Jim! What are the odds that of all people… *we* would be the ones to find them and be able to venture to this place?"

Reluctantly, Alexander had to agree. The fact they had discovered this much so far was astounding. Fitzgerald carefully removed the Paititi pendant from his neck. "You always were a better climber than me. You will need to fit this into the god's heart and turn it counter-clockwise one hundred eighty degrees —"

"Signifying the rising and setting sun like the riddle says. This isn't my first rodeo."

"Why is it always a rodeo? If this were an actual rodeo, it would be my first. I've never actually been to one! We just don't want to find out what happens if you accidentally turn it the wrong way."

Alexander took the pendant and held it over the chasm. "Or I could do this." All he had to do was let go and the pendant would be lost forever, swallowed by the earth. Fitzgerald rolled his eyes as if bored.

"Why would you be such a fool, Jim?"

"It's what I should've done when we first discovered this pendant all those years ago."

Fitzgerald narrowed his gaze. "If you drop that, you can say goodbye to your family. It would be such a waste for them to die so young."

Alexander squeezed the chain so hard, it bit into his skin. He could still find a way to save the kids. But even as he thought of it, he knew Fitzgerald would follow through with his threat instantly. A darkness filled his friend's eyes, one he had seen all those years ago. He should've found a way to help him back then, but he had failed.

Alexander withdrew his hand and spun on his feet. Fitzgerald chuckled behind him, but he ignored the man and worked on finding his way up the massive form of the sun god. Draping the chain around his neck, he carefully scaled up the platform from one stone crevice to another, all the while heading toward the right leg of the statue. He was so close.

He scraped his fingers as he hauled himself up the massive 20-foot sculpture, his feet struggling to find big enough footholds for his boots. His foot slipped and he hung by his fingertips, knowing what awaited him if he fell. Gritting his teeth, arms straining, he dragged himself higher and higher up until he was able to balance himself between its arms, the opening for the pendant in front of him. Leaning into the stone, he removed the pendant from his neck and pressed it into the opening. The fit was almost perfect and after another moment's hesitation, he turned it counter-clockwise.

The statue rumbled and Alexander held on precariously as something below scraped against stone.

"You did it, Jim!" Fitzgerald yelled excitedly, reaching into an opening that had appeared at the base of the platform.

Alexander slowly made his way back down to the wide ledge. Fitzgerald was clutching a large piece of leather that was rolled up and tied with a thin rope. He pointed to a small, stone tablet carved into the opening. "What does it say?"

"Hmmm. It's in Quechuan, the ancient language of the Incans." He took a moment to study it.

"Well?" Fitzgerald asked impatiently.

"You can see the large symbol of Paititi there," Alexander pointed. "And the rest of it? It's basically a plaque of sorts congratulating us on the beginning of their quest. It does warn that we must retrieve the medallion if we wish to complete our journey."

Fitzgerald slapped Alexander heartily on the back upon hearing this and his laughter filled the cavern. "The game's afoot, old chum!"

He then reverently held up what was in his other hand, "And I presume this is the map that will direct us to our beloved city."

With eyes wide with glee, the big man carefully loosened the knot and gently unrolled it.

"Glorious!" he whispered breathlessly.

Alexander's lips thinned as he peered over the man's shoulder, noticing that the writings on it and around its border were in Latin. He watched as the greed in Fitzgerald's eyes only grew, his hands trembling with excitement at the treasure they just uncovered.

"Sir? We should go," Beady Eyes called out, his finger pressed to his ear listening to his comm. "Fairchild says that we're about to have company topside!"

"Right, yes of course." Fitzgerald rolled up the map, retied the thin rope, and handed it to Alexander. "Hold this, if you please. I must now recover my pendent!"

He clamored up the statue, slipping several times in his haste. Using his knife, he unceremoniously tried to pry it from the heart of the statue.

"Be gentle, Adrian! If you're not careful enough, you might set off another trap!"

The medallion suddenly popped free, and Fitzgerald smirked as he held it once again in his palm. "See? Nothing to worry about."

The second the words left his mouth, the statue trembled and the stones beneath Alexander's feet began to crack and shift.

"I knew it!" the professor scowled.

Fitzgerald yelped, slipping off the statue and clawing his way down the body of it to slow his fall. He landed on the platform hard, but squarely on his feet unscathed.

He grinned with a wild look in his eye, "What a rush. Come on!" Fitzgerald jumped across the chasm, followed closely by Alexander. The statue began to collapse in on itself behind them and the wide cobblestone path they took to reach it shook violently. Fitzgerald selfishly launched forward from stone to stone as quickly as he could.

"Hurry up!" Alexander shouted as he knew he was just moments away from death if he had to wait any longer on the man. Once Fitzgerald reached the cavern threshold, Alexander took off at a run, dodging openings of the wedged stones that had given way from all the shaking. He could see now which stones were supported by the wooden beams and didn't have to guess which ones had the Paititi marking. *Oh God, please help me! One wrong move and I'll be impaled!* As he neared the entryway, the last supported stone gave out completely. He lunged headlong with as much force as he could muster and caught the ledge with one hand — his other still clinging nimbly to the map.

His hand slipped and he felt his body begin to drop toward the spikes below. Bracing for impact, he was about to cry out when suddenly two strong arms snatched his own. Beady Eyes and Goatee hoisted Alexander to the ledge. There was not a moment to lose as rock from the walls within the cavern began cascading downward. All four men took off at a run, barely remembering to jump over the tripwire and sprinting the rest of the way to the entrance beneath Torreón. Stones continued to fall and crash behind them, sealing the tunnel for good. As the dust settled, Alexander bent over, catching his breath and eyeing Fitzgerald like he'd lost his mind.

"That's one way to get the blood pumping!" the mercenary laughed uncontrollably through gasps, also struggling to catch his breath. He slipped the chain over his neck and nodded to the stairs. "Let's say we get out of here?" He patted Alexander heartily on the back, whistling as he climbed the roughly hewn steps. Beady Eyes signaled for the professor to go next.

Alexander reluctantly followed, clutching the ancient map to Paititi in his hands.

CHAPTER V

The ride away from Machu Picchu in the back of the van was anything but relaxing. Alexander's chaffed hands ached and every inch of him was sore. More importantly, he was anxious for Fitzgerald to make the call and release Drew and Kaci. So far, the man had done nothing but stare at the map they'd found.

Alexander cleared his throat to cut through the thick silence, "Adrian?"

"You really need to look at this, Jim," the man didn't look up, absorbed with the ancient artifact, "This is going to lead us to the greatest discovery of modern history!"

"Adrian," Alexander firmly pressed, and the man's eyes finally broke free. "We had a deal, remember? I help you get the map, you let the kids go. Make the call. Please get them home to their mother safely." Alexander's eyes narrowed. "*Now.*"

Fitzgerald slowly rolled the map back up, shaking his head. "You really think it's that simple?"

"You said you would let them go."

"True. But if you remember correctly, I specifically said, '*You help me and the kids go free.*'" He took a long look at Alexander then burst into laughter. "Oh, I get it! You thought I meant for you to just help me get the map! Well, the joke is on you, old chum. I suppose I should have made myself a bit clearer. You so hastily agreed to help me."

Alexander's blood began to boil. "What choice did I have? You kidnapped my niece and nephew!"

"That I did. I've placed you in a very hard predicament, but I *had* to get through to you somehow. Now that we have the map, we've got a city of gold to find!"

Alexander should have known the man would never keep his word. "You lying, conniving—"

"I would stop while you're ahead," Fitzgerald cut him off harshly. "Besides, they're a bit further from home than you realize."

Alexander's heart dropped.

"Ah, yes, now you understand. Why would I leave them so far away when having them closer at hand will make you complete your tasks that much quicker? And more efficiently. No, my friend, Drew and Kaci are only about forty miles from here. Don't worry," he added with a sneer, "they're being well looked after."

"You can't do this. You can't make me help you."

"Oh, but I think I can. You see, if you decide *not* to help me, why I'll just take your little monsters and drop them in the middle of the jungle somewhere," Fitzgerald said, his voice hard and cold. "They won't last a day in the wilds of this place. They'll just disappear forever. You probably wouldn't even find their bodies."

"They're just kids! What happened to you?" Alexander whispered.

The man's eyes narrowed. "I'm not sure what you mean."

"You weren't always this heartless. This quest — this lust for fame and immortality — has changed you. It's corrupted you to the core."

Fitzgerald smacked Alexander in the face, his brow furrowing as he whispered heavily, "How dare you judge me! You don't know anything about my life, not anymore. You have no idea what I've given up to finally be where I am today. What I've lost. My quest will not be in vain, understand me? I don't care what I have to do to find the lost city but find it I *will*."

Alexander was not surprised by the man's violent reaction; he gently daubed at the small trickle of blood at the corner of his mouth with a handkerchief. He knew sooner or later something like this would happen. But he *was* startled to see a glimpse of pain in Fitzgerald's eyes. It was real. *Something in his past must be haunting him,* Alexander thought to himself.

Fitzgerald leaned forward to speak tenderly, "If you help me, Jim, help me read the map and find the city, you have my word that I will let you and the kids go home unharmed."

"To be honest, it's difficult for me to believe you."

"I know that we have our differences. But we must work on building our trust in one another." Fitzgerald handed him the map. "And as much as I'd like to say I can do this alone, I can't. I need you, Jim. Besides, you have to admit deep down you want to find this place as much as I do."

Alexander crossed his arms and just stared at him for a long moment. He thought back to the map on the wall of his study. Over the years he had collected vague clues as to the city's possible location — tidbits from explorers he met while lecturing at archeological conferences. Occasionally, he received emails from contacts who would randomly hear stories from locals in the Amazon jungle. But that was all they ever were — just stories. Ever since his time with Adrian twenty years ago in Bloodfist's lair, he had a passing interest in finding the city. But it had never consumed him like it did the man sitting across from him. Many weeks would go by before he had a chance to follow up on a stray lead. His map had accumulated numerous pins over the years that signified clues, but nothing ever came of it.

"Fine," Fitzgerald grumbled, interrupting Alexander's train of thought. "I'll make you a compromise to put your mind at ease. You and I will follow this map. You find for me where we need to start and I will have my guards bring Drew and Kaci to us. You'll see they haven't been harmed and they can remain by your side throughout the journey." He held out his hand. "Deal?"

"How about you take me to them right now, Adrian. That's the only deal I'll agree to."

Fitzgerald let his hand fall and patted the driver, Goatee, on the shoulder. "Change of plans, boys. Take us to the kids." He grinned at Alexander. "Always with the dramatic flair. This will add an extra day to our trek, but if it makes you cooperate then I'll sacrifice the time. Just think of how much fun they'll have, spending their summer exploring the jungle with their uncle. It'll be like a vacation."

"Some vacation, constantly surveilled by armed guards," Alexander muttered. "This goes against everything I stand for, but for the sake of my family, I'll help you. The second we find Paititi, you will give us all a way home immediately. After that, I never want to see you again."

Fitzgerald's eye twitched, but he held out his hand a second time. Alexander shook it. "Then we have a deal, Jim. We have a deal."

Alexander turned to look out the window. *Oh God, please help me to be patient and keep my temper. It's so hard. I cannot give in to the frustration and anger of my flesh. I want to, but I know it's wrong. I need to be a testimony of You to this man. You love him and died for him. You want to save his soul! Lord... I need You. Please let him see You through me.*

Kaci shook Drew's arm, jerking him awake. "Something's happening," she whispered.

Her brother sat up, dragging the heavy chain with him. After their first attempt to escape, the siblings had tried two more times before the young woman in charge ordered them to be chained.

Kaci's stomach growled and she covered it with her hand. Every day they'd been given nothing but thick, sticky oatmeal for breakfast and bread, beans, and water for dinner. Since they never had lunch, Drew always insisted she take more at dinner, but after a few silent arguments, he agreed they'd split everything equally. She didn't want him being weak if a chance came for them to make a run for it. She shifted on the hard floor and her back ached. Any time she stood to stretch her legs, the guards would shout at her until she sat back down. She was exhausted, unable to sleep.

"Think she's back?" Drew asked, peering at the old stacked wooden boxes blocking their view of the door.

"I don't know, but I hope she's in a better mood today." She glanced at Drew, eyeing a slight bruise forming underneath his eye. He'd gotten that after their last escape attempt. The woman had head-butted him for his defiance. "How bad does it hurt?"

Drew chuckled, "I'll be fine. If they wanted us dead, they would have killed us a long time ago. They need us for something. I really think we're going to be okay. We've gotta keep the faith."

Kaci warmly smiled at her brother's positive spirit. She loved that about him; he always found the best in any situation. "Well, just think of the story we'll have for our youth group!"

"That's the spirit, little sister."

The two guards who had been watching over them stood the moment the young woman appeared, chewing on a toothpick as always. She waved toward Drew and Kaci, yelling, "Get them on their feet. Unchain them."

"What's going on?" Drew asked as he and Kaci were hauled to their feet.

The young woman smirked over her shoulder. "You'll see. Bring them, now!"

"Where are we going?" Kaci shouted. "Please, get your hands off me!"

She fought against the man holding her arm, yanking her away from her brother. She lost sight of him as she was dragged through the maze of oversized shipping crates and then was shoved through a door out into humid air. She sucked in a breath, confused by what was quickly coming into focus around her. Holding up her hand against the bright glare of the sun, she squinted, telling herself this wasn't real. It couldn't be. Suddenly Drew was thrust next to her, and he collapsed to his knees. He winced at the brightness of the sun. "Are we... where are we?"

Kaci shook her head. "We're not in Iowa, that's for sure. Why does this look like a jungle?"

"Because it *is* a jungle, sweetheart," the young woman replied with a smirk. "You're a long way from home. Something to keep in mind in case you decide to try and run again. What's out there is far worse than what's right here."

Drew stood up and Kaci leaned into her brother's side. Fear threatened to cripple her, when a familiar voice off in the distance reached her ears. She jumped at the sound, Drew looking frantically with her around the corner of the warehouse. Their eyes were now adjusted to the bright sun and they saw a makeshift camp of camouflaged tents among low-lying structures that stood out from the overgrowth. A rusty guard tower loomed over the small spread of buildings and a tall chain-link fence interwoven with barbed wire appeared to surround the perimeter.

Two men were walking toward them. One had a wild look in his eyes and was talking and gesturing broadly at the complex around them. The other man faced straight forward, jaw clenched, moving with wide determined strides. The moment they recognized who it was, the siblings took off at a run, throwing themselves into their uncle's arms.

Alexander set his duffle bag down and hugged them close, apologizing over and over for what they had endured. When his eyes landed on Drew's face, he whirled around on the other man, snapping, "You said they were unharmed."

The man peered at the bruise, then glowered at the young woman who had just walked up. "What did I say?" he growled through his teeth.

"They tried to escape," she replied nonchalantly. "Had to do something to keep them in line."

"Those were *not* your orders! Now get that toothpick out of your mouth and act more decently."

The woman shrugged, spitting it out in the man's face, and stormed away, muttering angrily under her breath.

"Adrian," Alexander sharply stated.

"It shouldn't have happened," the man responded quickly, raising both of his hands defensively. "Truly, I did not know." He then glared at the two young people. "It would have helped if you simply complied."

"Um, we don't know what's going on here," Drew boldly stepped forward, "but someone *kidnapped* us. What were we supposed to do? Huh?"

"Enough!" Fitzgerald interjected. "Jim, you have my word. For the remainder of our time together, they will not be harmed. Now if you'll excuse me, I need to speak with my men. We'll stay here tonight and head out first thing in the morning." He hurried off in the direction where the young woman had disappeared, leaving Alexander with Kaci and Drew.

"I never wanted this to happen to you," Alexander said, hugging them again.

"We're okay, Uncle James. Really. Besides needing a shower and a good meal, I think we're going to be fine." Drew looked in the direction Fitzgerald had walked and asked, "Who is that man? How do you know him?"

"His name is Adrian Fitzgerald. He was my friend a very long time ago, but everything about him has changed," Alexander told them sadly. "He's turned into a ruthless criminal mastermind. He kidnapped you to force me to help him on his quest for the lost city of gold."

Kaci's eyes brightened. "You mean Paititi?"

Alexander instantly turned his gaze to her when she mentioned the word. "How do you know of that place?"

She smiled. "Drew and I saw that word scribbled on the map in your office when we visited you last time."

"Ah, yes. Before our escapade in the Mediterranean." He shook his head, "Dabbling in the research of this city has been a passing hobby of mine."

"It really intrigued us," Drew mentioned. "After we got home, we looked it up on the internet. It was something like you said — a legendary city of gold that no one has ever been able to find."

"Until possibly now," their uncle grimly acknowledged. "We've found a map that might lead us to its location — but I don't know how real or accurate it is. I must say, however, that what we've seen so far seems to validate the city's existence."

"You agreed to help him, didn't you?" Kaci said quietly. "To keep us safe?"

"When I found out he'd kidnapped you, I had to do whatever it took to protect you. But it appears that he wishes to take you both along on our jungle quest as 'insurance' to make me cooperate. I've tried to talk him out of it, but he won't have anything to do with it. I'm so sorry."

Drew placed his hand on his uncle's shoulder. "It's okay. Kaci and I were scared, but we've been learning to pray a lot. To really have faith in God."

"Amen. And I am most thankful that He has kept you safe."

"Now we're with you," Kaci chimed in. "And together with Jesus, we can take on anyone!"

Alexander burst out in warm laughter, and a lop-sided grin began to slowly spread across his face. He motioned for them to sit on a large crate under the shade of a nearby tree. Supplies, boxes, and even trash sat in piles nearby against the wall of the warehouse.

"I must warn you that this journey will not be easy. It will be very treacherous," he peered at them over the top rim of his glasses. Both of their eyes were wide with excitement and a charged spirit. "But I know both of my little monsters are always up for a good challenge."

He knelt down beside his large duffle bag and pulled out a rolled-up faded brown leather backpack. His eyes twinkled as he tossed it to Kaci. "I know you two didn't pack for this trip, seeing as you weren't even planning to go on one in the first place. You'll need this. It's been a personal favorite of mine for many years on many adventures. Perhaps you can use it to keep any personal items you both might gather along the way?"

"Thanks, Uncle James!" Kaci took it with a grateful smile, opening it and discovering the various pockets within.

Alexander hesitated, then pulled a small silver case out of a pouch from inside his bag. "And maybe you could start your collection with this?" He held out the case. "Would you please keep this kit safe in there for me? I don't think I'll need it, but... well, you just never know."

"Sure," she nodded and quickly slipped it into the large opening. "I'd be glad to."

"Uncle James?" Drew stroked his chin, deep in thought. "This lost city... why does Mr. Fitzgerald want to find it so badly?"

"Adrian has become consumed by greed," Alexander replied softly. "I warned him a long time ago it would cost him everything he had if he tried to find it. But he ignored me and now he's become a twisted version of himself. If we find the lost city, I fear it's only going to break him further. I think there's something else he's after, not just the gold."

"What do you mean?"

Alexander gave Kaci a worried look. "I'm not sure yet. He mentioned something to me in passing the other day that struck me as odd — but we'll worry about it when we get there. If we do." He hooked his arms around both of the teenagers' shoulders. "Come on, let's see if we can get you both cleaned up. You don't look like you've been taken care of as well as I was told you were."

With their uncle there, Kaci and Drew were treated as if they were now a part of the team. The guards nodded and smiled at them. One even gruffly stated, "No harm meant. It's just business," then walked away clutching his AK-47. They were given clean water to drink and an actual meal. They sat down on makeshift wooden benches under a camouflaged canopy surrounded by a scattering of tents.

Fitzgerald, despite having kidnapped them, didn't seem too pleased with how they'd been looked after and sincerely apologized to Drew and Kaci. He sat across from them as the kids devoured their food and spoke fondly of their uncle, sharing memories from their college days. Kaci sensed he was simply trying to win them over and get them to like him.

As he finished an entertaining story of when they were on the rugby team together, she abruptly asked, "Can we call our mom?"

This caught him by complete surprise, and both teenagers saw his eyes narrow menacingly. But they softened as she continued with a quivering voice, "I miss her so much. I can't even imagine what she must be thinking or how she's feeling. It's been at least five days!"

For a moment, silence hung thick in the humid air.

Alexander leaned forward earnestly, "Adrian, you promised me that you would allow this."

"Fine! Fine. But, you are not to give her any names, understand?" Fitzgerald instructed, handing over a satellite phone to Alexander. "You have five minutes and not a second more. Make your call."

Alexander dialed out and waited. "Susan?" he said when she answered.

"James! I am *so glad* to hear your voice. The kids are gone!"

He shut his eyes, sighing. "Yes, I know, but everything will be okay. The kids are safe with me."

"Thank God! I've been so distraught. When they didn't come that night, I just knew something was wrong. But within the hour, I received a phone call from a disguised voice threatening me that if I contacted you or the authorities, they'd kill the kids instantly." She burst into tears. "They said to just sit tight and wait for a call from you. Can you imagine? Asking the mother of kidnapped children to sit tight? I've been a nervous wreck these last few days," she sighed. "But, James, I'm so glad they're okay! Does all this have to do with the Demeons?"

"No," he paused, his eyes flickering to Fitzgerald. "But unfortunately, I'm not at liberty to divulge any other details at the moment. Susan, I am *so* sorry this happened. I wish I could say more, but please pray for us with what lies ahead. I promise you that I'm going to get them home. Take just a moment and speak to them; then I'm afraid we have to go." He handed the phone to Kaci and she and Drew put it between them.

"Mom?" Kaci said.

Susan cried at the other end of the line. "What happened? Where are you? Are you both okay?"

"We're fine," Drew assured her. "We really are. We're with Uncle James. He's going to take care of us."

She sniffed a couple times and cleared her throat. "I'm so sorry this happened to you, Sweetheart, but it does give me some peace of mind to know your uncle is there with you. Where are you, anyway?"

He glanced around. "I don't know, a jungle or something."

"Watch it, son," Fitzgerald quietly snarled.

"Mom, we love you," Kaci stammered, trying to hold back the tears that she could feel welling up within her.

"But what happened? Can't you tell me *anything?*"

"Mom, everything is okay; I promise," Kaci added calmly even as she glared at the mercenary. "We're safe; just keep praying for us."

"Time's up," Fitzgerald growled, reaching for the phone.

"Please, just another moment!" Drew demanded, putting out his hand forcefully on Fitzgerald's chest. The man's eyes burned as he smacked Drew's hand away.

"Ow! You didn't have to do that!"

"Are you challenging me, boy?"

Two of the guards rushed forward and Alexander yelled for everyone to stop.

"What's going on?" Susan demanded with a tremor in her voice.

"Mom, we love you!" Kaci exclaimed as the phone was wrenched away and the call disconnected.

"You got a problem with us talking to our mother for a minute?" Red-faced, Drew was livid, adrenalin rushing through his body. He boldly stepped right in front of Fitzgerald. "Huh? HUH?"

The man stood silent for a moment and then laughed harshly. Bits of saliva landed on Drew's face. "Aww. Do we have a momma's boy on our hands?" Some of the guards who had gathered chuckled along with their boss.

"N-n-no." Drew's offensive stance lessened as he felt the tender yet firm hand of his uncle on his shoulder. "But there's nothing wrong with telling her that we're okay. It's been five days, sir!"

"And you did just that, my boy." Everyone stood still as Fitzgerald paced back and forth and stared at the two teenagers.

"This trip will go much better for everyone if you both play by the rules; and the rules are simple. I am in charge. You will do as I say. What I say goes! If you question my authority, you will regret it and there will be consequences. End of story. Work with me, and I will work with you. Have I made myself clear?"

Alexander cleared his throat and answered for them, "Perfectly."

"Good. Now I suggest, Jim, that you take some time to explain to your 'little monsters' how this is going to work." He flashed a chilling smile. "I know their cooperation will be greatly appreciated by both me... and you." He turned on his heels and began barking orders to his men about supplies that needed to be packed, equipment that needed to be double-checked, and weapon magazines that needed to be loaded and stored safely.

"How was *that* man ever your friend?" Drew asked his uncle once Fitzgerald left them alone.

"It's a long story from a long time ago," Alexander shook his head. "Come on. Let's find somewhere out of the way where we can talk."

They slowly walked together down the dirt road that led through the heart of the dilapidated complex.

"You know, I was actually planning to surprise you both with a visit after my trip here to South America." The professor chuckled. "Cambridge sent me, and we had no idea that Adrian was behind all of it. Somehow, he falsified a discovery and blackmailed a professor at the University of Lima to get me down here. When I walked into my hotel room, there he was, sitting in the darkness waiting for me. I was shocked. You know why?"

Both young people shook their heads, eagerly wondering.

"He supposedly has been dead for years."

"What?" Kaci blurted out.

"That's right. He faked his own death to become a ghost to the world. He founded some sort of criminal organization that engages in less than honorable activities including racketeering, assassinations, and gun smuggling."

"Add kidnapping to that list," Drew glowered.

"And there's that," Alexander remarked as he finished cleaning his glasses with a handkerchief.

"Wow. He really is a bad man," Kaci shivered.

"That he is. But he has a soul; don't forget Jesus loves him and died for him on the Cross, too."

"But how can we work with a guy like that?" Drew asked.

"It won't be easy, but we have to if we want to make it out of this alive." Their uncle put his glasses on and stuffed his handkerchief into his back pocket. "We must be careful. The Bible warns us to *'make no friendship with an angry man; and with a furious man thou shalt not go. Lest thou learn his ways and get a snare to thy soul.'* We must keep our eyes on the Lord." He paused. "I encourage you both to pray often and ask God for strength and for many opportunities to be a testimony for Him while we're in this situation." He pointed around them discreetly.

"Do you see all these men? We might be the only Gospel witness they'll ever get in their entire life." He pulled out his small worn Bible from the pouch on his hip. Drew and Kaci smiled fondly as the sight of it flooded their minds with scenes of their last adventure. "Everyone needs Jesus, and God wants to use *us* as living epistles."

"Hmmm," Drew rubbed his jaw. "I remember our youth pastor talking about this a couple of weeks ago in Sunday School. Something about how we should be living out God's Word through our words and actions."

"Yes!" Kaci interjected. "Like walking Bibles! Well, sort of. You know what I mean."

"Of course," Alexander laughed. "God wants us to be 'peculiar.' Not in the sense of being strange or 'weird' as you young people would say, but 'different.' We ought to act different from the world because we *are* different. Jesus lives inside us! II Corinthians 3 encourages us that His Word should be *'written in our hearts, known and read of all men.'"*

He stopped and hugged them both tightly. "I promise you that I'll do whatever it takes to keep you both safe. You and your mother are the only family I have left. But let's covenant together that we'll allow His Word to shine through us on this journey, okay?" The teenagers nodded their heads, and Alexander began to softly pray for boldness to face whatever lay ahead and God's strength to carry them every step of the way.

CHAPTER VI

Drew stared into their small crackling fire. Kaci opened an MRE and carefully shuffled out the contents onto a tin plate. She sat beside him on the soft ground, their uncle next to her in a camp chair.

"Enjoy those while they last," Alexander smiled. "I have a feeling we're only going to have enough for the first few weeks. After that, we'll be living off the land. What a way to spend your summer!"

The two young people grinned. Uncle James knew they were born for adventure. He remembered seeing the disappointment in their eyes when it was time for them to head home after their spring break. Of course, they wanted to be back with their mother again, but part of them wished they could all live with their uncle in England.

"This is going to be the ultimate camping experience," Drew remarked, still staring into the flames.

The three of them were allowed to share a tent; Alexander wouldn't have it any other way. He didn't feel comfortable leaving them out of his sight all night among so many "unsavory characters," as he called them. Fitzgerald generously gave them one of the best tents and promised that there wouldn't be any guards keeping a wary eye on them. They were a part of the team now. But Drew knew this freedom was only because they were hedged about completely by miles and miles of rainforest. There was nowhere for them to run even if they *were* able to escape.

Night fell and with it came the ambiance of the South American jungle — animals calling and howling, insects chirping, leaves rustling overhead as the humid wind blew. The lack of sun brought little relief as far as heat or humidity, but at least they were outside and no longer trapped inside the foul-smelling warehouse.

"How is everyone?" Fitzgerald asked as he approached. The two men exchanged nods while the two teenagers mumbled a greeting without looking up. "What do you think of this base, Jim? It's an old military prison that the Peruvian government abandoned decades ago. It's turned out to be an excellent base for our operations here in South America."

"Adrian, I mean no disrespect, but the less we know about your operations, the better off we are."

The man laughed, "Agreed! Lest you get all 'preachy' on me."

Drew saw Fitzgerald's muddy boots step in front of him. He looked up and noticed the man was pleasantly smiling and holding out his hand toward the teenager. "Let's try this again, shall we? A 'fresh start' as they call it."

Drew looked to his uncle who smiled and nodded. He looked back up toward Fitzgerald and firmly shook his hand.

"Ah! Quite a grip you have there. That'll sure come in handy as we travel into the heart of the Amazon." He opened up a portable folding stool and sat down across from them. The fire glowed on his face, accentuating the wrinkles caused by hardened years.

"I suggest you two turn in soon. It's going to be a long trip tomorrow."

"It'll be good to sleep," Kaci sighed. "It's been almost a week."

"And again, for that I am sorry."

"We forgive you," Drew and the man made direct eye contact. "And Mr. Fitzgerald, I'm sorry for how I handled myself earlier today. It just really saddened me to hear my mother so distraught, and when you cut us off from talking to her, it really made me angry. I shouldn't have gotten into your face. I wasn't letting Jesus live through me."

Fitzgerald snorted, not knowing how to respond. "Fine. Just… just watch your mouth next time, and we won't have any problems."

The teenagers could easily see that he was uncomfortable with spiritual things. An awkward silence hung in the air until Kaci spoke up, "Mr. Fitzgerald, who was the young woman that watched us? I've noticed she's the only other female here besides me."

Fitzgerald absently picked up a stick from the ground, poking the fire. The flames reflected in his eyes and for a moment, Drew noticed a mix of sadness, regret, and pain. "That is Jada. My daughter."

"Your *daughter*?" Alexander was genuinely surprised. "You never told me you had a child."

"You never asked," Fitzgerald curtly replied. "I've already given you plenty of chances to catch up with me as the friends we once were."

"What happened to her?" Drew asked quietly.

"What on earth do you mean, boy?"

"Well, she's not exactly the nicest person around," he muttered, gingerly touching his lightly bruised eye.

Fitzgerald frowned, poking at the fire again. "She hasn't had the easiest life, I'll grant you that." He smiled softly. "But she's younger than she looks; she's gone through a lot to make her tough."

"How old is she?" Kaci gently interrupted.

"How old do you *think* she is?"

"Like 20 or something."

"No. She'll be turning 18 by the end of the summer."

Kaci and Drew exchanged surprised glances. "What? She's *our* age?"

Fizgerald chuckled. "They grow up so fast. She looks just like her mother, but I'm afraid that's all she inherited from her."

"What was her name, your wife?" Alexander asked, leaning forward intently.

"That's another story for another time," a female voice coldly said just beyond the glow of the small campfire. Jada silently stepped forward and appeared behind Fitzgerald. Her gaze was like steel and her lips were firmly pressed together. "Dad, we barely know these people, and you're about to spill our family history? I'm not comfortable with that. Don't."

Fitzgerald was humored by his daughter's forwardness and shook his head. "These *people* are our friends — like I told you before, Jim here and I go back over twenty years."

"Well, I don't care," she snapped, stepping up to the fire to join the others. "They're not *my* friends. And they *won't* be until they prove their worth. The less they know about us, the better."

Fitzgerald sighed. "Oh, Jada, nothing like spoiling the mood. Just when I was about to get them to like me." He laughed. "You *are* your mother's daughter."

A smirk spread across her face, "Stubborn to the core." She gently punched him in the arm. "I think you had something to do with that, too."

"Undoubtedly!"

Drew and Kaci were shocked at the level of disrespect the girl showed her father and how it seemed he enjoyed it.

"Oh," Jada said with false concern as she noticed their eyes on her. "Does our relationship bother you? Good. Get used to it. But if I ever hear any of you talking to my father the way I do —" She gently half-pulled one of her throwing knives from its holster by her side.

"Jada, that's enough. You will treat the Professor here with dignity. He has earned my respect — he saved my life back in Machu Picchu! And you will be pleasant to Drew and Kaci. I've actually been thinking it might be good for you to spend some time with them on our journey."

"*What?*"

"You heard me clearly!" he half-snarled, pointing directly at her. After a moment, his mood suddenly lightened, and he lowered his hand. "You need some friends your age. Won't it be great to 'hang out,' as today's young people say?"

Jada's eyes blazed with fury as she darted a glance toward Drew and Kaci. She spun around without saying a word and stormed off.

Fitzgerald shook his head with a chuckle. "She's a handful, but she's a good girl. She loves this life I've given her and has an even greater drive than I do." He stood and stretched. His shadow flickered and loomed large against the jungle overgrowth and a few of the abandoned buildings. "Tomorrow will be the first day of our historic quest! In the morning, we'll start looking at the map together and you can begin using those translation skills of yours."

Alexander looked anything but thrilled. "I pray that it will lead us right. That map could be a false clue, a way to take searchers such as yourself *away* from the city, if it even exists. For all you know, it wasn't a city of gold, but just another city."

The man barked a laugh and folded up his portable metal stool. "Whether the walls are made of gold or not — there is believed to be over ten billion dollars' worth of Incan gold, artifacts, and jewelry within them. It's the largest undiscovered treasure trove in human history, old chum!"

Alexander stood and motioned for Drew and Kaci to head into their tent for the night. The two men lingered for several minutes, speaking to each other in hushed tones. Drew and Kaci could barely see them through the tent flap that was cracked open. Kaci strained to hear what they were talking about but was sound asleep within moments. Drew's mind was racing as he tried to think of what lay before them. They were with their uncle again, about to begin the adventure of a lifetime, facing countless dangers. Would they survive? He found himself shivering in trepidation.

Finally, Drew noticed Fitzgerald walking away and he lay perfectly still as his uncle came into the tent. The man quietly zipped the front flap closed and made his way to his cot. Instead of crawling into his bed to go to sleep, he slumped to his knees and began to pray. A tear formed in the corner of Drew's eye as he heard his uncle's whispered prayer for their safety, God's wisdom and power, and Adrian's salvation. Drew suddenly felt a wave of peace flood over him. He smiled and instantly fell asleep, knowing that God was in control.

Morning came far too quickly for Alexander. He awoke before Kaci and Drew as the bright sun began spilling over the horizon and through the jungle trees. He wearily rubbed his face as his feet touched the canvas floor of the tent, yawning as he put on his glasses. For a few moments he talked with the Lord silently, thanking Him for a new day and humbly asking for strength in what they were about to undertake. He glanced at his wristwatch; it was barely 6:30 am. He knew neither of the teenagers had gotten much sleep while they were locked up in that warehouse, so he decided to let them rest for a bit longer. He silently pulled out a thin spare Bible from his duffle bag and left a note on it, *"My little monsters, take some time each morning to let God speak to you through His Word. This book will be a light unto your path and the spiritual nourishment you need to make it through this adventure! Joshua 1:8."*

He quietly exited the tent, took some time to freshen up, and then sat down in his camping chair. He nodded at one of the morning patrols as they passed by on the dirt road leading through the compound. He smiled, pulling out his worn leather Bible. *Father, what have we gotten ourselves into?* He shook his head and sighed. *This is absolutely crazy. I'm thankful, though, that Your promises are real and can be claimed daily.*

His devotions lead him to a familiar passage of Scripture in Lamentations 3. In spite of the suffering that Jeremiah endured, he rejoiced in the face of adversity because of God's steadfastness. Alexander's tired eyes brightened as he mediated upon a couple of the verses in particular: *"It is of the Lord's mercies that we are not consumed, because his compassions fail not. They are new every morning: great is thy faithfulness. The Lord is my portion, saith my soul; therefore will I hope in him."*

He looked up to the sky above and smiled broadly. *Lord, thank You. That is just what I needed.*

He heard footsteps approach from behind.

"Jim, isn't it a lovely morning?" Fitzgerald called out boisterously.

Alexander quickly stood and put a finger to his lips, then pointed to the tent.

"Ah, yes," the Scott responded with a hushed tone. "Your little monsters are still resting. But they will have to rise soon because my men have already begun to break camp." He slapped Alexander heartily on the back. "Come along now. Can't you feel the excitement in the air? It's electrifying!"

As they approached the heart of the compound, men were scurrying about loading rifles and packing supplies in small protective storage cases. Others were taking down tents and carefully loading crates into the back of green camouflaged M939 transport trucks and jeeps. A few others were opening up a warehouse bay door and guiding out fuel tankers.

Alexander also observed that each man bore a similar red tattoo. While his former friend had a large, flying, tattered flag bearing two crossed fists running up both forearms, the men had a smaller version of just the crossed fists themselves on the under part of their left forearm.

A couple of patrols in M1161 Growlers — open-roofed two-seater vehicles outfitted with .50 caliber machine guns mounted in the back — passed by them, and the men saluted Fitzgerald.

"You've got yourself a regular army here," Alexander dryly commented.

"Impressive, isn't it? We want to be prepared for the worst," Fitzgerald replied.

"You're aware that we won't be able to bring all of this with us the entire journey?"

"That is understandable, but we'll most likely be going through territories overrun with guerrillas or owned by drug cartels. Who knows what we will run into, but nothing will stand in my way — our way — of finding Paititi." Fitzgerald stopped at a table that had been set up under a canvas canopy.

"Here it is," he wildly smiled. "Our guide that will lead us to destiny."

Before them, sprawled out on the wooden surface, lay the ancient map held down by several small rocks at the corners.

"How does it feel to know that you're about to become one of the most famous explorers on the planet?" the man playfully asked.

"I'm not in it for the fame. I just want to get my family back home safely."

"But, Jim, you and I both know that this is an archaeologist's *dream*," he prodded further. "Besides, you'll be rich. So rich, you'll never have to work another day in your life. You'll be able to take care of your niece and nephew and your poor widowed sister for the rest of their days."

"And we're back to the money," Alexander muttered.

"Money is *power* in this world. When are you going to finally learn that?"

"I don't want power, money, or fame. I want our find to be studied by the world. It's preserved history. And I want the integrity of our find to remain intact. Undisturbed."

Fitzgerald's eyes darkened. "Always with the ethics, old chum."

"I want you to promise me. Not that your word means much to me at this point."

Fitzgerald chuckled, but the sound was forced. At that moment, Girly approached them, holding out tin cups filled with a dark brew, "Coffee?"

Alexander nodded, breathing in the pleasant aroma, and took it without saying a word.

"Would you like to add something a bit stronger?" Fitzgerald's eyes twinkled as he removed a small aluminum flask from his cargo vest.

"Adrian, just stop. Stop with all the subtle temptations. I'm a Christian, and I'm going to glorify the Lord." Girly awkwardly looked at his boss and then slowly backed away.

"You don't have to be so dramatic," Fitzgerald laughed. "I was just having some fun with you!"

"Well, I don't drink alcohol and honestly neither should you. It will impair your abilities to reason. Besides, it's a sin. Do *not* offer it to me again!"

The burly man shrugged as he unscrewed the lid and poured a portion of its contents into his coffee. "Fine, fine I get it. Just more for me anyway!"

"Now leave me to my work so I can figure out where we're supposed to begin."

"Excellent, my good man!" He glanced at the watch on his left wrist. "We're leaving in less than two hours."

Alexander took another moment to drink his coffee as he studied the map. The writing was in excellent condition. In any other situation, he would've been thrilled to see such an artifact intact, but not this time. If the letters had been faded, if the images weren't readable, he could simply claim there was no way to read it. If he could find a way to ruin the map, Fitzgerald would have no choice but to give up on his search. *If I accidentally spill my cup of coffee....* Glancing around, Alexander noticed Beady Eyes and Goatee watching him. Their lips were curled with menacing smiles, and their hands rested on the butts of their handguns holstered at their hips, almost as if they could read the man's mind. That and there were about ten other men milling around, all armed to the teeth. He sighed, giving up on his idea and turning his attention back to translating.

Gingerly, he ran his fingers over the writing and then found a pen and pad of paper waiting there for him to use. He started with the text located in the bottom left corner of the map, the place he believed their path began, and worked his way around the edge of the map. He noticed that at each corner and in the middle of the top and bottom edge was an ominous stone face, angled and sitting upright. There were six in total. *Hmmm. That's something worth taking note of.* The morning heat was already sweltering and sweat broke out on his brow while he worked at roughly writing down the words in English. When he finished, he held up the page, reading them quietly to himself.

"*Where the land reaches up toward the sun in a jagged peak of stone, that is where the path begins. The guide waits. Its soul will point*

the way. Choose not to listen and you will turn down a path of despair."
Alexander's brow furrowed. *Well, that's cheery and good for the soul.*
He set the pad of paper down, removing his glasses to rub his eyes.
Guess we'll figure that part out later. As for this jagged peak of stone....
He put his glasses back on and dragged over a modern map of Peru,
searching for where this location might be. According to the ancient
map, this peak was close to a small lake. After a few minutes of
scouring the second map, he found the only location that made sense.
There was a lone, jagged peak that stuck up in the middle of nowhere.
There was no name for it, nor was there anything around it as far as
he could tell. A road led close to it and there was a small lake nearby.
Better than nothing, he thought to himself. *There's probably a village
there since there's a road. Maybe they will know something.*

Marking the place on the modern-day map for Fitzgerald,
Alexander returned to the ancient one to finish translating. Three
large areas were highlighted with beautiful drawings that had
somehow not lost any of their vibrant color over the years.

The first was a cliff with what appeared to be scribbles written
across it. Unfortunately, the writing was too small to make out if they
were actual words or not. Jungle surrounded the cliff with small dots
sprawling out in front of it in a semi-arc. He pinched his chin, curious
as to what that represented.

The second drawing further to the northeast of the cliff was a
waterfall crashing into a turquoise pool surrounded by vegetation with
a river stemming from it. The final image of importance was an island
with mountains on it. In the center of it was an open-mouthed skull
with the Incan symbol of Paititi encircled above it. The eerie face
almost appeared to be laughing at those who dared to look upon it.
Around the island was a lake containing a giant green serpent with a
head on each end of its coiled body lurking at the bottom as if waiting
to devour any who came too close. *This was a depiction of Amura, the
Incan god of the underworld,* he thought to himself.

Alexander didn't need a clue to tell him getting near that
mountain was not going to be easy. There was no telling how

treacherous this trip was going to be or how far the distance was between the locations. Nothing appeared to be drawn to scale. Without finding these guides the map mentioned, they'd be wandering around with no clear direction. He sighed, sipping his coffee. Sensing eyes on him, he glanced up to find Blondie glaring at him.

"Fairchild," Fitzgerald shouted, and the man jerked around. "Finalize the things on this list. Make sure the men double-check everything."

"Right away, Boss," Fairchild replied. His eyes narrowed on Alexander. He blinked and stalked off leaving the professor once again under the watchful gaze of Beady Eyes and Goatee. There was something off about that man. Something unsettling. Alexander had his fair share of dealing with unsavory characters in his line of work. But this man's unnaturally pale skin gave him goosebumps, and his sharp blue eyes seemed to be after more than just what lay at the end of this treasure hunt. Alexander could feel it. He was tempted to say something to his old friend. Then again, that was probably why Fitzgerald had hired him in the first place — similar devious nature.

"Uncle James?" Drew asked, appearing at his right side while Kaci was at his left.

"Why, hello there!" He stood to give them both a hug. "You two sleep okay?"

"Couldn't have been better," Drew answered.

"And thank you for the Bible!" Kaci cheerfully bounced on the balls of her feet.

"You are most welcome," the professor grinned broadly.

"The sleeping beauties finally rise and shine," Jada muttered sarcastically as she and her father marched under the canopy.

"So," Fitzgerald said, clapping his hands together, "where do we start?"

Alexander pointed to a spot on the map of Peru at the other end of the table. "Here. There's a chance I'm wrong, but if you trust my translation skills to be correct then that's where the path begins."

"At this jagged peak? Why do you think so?"

"It's my best educated guess according to the clue that was left to us," he handed Fitzgerald the pad. "You can check for yourself."

"'*Where the land reaches up toward the sun in a jagged peak of stone, that is where the path begins,*'" Fitzgerald mumbled to himself and scoured the map for a few moments. Then he nodded, resigned, "Fine. I'll trust your gut."

"Look," the professor lowered his voice, looked around, and took a step forward. "Let me just make something clear. You don't want me challenging your authority. I get that, and I will respect that. But I ask that you don't challenge mine. I know what I'm doing here." He backed away and tilted his head over to one side. "Now if you would like to find someone *else* to translate, then by all means please do because we would love to go home."

Fitzgerald chuckled. "Nice try, Jim. Of course I trust you!" Then his face twisted to a sinister smile. "If you lead us to our deaths, you only lead to yours as well." His demeanor instantly changed to be less menacing. "Now, what else have you discovered?"

Alexander cleared his throat and tapped the notepad. "It gets complicated."

"Complicated how?"

Alexander waved his hand over the ancient map. "Do you see any indication on this map of where to go?" he asked. "How to follow that little line connecting these three places that serve as checkpoints? There are no directions. No 'take twenty paces north of the crooked tree.' We have our starting point and, well, we have this." He handed the notepad to Fitzgerald.

The mercenary's brow furrowed when he read Alexander's scripted writing. "A guide? We're supposed to find a guide? And its soul will point the way? How is that even remotely helpful?"

"That's what it says. If we want to find this city of yours, we have to find the guide. I'm going to assume it holds the next clue to follow. Without it, we won't be getting anywhere," he explained. "Now, my guess is that there's a village near this road; maybe someone there knows more about this. But it's a fifty-fifty chance at best. You and I both know these guides are most likely going to be hidden or hard to find."

"What do you suppose they are?"

"I'm inclined to think that we're looking for something like what's on the map. Look here." He pointed to each of the four corners. "These faces might be of some significance since they are with this text. Maybe it will be that obvious, maybe it won't. But what's the harm in looking until we find out for certain?"

"Interesting, indeed," Fitzgerald scratched his jaw.

"Now, please understand — it has been centuries. These guides might not even be around anymore. And if we can't find the first one, it's over. That and I have no idea how many there even are. The map says nothing about it. There could be dozens, Adrian, scores of them in the jungle. You really think we'll be able to find them all?"

"If you're going to give me one more lecture on how this is a fool's errand, you can save it," Fitzgerald snapped, tossing the notepad back to Alexander. "We'll head to the first location and I suggest you use that time to figure out where we go next."

"Adrian," he tried, but the man stalked off, shouting at his men to finish up.

"Can we help?" Kaci asked their uncle. "Maybe help you brainstorm about what the guide might be?"

He smiled at her. "Always so optimistic."

She shrugged. "Well, if anything, it will keep our minds off of our current situation."

Alexander appreciated the help. He made sure they'd eaten before they climbed into the back of one of the jeeps. Jada and Baldy took the front seats. Fitzgerald had slid into the lead vehicle with Fairchild, Beady Eyes, and Goatee. Others scurried about with their last-minute preparations, securing cargo on the M939's.

Alexander climbed into the front passenger seat of the jeep behind his niece and nephew. He wanted to always have them in his sights. Girly hopped into the driver seat and when the big man realized that Alexander was sitting next to him, he murmured. "You're not gonna try some more to convert me, are ya?"

Alexander laughed, "No, not right now, unless you're interested."

The man grunted. Alexander smiled as they slowly drove off. *He's under conviction. Keep working, Holy Spirit!* He unrolled the map on his lap and set to work figuring out what the guides could be. The ancient cultures of South America had many creatures and gods that they might be referring to. The question was, what were they looking for? An animal? A totem? A statue of some kind? Alexander studied the map closely, looking with curiosity at all the intricate details, anything to give him a clue as to what they would be searching for. He leaned back and rested his eyes. "Hopefully, when we reach the village, we'll be able to find some answers."

"You better hope we do," Girly chuckled. "Adrian Fitzgerald isn't a very patient man."

CHAPTER VII

The trip to the jagged peak took longer than expected. After a few days of traveling, storms moved in and washed out the roads, making it impossible to go anywhere. The following morning as the rain subsided, Fitzgerald's men feverishly worked cutting down small trees and laying them in the road. The tall trunks sank into the mud enough to offer grip for the vehicles to move on once again.

Fitzgerald stalked around their camp, glaring and yelling at anyone who looked at him sideways. He hoped that this setback was not a sign of things to come. While he paced impatiently like a caged tiger, Kaci and Drew tried their best to avoid him. They kept helping with the map, looking at it with magnifying glasses until their eyes hurt. They studied every detail of each illustration, but there weren't any hidden messages as far as they could tell. All they could do now was wait.

That evening, Drew and Kaci sat beside their campfire. Kaci was sketching the turquoise flower she'd picked early that afternoon in a notebook she found in one of the supply crates. Alexander was under another canopy, his brow furrowed in deep concentration as he intently read in Latin Aapo's letter to the Pope. Past him was Fitzgerald's command tent with its canvas sides rolled up. Men came and went as their leader gave orders. Other guards who were not on duty loudly engaged in a game of poker that sprawled out on top of a large wooden crate nearby.

Drew tossed a few dried leaves into the fire, his mind drifting to how differently he imagined this summer would go. He thought the hardest decision he was going to have to make was figuring out what to do once he graduated from high school next year. He still didn't have any clear leading from God yet, and his heart was torn over a couple of different directions he could take. He thought about his friends back home, probably busy training for the next football season. *Do they wonder where I'm at? How's mom doing? And Pastor Mark? Is the youth group praying for us?* He shook his head. *I can't believe I'm back on a wild, dangerous adventure — and one that I might not survive.*

Fairchild suddenly walked passed them covered in dirt. "Children," he drily greeted them with a nod. The two teenagers just looked at each other and shrugged.

The man entered the command tent and Fitzgerald laughed at him, "Please tell me you have some good news after playing in the mud all day."

"Our patrols have gone further ahead and discovered that this was the only portion of the road that was affected."

"And?"

"We'll be ready by morning."

Fitzgerald yelled in exhilaration with such a force that it startled everyone. He smacked his lieutenant on the shoulder, "Good work, man!"

Fairchild gave a thin smile in return with what looked more like a wince and then slipped off into the night without saying a word.

The folding chair on the other side of the fire shifted and Drew glanced over to find Jada sitting across from him. She casually held one of her knives in her hand, whittling on a piece of wood in silence. Kaci looked up only momentarily, and then went back to her sketching. The first time they met her, she had greatly intimidated them. But the more they were around her — in the vehicle as they drove and eating meals together — the more comfortable they became. She wasn't as dangerous as she tried to appear. They had paid attention to her behavior and subtle facial expressions when she spoke with her father and were starting to wonder if she wasn't in some way trapped here just like the rest of them. Suddenly, she noticed Drew watching at her.

"What?" she snapped, glaring at him quickly before looking back down at her carving.

"Nothing. Just curious," Drew replied.

"You can keep your curiosities to yourself."

He shrugged, tossing a few more leaves into the fire. "Out of all the people that you could be with right now, you chose to sit down with us. That's got to mean *something*."

"It means nothing."

Drew chuckled. "Come on. You could be over there with those guys playing poker."

"Boring. They have brains the size of a bat. I beat them every time."

Drew crossed his arms and sat back. "So, you're wanting to get to know us a little better?"

"We're stuck together on this trip for a while," she looked up with a faint sinister spark in her eyes like that of her father, "*If* you can make it. So yeah, why not? You're tough kids. I kinda respect you for that."

Drew laughed. "Kids? What's with everybody calling us that? Honestly, how old do you think we are?"

Jada shrugged.

"We're your age. I'm 16. Kaci's 15. And we know that you're only 17."

Jada froze suddenly and sharply looked up. "Who told you that?"

"Your dad did," Kaci replied softly.

"Figures," she rolled her eyes and resumed whittling.

"I think he told us because he wanted us to connect with you. You know, to become your friends."

"Ha! Like that's gonna happen," she turned the wood around in her hand for a moment, studying her handywork. "Well, it still doesn't give him the right. He should keep his mouth shut. My age is nobody's business. The men don't even know and neither should you."

Drew leaned forward and gently declared, "You should be respectful of your father –"

"Don't you start trying to fix me like Alexander does with Dad," Jada cut him off. "It won't work."

Drew put up his hands defensively, "That's not what I was trying to do. I was just going to say, you should be respectful of your father, because you don't know how long you'll have with him."

Her eye twitched and her hand tightened around her knife. "What's that supposed to mean? You know something I don't?"

"No, but the Bible says —"

"Seriously? The Bible?" She scoffed. "You two are bunch of fanatics just like your uncle, aren't you?"

"Yep!" Kaci jumped in. "We love Jesus."

"And the Bible says in Proverbs, *'Boast not thyself of to morrow; for thou knowest not what a day may bring forth.'* Nobody is guaranteed tomorrow. Enjoy what God gives you today. You have your dad; you should be thankful for that."

"I thought you imagined him to be a very bad man."

Drew chuckled, "Well, he *is* a thief and a murderer. And I'm afraid he'll stop at nothing and for no one to reach his goal. But he's *still* your father. And for that, he deserves your respect."

Jada grunted. Drew looked at his sister and hesitantly continued. "You know, we lost our dad some years ago. He was an archeologist. There was an accident, and they never could find his body." Drew cleared his throat to cover up the emotions that were welling up within him.

Kaci finished with a wavering voice, "We miss him so much. Wish we could have him back. We'll never be able to tell him again that we love him."

Jada momentarily softened. "Oh," her voice trailed off. "I-I didn't know." Her features hardened again. "But that's life. We just roll with what it gives us. My mom died from cancer and I have no other family. Sure, he's all I have in this world now, but it doesn't mean that the old man can control my life." She stood and tossed her stick into the fire.

Drew shook his head. "Look, Jada, we didn't mean to argue with you; I'm sorry if this conversation got out of hand. I think Kaci and I are just processing a lot right now. But, we're grateful you took some time to chat."

"Don't get used to it," she snapped. "I suggest you both get some rest. We'll be leaving early, and we have a long drive ahead of us."

As she stalked away from the fire, Kaci softly remarked, "You know, my heart goes out to her. Her father's men might be intimidated by the tough act she's putting on, but I think there's much more to her than meets the eye."

"You're right. She's screaming for help, and I don't think she even realizes it. Kaci, we need to pray for God to help us be a testimony of Jesus to her. Remember what Uncle James said the other day? We might be the only Gospel witness she'll ever get."

She smiled, causing Drew to smile, too. His sister's joy encouraged him, and he was thankful for that. "I wonder if God brought us all the way out here to the jungle for Jada?" Kaci thought aloud. "Remember Pastor Mark's Sunday School lesson right before football camp?"

"Yep. I've been thinking a lot about that, too." Drew looked up to the star-lit sky high above the rainforest. *Just like You led Philip in the book of Acts all the way into the desert to meet the Ethiopian in his chariot... Lord, we believe you've led us to Jada. Please use us to help her find You.*

❁ ❁ ❁

Drew tried to sleep after they all fell onto their cots, but after tossing and turning for what seemed like an eternity, he sat up quietly and crept out of the tent. The air was still thick and muggy but at least it was slightly cooler than what they had felt during the day. He softly walked along the makeshift row of tents soaking up the jungle sounds of night when suddenly the sound of Fitzgerald's raised voice drew him to a large, oversized tent further down. He crept closer to the canvas, ducking out of sight from two guards straggling along on patrol, and peered through a slit in the dimly-lit tent.

"—billions of dollars of Incan gold. All for us and our organization!" He broke out into a gleeful laugh. "This is it, my girl! We're finally on the trail. I promised you, didn't I?"

"Yeah, you did," Jada replied. "Do you think you can trust Alexander?"

"But of course! He will not do *anything* to put his precious little monsters in danger. He is what you might call — a necessary evil."

Jada chuckled. "And he thinks *you're* the evil one."

"He can think whatever he wishes. But I've been given a divine sense of quest by the gods to discover this enchanted kingdom." The man spoke of himself with big gestures while staring into nothingness. "I can feel it in my bones. *I am* the chosen one."

Wow, this guy is full of himself. Drew thought. *A complete narcissist.*

"Alexander is merely a cog in the wheel, a means to my end, and I will stop at nothing to fulfill my destiny. Of course, you will be right there beside me. I will be handing down to you a great legacy!" The man paused and held up a couple of old leather-bound folders from off his makeshift desk.

"I have not dared to show these to the professor yet," he continued as Jada raised an eyebrow in curiosity. "These are the ancient Latin works of Andres Lopez."

"And he is?"

"A man of great importance, particularly in one's study of Paititi. He was a Jesuit priest that journeyed deep into Peru to spread Catholicism among the remote villages," he unwound the leather strap on one of the folders and gently pulled out its contents. "All of his exploits are here. He wrote of being led by some of his converts to

Paititi. When he beheld the great city, he described it as a refuge for the remaining factions of Incan royalty and as the vault of the fallen Empire's treasury."

"Why haven't you told Alexander about this?"

"Because he doesn't need to know. I stole these texts from the Vatican when I lifted Aapo's letter and medallion from the archives. The last thing I wish to hear is the good professor rambling on about ethics and thievery again," he snorted.

"You've got a point."

"Besides, unfortunately, there are pages missing from Lopez's writings." He pointed at the loose-leaf pages that he fanned out on the desk in front of him. "The sentence of this page doesn't match up with the next. If he *did* give any instructions on how to find Paititi, it has been lost to history. However, we can read of how he described the city's opulence. Listen to this!" He scanned his fingers over one of the pages, while Jada looked over his shoulder. "He wrote, *'The King is very powerful, and he has a court as majestic as that of the Grand Turk. His kingdom is rich and full of gold, silver, and many pearls. Such overabundance that they use these precious materials to make cooking pots and pans as others use metal or iron. Yet something far greater lies within....'*"

"Hmmm. Something greater? What does that mean?"

"Exactly. What *does* it mean?" He lowered his voice and Drew strained to hear his whisper. "I'm about to tell you something that I've not shared with anyone else. Look. Lopez declares right here," his finger traced along the Latin words, *"'Yet something far greater lies within, where there is power and life to do that which is desired.'"* Jada's eyes widened. "That's a rough translation at least, my dear. Comparing this documented account with other folklore tales, I believe that this man is directly speaking of immortality."

"Wait, what?" Jada looked at her father incredulously, then shook her head. "You've got to be kidding me."

"I am telling you the truth. There must be *some* sort of life-giving source there, such as a fountain or spring."

Drew froze at Fitzgerald's words. *Life-giving water? As in some sort of Fountain of Youth?* He shook his head. *So, that's what this guy's really after. Certainly, nothing like that exists.*

"Dad! Just listen to yourself. You're — you're crazy!"

"Come now, my dear. I believe the legend to be true. Why else would Aapo bury its secret? Why else would Mother Earth hide its location from the rest of the planet in dense overgrowth?"

"You're insane — believing in fables. Just like the professor and those kids believe in the fairy tales of the Bible! I can't believe we're even talking about this right now."

"Jada, I very well could be wrong, and I am willing to accept that. The discovery of the city itself would bring validation and legacy. But think of it! Since the beginning of time, mankind has been on the quest to discover a river of life or a fountain that gives immortality to whoever bathes in it or drinks from it. Alexander the Great, Genghis Khan, Nero, Ponce de Leon... the list goes on. You know I'm right!"

Jada shrugged her shoulders and refused to make eye contact with her father as he continued. "I believe there have been various locations where a fountain like this has sprung up across the Earth. Throughout history, legends speak of places from the Middle East to the foot of the mountains outside Polombe, India; on Bimini Island in the Caribbean to Ethiopia and even Central Asia. If immortality is at the core of Paititi, I will find it. It will make me the most powerful man in the entire world. I *will* achieve this and rule the earth from the shadows. Together, we will take whatever we want and no one will be able to stop us."

Drew could hardly believe what he was hearing. Trepidation had his heart pounding in his chest. He needed to tell Uncle James and Kaci. This knowledge changed everything. He was about to stand, ready to rush back to his tent, when the flap of Fitzgerald's tent suddenly opened. He pressed himself down as far as he could into the jungle overgrowth surrounding the tent.

"Dad, enough!" Jada muttered angrily. She turned and walked right in front of where Drew was hiding, then paused. Nothing could be heard but the swelling chorus of tropical cicadas. He expected her to look down any second right into his eyes. Instead, she closed her eyes and sighed deeply. Some of the anger he'd seen on her face was gone, and he saw genuine worry and sadness. Folding her arms, she slowly looked up into the starry night sky and walked off to her tent.

Shaking from the adrenalin rush, Drew quietly stood and slipped back to his own tent. He was tempted to wake Kaci and Uncle James right then to tell them what he overheard. But his sister was sleeping peacefully. His uncle looked like he was getting some much-needed rest, too. He took off his boots and crawled onto his cot.

What would Mr. Fitzgerald do to me if he found out that I had been spying on them? The man was unpredictable at best and looked like he would kill anyone he wanted to on the spot without hesitation. Kadir of the Demeons was a bad man, but Adrian Fitzgerald was just plain cruel. *If I tell the others, and he finds out, I could be killed! He has no reason to keep me alive.* Drew lay there wide-eyed, his head spinning with fearful thoughts and so many questions. *God, help me. Please calm my nerves.*

In that moment, a couple of Bible verses came to mind. They washed over his soul, and it was as if God was trying to speak to him in the stillness right then and there. *"Be careful for nothing; but in every thing by prayer and supplication with thanksgiving let your requests be made known unto God. And the peace of God, which passeth all understanding, shall keep your hearts and minds through Christ Jesus."*

Drew smiled. *Thank you, Lord. I know You'll lead me when it's the right time. I love You.*

CHAPTER VIII

Kaci peered out the window of the jeep. They'd driven another two full days and reached the jagged peak at last. They were deep within the jungle, far from any modern civilization. At the base of the mountain was a small village, a scattering of a few roughly-built buildings and huts that trailed off up into the trees along the side of the rise. For discretion's sake, Fitzgerald radioed his men to set up camp about a mile back down the road; they discovered a sizable clearing there that would nicely house their equipment and tents. When the rest of the team drove up in their mud-covered all-terrain vehicles, it caused quite a stir in the quiet community. Locals stopped their work in front of their dwellings and men came from the fields. Children pressed in close and surrounded them with curious smiles.

"Right, Jim, you're with me. Let's talk to the locals, see if they can tell us anything. Fairchild, get us resupplied," Fitzgerald ordered.

Alexander slung the leather tube that carried their ancient map over his shoulder; it had become inseparable from him. He followed Fitzgerald as the man took broad strides to where three tall male villagers had gathered, eyeing them closely.

Fairchild called out orders and approached one of the women with a smile that sent a chill down Kaci's back. The woman nodded at whatever he said, seemingly unfazed by his unnerving smile. She went with a few others into a supply hut and then reappeared, carrying out food and what looked like cans of gasoline for the jeeps. Kaci's observation was suddenly interrupted when a few young girls rushed up to her, giggling and babbling away happily. She wished she knew what they were saying, but with a friendly smile she hugged them all anyway. They grinned and raced off again, playing as they darted into the trees. She missed being little sometimes, being able to run around without a care in the world. Wiping the sweat already gathering on her forehead, she thought how different summer days were back home, with swimming pools and tall glasses of ice-cold lemonade. Here, there seemed to be no relief from the sun, heat and humidity. Yet, there was a peaceful joy in this place.

"How are you holding up?" Drew asked his sister, breaking her out of her reverie.

"Fine," she replied with a soft smile. "This place is beautiful, you know?" She tilted her head back, taking in the jagged peak that overshadowed the small village. She turned slowly about, spotting a hint of turquoise water through the huts of the villagers. "Think that's the lake from the map? We should check it out!"

"Don't wander off," Jada warned, approaching Kaci and Drew from behind. "We'll be loading back up as soon as they find the guide."

"We won't go far. I think they'll be a little bit." Kaci pointed toward Alexander and Fitzgerald. They were walking with the three men to one of the larger huts where an elderly man sat in a chair, watching them intently.

"Well, just don't get yourselves into any trouble," she growled, spinning on her heels to oversee the progress that Fairchild was making.

"Come on!" Kaci took off with a sprint. Drew chuckled and ran after his sister. A couple of the children followed along with them and giggled as they all disappeared into the trees.

They pushed carefully through the underbrush. Kaci ran her fingers along the waxy leaves of the local fauna, taking the time to smell the sweet violet and yellow flowers reaching out to greet her. Last night, Alexander had said they were most likely heading north and east, as that appeared to be the general direction the ancient map led. But he had no way to know how far. They were going to traverse deeper into the jungle and things would most likely become more dangerous. She had so many questions, and at times, Kaci worried they'd be lost in the jungle forever. That they'd never make it home. But then she'd pray and feel God's peace rush over her. She was thankful for another day to be alive and another chance to soak up all the beautiful nature that God created — such a testament of His might and glory.

She passed through the last line of skinny, tall trees and reached the water's wide edge. In the distance across the lake, she could see a babbling stream coming gently down the mountain feeding the lake. On the other side, she noticed the natives' ingenuity by damming and channeling the water out into their fields. Drew finally caught up to her with even more children at his side, excited to spend time with these foreigners.

The small lake formed a rough oval; its surface was perfectly smooth and the water was clearer than anything the siblings had ever seen before. Kaci could almost look straight to the sandy bottom. Colorful, tiny fish darted through the vegetation and played in schools.

"Incredible!" She exclaimed. "We would *never* have been able to see anything like this if we were back at home."

Drew smiled, "Gotta count our blessings, right?"

Kaci laughed, "Now you're going to have that tune stuck in my head all day!"

A couple of young girls began to pull on Kaci's hand in excitement, repeating, *"Hamuni, hamuni!"* A few boys were further down the bank, waving for them to come.

"What?"

"I don't know," Drew replied. "I think they want to show us something."

"Hamuni?" Kaci asked, doing her best to repeat the word to the girls. They look at each other and giggled some more while nodding enthusiastically, *"Ari!"*

Kaci looked back at Drew as she was being pulled along, "Maybe *arí* means 'yes'?"

Drew shrugged and smiled. For a moment, he felt free and like they belonged. Without thinking, he began to whistle the hymn they'd referenced moments before.

As they drew nearer, the boys pointed to the water.

"*Uya! Uya!*" They said over and over, gesturing with their hands around their faces.

"This is so strange. But cool!" Kaci remarked. She knelt and tilted her head to look down under the surface, trying to figure out what they were talking about. After a few yards, the ground gave way to a deep pool. She noticed a group of fish dart through the vegetation, and the disturbance in the water made it shift. And then she saw it. Nestled at the bottom on the side of the lake was a big face carved out of stone.

"Drew, it looks just like the pictures of the stone faces on the map! You don't think… could that be it?" she squealed. "The guide!"

"Where?" her brother shouted.

"Down there!" She pointed more directly. His gaze aligned with it and he saw it as well, discreetly located among the kelp and weeds. The children were nodding and laughing, thrilled to share with their guests what they believed to be their local attraction. "Wow! I get it now. *Uya!*" He said to the boys, giving them a thumbs up. "Face!"

"What's all this excitement about?" a voice called out. They turned to see Jada softly approaching through the trees. "I could hear you guys all the way back in the village."

"I think we may have found the guide," Drew pointed. "It's down there — a stone statue just like the ones on the map!"

"*In* the lake?" Jada exclaimed. "I guess it could be possible. I'd better contact my father right away." She pulled a radio from her hip. "Dad, we think we found it. Lakefront, 2 o'clock position."

"Astounding!" his voice crackled back. "We'll be there momentarily."

Jade came closer and took a look for herself. "That's got to be it." She glanced at the siblings with a faint smile. "Nice work, you two."

Drew looked to Kaci and then to the children. "You can thank our little friends. *Uya!*" All the kids laughed and began chattering away in their native tongue. They practically hung on the three teenagers, which didn't bother Drew and Kaci a bit. Jada endured it but was clearly annoyed by all the clamor and attention. A few minutes later, the men, along with the local chieftains and a few of Fitzgerald's team joined them at the water's edge. The leaders spoke firmly to the little ones in their native tongue and instantly the children stepped away from the Americans and stood at attention.

"Where is it?" Fitzgerald demanded.

Kaci pointed down into the lake. "If you look closely enough, you'll see it among the vegetation. On the right side toward the bottom."

The man leaned forward with an intense stare, "Fascinating how clear the water is." Everyone saw the moment he spotted it as his eyes narrowed and a dark smile spread across his lips. "Looks like you were right after all, Jim."

He turned, "Did you find this, young lady?"

"Yes, sir. But it was really the kids that led us here."

Fitzgerald grunted. "How would you like the honors of diving down there and seeing if you're right?"

"Adrian, you can't be serious," Alexander interjected.

"It's okay, Uncle James. I can hold my breath for over three minutes," she flashed a smile. "Lifeguard training for junior camp."

"Kaci —" Alexander said, shaking his head, but he knew it was too late.

Fitzgerald held up his hand. "Let the girl relish her moment, Jim. Don't take this from her."

"I can go. I'll just have to go down and maybe come up a few times. I'll be fine," Drew insisted, but Kaci put her hand on his arm.

"It's too deep for you, Drew. You're not the swimmer of the family, remember? You're the football guy. By the time you get down there, you'll have to come right back up. I'll be okay," she assured him, trying to hide her apprehension. She stepped out of her shoes and moved into the water. "You have a camera?"

The natives, now understanding what was going on, stepped forward and spoke anxiously with Alexander.

Fitzgerald snapped his fingers and Fairchild handed over a small waterproof case. Kaci slipped the loop around her wrist, first making sure she knew where the capture button was; then she immediately dove under the surface, praying for strength. Before the water closed in around her, she thought she heard her uncle exclaim something, but no one came in after her. *I must have been hearing things. I can't believe I'm doing this!*

The clear water made it easy to see and she swam deeper into the lake. Fish darted around her, then alongside her as if guiding her to the statue at the very bottom. When she finally reached it, she worked quickly to uncover the stone. Algae and some type of strange moss had grown over it. Her lungs were not burning yet, and she again felt gratitude for her previous water training. When the last bits of vegetation fell away, she came face to face with a set of piercing blue eyes. She flinched back, caught off guard by how real they appeared. She raised the camera to start snapping pictures, but felt herself freeze, half-expecting the statue to come to life. She shook her head. *How silly of me! But there is something odd with those eyes.* She took several photos and moved closer to see what was on the rest of this large stone face. At the very top was the faint, familiar symbol for Paititi. Beneath the face was an image similar to the one on the map of the cliff. She took a picture of that, too. Several Incan symbols had been carved into the stone. She snapped more images of those for her uncle to translate.

At the very bottom of the statue was another grouping of words, but these were not Incan. In fact, after studying them, Kaci realized they looked like Latin. She took several more pictures but knew her time was just about up as her lungs started to complain about needing air. She pressed her feet to the bottom and kicked off.

She suddenly felt the water around her become tumultuous and colder. Something large rushed passed her, sending a chill down her spine. She almost shrieked in terror as she saw an eel-like fish with beady eyes swimming about, making wide arcs in the clear water. The fish had to be at least 8 feet long. She gritted her teeth to preserve what air she had left in her lungs and propelled herself hard to the surface. With heart beating fast, out of the corner of her eye she saw a couple more eel-like creatures slither up from the depths and join the prowl.

Kaci closer her eyes and prayed as they circled closer and closer. One abruptly swam right toward her like a speeding bullet; she vaulted her body upward, feeling the sleek body barely miss her. Righting herself, she turned wildly one way then the other, but in the flurry of bubbles she could sense the others pressing in.

The water became a frenzy of scales, writhing bodies and Kaci's frantic limbs. Her lungs screamed for air, and she could barely keep her eyelids open. Darkness washed over her, sealing her doom, when suddenly she felt a hand — then two — grab hold of her and pull her out of the water. She broke through the surface and took in a huge, grateful gasp of air. Village men were in the lake with spears and a few of them wrestled with the large fish. They appeared to be enjoying themselves as if it were some sport.

Alexander and Drew helped Kaci out of the water, and she hugged them tight, thankful to be back on dry land. Then she remembered the camera, smiling weakly. "Here you go!" She tossed the camera to Fitzgerald.

He caught it effortlessly and looked through the gallery for a moment. His eyes glowed and he let out a shout, "Yes, indeed! You, my dear, are one incredible young lady. I'd say if we make it through this in one piece, you would be a welcome addition to my team."

"Thanks, but I think I'll pass," Kaci muttered. She slumped on the ground a few yards away from the lake's edge.

"What were those creatures?" she asked between heavy breaths. "They were huge!"

"They're called *arapaima* — they're the biggest fish in the Amazon!" her uncle explained. "To the locals catching one means fine dining since they're so big and rarely come to the surface. But, as you almost found out, they can be very dangerous under the water." He paused. "Right before you dove in, a chieftain mentioned the beasts. Immediately, I tried to stop you, but I was too late and Adrian wouldn't let me go in after you. The chieftains told me that occasionally they spot one of them if someone dives down too far." He removed his tortoiseshell glasses to rub his eyes. "Next time you're going to do something reckless, *ask me first,*" he said sternly.

"Yes, sir. I'm sorry."

He gave her a hug, then looked sincerely at both of them. "I have no problem with the two of you taking risks; that's going to come along with the territory. But this is nothing like our last adventure together. While we're out here, I am ultimately responsible for you. What do I tell your mother if one of you doesn't come home alive?"

Soberness settled upon the two young people. "Now if it's a 'hard call' moment where you must do something instantly, don't hesitate. Act. But in moments like these when there are variables at play, if you're able to, don't jump in before you know all the facts. I don't know how all this is going to play out with Adrian and his men. Who knows? He may again thrust you into some perilous situation that I'm powerless over." The professor smiled tenderly, which brightened Drew and Kaci's countenances. He lovingly placed a hand on each of their shoulders. "Just understand that your well-being weighs heavily upon me, and I am going to do my best with God's strength to keep you both safe."

By this time, more villagers had gathered. They cheered as the men dragged to shore the carcasses of three *arapaima.*

"Those fish are long!" Drew whistled.

"We'll be eating good tonight," Alexander smiled.

"I'm impressed," Jada commented softly as she slipped next to Kaci. "You're lucky to have gotten out of that alive."

"Luck had nothing to do with it. God protected me."

Jada raised an eyebrow, uncertain how to respond. "Well, maybe all your prayers to your God are paying off."

Kaci smiled. *Her tone is different.* It had always been cruel or condescending. Now for the first time, it was kind.

That night, they *did* eat good. The locals invited Fitzgerald, Alexander, and the three teenagers to stay; while the others joined the rest of the team stationed down the road. The fish didn't taste like fish at all. The meat was so tender and juicy, full of flavor from all the herbs and citrus that it was cooked in. It cut more like a prime rib than any fish Drew and Kaci had ever eaten.

For the first time the crew was happy together and got along. Drew and Kaci picked up a few more words and played with the children. Jada entertained the youth with her knife-throwing skills. Fitzgerald was pleased to gain a few more traces of information about the origins of the stone statue, while Alexander appreciated the time, though brief, to learn more of a culture he had never interacted with before.

With only a few rays of sunset left, they wished the natives farewell and climbed into their Jeep to head back before the darkness of the jungle swallowed them. As they drove into camp and saw the patrols with their AK-47s and the M1161 Growlers with their mounted .50 caliber machine guns, the sobering reminder washed back over Drew and Kaci of whom they were with and what they were doing.

Before getting out, Fitzgerald handed the camera over to Alexander, "I expect to have some answers by the morning. We've already lost enough time."

"I'll do my best. Paititi isn't going anywhere."

Fitzgerald grunted and looked into the rearview mirror. "Jada, with me."

The buzz of generators filled the night, drowning out any sounds from the jungle, and the faint crackle of bug zappers positioned throughout the camp interjected erratically as they attempted to keep down the invasion of mosquitoes. They found their tents set up as before. Two halogen work lamps mounted on a tripod lit up Alexander's station. The professor made a beeline to his open-air, makeshift canopy office, his niece and nephew trailing behind him. He spread out the ancient map once again, along with the modern-day one next to it. He held the camera in his hand and slowly flipped through the pictures Kaci took.

"I hope those are good enough," said Kaci.

"They're going to work just fine. Excellent job," he complimented her.

She immediately had flashbacks of the flurry of bubbles and scales and to the moment she was about to pass out for lack of oxygen. That sinking, hopeless feeling she had. She swallowed back her trepidation and nodded to the pictures on the camera. "So, what do you think all of it means?"

Alexander moved through the images until he was back at the first one she took of the face. "This statue head is definitely Incan," he said. Drew and Kaci crowded close to him as he angled the screen for all of them to see. "Those eyes are curious to me. I've never seen anything like it. I mean, used in a statue like this before."

"They were so vivid and life-like. The pictures don't do it justice!" Kaci remarked.

"Certainly. They appear to be crafted of aquamarine — the most prized gemstone in the Amazon. Since early times, they have been believed to endow youthfulness and certain healing properties." Alexander chuckled and shook his head. "Not that we believe a stone could grant such things. But that's what the superstitions have been over the centuries."

"Do you think those stones were selected for a reason?" Drew interjected, his mind going back to the conversation he'd overheard a few nights before.

Alexander furrowed his brow. "Hmmm. I don't know. Someone had to *specifically* choose them I suppose."

"Uncle James," Kaci piped up. "The eyes, don't you think they look odd?"

Alexander looked up suddenly, "What do you mean?"

"I mean, it's like the gems are in the sockets sideways or something." She politely took the camera from his hands and zoomed in on their orientation. "I noticed the points on each gem were pointing up and to the right. See?"

"Very interesting!" He pushed his glasses up the bridge of his nose and studied the gems more intently. "If you are correct, the eyes are trying to point us northeast. And that supports the clue on our map," he whispered.

"What do you mean?" Drew asked.

He shuffled through the notepad then tapped the page. "'*Its soul will point the way.*' The old expression is that the eyes are the window to the soul. Based on that, I think our next guide could be northeast of our current position. But that honestly is not a lot to go on."

"And how are we going to find it?" Drew leaned over both maps. "The jungle is so vast. I mean, we could get lost in this real quick."

"Absolutely. Hmmm. That's intriguing. Notice this passage here," he said, moving to the next picture of the Incan text. He paused, inaudibly mouthing the translation. "It has a sort of rhyme to it, '*Follow the crooked path. Don't lose sight of your feet, or the mighty raging you will meet.*'"

"Crooked path and losing your feet? That doesn't sound very helpful," Kaci sighed.

"It wouldn't be; but since we have the direction, I think it'd be a safe guess to say whatever rushing body of water we come across to the northeast, by following a crooked trail, that's where the second guide will be." A lop-sided grin slowly spread across his face as he looked at the blinking stares of his niece and nephew. He tapped the other map. "Remember, we have modern cartography at our disposal. This detail greatly helps us." He traced his fingers along the section where they were located. "Look here — that's the lake where we found the first statue. There's a ridge just beyond our jagged peak that runs to the northeast. See this dotted line? It must be depicting a narrow trail all along there. That's where we need to head next and look here," he said, pointing to a tributary. "This is the first bit of water we would come to if we followed it."

Drew rubbed his eyes. "Wow. You're really good at this."

He smiled, but it wasn't a very happy one. "It's just an educated guess with what clues we have at our disposal. I do hope I'm right. I'd hate to see what Adrian Fitzgerald would become if he doesn't find his precious Paititi."

He picked up the camera and sifted through the rest of the pictures. "Now here is what I find most fascinating. This part here, this Latin. '*Esto vigilans aquarum abyssi.*' It means — '*Be watchful of the waters deep.*'"

"Of the waters?" Kaci questioned. "Which ones? The waters I just went in to find the guide or the river we're headed to next?"

"I'm not sure. It wouldn't make sense that it refers to the lake," he mused. "My guess is that the statue was erected long before that body of water existed."

"Yeah, that mountain stream has had hundreds of years to fill in the lake, right?" Drew speculated. "Maybe it was like a smaller pond when the statue was built?"

"Most likely." Alexander glanced from the picture to the ancient map then back again with a puzzled look on his face.

"Maybe it's something for later?" Kaci suggested.

"Possibly. You never know with cryptic things like this. Let's tuck it away for now and focus on finding this second guide instead."

"So!" Fitzgerald called from behind them. "Do you know where we're going?"

Alexander set the camera aside, watching the man come around to stand on the other side of the table. "I think I do. Northeast would be my best guess." He traced the path along the map explaining all that they had discovered. "The second guide is most likely around here somewhere."

"That's quite a lot of ground to cover."

"Yes. But, as you can see, it's the best I can do with what limited knowledge we have." His eyes twinkled. "Do you think these guides were designed to make it easy? Don't forget your whole '*only the worthy will be able to find it.'"*

Fitzgerald's eyes narrowed. Kaci waited for the man to spew forth something uncouth, but instead, he clapped his hands and burst out laughing. "Well then, this calls for a celebration." He grinned at Drew and Kaci, but all they wanted to do was slip away from the greed and darkness in that one look. "Don't lose your touch, old chum."

As he was about to turn and leave, his eyes glanced over Alexander's opened notepad and lit up. "Hello? What's this? Youthfulness — Healing?"

Alexander frowned, disturbed by the man's sudden keen interest in something so trivial. He carefully shared his curiosity behind why the aquamarine gemstone was chosen.

Fitzgerald soaked up every word, gently nodding. Drew could only think of the man's obsession to find a fabled "fountain of youth." *When should I tell Uncle James and Kaci?*

"Fascinating," the mercenary commented shrewdly as he marched off into the night.

Alexander shook his head. "Adrian Fitzgerald is a strange man. No telling what he might be thinking."

"Maybe there's more to this than meets the eye," Drew suggested.

"What do you mean by that?"

Drew shrugged. His heart was beating fast, screaming for him to share what he'd overheard. But the fear of what Fitzgerald might do to him crept back into his mind and kept him silent. "I don't know. It's late; I think I'm going to turn in."

Alexander stretched out his arms, "Come here you two. I love you. We're going be fine. God will protect us." Kaci rested her head on his chest and smiled. Drew hugged him with a little extra squeeze, thankful for such a courageous and godly uncle. Then, under the canopy they formed a circle by holding hands together. Taking turns, each of them prayed aloud for God's wisdom and strength, illuminated by the halogen lamps for all the camp to see.

CHAPTER IX

Five days of hard travel had the group bouncing over rocky roads, following the path Alexander led them on. The only crooked trail Alexander and Fitzgerald had been able to see on the map was a ridgeline navigated by extremely narrow dirt roads that eventually ran into a snaking river. Drew had been surprised to see roads at all. But he found himself spending a majority of the time staring out the window, unable to look away as the tires of their jeep came dangerously close to dropping off the edge and plummeting them to what would most certainly be their deaths.

Jada got a kick out of how often he prayed. He didn't say anything audibly, but when she occasionally looked back in the rearview mirror, she could see his lips moving. Sometimes his eyes were open, sometimes they were closed. One thing she noticed about the siblings was that they were real. Not just real, but consistently real. She found herself being jealous of the peace and joy they constantly possessed despite being kidnapped and enduring rugged conditions.

When they finally came to a stop for the day to make camp, it wasn't anywhere like the first few stopping places. Tonight, they used the vehicles as a makeshift barricade, tucking themselves back into an alcove against the rocky slope. Just beyond the vehicles was a straight shot down into nothingness. They'd stopped for good reason as the sun was setting. The roads were treacherous enough during the day. But one could barely make them out in the dark of night as a thick fog would settle upon the high mountain ridge.

Drew climbed out of the jeep and wandered up to where his uncle stood, his brow furrowed as he muttered in what sounded like Latin. He'd been pondering those strange words found on the first guide and, so far, had no idea what they could mean. Alexander removed his glasses and rubbed his aching temples. He offered Drew a weary smile.

"You okay, Uncle James?"

"I should be asking you and your sister that," Alexander chuckled. "I've been having a rather intense philosophical discussion with my notepad. This phrase in Latin, it seems a bit out of place. I'm not sure what to make of it. It has nothing to do with the rest of what's here."

Drew bit his lip. "You know, I was thinking about that, too. This may sound crazy, but from the pictures, I thought it looked like it was added later. Maybe by someone else?"

"Interesting that you'd say that. I'm starting to think that's the case, but why?" The professor put on his glasses, his mental wheels turning again. "Why leave another clue at all and for what? My gut says it was left for a different purpose, a warning maybe. I don't know. We'll just have to wait and see, I guess, once we find the second guide. The best that we can do is to keep heading northeast toward the river and see if we find anything. Adrian got lucky where we found that first one. We're likely to run into villages that will be *less* hospitable."

Drew shuddered, the sudden high mountain breeze not the only source of his chill. "I'm just glad Kaci made it out of that lake okay."

"What about me?" Kaci piped up as she sauntered toward them out of the light fog with her hands on her hips. Both men laughed.

"Nothing, sis," Drew teased. "Just talking about how you snore way too loud at night."

"Hey!" she jabbed him in the arm. "That is *not* me."

Drew threw up his hands playfully to defend himself as she continued her attack. "Okay! Okay! I surrender."

"You're not getting off that easy," she challenged.

Alexander laughed. *They must be stir-crazy, sitting in a vehicle all day.* He was thankful that his niece and nephew hadn't lost their joy. It invigorated him, and sometimes he wondered if they actually understood how dangerous this situation was. He shook his head. *Thank you, Lord, for showing Yourself strong to them. They are both so young, but Your grace is always sufficient.*

While the two of them tussled for a bit longer, he began to set up their makeshift quarters — three sleeping bags on the ground forming a triangle with a fire starter kit in the middle. He tried to find the smoothest, flattest place, but there wasn't a lot of room to move around in their little section of angled vehicles. Their small flame danced off of the rocky slope that towered high overhead behind them.

"All right, you two," a voice cut through the darkness, "Knock it off." Jada walked up with MREs in hand.

"We were just messing around," Drew said in their defense.

"I know, and you were embarrassing yourselves," she commented drily and then glanced at Kaci. "I could teach you how to throw a *real* punch."

Drew was surprised that Kaci actually smiled in return. He thought she would've taken offense to that, but she didn't. "That would be awesome," his sister replied. "Then I would know how to really put him in his place." She turned to her brother with a twinkle in her eye.

"What have I done to cause you both to gang up on me?" he joked.

"We girls have to stick together," Jada proclaimed, smiling at Kaci. Her smile lasted only for a moment, however, before she slipped back to her normal cold self. "Here you go," she tossed them their meals and one to Alexander. "My father doesn't want there to be a lot of noise tonight. Keep the fire low. We don't want to attract any unwanted attention."

"Does he know something that I'm not aware of?" Alexander asked carefully.

Jada shrugged. "How am I supposed to know? I'm guessing it's just because we're up so high. Others might hear or see us, and you know him — he's quite determined to keep our mission a secret."

Before Alexander could respond, she abruptly turned on her heels and disappeared into the night. The man just furrowed his brow and kept the comment to himself with a soft "Hmmmm."

The three of them huddled up near the fire, sitting across from each other on the ground. The illumination allowed them to see their food as they tore into the MREs. Then Alexander prayed aloud, thanking God for their meal and for safety on their journey thus far. They ate in silence for the most part, staring into the fire and soaking up the cooler mountain air which they welcomed as a reprieve from the normal jungle heat.

Kaci cleared her throat after drinking from her canteen. "Uncle James? Can I ask you something?"

"Of course, my dear. What's on your mind?"

Kaci hesitated, pondering over her words, "Why do you think God allowed this to happen to us?"

Alexander breathed in deeply. He'd been praying for wisdom about how to address this. He had known that the time for this question would come. He set aside the dinner he was almost finished with and reached for the small worn Bible at his hip. He held it reverently with both hands and leaned forward toward the small fire.

"Do you both believe that God loves you?" he began.

The two teenagers nodded. "Absolutely," Drew stated softly.

"Do you believe that He has your best interests in mind?"

"Yeah, but if I can be honest, sometimes I wonder. How could all of what we're going through be God's best? I mean, with Dad dying and now this...." Kaci's voice trailed off. "Sometimes I just wonder why, that's all."

"I do, too," Drew interjected.

Alexander chuckled, "I completely understand; unfortunately, I don't have all the answers. But I know Who does."

"God," Drew and Kaci said almost in unison.

"That's right, and I'm thankful He's given us His Word. God encourages us to seek Him." He flipped open His Bible. "Isaiah 55:6 says, *'Seek ye the LORD while he may be found, call ye upon him* — or talk with Him and ask Him — *while he is near:'*" He flipped back a few pages. "Isaiah 34:16 says, '*Seek ye out of the book of the LORD, and read: no one of these shall fail,*' God will always be true to His Word." He looked up keenly over his glasses, "I know that the both of you became very familiar with His Word on our last adventure."

The two teenagers smiled as a flood of memories instantly flashed through their minds.

"You know, even Jesus encouraged His disciples to ask questions. It's healthy to do this so you can grow in the Lord." He stroked his jaw slowly. "I tell young people all the time, there's nothing wrong with asking 'why.' What really matters is the attitude behind your question." He smiled. "You see, if someone asks 'why' with a rebellious spirit, that is absolutely wrong; it's sin. But if someone asks out of a desire to gain wisdom and receive truth, this is good and right."

"God knows my heart," Kaci responded sincerely. "He knows that I ask wanting to understand more. I feel closer to Him now than I ever have in my life!"

"Same here," Drew continued. "His Word has become so real to me. It's amazing! Maybe this sounds strange, but I can *feel* His presence helping me be the right kind of person."

Alexander warmly smiled. "I am so very proud of you both. It's evident, the work of grace that God is doing in your lives. I'm thankful you've been getting up early to read the Bible every morning. Doesn't it stir your hearts to keep living for Christ and give you strength to go another day?"

Both of the young people nodded happily, but Alexander paused for a moment, choosing his next words carefully. "If I were to venture a guess, however, the two of you were *not* doing this as much before you were kidnapped and brought here."

They looked down, and Drew cleared his throat. "Yeah. We went to church every Sunday and Wednesday, but I know that I was only reading my Bible a couple of times a week. I was beginning to get so caught up in other things... school, friends, sports," he looked up sheepishly. "It wasn't bad stuff, but I see now that my heart was becoming cold toward the things of God." Kaci nodded in agreement.

"Well, that is all behind you," Alexander encouraged them. "You know, this wonderful closeness you're now enjoying with Christ doesn't have to come and go. You can enjoy this *daily* as you go forward in your lives. Maybe this is one of reasons why God has allowed you to go through this experience. To draw you closer to Himself. To help you live a life completely dependent upon him."

Their uncle gazed up into the night sky before looking back at them. "I don't claim to know the mind of the Lord. I'm just so happy to see you both walking closer with Him. It is evident!" He paused to turn in his Bible to another passage of Scripture. "To get back to your question, Kaci, I honestly don't fully understand why God is leading us down this path of such radical circumstances." He smiled, looking around them, listening to the jungle's night sounds. "We must come to the same conclusion as Job did, *"He knoweth the way that I take."* God knows, God sees, and there is nothing too sudden that catches Him by surprise. Do you both still have Psalm 139 memorized?"

Drew and Kaci looked at each other and grinned. It brought back fond memories of when they were children. Their parents had patiently taught them the entire chapter, and it had stuck with them all these years.

"Remember verse 7? A couple of questions are asked —"

"*Whither shall I go from thy spirit? or whither shall I flee from thy presence?*" Kaci blurted out.

"Exactly," Alexander chuckled. "And what is the answer in verse 10, Drew?"

"*Even there shall thy hand lead me, and thy right hand shall hold me,*" he responded, his eyes bright with God's promise.

"Isn't that wonderful? He will never leave us or forsake us. I love Deuteronomy 31:8," he leaned his open Bible closer to the fire to read it clearly, '*And the LORD, he it is that doth go before thee; he will be with thee, he will not fail thee, neither forsake thee: fear not, neither be dismayed.*'"

"That is so beautiful," Kaci said softly.

"Yes, it is. God will be with us every step along the way, but He is omnipresent — '*And the LORD, he it is that doth go before thee.*' He's also one step ahead. He's already in our tomorrow. He's standing at the next crossroad with a solution and with the strength for us to accomplish what we are to do. There is no reason to live in fear." He set his Bible down on a large rock beside him and took off his glasses to clean them with a handkerchief.

"There are a lot of people today that live in fear. Even as Christians, we can readily find reasons to live in fear, but you'll never find a Biblical excuse to do so. The Bible encourages us in Psalm 56:3, *'What time I am afraid, I will trust in thee.'* Please understand that feeling fear is natural; it's a part of being human, how God made us. But to respond in fear or make decisions based on fear is sin. We instead need to trust God and obey Him by *faith*, the opposite of fear. If you are afraid, ask God to give you grace to face whatever is causing this fear. Don't be ashamed to admit to Him when you're fearful. Simply and sincerely pray, *'Father, I am scared to death. Please help me.'* Or, if your faith is weakening, remember that we've been taught to pray, *'Lord, increase my faith.'* Never be afraid to trust an unknown future to a known God."

He put his glasses back on, leaned back and crossed his arms. "I know that this is a lot for you both to take in, but thank you for being willing to listen."

Kaci smiled, "We've missed our long spiritual talks with you, Uncle James!"

Drew nodded in agreement, "Yeah, you've really encouraged us." He leaned forward eagerly. "Please, continue."

Alexander picked up his Bible, "Well, there's no doubt in my mind that God has a purpose. He has a purpose for everything He does and perfect reasons for everything He allows. It will always be for our good and His glory." He flipped through the pages, "I love this verse here in Psalm 52:1 —"

"You love them all, don't you, Uncle James?" Kaci giggled.

A lop-sided grin spread across his face. "Guilty as charged!"

"I know that verse," Drew interjected. "Mom has it as wall art in her bedroom. It says, *'The goodness of God endureth continually.'* That verse really helped her after Dad died."

"Exactly. And if anyone truly understands this, it's your dear mother. She has gone through so much, yet her faith in God and love for Him is so strong. Even in the bad times and the hard days, God is still good. Do you remember what Romans 8:28 promises?"

"That all things work together for good," Drew and Kaci said together.

Alexander put his hands up, "It does not say that everything *would* be good, does it? Rather, it says that everything, good or bad, difficult or easy, will work *together for* good. We may not fully understand His purpose until we get to Heaven, but we can rest upon His promise that He'll never make a mistake. The older you both get, the more meaning these truths will take on, and, if you're like me, the more special they will become to you," he smiled lovingly at his little monsters. "But if you're able to learn them now, they will help you navigate through so many things you will face in life. Basically, it all boils down to this: if you can learn to focus on God and Who He is in all His power and majesty as the Bible references in Ephesians 3:20, you'll never have to live in fear. If you can learn to focus on God's promises — or what He has said as Jesus taught in John 16:33, it will make living in fear an impossibility. Your hearts will remain completely fixed on God in faith no matter the circumstances, and He will give you His strength and peace."

The professor paused a moment for the teenagers to soak up what he just shared, then beamed from ear to ear, proud of the fact that they were so attentive to these life-changing truths.

"Of course," he continued, "We must remember that our view of peace is sometimes different than the kind of peace God gives. Biblical peace is not defined by the absence of a crisis or a hardship; it is defined by remaining in the presence of Jesus. If you let Jesus be in control, He will create a stillness within you that's greater than what's going on around you. The Lord says in John14:27, *'Peace I leave with you, my peace I give unto you: not as the world giveth, give I unto you. Let not your heart be troubled, neither let it be afraid.'"*

Kaci began to understand. "Wow. *That's* why we've been able to see so many people we know face trials and never lose their joy.

They're so happy in Jesus."

Alexander smiled broadly. "Reminds me of someone I know very well."

Both he and Drew looked at her, and she blinked, "What? Who, me? Oh, no...." She shook her head and looked down, a little embarrassed.

"Young lady, you have been experiencing Biblical peace in your heart and it shows. God is working through you, and it is a tremendous encouragement to me. You've been a beautiful testimony for the Lord on this journey," he also nodded to Drew, "As have you."

He shook his head, realizing what he'd said, and broke out into a crooked smile. "Well, maybe I shouldn't have referred to your testimony as *beautiful*," he remarked to his nephew.

Drew chuckled, lifting his arms to flex his biceps. "You meant ruggedly handsome, right, Uncle James?"

"I wouldn't push it!" Kaci teased, and they all laughed together.

"Let's continue to fervently pray that God would use each of us to shine Jesus' light to those around us who are lost," Alexander concluded. The young people nodded in agreement as they joined hands and bowed in prayer with their uncle, grateful for these few quiet moments together.

Unbeknownst to them, sitting perfectly still in the shadows, Jada brushed away tears trickling down her face. She'd never heard anything like this before. She knew nothing of the Bible except how much her father hated it. But everything she was able to make out as Alexander softly spoke washed over her soul and filled her heart with so many emotions and so many questions. Part of her wanted to rush to them and beg for more. She craved their peace, their joy, their faith. Almost as quickly as those thoughts came, they left, however. She shook her head and pulled herself back to her reality. *I can't just walk up to them and have an open discussion about all this. What would they think? I've got to keep up appearances and not show any sign of weakness.* She wiped her face clean and silently slipped into the night toward her Jeep where she slept the way she lived — all alone.

CHAPTER X

The narrow dirt road along the mountain ridge finally gave way to a wider well-worn path, taking the convoy down into a sprawling rainforest valley. The region up the side of the mountain was covered in massive rocks and tall grass and appeared to be used as grazing lands for llamas led by nomadic shepherds. The group had to pause a half-dozen times for these Peruvian herdsmen to slowly coax their flocks out of the road. The long-necked animals would look up inquisitively and jostle about whenever Fitzgerald blared his airhorn impatiently and yelled at them to move out of the way, but it didn't make them move any faster. Kaci giggled at how they would go back to grazing without paying the man any further attention, sprawling all over the road before them.

"I don't know how much more of this I can take!" he exclaimed to Alexander who was sitting in the passenger seat intently peering at the map. "I'm about to order the .50 caliber to start blasting them out of the way!"

Alexander shook his head. "Adrian, will that *really* help matters? Then you'll just have several dead animals in the way that you'll have to move off the road before we can proceed."

"Point taken. But it would feel so... *liberating*. These incompetent herdsmen appear to have no respect for all our equipment coming through. It's disgusting."

"Adrian, come on. *We're* the ones encroaching on *their* ground. Just be thankful they're at least trying to work with us. Patience is a virtue, and you need some," he reasoned, giving his former friend a sarcastic smile.

Fitzgerald sharply looked at him and changed the subject. "Are we still on track? How much further to the river?"

Alexander frowned, becoming absorbed again in his calculations. "That's a good question. I'm trying to get a sense of our bearings. This road that we're on is not on this map. The river is close," he pointed out the front window, "See that group of herons flying in the distance? But it appears our road veers west, and we need to continue heading northeast."

"We could leave the vehicles with a small group of my men and go forward on foot."

"Possibly. Or maybe there is a better idea. See that shepherd waving at you?"

Fitzgerald grunted.

"Why don't you pull over and thank him for moving his herd off the road for us," Fitzgerald turned to give Alexander an incredulous look. "We could ask him if there's a village nearby, perhaps farther along this road even though it's not going in our direction. We could find answers there."

"Fine," Fitzgerald cleared his throat. "But *you* can do all the thanking. I have no interest in speaking with this lowlife."

The nomad approached smiling, only to reveal most of his teeth missing. Fitzgerald winced as the man, clearly in need of a good bath, leaned in the driver's side window to talk with Alexander.

"What did you discover?" Fitzgerald probed as they drove away a few minutes later.

"My hunch was right. There's a large fishing village only about thirty miles from here. It's primitive but seems to be the hub of this region — fishermen coming and going and a weekly market tomorrow. My advice would be to head there."

"But the road takes us in the opposite direction!" Fitzgerald exclaimed in frustration.

"Yes, it does look that way, but according to our shepherd

friend, it goes west for a bit before cutting back to run along the river. I think we'll be fine. Besides, it's been a while since we've been near any type of civilization, and we'll at least be able to get a decent hot meal."

Fitzgerald understood there was no arguing with that. If anything, they could divide up to follow any leads that the locals might have as they asked around in the market tomorrow.

Fitzgerald used the same tactic as he had done before as they approached the small village — only a few of them would venture forward while the bulk of his men made camp away from the prying eyes of the locals. When they drove up to the outskirts of the community, their reception was not as they anticipated. Men made eye contact with them briefly, then looked to the ground in humble submission as they quickly strode away with their nets and gear. Women gathered their children into thatched roof huts on stilts and people scattered quietly into the trees. Within moments, the dilapidated fishing pier and dusty lanes of the third-world village became strangely quiet. So quiet that when Drew climbed out of the Jeep and closed his door, the sound was abnormally loud.

"Something's not right here," Alexander muttered.

"Fairchild," Fitzgerald motioned, and the men silently slipped their weapons over their shoulders from the back of one of the Jeeps.

They wove through the village toward its center, where a giant thatched roof hut with open sides stood. There, they could hear the crackling sound of an old radio sitting on a tree stump announcing a soccer game in Iquitos. A few abandoned chairs lay on their side around it. Underneath the hut, a deep circular-shaped cast iron pot about 6 feet in diameter built on supports hung over a fire pit. Kaci looked inside. Long grain rice simmered in liquid not yet boiled out.

"There's enough here to feed an entire village!" she said.

"Yes," her uncle replied. "A lot of people in the jungle do it this way. It's a sort of communal rice cooker; women take turns preparing it."

"Quiet, you two," Fitzgerald harshly whispered, then pointed with his chin. "We've got company."

Five men dressed in long brown robes and headbands and armed with axes and fish harpoons deftly approached; others could be seen getting into position in the shadows of nearby huts, holding long poles that Alexander guessed to be blowguns. Fitzgerald calmly looped his thumb in his belt near the butt of his chrome-covered revolver. Jada stepped in front of Drew and Kaci, and they noticed a throwing knife tucked in the palm of each hand. Other men unshouldered their AK-47s and clicked the safeties off. They were ready for anything but carefully kept their gun barrels pointed to the ground, understanding that they were outnumbered *and* surrounded.

"Can we please try to avoid any bloodshed?" Alexander muttered in frustration. He raised both hands and stepped forward, choosing his words carefully.

"We come in peace," he began in the Asháninka dialect the herdsman had used on the road.

The men stopped suddenly. "You speak our native tongue?"

"Only some. I am learning. I love to learn from all cultures. I am a student and teacher of languages. But I prefer the Quechua dialect."

"Ah," the man in the middle spoke, switching to that language. He was much older than the others. His face sagged with wrinkles, but his eyes squinted with keen observation. "The language of the jungle. I will honor this. What do you want with us?"

Alexander's eyes slowly went from man to man. He presumed this gray-haired man in the middle was their chieftain. The others' stances hadn't changed nor did they lower their weapons. Those he could see vaguely in the shadows were still poised. From their body language, he understood their intentions were genuine; these natives were committed to defend their homes at all costs. The chieftain only needed to speak the word, and they'd all be either incapacitated or dead.

"What's going on here?" Fitzgerald gruffly spat, breaking the thick silence.

"Speak kindly, Adrian. Nobody move. I'll handle this," Alexander replied softly. Though the men before him couldn't understand English, he knew that even with the wrong vocal inflection their current situation could escalate quickly.

The professor smiled and offered a short bow. "My name is James Alexander, professor at Cambridge University in England. You have probably never heard of such a place, but it is a school where people come from around the world to learn. My colleagues and I are merely passing through on a deep jungle expedition."

The older man slightly relaxed but didn't let down his guard, "You are not with the *hampi qhapaq*?"

Alexander immediately stiffened, "What? No! Do you have problems with drug lords in this region?"

The man nodded warily. "We have always been a peaceful valley, but very bad men have come upon us in recent days." He paused and exchanged glances with the others on either side of him. "They take our people and make us work in their fields. But we have decided that they will do this no longer. We would rather die first. One of our young men overheard the *qhapaq* speaking together late in the night. They are planning an assault on our village because we do not obey. When you approached, we thought they had hired you to strike us!"

Alexander quickly raised his hands again in peace and urged, "I assure you that we do not work for them. We mean you and your people no harm!"

The older man pointed an aged finger at the automatic rifles. "But your friends' weapons speak another story. They are the same ones that are used to kill our people by the hands of the *qhapaq*." He suspiciously eyed Fitzgerald's large red tattoos on his forearms. "I don't trust him. Why do the other men also wear his mark?" referring to the smaller crossed-fists tattoos on the forearms of Fitzgerald's men.

As much as Alexander wanted to tell them that Adrian and his men were black marketeers called the *Bloodfists*, he understood that the less information he gave and the more simply he answered their questions, the better off everyone would be.

"They are a family of warriors that travel together," he responded. "They have sought my help in their quest... for Paititi."

The chieftain and his men gasped. "The city of the ancients? Many have sought for it, but none have found it."

Alexander smiled weakly. "True. But we have been blessed with clues that no one else has ever discovered." He slowly reached to take off the lid of the leather tube that hung from his shoulder and pulled out its contents. "A map from the heart of *Terreón* left by the remnants of the Incan Empire has guided us here."

Fitzgerald resisted the urge to move but his face turned livid as he did his best to whisper, "What on earth are you doing, Jim? They could kill us for that! It is *mine!*" His demeanor instantly put the warriors on high alert, axes and harpoons immediately raised.

Alexander cut through the tension, "It's okay, my friends. These with me do not understand of what we speak. This map is just important to them. We mean you no harm." He calmed stretched a hand toward Adrian and murmured in English, "Trust me."

Bending down to lay the map on the ground, Alexander beckoned the chieftain to join him. Both men sat in the dirt with their legs crossed, one on either side of the map.

"We have come to seek your guidance on our journey."

"I will consider this." The older man reached out to firmly shake Alexander's hand. "My name is Tenoch, head chieftain of *Punku-Qhichwa*."

"It is an honor to meet you, Chief Tenoch," Alexander glowed, shaking his hand with a slight bow of his head. Then he pondered aloud, "Your village name. It means 'door to the valley'?"

"Very perceptive, James Alexander. We serve as the seat of power over this entire valley. Our sister village, *Punku-Amaramayu*, is far to the north and stands as the last outpost of civilization that can be reached by road before one proceeds into the vast expanse of the

Amazon Basin."

"Fascinating," the professor scratched his chin, "'Door to the Amazon.' After that, I assume travel must be primarily by boat?"

Tenoch nodded. "That or on foot. You will find some dirt paths used for oxen and carts, but it is very rugged."

"I see. This knowledge will greatly help us on our journey." He slowly rolled out the map between them. "We have already ventured far," the professor began, "But there is still much more ground to cover, I fear. There are three landmarks —"

"The Guardian!" Tenoch interjected, pointing to the stone-faced statue illustrated on each corner of the map.

"Ah, he knows of the guide," Fitzgerald quietly commented. "Find out more, Jim. He *must* tell you."

Alexander furrowed his brow, trying to block out Fitzgerald's persistence. "You are familiar with these? Have you seen one before?"

"Yes, he stands atop his elevated tower as a lone sentential looking over our entire valley."

"Where is he located? He and his brothers serve as guides on our journey to point the way."

"He rests downriver farther up the mountain from where you came. For many generations my people worshiped him as their god." The chieftain shook his head. "But we know now that a carved stone has no life force within itself. We have heard such truths on our radio."

Alexander hesitated, wanting to inquire further about the stone face, but feeling pressed by the Lord to pursue a different path. "Are you talking about broadcasts about God's Book, the Bible? Do you get signal all the way out here from a Christian station?"

"Sometimes when I was a boy we did. But now it is silent," Tenoch slowly stroked his chin, giving the professor an inquisitive look. "I remember hearing about the Book you mentioned. Do you know of it?"

Alexander felt the tears welling up in his eyes. He slowly pulled his worn leather Bible from his hip pouch and handed it to the chieftain. "Here, hold this."

"Jim, what are you doing *now?*" Fitzgerald whispered in a forcedly kind tone.

Alexander turned to look at him, "Making a friend. You will have answers soon."

The chieftain observed the cross on the front and traced it with his wrinkled fingers. "Is this... is this God's Book?"

"Indeed, it is. It contains my native language, which is English, and the original languages the Bible was written in — Hebrew and Greek." By now he noticed that the warriors had lowered their weapons and gathered closer around Tenoch, intrigued, leaning in to look at the pages as he respectfully turned each one.

"We have heard much of this Book but have never seen one. I cannot understand yours because it is not in our tongue, but to at least hold it is a treasure." He looked up at Alexander. "I must share this with my people. Would you be willing to tell us more of what it says? No man has ever done so before."

Alexander smiled tenderly as he felt tears trickle down his cheeks, "Gladly, Chieftain Tenoch. Gladly."

The man beamed with a wide toothy grin and returned the Bible to Alexander. "Very good. After you tell us all that you know of this Holy Book tonight, we will tell you everything we know about the Guardian tomorrow." They stood to shake hands, and the chieftain whistled. The warriors that had surrounded the entire group lowered their blowguns and came out of the shadows with eager respectful faces. Tenoch raised his voice to address them in their native tongue, and Alexander picked up only a few words.

Fitzgerald approached, shaking his head in bewilderment, "What is happening now, Jim? What did he say? Did he tell you about the guide?"

"All in due time, Adrian," the professor sighed, placing a hand on the man's shoulder. "Right now, let's just be thankful we made it through this unscathed."

The man's face darkened slightly. "Are you keeping things from me?"

"No. I'll explain everything to you very soon. But right now, I have more important work to do to get you your answers."

"More important work?"

The village around them came to life. Children ran out of their huts with laughter; women bustled about mixing the rice in the communal cooker and preparing fish and plantains.

"James Alexander!" Tenoch interrupted warmly, hobbling back over to where Alexander and Fitzgerald stood. "You and your friends will be our guests tonight!"

"Thank you, Chief! Please allow me to introduce you to my associate."

After a brief translated exchange of pleasantries, Fitzgerald pulled Alexander off to the side and demanded with a hushed tone, "Tell me everything *now*."

When he got to the part where the chief asked for more teaching about the Bible, Fitzgerald viciously whispered, "We don't have time to *waste* on religious frivolities."

"You want answers, right? The only way they'll talk is if I tell them more about the Bible."

"Utter nonsense!" he half shouted with his fists clenched at his side.

Alexander sighed again, "This is the way, Adrian. Please be patient. We should know something by tomorrow. Let's just enjoy the night, get a fresh meal, and good rest. We all need it." He removed his glasses and wearily rubbed his eyes as he said to himself, "But *'I have meat to eat that ye know not of.'*"

"What are you babbling about?"

"Nothing," he replied, putting his glasses back on. "Just a Bible verse from the Lord Jesus that popped into my head."

The man rolled his eyes and grunted as he walked off to speak with his men. "Tonight, we feast! But keep your eyes open," he warned. "They've been having cartel troubles."

As the villagers came together to eat that evening, Alexander realized he wasn't hungry. He was nervous. Nervous about what to say and how to present the truth of God's Word. He prayed as he gazed at all the faces of the people that had begun to gather round. More verses from John 4 came to mind, *"My meat is to do the will of him that sent me, and to finish his work. Say not ye, There are yet four months, and then cometh harvest? behold, I say unto you, Lift up your eyes, and look on the fields; for they are white already to harvest."* James Alexander was about to serve the best meal these natives had ever eaten — the Bread of Life to fill their hungry souls and Living Water so sweet, they would never thirst again.

CHAPTER XI

Early the next morning, the quiet village began to buzz with life as people from all over the region came on their motorized dugout canoes to sell their fruits, vegetables, and goods in the weekly market. They lined the dusty street along the dilapidated wooden pier, surrounded by thatched roof huts raised on stilts. Kaci and Drew walked along with Jada and Goatee, fascinated by all the stalls of brightly-colored bead necklaces, woven rugs, wicker baskets, fishing supplies, and crates containing exotic fruits and nuts. Goatee seemed especially drawn to the nut crates.

"His sunflower seed stash must be running low," Kaci snickered to her brother. Jada must have overheard because she glanced at them with a small smile, as if she were trying to hide a laugh.

Drew swatted away the annoying flies that buzzed around his face as they walked passed the butcher's corner. Goat, lamb, and cow carcasses hung by their rear limbs from a nearby tree. Portions of meat were being sold, freshly cut from the suspended dead beasts, then wrapped in banana leaves.

Unlike the hostility shown them from the day before, the natives greeted them with nods and smiles, now grateful that the team had invaded their little community. Though Drew and Kaci had no idea what exactly had been said last night, they had sat enthralled as they watched their uncle stand before a large fire in the center of the village and share truths from God's Word to the people for three hours. At times, he paced back and forth and pointed to the worn pages of his Bible; and in other instances, he wept and stretched out his arms representing Jesus on the Cross. The people remained motionless, their attention fixed on Alexander, soaking up every word he spoke.

Fitzgerald had sent his men back to camp, while he and Jada stayed, not trusting anyone else to keep a watchful eye on the professor and the teenagers. After the first hour, the man muttered underneath his breath and wandered off to sit in his Jeep. But Jada couldn't help but be intrigued by all that took place, though she did her best to conceal it. At times, she saw Kaci looking at her and the girl would smile. This startled Jada, hoping that she hadn't let her guard down or accidentally revealed that she was curious.

At the end of Alexander's message, Drew and Kaci saw many of the natives bow their heads in prayer. Chief Tenoch got on his knees with his hands raised in the air crying out, *"Iñiy! Iñiy!"* Later, Drew and Kaci found out he was proclaiming, "I believe! I believe!" He then told his people that he had never heard the Gospel explained like this before. "James Alexander was sent to us by the God of this Book!" he declared as he held the professor's Bible up in the air. Alexander was so stirred in that moment, his heart swelling with love for these new brothers and sisters in Christ. He publicly promised that as soon as he got home to England, he would commission a missions' agency to send a pontoon plane filled with Bibles in their language for all the people of the village. There was so much excitement among the people that the men rushed toward him and raised him up on their shoulders. With torches leading the way, they paraded him through the dusty lanes among the huts, singing and cheering. Finally, around midnight, the team returned to their camp and got what sleep they could.

As they wandered through the marketplace, Kaci's thoughts drifted back to early that morning when she and Drew had overheard Fitzgerald and Alexander talking.

The Scottsman paced back and forth nervously under their uncle's canvas work tent. "During market today, Tenoch *must* tell us all that he knows about the location of the next guide," he had threatened.

"He will," Alexander promised, holding a tin cup of steaming black coffee. "I am certain of it."

"For your sakes, he better. And one more thing," Fitzgerald stepped forward and pointed his finger in the professor's face, "Don't even *think* about turning this venture into some sort of blasted missionary trip."

Alexander bit his tongue, "But Adrian, if I wasn't sensitive to their spiritual need, we would have *never* found answers."

Fitzgerald's face darkened, and for a moment, Kaci and Drew had feared the man was going to smack their uncle across the face. "Just keep your Bible and your Jesus out of our business!" he screamed, then whirled about and tramped away.

Alexander sighed and gently smiled at his niece and nephew, "The Lord led us here to share the Gospel. I have no doubt of that!"

Suddenly, the rapid fire of machine guns cut through the air in the marketplace, snapping Kaci back into the present. The market's buzz of excitement turned into panic as people stumbled over one another fleeing from the half dozen flat-bottom airboats speeding to shore. More bursts of gunfire ripped along the tops of the thatched roofs close to the water. A short, stocky Peruvian with two bullet belts crisscrossing his chest climbed onto the dock with a loud thud as his men filled in behind him, weapons raised. Their faces were greasy and their tattered guerrilla clothing looked like it hadn't been washed in weeks.

The village fell eerily quiet. Drew and Kaci could feel their hearts pounding as they remained motionless behind an overturned cart. Jada and Goatee were a half dozen yards away lying flat on the ground by the butcher's clump of trees. She put a finger to her lips and quietly unsheathed two knives from her hip. It was only going to be a matter of moments before they were discovered.

This must be that drug cartel Uncle James told us about, Drew thought to himself. *How are we going to get out of this one?* The men had already fanned out and were slowly approaching, kicking over crates and smashing anything in sight that could be broken. *Father, we need you. Please keep us safe,* he prayed silently.

"Tenoch! Your day has come!" the man yelled out in Spanish as he shot a hole through an old guitar amp supplying music for the market from a radio.

"That's him!" the chieftain gasped in horror as he peered through the wooden slates of his council chamber where he met with Alexander and Fitzgerald. "That's Bruno, the *qhapaq* I spoke of! He has come to kill my people!" He motioned to four guards that stood with him and they ran out with a war cry. A few others who were brave enough emerged from the shadows and joined them.

"Tell them to stop!" Fitzgerald yelled, but it was too late. After a few erratic spurts of gunfire, everything fell silent again.

"No! No! This cannot be!" Tenoch moved toward the door but Fitzgerald forcibly restrained him.

"Don't move, you old fool!" he commanded as they struggled back and forth. "If he finds you, he'll kill you, and you haven't told us yet about the location of the guide!"

Tenoch stared at Fitzgerald in fear, anger, and confusion.

"Adrian, he can't understand you!" Alexander interjected.

"Tell him I'll handle this," he snarled and let go of the chieftain's arms with a shove. Before Alexander could respond, Fitzgerald was out the door.

Bruno stilled as he saw Fitzgerald stride toward him up the dirt lane that led from the heart of the village. He warily held his automatic pistol down by his side. His men ceased their ransacking and raised their AK-47s, carefully training them on the tall, muscular, tattooed man as he stopped about twenty yards away.

"What is a gringo doing way out here?" Bruno said in Spanish, smirking at him, his gold tooth glinting in the sunlight. "Who are you?"

Fitzgerald nonchalantly hooked his thumbs in his front beltloops. The medallion of Paititi dangled around his thick neck for all to see. "Just a concerned party interested in why you've come," he responded fluently.

"That is none of your business. I suggest you move out of the way before I have you moved!"

"Don't threaten me with empty words. *You* are the ones who should turn around and walk away while you still can."

"Oh really?" Bruno mocked. Beads of sweat trickled down his grimy face. "And if we don't? You're gonna stop us?"

"This village is under my protection —"

"You and what army?" Bruno's men roared with laughter as he gestured around him with outstretched arms. "You fancy yourself to be some tough guy, no? I've met many in my time, *muchacho*, and it never ended well for any of them. I don't think it's about to end well for you either."

"I know what you are thinking. Don't. This is your last warning. Leave the village with your lives. You cannot have Tenoch; he is far too valuable to me!"

"That old man?" Bruno glared at him. "He will die. *Slowly.* I *own* this valley! It is under my control now. No one tells me what to do!"

In a rage, Bruno lifted his handgun to fire but before he could pull the trigger, he saw a flash of light erupt from the tall gringo's hand and felt something slam into his chest. Fitzgerald held a large smoking revolver with a smile curled on his lips. In that same moment, the trees around the *qhapaq* roared to life. Bullets tore through limbs, spraying out large splinters and plumes of leaves from the jungle forest. The air filled with blue smoke and the smell of gun powder. It ended as fast as it had begun with no cartel members left standing but the drug lord.

Bruno stared at Fitzgerald in bewilderment as blood gushed forth from the wound in his chest. His handgun clattered to the ground and he slumped to his knees attempting to mutter something before collapsing in the dirt.

Fitzgerald whistled. His men immediately slid down from where they had been hiding up in the trees and came out into the open, reloading their weapons. Jada re-sheathed her unused knives and move forward with Goatee to kick the guns away from the hands of the fallen *qhapaq*. Drew and Kaci slowly stood, their bodies shaking from what they had just witnessed.

"Drew! Kaci!" Alexander ran toward them. His eyes widened at the sight. "Adrian, what have you done?"

"What I had to." Fitzgerald holstered his revolver with a haunting, wide-eyed smile. "Nothing will stand in my way! And now these people are safe, Jim; they will herald me as their savior!"

Alexander ignored the subtle insult and hugged his niece and nephew. "You two alright?"

"We'll be fine, Uncle James," Drew tried to say strongly, but Kaci just buried her face in her uncle's shoulder and cried, releasing the emotions of what they just experienced.

"I'm so sorry that you had to go through that. We are in a very dangerous part of the world. I'm just thankful that you're okay."

Chief Tenoch came down the dusty path with a growing number of villagers surrounding him. They took in the scene as they wandered through the marketplace and surveyed the damage. Then he finally spoke, breaking the silence. "I am saddened at the passing of life, James Alexander, and many of my people's goods are destroyed. But we can always replant and rebuild. You… you and your team have given us something that we can never repay. Hope in God and freedom from our oppressors! Come now, and I will tell you everything I know to help you on your quest."

⊗ ⊗ ⊗

Fitzgerald listened gleefully as Alexander translated for Tenoch. *Finally, we can make more progress on our journey,* he thought to himself. The three men, together with Drew, Kaci, and Jada sat in a circle on the woven flax mat covering the floor of the council chamber. Multi-colored cloths, strings of beads, and crude scenic finger paintings decorated the large circular hut. A couple of young ladies silently waited on them and served a hearty lunch of beef stew and plantains.

With a pencil, Alexander lightly traced along their modern map to show Tenoch the route they'd taken to reach their village.

"Ah," the old chieftain said. "You must go back to the main road and follow it to here." He pointed to the spot where it made a sharp turn and led down to the valley. "There you will find an old trail. You must look carefully, or you will pass by it. To reach the Guardian, you will have to travel on foot. This path will weave you through the rocks steeply up the mountain."

Tenoch turned back to the ancient map of Paititi, his wrinkled eyes taking in the details. "There is something else, and I wonder...." His voice trailed off as he stared.

Fitzgerald leaned closer, "What is it, man? Spit it out!"

Alexander shook his head with a lop-sided grin. "Adrian, I'm not translating that."

Tenoch nodded, "This place. I have heard tales of it in my youth." He gingerly tapped where the artifact depicted a vine-covered cliff with writing upon it. "It lies deep in the jungle, two days' journey beyond our sister village *Punka-Amarumayu*."

Fitzgerald squeezed Alexander's arm, "We've hit the jackpot, Jim!"

"It stands tall over a sacred burial ground belonging to our ancestors." Tenoch eyed each of them with great concern. "But I must warn you; we call it *Pachawañu*."

The professor raised an eyebrow. "*Pachawañu?* The place of death?"

Drew cleared his throat and whispered to Kaci and Jada sitting next to him, "Well, that sounds real inviting."

"Yes, the place of death. When I was a boy, some from my village took a pilgrimage there. Our crops were diseased, and the fish were washing ashore from harmful algae blooming in the river. My people went to pray for our ancestors' blessing." The chieftain bowed his head. "Only a few returned, crazed with horror, speaking of a giant creature the height of three men! It was savage, covered with rough knots like that of a crocodile and had a snakelike neck with horned face and jaws. The survivors died soon after from madness. The entire valley was in shock. From that time, no one has gone there, in fear of meeting this deadly beast. That is why the place has been called *Pachuwañu*."

"My, my!" Fitzgerald stroked his beard as he took in Alexander's translation. "Our adventure grows more exhilarating!"

"Uncle James, this sounds crazy but — do you think he's talking about a dinosaur?" Drew speculated.

"There's no way." Kaci chimed in. "I thought those didn't exist anymore!"

"They don't; they died off after the Genesis Flood," their uncle replied.

"Ha! You and your Bible again," Fitzgerald muttered. "Noah and his big bad boat? You have no proof of that! It's a fairy tale."

Alexander looked at the man warily, "I'm not getting into this with you right now. We all know the dinosaurs are gone. But over the years, there *have* been rumors of dinosaur-like creatures roaming deep in the jungles of Africa, Asia, and South America. Creationists speculate that these rainforests have a slightly similar ecosystem to that of the earth before the flood."

He turned to the chieftain, "Have there been any other sightings of this creature?"

The old man shrugged. "Not that I have heard. This was many, many years ago." He paused. "If your path leads you there, James Alexander, then go with God. You will never make it without Him, I fear."

Alexander smiled warmly. *Yes, Lord, guide our steps.*

The group talked together just a little longer. Fitzgerald advised the chieftain to secure the drug cartel's weapons to protect themselves against any future attacks. Tenoch assured him that they would, and his eyes twinkled as he told them how his men were already burning the *qhapaq's* drug fields to the ground. "And we will put their airboats to good use," he mentioned. "They will make excellent transports along the river for my people."

At Alexander's request, Tenoch sketched out directions to *Punka-Amarumayu* on their modern map. He chuckled, "They are not really roads, just dirt lanes used for carts and wagons. My people mainly traverse by boat or on foot. I think that your vehicles will soon become useless as well. I do not know of any roads past our sister village and even getting *there* will be difficult."

"Hmmmm," Alexander furrowed his brow and looked at Fitzgerald. "That's something we need to take note of."

The mercenary clenched his jaw and accepted the challenge, "If there is no path, then I'll make one!" He stood and stretched; his brawny form loomed large in the dimly lit council chamber. "We have what we need, Jim. Let's go! I want to reach our next guide before nightfall."

Tenoch raised his hand to still the group. "Please. Before you leave, you must take this." He stood and reached for a small intricately carved wooden figurine on the ledge behind him. It was small enough that it could fit in the palm of the man's hand. He handed it carefully to Alexander. "This is the highest symbol of honor that one could obtain in this valley. Show this to Centehua, chieftain of *Punka-Amarumayu*, so he knows that you arrive with my blessing. Be safe, James Alexander. Go with God!"

It seemed like the whole village came out to say farewell. Kaci and Drew teared up as they watched Tenoch give their uncle a warm embrace. The chieftain cried and repeatedly expressed his thankfulness to God for bringing the team to their remote village. He then smiled and wagged a wrinkled finger in the man's face.

"Do not forget your promise to us, James Alexander!"

"I won't, my friend. As soon as I return to England, I will send you that plane!"

The people crowded around the mud-covered Jeep as the team of five prepared to leave. Fitzgerald and Jada climbed up front while the others sat in the back with Kaci in the middle. Tenoch and his people showered them with farewells and stood in the dirt lane waving until they could see the vehicle no more.

"I feel like a piece of my heart is going to stay here forever!" Kaci whispered as she wiped tears from her face, freckled and tanned from their many days in the sun.

Drew reached over and squeezed her hand. "Me, too."

"Shards of my heart have been buried in a thousand different places," Alexander softly commented.

"I don't know how you do it, Uncle James!" Kaci replied.

His face glowed, and he spoke a little louder. "I've found that the more you go and the more you give, the more of a heart God grows within you. You know, there are people like Tenoch and his village all over the world. People sitting in darkness. Who will reach them with the Gospel?"

Fitzgerald loudly cleared his throat, annoyed by the conversation. "After we visit the guide, we'll stay tonight at base camp. But we're moving out first thing in the morning." He looked in the rearview mirror. "To the burial grounds and its cliff, I presume?"

Alexander shrugged. "If I was to make an educated guess — yes. But I'm not sure. It depends on what we find with this next guide. We cannot allow other landmarks and locations to distract us from finding each one of the guides. I haven't figured it out yet, but I believe they all hold important clues — clues to the great mystery of discovering the location of Paititi."

"Agreed!" As they pulled back onto the main dirt road, Fitzgerald pulled out his radio. "Fairchild! Do you copy?"

After a few moments of static, "Fairchild here."

"Gather some of the men and join us in Transport B. We'll pass by your location in five. We've located our next guide."

"10-4."

Fitzgerald replaced the walkie in its holder on the dashboard and his eyes flickered to look at Alexander in the mirror. "Here we go, old chum!"

CHAPTER XII

The distant sound of rushing water met their ears as the team climbed out of their vehicles at the center of the sharp curve Tenoch had described. They fanned out on the narrow road running along the mountain ridge and hunted for an opening among the jagged boulders.

"Here!" Drew shouted. He stepped sideways between two massive rocks and disappeared from view. "I think this is it!"

The rest of the team scurried over to where he'd called from and as each of them passed through the thin entryway, they beheld a broad dirt path weaving steeply up the mountain with broken rocks strewn across it. On either side of the shaded passage, rock walls loomed high overhead with faded symbols and worn scenes crudely painted on them.

"Do you mind if I take some pictures of these?" Alexander asked Fitzgerald. "I doubt this has anything to do with our journey, but I find it very fascinating."

The man nodded, the trained archeologist within him briefly coming out, as he too was intrigued by the history covering the stones.

Kaci ran up to where her brother was, leading the group in the front. He grinned at her. "Can you feel the burn?"

"I don't know what you're talking about," she teased. "Why are you so winded? I thought you were in shape from all that football practice." She sprinted ahead of him a couple of steps. "I can do this all day!"

"We'll see about that!" he challenged, and they were off, taking big strides up the pathway.

Jada rolled her eyes and found herself smiling. The two had grown on her. Despite all their "Jesus talk," they were actually pretty nice and always friendly. And it wasn't anything fake. They were the real deal, and Jada liked that about them. She climbed over a small boulder. *They definitely have something I know I don't have. But what exactly?*

Her eyes glanced up to some of her father's men in front of her and caught Goatee staring at her. "What are you looking at?" she snarled. The man blinked and turned his face toward the ground. *Come on, Jada. You can't let anyone see that you have a soft spot. You've got to be tough.*

Far above, Kaci doubled over with her arms around her waist and blurted out between gasps, "Okay, big brother! You win!"

Drew chuckled as he rushed forward, "No pain, no gain!"

When he neared the top, his eyes widened and he yelled over his shoulder down to the rest of the group, "Come on! You've got to see this!"

His words spurred them forward with a buzz of curiosity, and Fitzgerald laughed with exhilaration, sending echoes along the rocky passage. As they approached the top of the steep incline, the ground leveled out to a wide sandy landing with an engraved stone archway covered in tangled greenery. The hot sun shone intensely upon them, and they squinted at the overbearing brightness. A few of them staggered forward in exhaustion, trying to catch their breath.

"Wow, careful," Drew held up a hand in warning. "This ledge drops off crazy steep! See? It's exactly like the last clue said! *'Don't lose sight of your feet, or the mighty raging you will meet.'*"

"Very astute, my boy!" Fitzgerald complimented, his eyes now almost adjusted to the glare.

A sheer cliff wrapped around the landing with moss and low-lying vines creeping along the edge. Far below, a river cascaded down the mountain forming furious rapids. But what gripped all of their attention was what stood tall on a rock pillar jutting up from the middle of the river.

"Look at that," Fitzgerald whistled, placing his hands on his hips. "Isn't it beautiful, men? Our second guide."

Alexander shook his head, "Adrian, that is *not* going to be easy to get to."

A single dilapidated rope bridge stretched loosely across the void, far above the raging rapids, from the ledge between the stone columns of the archway where they stood to the pillar holding the guide, about 40 yards away.

"That's doesn't look safe at all," Kaci muttered.

"Maybe not, but we *must* know what is on the statue! It's too far away for the camera we have," Fitzgerald began to look around with a wild look in his eyes. "Someone has to go over there."

"Send one of your men," Alexander suggested. "Isn't that why you pay them?"

"Perhaps… or perhaps Drew can do it," the man slid his arm around the teenager.

"What?" Alexander started. "No. Absolutely not. Sending Kaci into that lake was one thing, but this? He could fall to his death. It is *not* happening. Send someone else!"

"Jim, it's the only logical choice." The man turned to squarely face his former friend. "He's lightweight with quick reflexes. It was nothing for him to climb this mountain!" He momentarily flashed a wicked smile. "Unless you wish for me to send Kaci again…."

At the sound of her name, Kaci stumbled backward away from the ledge, horror gripping her. "No! No! Please!"

"Fine, I'll do it." Alexander began taking off the cylindrical map case slung around his neck.

"No," Fitzgerald shoved a strong finger in the man's chest. "You are precious commodity. I cannot allow you to put your life at risk, old chum."

"Adrian, you cannot send a teenage boy out there to his death! I won't let you!"

"Then you leave me no choice." In an instant, his revolver was in Alexander's face.

Everything and everyone froze, poised to see what would take place in the next few moments. The professor stared coolly down the barrel. "What are you going to do, shoot me? That's really smart. You just said you needed me."

"I do. This is just a preventative measure to keep you in your place while I do something drastic." Without taking his eyes off of Alexander, he snapped his finger. "Fairchild. Do it."

The pale, thin mercenary snatched Kaci by the arm. She screamed, instantly causing Alexander and Drew to rush forward. They didn't make it far, however, with Goatee and Beady Eyes aiming machine guns at their chests. Fairchild dragged Kaci to the ledge and pushed her toward it. She shrieked in panic as the only thing stopping her from falling was his grip on her arm.

Fitzgerald grinned. "Now then, Drew, if you would be so kind as to cross the bridge and get to the statue, I would very much appreciate it. If not, well, your sister will be taking a swim in that river."

Jada stepped forward, her heart pounding and her hand impulsively tightening around the butt of her knife, "Dad, this is madness —"

"Are you threatening me?" he snarled. "Stay out of this!"

Drew grabbed hold of the frayed ropes of the bridge and took a step on the first rotted wooden plank. "Everybody, enough!" he yelled. "Mr. Fitzgerald, I'm doing this. Give me the camera. Just… just get her away from the ledge. Please!"

Fitzgerald nodded, his eyes glistening. Fairchild dragged Kaci back a foot but kept his hand firmly on her arm. With another snap of the finger, Drew had no doubt he could be watching his sister be pushed over into the river. Jada stepped forward and slung the camera around his neck. She looked at him with a piercing stare, "Don't drop this or you might as well fall in yourself." For an instant, Drew glimpsed fear and concern flash behind her hardened eyes, which surprised him.

He smiled nervously and turned back to the bridge, shutting his eyes as he felt it sway with the wind. *God, You've got to help me with this. I need Your strength! Please guide my steps.*

"Come on, boy. I don't have all day. Get on with it! Just don't look down," Fitzgerald laughed.

"Don't rush him," Alexander scolded then put a hand to his mouth, calling, "Take your time, Drew. Trust in the Lord! You can do this."

"Be careful!" Kaci pleaded.

Drew's heart pounded and he did his best to keep his eyes focused on the stone statue ahead of him, not the flimsy wooden bridge he stood on. He tuned out the noises of the river rushing below and the constant creaking of the weak boards in front of him. He gripped the rough ropes and took another step, testing each board before putting his full weight down.

As nervous as he was about the security of the bridge he was crossing, Drew couldn't help wondering about Jada. That insecure, scared look in her eyes had caught him off guard and got him thinking. *God, are you working in Jada's heart?* She'd always been so firm and unforgiving — sometimes even cruel with her words and demeanor. Yet even though she had just been harsh with him, he sensed that something was different. It seemed like more of a show to keep up appearances than anything else. He took another step, then another, his body rigid with decisive poise for every move he made.

Even Kaci has had brief moments of kindness from her over the past week, he thought. *Since that lake incident.* He smiled to himself. *And I wonder what she thought about that evangelistic service back in the last village?* Now this — that brief moment of hardness disappearing to reveal someone who was confused and all alone. He picked up the pace slightly in his excitement. He and his sister, along with Uncle James, were praying every day that God would use them to be a testimony of Jesus to everyone around them, including Jada. Now, in this moment, he realized that just maybe, their prayers were working.

Suddenly, the board beneath his right foot cracked. He barely had time to pull himself backward, the ropes burning into his hands as he steadied himself. The bits of plank tumbled into the river below, dragged under by the current. Struggling to catch his breath, Drew stared wide-eyed at how far the drop really was.

"I've got to focus," he said aloud.

"Move!" Fitzgerald bellowed.

Drew gritted his teeth, "I can do all things through Christ which strengtheneth me!"

He steadied himself and stepped over the gap. He was just past the center of the bridge, and it seemed like the wind was strongest here. He steadied himself as it rocked back and forth. Back and forth. He made it a few more steps when more planks gave way, and he felt himself falling forward unable to catch himself. He momentarily landed his foot on the suspension rope, but his leg slipped and he yelled, falling through the bridge.

Kaci's bloodcurdling scream mixed with Alexander's shout of horror. The entire team was riveted by the young man's plight. Drew flailed his arms as he fell, his hand catching the rope where the broken boards had been attached. He felt the frayed fibers dig deeply into his skin as the bridge bounced wildly from the momentum.

"Enough," Jada panicked. "He's not gonna make it, Dad."

"He will if he wants his sister to live," Fitzgerald replied. "Did you hear that, boy? Get up and get moving! Or your sister will be the next thing you'll see falling into the water."

Fairchild gave a sinister laugh and shoved Kaci closer to the edge, scattering pebbles and sand over the side.

"Adrian!" Alexander raised his fists to fight with the man, but Goatee and Beady Eyes roughly jabbed him into a corner with the barrels of their AK-47s.

"Stop this *now*, Dad!" Jada demanded, stepping forward with one of her knives instinctively drawn. Abruptly, a gunshot went off.

Drew jerked at the sound, whipping his head around to see

Adrian holding his gun in the air, having a stare-down with his daughter. "What has gotten into you?" he screamed.

Drew shook his head as the two loudly argued. *I can't worry about them right now.* He felt something moving on his body. The camera! Somehow in his thrashing it had slipped around his waist, and now he felt it slowly sliding down his legs. He bent his knees and carefully reached with his other hand to grab it by the strap. He felt sick to his stomach as he looked down, his eyes taking in the furious rapids far below. He smelled the ominous mist that ascended from the river; it seemed like it was reaching up to him to drag him to his death. *Stop! Just get the camera!* Almost there. Just a little more. *Got it!* His fingers nimbly wrapped around the lanyard, and Drew quickly looped the camera over his head once again. He threw up his hand to grab hold of the rope, hoping to relieve the strain from his other hand that stiffly ached.

He felt his muscles burn as he slowly hauled himself back up. His foot found the next plank to steady himself on, and he kept gingerly repositioning his hands along the ropes as he pulled his body forward to an upright position. He looked back and saw Fitzgerald and Jada still arguing. "Look! Look! I'm fine!" he yelled, interrupting. "I can make it, guys! I'm almost there!"

Jada's gaze flicked to him but only for a second. She said something to her father, but whatever it was, it was too quiet for Drew to hear. The man lowered his gun, and she sheathed her blade. Fairchild backed away from the edge with Kaci.

"I said let her GO!" Jada roared.

The man looked to Fitzgerald, who nodded, and Drew saw his sister reunite with their uncle in a relieved embrace. Goatee and Beady Eyes lowered their weapons but carefully kept an eye on the two to make sure they didn't make any sudden moves.

"Let's go, son, let's go!" Fitzgerald's command stirred Drew to cautiously move further down the bridge. Each step sent a jolt of fear slithering down his spine, but he focused on Christ and gained strength to continue on. He breathed in and out steadily through his nose, keeping his eyes on the stone guide. With three planks to go, he leapt the remaining distance to solid ground and happily slumped to his knees in relief that, for the moment, he was safe.

How am I going to make it back across? He shook his head. *One thing at a time.*

He carefully climbed his way to the front of the statue. The stone pillar upon which it sat was barely large enough for Drew to move around on without falling off. The face stood as tall as he was and was similar to the one Kaci had snapped pictures of at the bottom of the lake. Gently, he ran his hands over the carvings, fascinated by the detail. He stared into its bright blue eyes that, this time, pointed straight up.

"That must mean we've got to go North," he whispered to himself.

The symbol for Paititi was just below the face. He took a few pictures then shifted his gaze to the Incan writing beneath the face. He made sure to get clear shots so his uncle would be able to translate it easily. *What's this?* An image of a cliff, like what they'd seen on the ancient map, was etched into the stone over the mouth of the statue. *Fascinating.* Click!

He looked further down and noticed dark red flowers covering the base of the statue around its neck. He knew every single clue and message was important to their mission, and ultimately to their lives. Not wanting to risk missing anything and moving carefully so as not to lose his balance, he crouched and gently pushed the foliage out of the way. Here he discovered more writing, this time in Latin. He snapped a few images of that, too, before moving around the face for a second time to make sure he hadn't missed any other clues.

"What is taking so long?" Fitzgerald shouted, his impatient voice echoing across the ravine.

Drew rolled his eyes, turning around slowly. "I'm headed back now," he called back. He tucked the camera in the zipper pocket of his cargo pants. The photos on that camera were far too valuable to risk losing it a second time.

"Wait!" Fitzgerald yelled. "Before you come back — try to take the eyes out!"

"What?" Alexander stepped forward. "That is extremely unwise. The whole thing could be rigged."

Fitzgerald threw his thick, muscular arm in front of his old friend, "Back off, Jim."

Drew couldn't hear what his uncle said but he saw him throw his hands up in the air and shake his head in disbelief. Fitzgerald shouted again, "The eyes! I *must* have them. Take them out!"

Drew frowned. *Why in the world would he need....?* Then he froze as he felt goosebumps crawl up and down his back. *This probably has something to do with his quest for immortality. I've really got to tell Uncle James!* He reached around to the front of the face and tried to pull on the bright blue gemstones.

"Boy, use your knife if you have to!"

Oh yeah! Drew suddenly remembered that some time ago the man had given both him and his uncle a nice multi-tooled pocketknife. Kaci was jealous and wished she had one, too. But Fitzgerald had merely laughed and replied with a sarcastic look over to his daughter that girls shouldn't play with knives.

Though the gems were carved to fit into the stone and point a certain direction, Drew was surprised how easily they slid out as he scraped his blade along the rim of each socket.

"Did you get both of them?"

"Yes, sir!" The empty sockets now stared at him like a skull.

"Good lad! Come back to us. Careful now!"

Drew zipped the gems into his other cargo pocket. Then he froze. Something didn't feel right. Did the stone pillar just move? Drew steadied himself by holding on to the face. Confused, he glanced down, wondering what was happening. The trembling came again, but stronger. A sharp crack shuddered him to his core. He rushed to grab hold of the rope bridge as stones began to break off the pillar and plummet into the water. *How is this happening?* Another crack resounded, sending him to his knees.

"Drew!" Alexander bellowed, "Run! It's a booby trap!"

The statue shifted as if warning Drew of the penalty for removing its "soul," and then the top of the pillar swayed as the bottom began to cave in. Drew darted as fast as he dared across the bridge, which swayed viciously back and forth threatening to throw him off. He leaped and shimmied his feet along the bottom suspension ropes in the spots where the boards had broken away.

Praying with everything he had, he put his head down and ran. One of the rope railings collapsed and he was left with one slack rope to hold on to as he tried to balance on the planks suspended by the other two fraying ropes. He froze, feeling the bridge about to fall beneath him. He was only a few yards from the ledge, but each time he tried to move, the planks crumbled. Kaci began screaming in terror, but it wasn't his sister's face his eyes landed on.

Jada stared at him in open panic. The ropes beneath him suddenly snapped and Drew felt himself now falling. He grabbed hold of the single remaining rope with both hands, thankful it was still attached to the ledge. Holding on for dear life, his body swung wildly from side to side as the collapsed bridge ricocheted against the side of the cliff. The old rope strands groaned and began to slowly snap apart under the weight it supported. Just when Drew expected it to give way, two hands reached down, grabbing hold of his arm. Jada. They heard the final snap of the rope, and the bridge cascaded downward, splintering violently in the foaming depths below. Drew looked up to find Jada precariously leaning over the ledge with Fitzgerald and Alexander holding onto her belt to keep her from going over with him.

Drew propped his feet up on the cliff and climbed up as the two men drew them both back to safety. They collapsed to the ground, Drew falling onto his back, thankful to be alive. Kaci was at his side a second later, hugging him and ensuring that he was all right. His hands and legs shook. Jada sat a few feet away, catching her breath.

"Thanks," he told her. "You saved my life."

Her eye twitched and she held out her hand. "Wasn't saving you. We need that camera."

Drew sensed she was lying for the sake of her father and the men that stood by, but he let it go. He removed the camera from his pocket and handed it over. "All yours."

He stood slowly and Fitzgerald gave him a hearty slap on the back. "I guess it *was* a booby trap!" He laughed. "Good show, my boy. You have your uncle's blood in you!" His eyes narrowed. "And your father's, for that matter."

Drew and Kaci looked at him sharply. "You knew our dad?"

The man dismissed the question with the wave of his hand, "A long time ago in a different life. Now, the gems please?"

As soon as Drew pulled them out, the mercenary eagerly snatched them, his eyes gleeful.

"Just as beautiful as the others!" he said to himself.

"What's that supposed to mean?" Alexander interjected.

"Oh, nothing that concerns you, old chum," he laughed while reaching out to help his daughter up. Jada was puzzled by this suddenly kind gesture but welcomed it. As soon as she stood, Fitzgerald smacked her hard across the face, sending her back to the ground. Jada furiously jumped to her feet and cleared the disheveled hair out of her face to reveal blood trickling from the corner of her mouth.

"Don't you *ever* threaten me again!" he snarled with eyes ablaze. "Have I made myself clear?"

Fairchild chuckled and smirked broadly while everyone stood motionless. Jada flashed him a piercing glare and then looked at her father in hatred and slowly nodded.

"I can't hear you, girl."

She gritted her teeth, "Yes, sir."

"Louder."

"Yes, sir!"

"Good. And let this be a lesson to all of you," he commented without taking his eyes off Jada. "Now let's go!" he ordered, rolling the two aqua gemstones around in his hand as he walked away.

Kaci shook her head in disbelief at what just happened and

walked over to the two pillars of the stone archway where the bridge had been. Far below, the stone statue could be seen laying on its side among the pile of scattered rocks that used to be the pillar. "It's a miracle you're alive, Drew."

"It's a miracle that any of you are alive," Jada interrupted. "Adrian Fitzgerald is a madman." She stormed off, ordering her father's men to move ahead of her.

Alexander, Kaci, and Drew brought up the rear as they all descended the mountain. Drew intentionally slowed down and whispered, "Uncle James?"

Alexander could sense the uneasiness and urgency in the young man's voice.

"There's something that I've *got* to tell you. I've kept this to myself long enough. Fitzgerald, he's...he's not just after the gold!"

CHAPTER XIII

J ames Alexander sat in silence, staring out the window. Sunset spilled its golden rays through the trees, and black howler monkeys swung from limb to limb chattering loudly as they followed the vehicles returning to camp. The professor pondered over everything his nephew had told him and clenched his jaw. *Immortality. The Fountain of Youth.*

Despite all that had happened, Fitzgerald was in an unusually happy mood as he rambled on about what might be laying ahead of them in their quest for Paititi.

"Jim? Are you listening?" the man jabbed Alexander in the arm, startling him out of his deep thought.

He took off his glasses and wearily rubbed his eyes. "We don't know anything just yet, Adrian. Yes, Tenoch told us about the cliff, but we must follow the guides. I believe they hold the key to everything."

"Good point. I suppose if we accidently pass one up, we could miss out on finding the ancient city entirely," Fitzgerald muttered grimly. "And we haven't come this far to make mistakes."

As they drove into their base of operations, the mercenary snatched his radio and began barking instructions to different squad leaders. He wanted patrols doubled, just in case there were any remaining *qhapaq* in the region; and he expected things to be ready for transport by 6am.

He replaced the walkie in its holder as they pulled up to the center of camp. "We have no time to waste. Come on, Jim!" In a flash, he was out of the vehicle and unfolding their large modern map on the makeshift wooden table under Alexander's station tent. The professor reluctantly grabbed the camera sitting on the dashboard. *Lord, please help me. I need Your wisdom and guidance with how to handle Adrian.*

Jada slammed her door, murmuring loudly, and stormed off into the shadows. Some of the men who sat close by quietly cleaning their weapons and reloading magazine clips exchanged glances, then shrugged before getting back to work. Drew, curious to see where this next statue would lead them, followed his uncle and helped him carefully roll out their ancient map. He looked to Kaci and waved her over to join them, but she shook her head and silently pointed in the direction that Jada had disappeared. He knew what she wanted to do. What she had to do.

Alexander slowly moved through the pictures on the camera. "Good job getting all these pictures, Drew. They are very clear and orderly."

"You're welcome. God helped me!"

"Yes, He did," his uncle replied thinking over Drew's harrowing escape.

Fitzgerald cleared his throat. "Any *luck* with the clues, Jim?"

"Interesting," the professor commented, ignoring the man. He angled the viewscreen toward Drew. "So, there was Latin on the bottom of this guide too?"

"Yeah, it was weird. Underneath some red flowers growing around it."

Alexander smiled. "I'm glad you checked! Way to be thorough!" He jotted down some notes on his pad, his face changing to an expression of deep concern. "*'Ne torporem e somno excites.'*"

"*'Lest you wake the writhing from sleep.'*" Fitzgerald translated aloud. "How exhilarating!"

"To what and where this refers, I do not know," the professor stroked his bearded chin then shrugged. "At least it seems to go along with the other clue."

Drew read over the first set of words again followed by the second. "'*Be watchful of the waters deep, lest you wake the writhing from sleep.*' Well, whatever it's for, it doesn't sound like it's going to be a fun time."

Fitzgerald interjected a jovial laugh, "All part of the adventure, my boy, all part of the adventure. With great risk comes great reward."

"Great risk? You mean Kaci almost getting eaten by underwater beasts or me almost falling to my death on an ancient bridge?" Drew fumed. "So far, you've had *kids* do all your risk taking. I haven't seen you lift a fingernail yet."

"The insolence!" Fitzgerald bellowed. His face grew red — whether by embarrassment or anger, no one knew.

"Adrian, Drew has a point. You cannot keep putting these young people in such danger. But thankfully, God has protected them and they are fine for now. We need to focus on the task at hand. Please."

Drew nodded his head in agreement.

Fitzgerald sighed, "Fine. Where are we going next?"

"Let's go back to the beginning here to find out," Alexander scrolled through the photos to the first one Drew had taken. "Okay. The eyes are pointing North," he peered at Adrian over his glasses. "This leads us toward *Punka-Amarumayu*, yes?"

"Correct!" Fitzgerald replied as he aligned a straight edge between the point of the guide with the light circle Tenoch had marked. "The old man was right. What else?"

Alexander continued scribbling notes on his pad. "These writings speak of our first landmark — the cliff — and has this clue, '*Deep with the dead by tilted head, away from moon and sun lies the search the ancients have begun.*'" He looked up, concerned. "Our next guide must be buried somewhere in the vicinity of *Pachawañu.*"

Fitzgerald beamed, slapping his hands together. "The hunt's afoot! I know we'll find it; and no mythical beast will stand in our way!"

"But Adrian, if the guide is hidden there, we cannot simply

waltz into an ancient burial ground and start digging around. Tenoch and his people may not worship their ancestors any more, but you and I both know what a place like that means to people around here. It's a place of deep respect. Besides, it's also against federal and international laws to desecrate burial grounds. We simply can't."

Drew was in full agreement with his uncle's words. Fitzgerald, however, didn't seem phased in the least. "We go where the guide takes us. It was *meant* to be found, Jim." He smiled wickedly. "They haven't made it easy for us. But I will not let tradition or some government stand in my way."

Alexander shook his head, "I cannot support that; it's wrong."

Fitzgerald stilled and his eyes narrowed. "You can, and you *will* if you know what's best for you."

The professor sighed, "Drew, go find your sister. She probably went to get an MRE. Don't stay up too late; we have an early morning ahead of us." He turned to Fitzgerald and crossed his arms. "You and me? We need to talk. Somewhere private."

"Fine," the large man muttered harshly under his breath, "To my tent, if you please."

Ⓧ Ⓧ Ⓧ

Jada tramped under the moonlight through the knee-high grass with her head down and fists clenched by her side. She was confused by the emotions raging within her. Before she met Drew, Kaci, and the professor, she had never questioned any of the methods her father used. She even relished in the moments that he was cruel at times. She knew he was grooming her to take over the *Bloodfists* when he grew too old to keep up with their global activities. He already trusted her enough to give her small missions, like the most recent one of kidnapping Drew and Kaci, bringing them to South America, and keeping them imprisoned until he arrived with Alexander. Now, something inside of her was screaming that this was all wrong. A battle raged within her. *I should never have listened to dad when he told me* to hang around those two. *Their dumb Bible talk is rubbing off on me.* She sighed. *And yet, there's something about them that so different. Something I've never seen before.*

The joy they possessed. The peace that filled their eyes. The genuine smiles they always glowed with in spite of the hardships. Sometimes she wished she could punch their faces in because of how content they always were. *How is it that they're so cheerful and I feel so...miserable? I'm the daughter of one of the wealthiest mercenaries in the world!*

She stopped as she approached the jungle tree line at the edge of camp. A hard knot formed in her throat, and she couldn't do anything to stop the hot tears from streaming down her cheeks. She let her shoulders slump as she stood alone, the questions swirling around in her mind. *Does my father even love me? Will we make it out of this alive? What am I supposed to do with my life? God,* — She shook her head. *What am I doing? I'm no saint. He wouldn't ever listen to me.* She suppressed her feelings and wiped her eyes clean, then looked to the bright stars above. *I suppose it couldn't hurt to try.*

"God," her lips moved silently. "If You're really there, can you help me understand?"

Suddenly, she heard a faint noise behind her and whirled around with both throwing knives in her hands, "Get away from me!" she yelled. Then she stilled as she saw Kaci with her hands up in front of her face, frightened by Jada's threatening pose.

"Oh, it's you," she said drily, throwing up her strong front, "What do *you* want?"

"I wanted to say 'thank you.'" Kaci replied hesitantly.

"For what?"

"Um...for saving Drew's life? For standing up for me today?"

"Yeah, well, look where that got me."

Kaci lowered her hands and calmly took a step forward. "And that's another reason why I wanted to come out here to you. I didn't know if...maybe you'd want to talk."

Jada rolled her eyes and sheathed her blades, "I'm fine. Leave me alone."

Kaci thought she could sense a plea for help behind the hard facade that Jada was trying to maintain. *Lord, help me break through to her,* she prayed. "Are you sure? I was just a little worried about you. You know, after what happened up on the mountain. I would love to sit and talk...if you wanted."

"I said no. Besides, I didn't ask for you to worry about me. You have enough going on trying to stay alive out here without wondering how I'm doing. Why don't you run your happy little self back to camp and get some dinner."

Kaci smiled, "Okay... I just wanted to spend some time with you."

"I said I'm *fine!*" Jada yelled harshly. She turned and crossed her arms, but she didn't walk away. "Adrian Fitzgerald cares only about one thing and that's finding this lost city of his. It's the story that was driven into my head every night when I was little and every day after he took me from my home and my friends when my mom died. I'm nothing to him but another tool. Sometimes I wonder if he even sees me as his daughter." Frustrated, she turned to hide the rush of tears that she hastily wiped away in rage.

Kaci reached out for her arm, "Oh, Jada —"

"I said leave me alone!!" She snatched Kaci's wrist and twisted her arm behind her back. Her knife was in her other hand a second later and she pointed its tip at Kaci's throat. Her eyes were filled with a pain and anger that ran deep, deeper than Kaci had realized. Jada's hand shook as she glowered at her.

"I want to be your friend," Kaci tenderly smiled.

Jada blinked twice, stunned by what she heard. Trembling, she released her tight grasp and hung her head in shame. The knife slipped from her fingers. "I— I'm sorry. I shouldn't have attacked you. I don't know what I was thinking. I'm just so...angry."

"I understand, and you have every right to be." Kaci picked up the ninja blade and handed it back with another soft smile. "But everything's going to fine."

Jada was bewildered. "How can you say that? And how can you even be *happy* right now? I just threatened you."

"Because God is in control, and his presence is with me. And He's with Drew and Uncle James. We're Christians, which means we have a relationship with Jesus…He's our Savior! We've asked Him to forgive our sins and save us from Hell and He's promised to take us to Heaven when we die. Whenever it's our time to go, we're ready."

"That's *crazy* talk," Jada muttered quietly.

"Not really. It's truth. It's what God teaches in the Bible —"

Jada rolled her eyes and interrupted, "The Bible? Seriously? What does *that* have to do with anything?"

Kaci hesitated, "It has to do with…*everything*."

Jada stepped back and raised an eyebrow. "Wait, so you're telling me that the Bible is why you all act like there's no problem in the world?"

Kaci nodded.

"Huh." She rubbed her jaw. "I see you guys praying and reading that Book at night around the fire. You're always laughing and having a good time. And then during the day you're so joyful, even when things go wrong. You have a sense of peace, even in danger. But, that's got to end at some point, right? I mean, we could all die out here! You're kidnapped, for crying out loud! Your uncle is being forced to help my father."

Kaci smiled, instinctively tucking her golden-brown hair behind her left ear. "I promise you that we're not putting on a show. Any happiness that you see in us comes from God as we walk with Him and read His Word. Jesus says in John 15, *'These things have I spoken unto you, that my joy might remain in you, and that your joy might be full.'* He keeps us happy in spite of the troubles."

Jada grunted.

"And by the way, did you know that today you actually lived out another verse in John 15?"

"Oh?" Jada raised her eyebrow again, slightly curious.

"Yeah — *'Greater love hath no man than this, that a man lay down his life for his friends.'* You showed yourself a friend when you risked your life to rescue Drew."

For a moment, Jada didn't know how to respond. "I wouldn't push it. I don't consider you both my friends."

"But we think of you as one," Drew replied, walking up out of the shadows.

"What?" Jada scolded, a little surprised by his sudden appearance. "How long have you been standing there?"

"Not long. I just didn't want to interrupt." He smiled. "And thank you for what you did for me today. You saved my life."

She crossed her arms and looked away. "I already told you that we needed the camera."

"Oh yes, of course!" Drew laughed. "But seriously I mean it, thank you. What you did was exactly what Jesus did on the Cross. He laid down His life for us — for you, Jada. So that each of us could have a relationship with Him. And an eternal home with Him one day in Heaven."

She shook her head, "I don't know about all that. You guys might believe in Jesus, but I'm not sure if I do."

Kaci linked her arm around her brother's and said, "That's okay. Whether you believe or not doesn't change the fact that He's real, and His love for you is real. *'For God so loved the world, that he gave his only begotten Son, that whosoever believeth in him should not perish, but have everlasting life.'*"

Jada's gaze softened. She bit her lip and whispered, "I've got to go." In an instant, she slipped into the night, making her way back to camp. Drew and Kaci looked up at the bright star-lit sky.

"You know, I think before this is all over, she's gonna get saved," Drew commented.

"I agree; I'm so glad I was able to squeeze in John 3:16!"

Drew nodded. "We've *got* to keep praying for her."

"Yes, and we've got to pray that God will give us another opportunity to talk with her before it's too late. Come on, let's go grab something to eat. I'm starved!"

(図) (図) (図)

As the flap of the tent closed behind him, James Alexander allowed his eyes to adjust to the dim flicker of candles that Fitzgerald lit. They rested in a bronze candelabrum on a small circular table in the middle of the canvas room.

"Do you remember this?" Fitzgerald grinned.

"Wow." His mind flooded back to memories of their first adventure together. "You've had it all these years."

"It helps me never lose sight of my life's work."

"What is that? To be ruthless like Bloodfist?"

"Ha!" The man took off his gun belt and holster and threw them on his disheveled cot lying in the corner. Alexander noticed the old pirate's chest sitting next to it. *So, he stole that too.*

"You can stop with your righteous crusade, Jim. It's just you and me now. Speak freely."

"Are you sure? Or are you going to smack me like you did your daughter today."

"Is that what this is about?" the man gruffly chuckled. "We both know she needed to be put in her place."

"But not like that. She's your *daughter*, Adrian."

"Yes, and she knows better. I don't know what's gotten into her!"

Alexander sat down on a collapsible metal chair by the table and folded his hands, "Maybe she's bothered by how reckless you've become."

"I don't know what you're talking about."

"How about forcing Drew to cross the bridge?"

Fitzgerald took out the two aquamarine gemstones from his pocket and tossed them on the table like giant dice as he plopped down in a seat across from Alexander. "Jim, the boy was the only one who could do it. You saw the bridge. It certainly wouldn't have supported you or me or any of my men. And the girls? They couldn't have gone.

Kaci would have been stiff with fear, and Jada isn't as quick on her feet as Drew."

"But threatening me and my niece?"

"He needed some motivation," Fitzgerald smirked. "I would have *never* shot you or let Fairchild kill the girl."

Alexander shook his head. "Adrian, your mind is unstable. You are ruthless, cold, and relentless."

"Thank you, old chum! I take that as a compliment."

"ENOUGH," the professor stood, his fist slamming the table. "Stop messing with my family. Don't you *ever* put their lives in danger like that again."

"Sit down, Jim." Fitzgerald said coldly. "You and I both know it was good for the boy to prove himself. Helps him become more of a man."

"You are not his father. And Benjamin Howard would never have made his son cross that bridge."

The mention of Drew and Kaci's father made Fitzgerald stiffen. He'd been close friends with both men all throughout college. Adrian and James had constantly teased Ben over his Yankee sound, being from the United States; but Ben dished it right back at them, butchering Fitzgerald's Scottish and Alexander's British accents. Together they planned the summer expedition to Dominica, but at the last minute, Ben bowed out, deciding to take his girlfriend — James' sister — to visit his parents in the U.S. instead. It was on that trip that he proposed to her.

Something flashed in Fitzgerald's eyes like he was hiding something; he opened his mouth to speak but hesitated.

"What is it?"

"It's — it's nothing." He leaned forward. "Okay, fine; tell you what. Now that your niece and nephew have proven their worth, I'll avoid any further risks. But I *expect* them to pull their weight."

"Of course. They're responsible. Maybe even more so than some of your men. I just don't want them unnecessarily thrown into harm's way. Drew was right earlier: you've got to stop giving the most dangerous jobs to kids."

"Deal," Fitzgerald extended his hand.

"Hmmm. Nothing like shaking hands with an unpredictable lunatic."

Fitzgerald let out a boisterous laugh that vibrated the canvas sides of the tent. *This is the moment,* Alexander thought to himself. *Give me wisdom, Lord. Please.* As Fitzgerald was about to withdraw his hand from the rigorous shake, Alexander squeezed it tightly, startling Fitzgerald into a serious mood. He chose his words carefully.

"Why haven't you told me the truth?" he asked, eyeing the mercenary closely.

"The truth? About what?"

"What you're really after." He released his grip slowly and the man jerked his hand away.

"I don't know what you're talking about."

Alexander picked up one of the jewels on the table and glanced at one of the flickering candles through it. "Why *did* you want Drew to take the eyes out of the statue?"

The man crossed his arms and smirked. "It's quite simple. I realized that if we cannot find Paititi, then nobody else should be allowed to. I've given my life to discover its location; *no one* has the right to find it but me."

He snatched the jewel out of Alexander's hand and placed it back with the other one on the table. "Don't you think these will make a lovely necklace? I plan to collect them all." He unzipped the pocket on his cargo pants, pulled out a small leather pouch, and spilled its contents. Two more light blue gemstones rolled out next to their siblings. The professor stared at them in disbelief. "My men fetched the eyes out of that first guide in the lake before we left." Fitzgerald explained. "It wasn't boobytrapped like the second one. I honestly didn't expect that other guide to crumble like it did."

Adrian is mad! Alexander thought to himself. He looked the man squarely in the eyes, careful to not let on anything he knew from his nephew. "This only confirms my suspicions. You're on the hunt for immortality, aren't you?"

Fitzgerald laughed, "Preposterous!"

"Is it? You know the superstition behind these stones as well as I do. The Amazonians believed they endow youthfulness and healing."

Fitzgerald couldn't help but let the dark, evil smile begin curling on his lips. "One has to wonder why Aapo and the others decided to choose *that* specific gemstone out of all the ones they could have used."

Alexander sensed the man was about to tell all. He continued to gently press further.

"Exactly. Do you remember back when you first cornered me in that hotel room in Lima? You said that Paititi was *'a city of gold that contained immortality at its core.'* That's always been the legend. But you said you had proof. Back then I thought you meant proof of Paititi existing. But now I think you must have some sort of proof that a *'fountain of youth'* exists."

Fitzgerald leaned forward, his eyes wide and his face glowing with lust. "So, you figured me out, old chum. How?"

"You keep talking about power. But I know it's not power from money, because you've amassed fortunes. You also already have your hand involved in the rise and fall of governments around the globe. But it's that look in your eyes that reveals it. It signifies something more. Something greater." He paused for a moment. "You do realize that the fountain is a myth, right? It doesn't exist."

Fitzgerald shrugged. "Maybe. Maybe not." He went over to the wooden chest beside his cot and lifted the latch. He looked at Alexander over his shoulder. "I'm about to share something with you that no one has seen except for my daughter."

The Scotsman pulled out a couple of leather scrolls. "These are the writings of Andres Lopez."

Alexander was stunned. "The Jesuit who ventured into the Amazon?"

"So, you've heard of him."

"Of course. But his journeys were only folklore, nothing

documented."

"Maybe to you and the rest of the world. But not to the Vatican. He was very real."

"Is that where you stole these from?"

Fitzgerald smiled. "They were doing no one any good collecting dust in their vaults, so I 'borrowed' them." Alexander rolled his eyes. Fitzgerald continued to wax eloquent about what the priest had found in his travels throughout South America while Alexander poured over the ornate calligraphed documents.

"Look here!" Fitzgerald pointed to a passage.

The professor read it aloud, "'*Yet something far greater lies within, where there is power and life to do that which is desired.*'" He took off his glasses. "Adrian, this could mean anything."

The man shrugged. "Perhaps. But all the evidence —"

"There is no evidence! It's just a bunch of conjecture."

"Ah, but what is it that you're always trying to tell me to do? Yes, I hear you pray, and I pick up on your subtle remarks. You talk about having faith. Believing! Trusting in God. Well, that's exactly what I'm doing, Jim. Having faith — but in something that is real, not your Jesus or your fabled Bible."

"Adrian, your faith is in the wrong place," Alexander argued. "The Bible says, '*It is better to trust in the LORD than to put confidence in man.*' Whether you believe that Jesus exists or not doesn't change that fact that He *is* real, and His Word is true. It's not too late for you to put your faith and trust in Him and stop this madman quest."

"Enough!" Fitzgerald exploded, standing abruptly. "I'll not have you preaching to me. In the morning, we're setting out for the cliff and you will help me find the next guide. If you're uncomfortable with the means that I must take, I respect that. But do *not* stand in my way or stop me from finding Paititi. Nothing will keep me from achieving immortality. Now, leave me!"

"Adrian —" Alexander stood.

"OUT!"

CHAPTER XIV

Awkward silence hung in the vehicles for a majority of the next couple of days. Though Jada had briefly opened herself up to Drew and Kaci, she went back to her cold withdrawn self. From her body language and how she constantly avoided eye contact, they got the idea that she didn't want to talk. Fitzgerald was in no chatting mood either and if the topic didn't have anything to do with their present journey to *Punka-Amarumayu* and the tombs beyond, he wasn't interested in carrying on a conversation with Alexander.

The team carefully made its way through treacherous ravines and across makeshift wooden bridges over shallow brooks. Once, a tire on one of the heavier transport vehicles snapped through the thin planking. As the bridge sagged under the immense weight, Alexander thought they were going to lose it, but once the bridge steadied, the men were able to gingerly push it up out of the hole with great exertion.

The thick rainforest canopy high overhead only allowed isolated beams of bright sunlight to spill forth to the mossy floor below. Bright colored toucans squawked with impatience and sloths hanging from gnarly trees slowly turned in curiosity as the convoy made its way through the jungle. Occasionally, they passed obscure settlements recessed deeply in the trees, comprised of no more than a dozen huts. Happy boys and girls always skipped down inquisitively to greet the long procession as it drove by, while parents often stared from afar off with disdain at the vehicles plowing over any small saplings or ferns that stood in their way.

Jada rolled her eyes whenever Kaci would stick her body through the window and wave at the children, shouting with a big, bright smile, *"Hello there! Allillachu!"* The boys and girls always giggled and waved in return, replying with warm greetings as she passed.

The deeper the team traversed, the smaller the cart path became until it was a single lane for a person or animal to walk down. Despite the looming overgrowth and vines threatening to stop their large vehicles dead in their tracks, they pushed forward. It soon became "all-hands-on-deck", and anyone not driving was under Fairchild's supervision to help clear a path wide enough to allow them through. Several men with chainsaws cut away at tree limbs, vines, and brush, while the rest carefully cleared away the debris.

Alexander sought to catch his breath after he heaved a heavy branch off the road with Drew, Baldy, and Beady Eyes. "Tenoch was right. By the way things appear, after *Punka-Amarumayu*, I don't think we're going to have any road left! It'll be solid jungle."

"It is no matter!" Fitzgerald boomed from his lead vehicle as he slowly drove past. "We will plow through! Pioneers to Paititi!"

Baldy grunted. "Easier said than done."

Drew plopped onto the ground. "By the way my arms and legs burn, I can only imagine what the early pioneers must've felt like!"

"Come on, kid; get up." Beady Eyes teased him. "This is the kind of stuff that separates the men from the boys. Stop being such a wimp."

Alexander chuckled as Drew struggled back to his feet, cheeks turning red from the criticism as well as the heat. "Well, maybe the road will open back up the closer we get to *Punka-Amarumayu*. There's always that chance. Until then, we've got our work cut out for us. I suppose, *'Whatsoever thy hand findeth to do, do it with thy might.'*" He grinned broadly. "And right now, that's moving tree limbs."

Finally, during the middle of the next day, the narrow lane did open back up into a wider path as Alexander had surmised. The men cheered and wearily climbed back into the vehicles to ride the rest of the way to their next destination. When they rounded the final bend in the road and emerged from the dense overgrowth, Alexander grabbed Fitzgerald's walkie talkie from the dashboard and commented, "Everyone, say hello to the last outpost of civilization. This is the only thing that stands between us and the vast expanse of the Amazon."

⊗ ⊗ ⊗

Punka-Amarumayu was teaming with life. The docks were full of fisherman bringing in the day's catch; emaciated oxen pulled carts loaded with sacks of grain and rice to be loaded on a riverboat; children chased one another down the dirt lanes that wove through the myriad host of thatched roof huts, laughing and playing soccer. Fitzgerald and Alexander strolled into the bustling village square followed by Drew, Kaci, Jada. A handful of the mercenaries — Girly, Beady Eyes, Baldy, and Goatee — tailed farther behind with their weapons tucked away and out of sight. A small band of street performers played a merry tune on tribal instruments under a cluster of palm trees that made Kaci smile.

She took a deep breath in as her wide eyes followed her nose over toward the large cooking hut that stood tall in the center of the square, "Mmmm! Those fried plantains smell *so* good! Can we get some? Please?"

Alexander chuckled and handed Drew a few Peruvian coins, "You all stay close. Don't get into any trouble!" In an instant, the two mingled into the crowd with Jada tailing behind, shaking her head.

"We'll re-stock here and head toward the ruins in the morning." Fitzgerald signaled to his men, and they began to spread out and barter with vendors for fresh food and supplies. Passing villagers observed them curiously but kept about their business; several children stared at them like they had never seen another human with different skin color before.

"Tenoch said that it would take two days to reach *Pachawañu*. But I doubt that," the burly man continued, running his fingers through his black curls. He left his hand on the back of his neck as they slowly walked, and he flexed his forearm, causing his red tattoo to ripple like it was flying. "Maybe it would take two days to walk. But I'm guessing it will only take us four or five hours to drive."

Alexander nodded. "Certainly. *If* the path is a wide enough."

The thought of the past few days made Fitzgerald bristle. "We lost too much valuable time cutting through that blasted rainforest!"

"Yes, but setbacks like these are bound to happen now that we are in the middle of unchartered territory. We must have patience! Paititi won't be going anywhere." He chuckled and then paused for a moment in serious reflection.

"What? What's on your mind, Jim? Speak freely."

"Well — I'm concerned how much further we'll be able to make it with your entire convoy. This far out, we need to consider possibly moving forward by boat, and this is probably the only place where we would be able to find something that we could use."

"What? And leave all my vehicles and supplies behind? Nonsense! What if the guides point us in a different direction?"

"It's your call." The professor shrugged. "But I'm sure we could manage a way to follow them. You and I both know that the Amazonian tributaries form a vast network all throughout this entire part of the world. The waterways will be the main source of transportation from here on out."

Fitzgerald grunted, "Let's just take it one guide at a time. I'm *not* leaving any of my men or vehicles behind. We're too deep into the jungle to do that now! I think a direct route on land is more efficient than your boat idea. You would have us zigzagging all over the map!"

Alexander wanted to say more but just bit his tongue. *I wonder if he's trying to find Paititi with all his trucks so he can go back on our agreement and haul the wealth of the city back to civilization?* He shook his head half-inclined to believe it, then changed the conversation.

"Adrian, we still need to find the exact location of *Pachawañu* before we can go anywhere. First things first. We must find Chief Centehua."

"I think he may have found us." Fitzgerald pointed across the village square. A strongly-built, middle-aged man wearing multicolored ceremonial bead necklaces and sporting a bowl haircut strode toward them surrounded by an entourage of young men.

"Greetings, travelers!" he spoke in Quechua. "My name is Centehua, chieftain of this tribe. Very few of your kind have ever come to our village. What are your intentions?" The man eyed Fitzgerald's large revolver holstered on his hip.

Alexander could sense uneasiness behind Centehua's bluntness and then noted the poised hands of his young men hovering around the hunting knives on their string belts. The music stopped, and all the people stilled, watching and listening intently. Though they weren't near the confrontation, Jada instinctively pulled Drew and Kaci back from the crowd and slipped in front of them, ready for whatever was about to happen.

The professor smiled warmly, kindly bowed, and held up open hands to signify they meant no harm. "Chief Centehua, we are merely explorers in search of a lost civilization. Our travels bring us to your region, but we come in peace."

He slowly reached into his side cargo pants pocket and withdrew a small figurine. The man's concerned stare melted into delight, "Ah! You come with the blessing of Tenoch! Anyone who has received the token of the valley is always welcome here." He turned to his people and thundered, "We have among us — friends!"

The music instantly resumed with a peppy tune, and the large throng that had gathered cheered happily. Everyone pressed in with bright smiles, hoping to touch the two men on the shoulder as a form of greeting. Fitzgerald looked to Alexander with a wry grin. "What did you tell them, Jim? They're treating us like gods!"

Alexander shook his head. *Everything with him is about 'power'.* "They're just welcoming us, Adrian. Nothing more."

Drew, Kaci, and Jada breathed a sigh of relief.

"Praise God nothing happened!" said Kaci, taking another bite of plantain.

Jada cleared her throat. "Your uncle certainly has a way with words."

"Yeah," Drew smiled. "He always seems to know what to say at the right time, and he's always so gracious about it."

"Why do you think that is?"

"My honest opinion? I really believe it's because he walks with God, and God gives him the wisdom of what to say and how to say it."

Jada grunted and rolled her eyes.

"No, for real! The Bible actually talks about that. It's amazing. And Uncle James is one of the godliest people we know."

"That's nice," Jada remarked curtly and then changed the subject. Drew and Kaci exchanged glances, happy that she was finally talking to them again. Together, they strolled around the square, weaving around the different booths of fruits, vegetables, odds-n-ends, and fish.

Some of the young men who waited on Centehua had disappeared in the crowd and now returned with tree stump seats on their shoulders. "Come!" the chieftain beckoned to Alexander and Fitzgerald, "Sit with me. Tell us why you have come and how I and my people can serve you."

Alexander thanked them for the stools, introduced themselves, and began explaining their journey. Part way through, a young lady brought the three men a warm clay mug of chapo — a beverage made of sweet plantains, water, cinnamon, and honey.

As Alexander continued, he noticed that Centehua took special interest in the part when Tenoch and his people wanted to know more about the Bible.

The chieftain leaned forward, "What is this book you speak of?"

"It is the Book of Heaven. It is the only source of eternal truth written by the One Who made all things — the stars above and the earth beneath. It is the Word of God."

Centehua seemed visibly touched by this. "Very fascinating. And you have this Book?"

Alexander paused and glanced over to Fitzgerald, who sat beside him with his arms crossed, not really paying attention to the conversation since he had no idea what was being said. *If I pull out my Bible, he will explode.* A verse immediately popped into his mind where Jesus said, *Behold, I send you forth as sheep in the midst of wolves: be ye therefore wise as serpents, and harmless as doves.*

"James Alexander, do you have this Book of God?" Centehua interrupted his thoughts.

The professor smiled and decided against reaching for his hip, "Yes, I do, in my language, and I promised Tenoch that I would send a crate filled with them to his village by airplane."

"In what language?"

"Quechua."

"This pleases me, for I also read that language. I need this Bible as well. I will write to Tenoch to get one for myself. I *must* know of this God Who you say made all things. For generations, my people have sacrificed offerings to the sun, the moon, and even the earth as it brought forth our food. They prayed to our ancestors for a divine blessing. They even worshipped gods carved out of wood and rock. But ever since I was a child, my father would say to me, *'How can these things be God? They cannot see or hear or speak. Who made the rocks and Who made the trees? Who made the sun, the moon, and the earth? There must be another Being Who made all these things.'* Since then, though my people continue to worship and pray to whatever they wish, in my heart, I have wanted to know if a God like this exists. And now, James Alexander, you come to my village and you speak directly of Him and His book!"

Alexander could feel a lump swelling in his throat as he fought back the tears. *Oh God, all these people are sitting in absolute darkness.*

"Centehua, He is the one true God, and He wants to be your Friend. He has a name. It's Jesus."

The chieftain didn't know how to respond as this truth rushed over him for the very first time. "I…I have never heard of this name before. This word. Did you say, 'Jesus'?"

"Yes, He is the Saviour of the world, and He loves you with all of His heart. I believe that it's no accident that God has brought us here on our expedition. We came in search of something, when all along, the God of Heaven was searching for you. Centehua, He has heard and answered your prayers!"

There was no holding back now; tears began to stream down Alexander's face. The chief was also physically moved by this powerful realization.

"What?" Fitzgerald sat up straight, placing his hands on his knees and narrowing his gaze. "What is the meaning of this?"

Alexander bit his lip, "He uh… he was just telling me about some of his life story, and…"

"Seriously, Jim? We don't have *time* for that. We need to break camp and get prepared for tomorrow. You got any answers yet?"

"Almost —"

"Almost means 'no'; hurry it up."

"Of course. Just give me a few more minutes." He paused and looked at Fitzgerald intently. "May I *please* speak with him a bit further once we get everything figured out?"

"Fine," the brawny man grumbled, crossing his arms again. "But just don't waste *my* time with your needless curiosity. This isn't a field trip."

Alexander wiped his eyes and grinned, "Thank you." *And thank you, Lord!*

He quickly gulped the last few mouthfuls of his chapo. "Chief Centehua, I would be honored to speak with you more about Jesus."

"Yes. I wish for you to tell me all that you know."

"Gladly. But first, my associate here would like for me to finish talking about how we got here and where we are seeking to go next."

The man nodded. "I understand. This man is not like you, James Alexander. Darkness is on his face, and he looks very cruel. Why do you keep company with him?"

The professor shook his head. "It's a long story. He *is* a bit rough around the edges, but I'm trying to tell him about Jesus too."

"Ah," Centehua smiled. "You are a good man; you glow with happiness. Please continue."

Alexander carefully chose his words as he shared the last few details of their expedition. He kept the purpose of their quest vague but knew it was finally time to reveal where they were seeking to go next. He looked Centehua in the eyes and said slowly, "And now, under the advisement of Chief Tenoch, we seek your counsel for how to find...*Pachawañu.*"

As soon as he said the name of the cursed burial grounds, it was as he feared. Everyone who'd gathered enthralled with their conversation gasped and slowly backed away from the two men. The chieftain's brow creased with concern and disapproval. Fitzgerald threw his hands up in the air and exhaled in frustration.

"What *now*, Jim?" But Alexander ignored him, not taking his eyes off the chief.

"You wish to visit *Pachawañu?*" Centehua said slowly.

"Yes, we believe it holds the clue of where we're to go next."

"Then you wish to visit with death itself!"

"We've heard stories —"

"Stories?" the chieftain stood in disbelief. "You take this lightly, James Alexander? The 'stories' are true."

Alexander stroked his chin in deep concentration, trying to process what he couldn't believe to be real. *A dinosaur-like creature roaming the deep jungle?*

Centehua slowly sat back down. "It has been many years since we have seen the devil beast. But because of it, no one ever visits the resting place of our ancestors."

"I'm not sure how else to say this, but this is a risk that we *must* take to continue our journey." He pulled out his large map of the region and spread it on the ground in front of them. "Would you please show us how to get there?"

Centehua said nothing for what seemed to be an eternity.

Finally, he sighed, "If Tenoch believed in you, then I will do the same. Yes, I will show you, James Alexander. But beware. It may cost you your lives."

Drew and Kaci could hear their uncle whistling from some distance as he walked down the narrow lane out of the village to their camp located just beyond the last row of huts. The melody of *Jesus Loves Even Me* soared above the sounds of the night that had already settled in around them. Kaci was sketching another flower in her notebook while sitting Indian style on the ground under the LED lantern that hung from the ceiling of their tent while her brother rested.

She stopped for a moment and smiled, "Something good must have happened!"

Drew agreed and sat up in his cot, then swung his feet to the floor.

Suddenly, the whistling faded. They both peered out of the small crack in the canvas door of their tent to see their uncle being stopped by Fitzgerald. They could barely make out the conversation above the night sounds of the jungle crickets, but it was enough to discern that the man was upset. Something about Jim spending too much time with the natives and slacking off in his responsibilities to the expedition. They held their breath as Alexander reasoned that there was only so much time he could spend studying a map or pouring over ancient documents. Fitzgerald froze, and it looked as if he was about to punch their uncle. But Alexander diffused the tension by calmly placing a hand on the man's shoulder and saying, "Everything will be fine, Adrian. I believe we will get to the location of the next guide tomorrow."

Fitzgerald pulled his shoulder away and snapped, "We'd better. We leave at 0600. I expect you and your 'little monsters' to be ready before my men are fully loaded so we can go over the details again.

There is no more time to waste, Jim!" He spun on his heels and disappeared into the night. Alexander shook his head and began to softly whistle again as he headed toward their tent. Drew and Kaci quietly scrambled back to their cots.

The canvas flap lifted, and Alexander bounded in with his eyes aflame with excitement.

"Well, God is good!" He seemed unphased by the confrontation he just had with his old friend. "He's opening up some incredible doors. Centehua soaked up everything I shared with him. He's so eager and hungry to believe on Jesus!"

"That's awesome!" Drew grinned.

"When we get back home, I've *got* to get a missions' team down here to reach all these people for Christ."

"Maybe they can bring all the Bibles with them!" Kaci softly interjected.

"Yes! I want every family to be able to get one. The task won't be easy, but I think I know of a group that would be willing to come." He dropped down onto his cot, exhausted from the long day, but his face glowed with spiritual bliss. "There is nothing that brings me greater joy than sharing God's love with others. That's really what life is all about — Christ's last command should always be our first priority."

"'*Go ye into all the world and preach the Gospel to every creature,*'" Drew quoted.

"Yes," Alexander smiled. "And now, because we've had the opportunity to meet these people through the craziest of circumstances, they too can have hope." He lifted his hands and closed his eyes overwhelmed by the thought. "'*The people that walked in darkness have seen a great light: they that dwell in the land of the shadow of death, upon them hath the light shined.*'"

He chuckled, "Think of that! How wonderful! Thank you, Lord."

Kaci tucked her long golden-brown hair behind her ears, "Uncle James, I can't help but think that maybe this is why God has allowed all of this to happen to us."

He nodded, "One of many reasons possibly." He looked at Drew for a moment and saw he'd grown deep in thought. Over the past few weeks, he could tell that there was some sort of spiritual struggle going on inside of his nephew, and it was in tender moments like these that his face showed it. "The Lord always has a purpose for everything He does — even in our trials. Many times, it's an opportunity — and yes, I'm specifically using that word, because it *is* an opportunity whenever we can be more vocal about the Gospel. If we are yielded to God's leading, He can take our suffering and hardships and use them to build His kingdom. And in this, we should find no greater joy — the very God of Heaven is using us to spread the hope of Christ to those desperately in need of it. There is nothing more exhilarating or fulfilling in life than this! With this understanding, any Christian should boldly say, *'God, let Your glorious work be accomplished through my life in any way You please.'*"

A lop-sided grin gently formed on the professor's face as he stared blankly into space. "Think of Paul and Silas. God used their suffering to ultimately lead the Philippian jailer to the Lord, along with his family, and start a church. That probably wouldn't have ever happened if they weren't first arrested and thrown into prison. How about Hananiah, Mishael, and Azariah? God used them to reach a heathen king and culture in the land of Babylon. But it was only in a fiery furnace that they were able to become a visible testimony for God's glory."

"Wow, I never thought of it like that," Kaci replied.

Alexander smiled and began taking off his boots, "There are so many other examples in the Bible that prove to us that God makes no mistakes, but rather *'He hath made every thing beautiful in his time.'* Psalm 18:32 reminds us, *'It is God that girdeth me with strength, and maketh my way perfect.'*"

He leaned forward and sincerely looked back and forth at the two young people, "God is in control. We must simply trust Him and obey. He will give us the strength to bear what lies ahead."

Drew thought back to his experience on the swinging bridge and warmly smiled, *"I can do all things through Christ which strengtheneth me.'"*

"Precisely, and another thing — we must be careful to not let things discourage us. Remember that *'The joy of the Lord is your strength.'* I just had a run-in again with Mr. Fitzgerald." Drew and Kaci glanced at each other.

"And the two of you saw it, didn't you?" Alexander chuckled. "The Devil would find no greater joy than to let that man's belligerence dampen my spirit — all of our spirits. I'm resolved to keep my eyes on the Lord, and you both must do the same. I know He's working through this, even though at times it's difficult to see. He will work it all out for our good! Let's make the best of it and allow God's glory to shine through us in the darkness of our valley."

Together, they knelt on the floor and prayed for continued protection and wisdom for what might lie ahead. Alexander knew the days would only grow tougher as they journeyed deeper into the unchartered jungle. His heart swelled with pride as he listened to his niece and nephew pray aloud. *They have grown so much.*

Once they crawled into their sleeping bags, Drew and Kaci were sound asleep within minutes, but Alexander's mind still raced. *Will Centehua get saved? What is Drew struggling with in his heart? Will we find the next guide? What's this "Devil's beast" the natives are so afraid of? What will happen to the children if we hit a dead end?* Chills ran up and down his spine as thoughts of horror flooded his mind. He gritted his teeth together and began to pray again. Soon, peace flooded his heart, and his eyes slowly closed as he fell asleep in the presence of God.

CHAPTER XV

Alexander couldn't believe it. He glanced from the ancient map in his hands to the massive cliff stretching up into the sky. They'd reached the first landmark. The smooth rock face was covered in etched petroglyphs and an overhang covered in vines had protected most of them over the centuries. He breathed a sigh of relief. *Could it be that we will actually find the lost city of the Amazon?*

Their trek through the jungle hadn't been easy, but Fitzgerald was determined to push forward. The vehicles that had gotten stuck along the way, he left, ordering the men who stayed behind to catch up with them when they could. By mid-afternoon, the jungle naturally cleared as they came over a small ridge and the region sprawled into a lush shallow valley before them, surrounded partly by the giant cliff. Leaving the convoy there, the team walked down into the sacred burial grounds.

Rock mounds and wooden posts stuck in the ground formed a vast semi-arc as depicted on the map. Several stone statues stood scattered about. At one time, they'd probably made fierce protectors over the graveyard. Now, they were nothing but crumbling bits of history lost to the jungle. Beyond, at the base of the cliff, lay ruins of what once was an impressive Incan temple built for ancestral worship. Smaller structures — probably humble dwellings for the priests and keepers of the cemetery — jutted up around it, taken over by moss and gnarled vines. Trees sprouted from the ground, not caring for what they destroyed in their search for the sun. One day, the ruins would disappear altogether reclaimed by the jungle. Alexander shut his eyes, able to picture the streams of people who would come here on their pilgrimage.

"We made it!" Fitzgerald exclaimed, snapping him back into the present. Alexander felt the man's hand squeeze his shoulder. For just a second, he spotted a glimpse of his old friend buried beneath the decades of greed, but then it was gone as a wicked smiled crept across his face.

"Faith is becoming sight just like your good book says, eh, Jim?" He breathed in deeply. "How do you think we should proceed to find our next guide?"

"Hmmmm. I've been giving that a lot of thought. I need to make my way closer to the cliff so I can study those markings to see if they bare any significance. Meanwhile, I believe the first thing you and your men should do is search the area for anything that might have the symbol of Paititi."

"Sounds reasonable," Fitzgerald agreed.

Alexander turned to Fairchild who had just approached. "Mind if I borrow your binoculars?"

The pale, blonde haired man just stared at him, being caught off guard. "So that I can see everything on the cliff a bit easier; my eyes are not what they used to be," he chuckled.

Awkward silence hung in the air as Alexander stretched out his hand.

"Well? Don't just stand there, give the man what he needs!" Fitzgerald snapped.

"I prefer not to. You know that I don't like giving out my things."

Fitzgerald's eyes narrowed, "Stop being so ridiculous."

Annoyed, Fairchild took off the pouch and smacked it into Alexander's palm without saying a word.

Alexander slung it over around his shoulder, "I'll be sure to take good care of them; don't worry." He motioned for Drew and Kaci to join him, and the three made their way through the graveyard to the cliff face. Beady Eyes and Girly trailed behind them, clutching their AK-47s in both hands.

"We're not gonna try to escape, you know," Drew commented to them.

"It's for your own safety, boy," Beady Eyes stated as he scanned the horizon without blinking. "You never know what might be out there; besides, your uncle is too valuable to lose."

Alexander cleared his throat. "I'll be fine, but my niece and nephew are to be protected at all costs."

"Those ain't our orders," Girly spat.

"But if we all stay together, then everybody will be okay, right?" Kaci, always the peacemaker, chimed in.

Behind them, Fitzgerald began barking out orders to his men, dividing them into two teams. One would remain on patrol with Fairchild in case they were visited by what he sarcastically called "the fabled beast the natives are so paranoid about." The other group formed a search party with him and were instructed of what they needed to carefully look for as they slowly spread out through the tombs and overgrowth.

"I'm still trying to figure out our last clue," the professor mentioned with a furrowed brow. "It said, *'Deep with the dead by tilted head, away from moon and sun lies the search the ancients have begun.'* The next guide has got to be at this location somewhere. Now that we're here, what do you both think?"

Drew shook his head as he carefully made his way over several knotty roots, "It sounds like it's something buried. In a grave maybe? But how could they cover something like that? Those guides are so big!"

"Well, I think the key has to do with the phrase, *'by titled head,'*" Kaci mentioned. "Out of everything that was mentioned — why that?"

"I presume it has something to do with angles," Alexander replied. "Hopefully we'll be able to make sense of all of this soon."

He came to a stop about 50 yards from the base of the cliff and looked up at the smooth face as it loomed high overhead. "We are certainly tilting our heads to look at this," he drily stated. "Maybe the key lies in the symbols?"

He pulled out Fairchild's binoculars to get a closer look.

"My, these are old," he admired them for a moment, distracted by the craftsmanship. "Dienstglas. German. They don't make them like they used to."

Something caught his eye, "Hello? What's this?"

Drew and Kaci leaned in as their uncle's curiosity peaked their own. On the right back side of the binoculars, his thumb gently brushed over a machine-imprinted serial number with "HM88" underneath it.

"Fascinating," he said to himself.

"What?" Drew asked.

"Oh, nothing," he dismissed with the wave of a hand and a lopsided grin. "I like old things. Now let's see what this cliff will tell us!"

Drew and Kaci glanced at each other. They could tell their uncle had discovered something of significance, and that he preferred not to tell them. As difficult as it was to not press him for further details, they remained quiet so he could focus on the task at hand. He squinted, moving closer to the wall. His lips moved, but whatever he said was too quiet for them to hear. After several minutes of silence, he sighed, "There is absolutely nothing on the cliff that resembles Paititi. Most of it is just ornate scrollwork, representations of spirit animals and gods they worshipped, and an homage to their buried ancestors. I do find it interesting, however, that Amaru is in the very center of the cliff, and it's just like the one on our old map."

"Wait — what's an Amaru?" Kaci asked confused.

"Oh, sorry," he chuckled and pointed up to an oddly shaped petroglyph of a coiled serpent with a head on each end of its body. Both mouths were opened wide and faced each other with their forked tongues meeting in the middle to form a complete circle. "The snake had a lot of significance in the Incan culture. They believed it represented the underworld and typified the beginning of a new life.

They called it Amaru."

Kaci shivered as she looked at the beast, "Where do people come up with these things? That looks so creepy. It reminds me of the Devil!"

Alexander somberly grimaced, "Well, there is no doubt that Satan kept the Incans in spiritual darkness; their religion certainly dabbled in the occult. Now look at this," he pulled out the ancient leather map and pointed at the skull island along with the two-headed serpent curled up over the image of the lake. "At the end of our journey, we find this same snake depicted. I wonder if they are somehow connected?"

"Like a clue!" Drew exclaimed.

"Exactly. Many times, people will leave 'breadcrumbs' by using similar objects or themes throughout the clues they want followed." He peered again through the binoculars. "In fact, I didn't notice this before. Do you see what looks to be cracks in the rock? I believe they're actually narrow ledges that weave back and forth up the cliff face." He shook his head in disbelief. "Sometimes I marvel at the ingenuity and bravery of early craftsmen as they undertook some of the most perilous circumstances to create the most epic feats of architecture. Imagine! All these petroglyphs were carved without a stitch of repelling gear!"

Drew and Kaci stood in shock as they took in the massive cliff spanning high overhead.

"It must have taken so many years," Kaci remarked.

"Yes — for most of them involved, probably a lifetime," Alexander added.

Suddenly from over by the temple ruins, Fitzgerald whistled loudly with his fingers and began to wave his arms. Beady Eyes gestured with his elbow to the others to follow him as they made their way over to where the rest of the team had congregated.

"This is it, Jim!" Adrian yelled. "We found it!"

They hustled to where he stood next to a stone archway that faced the cliff. The Paititi symbol resided at the top of the arch with two carved Amaru figures slithering up the columns on both sides, mouths open toward the symbol.

"We've searched the entire area. This is the only place that has our marking. What do you think it means?"

"Let me take a look," adjusting his glasses on the bridge of his nose. He walked around the arch slowly, glancing from the serpents to the symbol, then the large Amaru petroglyph on the cliff face.

After a moment, he commented, "Drew and Kaci, you see what I mean by 'breadcrumbs'? These snakes bear the resemblance of the one on the cliff face and the other on our map."

"That is of no coincidence," Fitzgerald stepped forward. "I believe you're on to something, old chum! But how does it all tie together?"

Alexander stroked his jaw slowly and lifted his voice to address the entire group, "The clue. The answer lies in the last clue. '*Deep with the dead by tilted head, away from moon and sun lies the search the ancients have begun.*' As my niece and nephew pointed out to me earlier, the third guide is most likely buried somewhere here and the key to locating it is probably by the phrase '*tilted head.*' I believe that they are correct."

Drew and Kaci beamed as all eyes pleasantly flickered toward them, then back on their uncle.

"The Incans were very much a geometrically orientated people, obsessed with right angles, squares, and symmetry. To them, a perfect tilt was exactly 45 degrees. I believe if we triangulate our position using 45 degrees between the point on the cliff where the two tongues of the Amura meet with the center of this Paititi symbol on the arch, we will find the next place we need to search."

"Brilliant!" Fitzgerald exclaimed and radioed Fairchild for one of the men to bring down the surveying equipment from the back of his jeep.

"It's just a wild guess, but it's a start in the right direction."

The next hour felt like five as Alexander doubled-checked his work before sharing where the two trajectories intersected each other.

Baldy was in charge of carrying around the survey tripod and placing it where Alexander needed it. Fitzgerald paced back and forth impatiently, muttering under his breath for the professor to hurry up. Within a few minutes of this, Alexander looked at him squarely in the eyes and declared, "If I don't take the time to get this right now, it's going to cost us a lot of extra time later. And I don't think you want that. So please be patient and give me some space."

Grumbling, the man stalked away and busied himself by cleaning his revolver. When he noticed a majority of his men were idle among the ruins, he snapped, "I'm not paying you to sit around! Get back to the vehicles and set up camp!" And then he added with a wicked grin, "We're sleeping with the dead tonight, boys."

Jada rolled her eyes and walked over to where Drew and Kaci stood, talking between themselves.

"What do you think about sleeping with dead people?" she commented drily, fiddling with the camera around her neck.

"I don't know." Drew replied looking at his sister, then smiled. "Never slept in a cemetery before. I guess there's a first time for everything."

An awkwardness hung in air for a moment until Jada broke the silence again, "So, kudos on helping your uncle out. I guess you both are smarter than you look." She frowned, "Wait, that came out wrong...."

Kaci giggled, "It's okay, Jada. We know what you mean. I guess we've had a lot of time on our hands lately to think about it, and it was really the only thing that seemed to make sense to us. Now let's see if any of it was actually correct!" She pointed toward her uncle who was making his way up to them from where he was by the cliff. Baldy was a bit behind him, perspiring heavily as he carried the equipment on his shoulders back to the vehicles on the ridge.

"I think I've got a location!" Alexander waved his notepad in the air.

Fitzgerald reloaded his weapon and holstered it quickly. "Excellent work, Jim! Where to?"

"Let me show you. But I'm a little bothered about where it's located..." His voice trailed off as they walked some distance and approached a burial rock mound. "Here."

"Ah!" Fitzgerald shrewdly remarked, moving forward. "The clue was quite literal — *'Deep with the dead.'*"

Alexander planted himself in front of the man. "You know how I feel about desecrating tombs. It's morally and archeologically wrong."

Fitzgerald smiled, "Back with the ethics again, I see. Well, if you won't tell anyone, I won't tell anyone either."

"Adrian, we *cannot* do this."

The man's face darkened instantly, "Yes, we can, Jim, and we will." He pulled out his revolver and kept it down by his side. "Step aside. Now."

"Adrian —"

The gun went off, startling everyone but Fitzgerald. Smoke curled up from a hole in the ground less than a foot from Drew's feet.

"Dad! What in the world?" Jada shouted.

The man ignored her. "I said step aside, Jim, and I would *strongly* encourage you to do so."

Alexander moved as ordered but held up his hands in protest. Fitzgerald radioed for Fairchild to bring shovels and a sledgehammer along with a couple of men. Then he turned to Drew and said with no emotion, "Young man, I don't forget things. That was payback for your insolence toward me the other night. Now watch closely as I lift more than a fingernail to get the job done."

He took off his cargo vest and sweat-stained shirt to begin moving the large stones by hand. The medallion of Paititi dangled wildly about his thick neck outside of his tank top with each move he made. His muscles rippled beneath his undershirt, and Drew realized in that moment that this man was a great force to be reckoned with. *If he ever lost control of himself, he would be unstoppable.*

"Is this the spot?" Fairchild asked as he approached, and Alexander gratefully handed him back his binoculars.

"Our dear professor believes so; get in here and give me a hand!"

Once the rocks were cleared away, the men began shoveling out the dirt. About 5 feet down, Fairchild's shovel hit something hard. As they carefully scraped away the excess dirt from the top and along the sides, a large rock slab was exposed with an Amaru coiled around the symbol of Paititi in the center.

"Look at this, Jim!" Fitzgerald teased. "All of your fussing for nothing! We haven't desecrated anything. This was *meant* to be found." He picked up the sledgehammer. *Thwack! Thwack!* The man's sheer force sent stone chips flying everywhere. After another dozen slams the rock began to fracture in multiple places and cascade down into a tunnel.

"Yes!" he shouted. "This is it!"

He motioned for his men to remove the rest of the stone with their shovels while he handed the sledgehammer up to Drew, "That's how a *man* gets it done. Now toss me my shirt and vest."

Once the passageway was clear, Fitzgerald removed a flashlight from his belt, clicked it on, and jumped down inside. "Jim, Jada, Drew, and Kaci, I want you to come with me. Fairchild, bring up the rear. We've got a guide to find!" And then he disappeared in the darkness.

The tunnel was tall and wider than Kaci expected. Jada handed her a flashlight and she used it to check out the walls. More petroglyphs were carved into the rock, these were well preserved being sealed away for all this time. The air was musty, and she found it hard to breathe. The tunnel angled down several yards and opened into a large room with an odd, flat ceiling.

"What's this?" Fitzgerald expressed in frustration. "A dead end? You've got to be *kidding* me!"

"Over there!" Fairchild gestured with his light. Close to the floor on the opposite end of the square room there was a bronze panel with six different vertically rotating rings lined up next to each other with a crude lever on the end.

Alexander knelt to take a closer look. "Interesting. It appears to be some sort of large archaic combination lock." He began to slowly turn the first ring. It grated against the stone wall but turned somewhat easily. "I see symbols of Amaru, a stone, Paititi, the profile of a face, a skull, and water being poured. I'm guessing each ring has the same set of symbols on it and they're out of alignment? —Hey, what are you doing?"

Fitzgerald shoved Alexander out of the way and began moving the first ring, then the next and the next, working at all six while Alexander stared at him with surprise and concern.

"I don't know why you're so worried," Fitzgerald commented, smirking like this was some great game. "Nothing's happening."

"Yet," Alexander firmly reacted.

Drew shifted closer to Kaci, just in case, anything did happen. He wasn't about to let them get hurt because of that man. Jada also took a few hesitant steps away from the wall to stand on the other side of Kaci. Her eyes were wide, and she kept staring at the ceiling, then over her shoulder at the tunnel they'd taken to get here.

"What's wrong?" Drew whispered.

"Something about this room feels off," she replied quietly. She nodded to the ceiling. "Why is it so flat like that?"

He tilted his head back, studying the smooth stone above them. "I don't know."

She seemed to be debating something then stepped forward in a hurry. "Dad, wait."

"Not now, Jada."

"Just listen to me. Something's wrong. I just know it."

"You'll stay quiet," he snapped, glaring at her. "Understand?"

She glared right back, crossing her arms. "You don't know what you're doing, do you? Why don't you let Alexander look at it?"

Fitzgerald stilled then whipped around. "Questioning me again?"

"I'm not questioning you," she argued, "I'm telling you — there's something off about this room. Let's just take a second to figure this out before you do something stupid."

"Go wait outside," he ordered, coldly and quietly.

"Dad," she tried to reason with him, but he yelled over her, thrashing his arms in a rage like an angry beast. She lifted her chin and stalked over to the very threshold of the room's entrance and waited, muttering to herself.

"It's all very simple enough really," he explained matter-of-factly, lining up all the rings to show the symbol of Amaru. When he was done, he stepped back, wiping the dirt from his hands. "It *has* to be this since Amaru is the emphasis on this part of our journey. Now we see what's been hidden away all this time."

"Adrian, hold on! —" Alexander reached out to hold back the man's arm, but it was too late. Fitzgerald pulled down the roughly-hewn bronze rod and the rings shifted, undoing the formation he'd created.

Behind them, Jada leapt back with a startled yelp as a stone slab crashed down in front of the doorway cutting them off from her and the tunnel. Drew dragged Kaci into his side as more stones groaned and pebbles fell around them.

"Why did you do that?" Alexander yelled above the rumbling. "From my experience, you need to figure out the correct combination *before* pulling the lever!"

"I don't understand," Fitzgerald stammered. "That should've worked."

"Well, it didn't," Alexander muttered, his eyes flicking from the rings to the room shaking around them.

"How was I supposed to know that wasn't right?!" Fitzgerald spit back.

Suddenly, the ceiling Jada had been so worried about began to slowly lower.

They were going to be crushed to death.

"Let's try another combination!" Fitzgerald exclaimed. "How about Paititi," his hands swiftly moved to align all the symbols and then pulled the lever again. The rings shifted back to their original position with the ceiling lowering even faster. Fairchild let out a bloodcurdling cry of terror and tried to push up on the ceiling to slow it down.

Kaci clasped her hands together and slumped to her knees, whispering under her breath. Drew considered joining her in prayer, but the only way to stop that ceiling was going to be getting the right sequence lined up. He ran forward to stand between the two men who were rapidly discussing the options of what to do next.

"Let's just quickly try them *all!*" Fitzgerald bellowed.

Alexander shook his head, "We'll be dead by then!"

"I think I got it!" Drew shouted, his mind racing as he rotated the first ring, taking in all the symbols.

"No time to waste, boy," snapped Fitzgerald, trying now a third option comprised of a mix-and-match of the Amaru and Paititi symbols.

"No, no, that's not it!" Drew stopped him, pushing his hands out of the way. "The map! It's all about the progression on the map!" He deftly worked the rings to form a sequence.

Alexander's eyes widened. "Yes, I think you're right! But we'll only have one shot at this!"

Everyone was now on their knees, the stone ceiling closing in fast.

"Drew, hurry!" Kaci cried out.

"Please, please do something!" Fairchild screamed, then proceeded to shriek in German.

"We've got this, Drew," Alexander stated calmly in spite of the chaos. "I see what you're doing. We must follow each step of our journey!"

"But what if we get it wrong?" the young man almost broke down.

"Don't stop now or it will be too late!" Fitzgerald gasped.

"Focus on my voice, son," Alexander placed his hand on Drew's shoulder and squeezed. "Face, stone, water, Amaru, skull, Paititi."

The team was now on their stomachs, laying prostrate on the floor. Drew clamped his eyes shut and swiftly pulled the lever with all of his might.

The grinding came to a halt with the ceiling jerking to a stop right above the bronze plating and the rings. Too slowly for Drew's liking, it rose back up and the slab sealing them off from the tunnel crumbled. Jada pushed through the rock and rushed forward to see if everyone was okay. Fairchild scrambled past her hysterically repeating to himself, *"Lass mich raus... Lass mich raus..."*

Kaci was slowly getting to her feet, visibly shaking and wiping tears from her eyes. Jada helped her the rest of the way and gave her a hug.

"Everything is going to be fine," she said softly while glaring at her father. It was the first time anyone had ever heard her speak tenderly.

"Thanks," Kaci began to laugh and hugged her back. "It's always been a dream of mine to almost be a pancake."

Jada shook her head and playfully smacked her on the arm, "Goofball."

"Are we going to talk about what just happened?" Alexander mentioned, as he and Drew sat up and rose to their feet.

"We made it out, didn't we?" Fitzgerald replied shakily, still laying on his back and staring at the ceiling.

"No thanks to you."

Fitzgerald grunted.

"Next time, let's please talk about things before you do something brash like that? I'd prefer to stay alive as much as possible."

"Whatever, old chum." the big man muttered, now too busy staring at a wall that had opened to reveal another chamber ahead of them.

Drew wasn't sure they should go in there after what just happened, but Fitzgerald was already walking inside, his flashlight illuminating a magnificent dome shaped room. He clapped his hands in glee, "Exquisite!"

Alexander shook his head with a sigh, "Always rushing forward with a death wish."

Kaci collapsed in her brother's arms, "How did you know what to do?"

"Honestly? I'm not sure. It just suddenly hit me that all these symbols represented places on the old map. Thanks for praying, sis." He lovingly squeezed her then pointed his flashlight toward the bronze rings, "The profile of the face looked kinda like the guide I thought, which led us here to the stone cliff — the first landmark, followed by the second landmark of water pouring or a waterfall, then the snake in the lake in front of the skull island at the end. Somehow that must be how we find Paititi."

Alexander put his hand on the young man's shoulder, "You remind me so much of your father. He was always able to think quick on his feet." His features softened, "He'd be proud of you, as am I. Now come along and let's see what we've found!"

The next room was a perfect sphere with flawlessly smooth walls and ceiling. Three steps led down to the middle of the space where their next guide sat, its face ornately carved into the preexisting stone. Its bright blue eyes sparkled as the beam from Kaci's flashlight caught them, sending ribbons of blue all across the chamber.

"They're pointed to the right," she noticed. "I guess that means we go east?"

"It appears so," her uncle replied. "Let's see what we've got here." He pulled a small notebook and pen from his back pocket and knelt down, studying the writing etched along the base. "As I suspected, more Incan and Latin."

"Let me know when you have something," Fitzgerald boomed from behind them as he wandered the full length of the room.

"Certainly." Alexander then peered up momentarily over his glasses and smiled, "Jada, could you and Kaci work together to take pictures of everything for further analysis? Drew, shine your light down here for me please so I can read all of this a bit easier."

He carefully examined the Incan symbols with furrowed brow, whispering to himself and jotting down various combinations of interpretations.

"This work is tricky," he commented. "A lot of it is subjective when translating to English, so I've *got* to be sure that it's as close as possible to what the architects originally intended."

Drew nodded, "Otherwise, we'll be led astray."

"Exactly."

"Well, I'm praying for you."

"Thank you, Drew. I need it."

After a few more minutes, he happily circled a statement that was scribbled in the margin. "I think I got it!"

Fitzgerald approached and cleared his throat. "You either have it or you don't, Jim. Where to next?"

"Hold on just a moment; let me copy over this Latin," he said and then proceeded to slowly recite it aloud while writing, "*Sine lapidibus mortem oppetere.*"

Fitzgerald flashed a devilish grin, "Why, how thrilling! '*Without the stones you face your death,*'" he quietly uttered from his own knack of the language.

Alexander looked up, "Exactly what I have." He underlined the translation in his notebook.

"Why does everything have to be so creepy and about death?" Kaci shivered.

"The journey is not for the faint of heart," Fitzgerald chuckled. "They are trying to intimidate us to not continue."

"Well, it's working."

He bellowed a laugh that reverberated off the spherical chamber.

Drew frowned, "What stones do you think they're talking about?"

"Your guess is as good as mine. I'm sure it will come to us," his uncle reassured them.

"And if not, we will all die," Jada muttered cynically. "What else did the writings say?"

Alexander fixed his glasses and read, "'*Near forked tongue great life has sprung; where a soul that lies amidst the tree watches o'er all who breathe.*'"

"Cute," Fitzgerald sounded irritated more than he did sarcastic. "Did it really say that?"

"Yes, all of the key elements are there. It's just easier for me to remember things poetically, so I arranged it in this fashion."

"So —" Fitzgerald cut in, "We head east and we look for a forked tongue. Simple enough. We need to find where a major river splits into two tributaries. Jim, do you have the map?"

The professor nodded, pulling it out of the leather tube that hung around his chest, and spread the large chart on the floor. All the flashlights illuminated it brightly making it easy for everyone to see. He traced his finger from their position directly east. "How about that," he chuckled, tapping his finger. "There it is."

"Fantastic, old chum! How far do you think that is? Two hundred miles?"

"Give or take. Maybe a five-day trip?"

"Five? Ha! Three at the *most*."

"Really? With all the dense jungle we've got to weave through?"

"What about the other parts of the clue?" Jada interrupted. "What are we looking for?"

"Well, I think that '*a soul*' refers to our next guide," Kaci said.

"Based on what we've previously experienced, yes, I agree with you," Fitzgerald remarked.

"And I don't believe we should make it that complicated," Drew stated. "Maybe it's gonna be just like it says.... The guide is in the middle of a tree? Or a tree is growing up on top of it? It's up high though because it's '*watching o'er all who breathe.*'"

"Look at us working so well together!" Fitzgerald beamed. Then rather ceremoniously, he marched over the stone face and pulled out his knife. "Saving the best part for last."

He began to gently scrape away at the sockets to remove the eyes. Kaci turned away, not bearing to watch and feeling weirded out by the whole idea.

"If they didn't want them taken out," the big man reasoned, "they wouldn't have made it so easy." But staring into the vacant holes left even him a bit unsettled. He laughed it off, "Come along now, I think we all could use some well-earned rest before the next phase of our journey. The game's afoot, and nothing shall stand in our way!"

As he hastily exited the room, he could hear his old friend quietly say to the other three, "Boast not thyself of to morrow; for thou knowest not what a day may bring forth."

Probably more Bible trash, he thought to himself. *I should put him in his place. Oh, never mind. I want to eat, and the man has been through enough today already.*

He went back down the tunnel and up the entrance into the jungle night. The moon was crescent-shaped, hanging like an ornament just risen above the towering trees. Not too far away, a jaguar cried out, the noise carrying over the ruins. And even though there wasn't a cloud in the sky, distant thunder rolled and bounced off the cliff. *Odd, but such is the way of things I suppose.*

He held a blue gemstone in each hand and shook his fists toward the stars. *Boast not myself, eh?* He grinned wildly. *I dare you to try and stop me, God! Paititi will be mine!*

CHAPTER XVI

Machine gun fire rang out sporadically through the still morning air. There was a distant scream and the rumble of thunder. Drew and Kaci both jumped out of their beds disoriented by the sudden outburst and found their uncle hurriedly exiting the tent.

"What was that?" Kaci rubbed her eyes and sat down on the edge of her cot, feeling sick from being so suddenly startled out of a deep sleep.

"I don't know," Drew stumbled around trying to find his boots. "Whatever it is, it can't be good."

"Where are you going?"

"To catch up with Uncle James. We can't just sit here. Come on!"

Outside their tent, they saw men darting about the camp with nervous frenzy. Fitzgerald was grumpily barking out orders from under his open-air command tent, and everyone looked sleep-deprived. Most were hastily loading supplies and taking down tents while others were grabbing their AK-47s and an extra clip or two from the supply crates in front of the munitions tent. Jada walked up, sheathing her throwing knives, her straight blonde hair a little matted from sleeping.

"Good morning," she said with no emotion. "If you can call it that."

"Right!" Kaci smiled. "Nothing like starting the day off at 5:30."

"And with no breakfast," Drew chuckled.

"Or coffee," Jada added.

Kaci opened her small backpack and tossed them both a protein bar, "Maybe these will help?" Her sleepy eyes twinkled. "I've been saving them for our MREs!"

The early morning sun filtered its golden rays through the jungle down onto the ancient cemetery and illuminated part of the cliff, causing its petroglyphs to glow. Dew remained undisturbed on the fields surrounding the camp, and the hot humid atmosphere covered the entire region with a haze. Without a cloud in the bright blue sky, thunder continued to echo across the valley from beyond the ridge.

"Well, that's slightly unnerving," Jada remarked.

The three teenagers hurried over to Alexander and Fitzgerald who were leaning over a large wooden crate with the regional map sprawled on top of it.

"I'm telling you, Jim, we can make it in three days if we push it."

"But there is a multitude of unexpected things that could happen along the way," the professor replied emphatically, setting down a tin cup of tea on the edge of the plywood surface.

Fitzgerald put up his hand, the large red tattoo on his forearm glistening with sweat in the morning sun. "I will not hear another word of it. We will follow the route you've advised, but *this* will be our first checkpoint." He roughly circled a spot on the map.

"What's going on?" Jada interrupted.

"We're packing up early, my dear."

"Dad, I can see that. What's the rush?"

The big man looked at Alexander, and after the professor nodded, Fitzgerald continued, "Our perimeter patrol encountered something. Not sure what." He gestured toward his walkie talkie standing upright on the crate holding back a corner of the map. "Their comms died before they could explain, but they sounded petrified. Something is out there."

"Is it the 'Devil beast'?" Kaci blurted out, fear filling her eyes.

"Stop calling it that," Fitzgerald murmured harshly. "There's no such thing!"

"Has anyone else made contact with them?" Drew asked.

"Negative. They've fallen off the grid, and we have no idea where they are. I just sent another squad out to see if they could locate them before we roll out."

Kaci's mouth dropped open. "You mean, you're... you're just gonna leave them?"

"If we can't find them, yes," he said heartlessly. "They knew what they were signing up for when they accepted the mission. They should actually be thankful that I'm sparing a few more men in attempts to locate them."

Suddenly, multiple AK-47s exploded in rapid fire somewhere in the jungle. A crop of white birds rose from the trees and scattered into the sky.

Fitzgerald snatched his walkie-talkie, "Status report!"

A second round of machine gun fire and frightened yells echoed through the crackle of the receiver, cutting in-and-out, as Beady Eyes shouted, "I don't know! This — it came — nowhere! Get out — before —!"

Fitzgerald's eyes narrowed. "Come again?" he asked.

Static.

"Before what?" Kaci stepped forward nervously.

"Do you copy?" the man pressed further, only to be greeted with more prevailing static.

"Dad, that machine gun fire was a lot closer than before. We'd better prepare ourselves," Jada instinctively gripped the hilts of her sheathed knives. "Whatever it is, it's headed this way."

"Impossible! My men are just seeing ghosts!" Fitzgerald slammed his radio down onto the makeshift table.

But heavy thuds could now be heard emanating from deep within the rainforest. They all looked at each other very slowly. Even the men scurrying about the camp noticed the methodical hollow crashing sounds and stopped to listen.

Alexander nodded toward his cup of tea. Faint vibrations rippled across the surface. He looked up at Fitzgerald, "You were saying?"

"Over there!" shouted Drew, pointing to the tree line on their left. Whatever was coming caused the tops of the trees to move as it worked its way down from the ridge.

A deep, guttural roar shook the air.

"That's no thunder! We've got to get out of here!" Jada shouted.

Everyone jolted into frantic motion. Fitzgerald bellowed for Fairchild, "As soon as the convoy is ready, get it out of here. Follow this map to the first checkpoint. *Go, go, go!*"

Drew and Kaci raced back to their tent to take it down and gather their belongings.

"Only bring what is absolutely necessary," Alexander instructed when he joined them. "Those things will be of no use to us if we're dead." The tone of his voice made the two teenagers move even faster.

He's genuinely concerned, Drew thought to himself. *As much as I'm dying to ask questions, there'll be time for that later... I hope.* Goosebumps made the hair on his arms and neck stand up.

Alexander began praying aloud as they packed the last few items together, "Father, we need Your help. You are the maker of all things, and in Thy great wisdom and power, it appears You have seen fit to preserve the existence of one of Your creatures. I don't know how that's possible, but You do. If it is indeed this beast the natives have described, we are no match for it. Please place a hedge of protection about us!"

They set their bags in the back of Fitzgerald's all-terrain vehicle next to his things.

"Any word from either of the two squads?" Alexander asked him.

"I've finally made contact. A few of them are still alive and coming this way!"

All around them, trucks and jeeps were starting up and driving off once they were fully loaded with supplies, equipment, and men.

Fitzgerald tossed the keys of his jeep to Jada, who caught them, a bit surprised.

"What are these for?"

"No time to explain. I trust only *you* with my things. Have someone else drive your vehicle. Take Kaci and get out of here. *Now!*" He turned to Alexander and Drew, "I need the two of you with me."

Kaci squeezed her brother and uncle with a quick hug and once she'd climbed in, Jada punched the gas to catch up with the rest of the convoy.

Only a half mile away now, trees were swaying, groaning, and falling as the earth shook with every passing *THUD! THUD! THUD!* Fitzgerald's radio crackled to life, "We're almost there! Don't leave without us! We're coming in hot," gasped Beady Eyes.

"Adrian, I'm shocked you weren't the first one out of here," Alexander commented breathlessly.

The man's eyes gleamed with a wild excitement, "And miss out on the opportunity of a lifetime with the thrill of this hunt? You must be mad!"

"Well, I hope you've got a plan!"

"Of course, I do. At least... half of one." He pointed to one of the last vehicles that still remained — an M1161 Growler. "We're taking that!" He leapt up onto the back, opened the side bolt of the mounted .50 caliber weapon, and loaded the first shell on the bullet belt into the chamber.

"It will be like old times, Jim!" Fitzgerald laughed. "You drive; I'll shoot. Just like back in Bangkok!"

"Bangkok?" The professor shook his head, "I've got a bad feeling about this."

"What happened in Bangkok?" Drew asked nervously, while climbing into the front passenger seat as Alexander started the vehicle.

"It was back in our post graduate days. Another story for another time, perhaps."

"Your uncle and I made quite the team. Until life brought its... *challenges.*"

Suddenly, they heard shouting in the distance. Beady Eyes and one other man staggered out of the jungle, their faces filled with terror and confusion.

"Only two of them survived?" Fitzgerald muttered.

The man with Beady Eyes tripped over a sprawling tree root and fell hard to the ground. Before he could pick himself back up, he was abruptly dragged back into the dense brush by some unseen force, screaming and firing his machine gun erratically. Beady Eyes froze in shock, looking at where the man had just been.

For a moment the trees remained motionless, then they burst to life with a flurry of crackling branches, falling limbs, and flying leaves. Beady Eyes dropped his AK-47 and stumbled backward in horror. As he saw what was coming, he frantically turned and yelled over and over, "Wait for me! Wait for me!" as he sprinted toward them as fast as he could.

A massive ugly beast with a long neck and a wide knot-covered face emerged violently from the jungle. It roared with all its might, sending bits of saliva and mucus out of a mouth filled with razor-sharp teeth. Gray stone-like plates were set into the creature's leathery dark green skin and a spikey tail wagged in annoyance from behind.

"I can't believe I'm seeing this!" Drew's voice quivered in a shout. "How is this possible?"

The creature remained still, its yellow eyes blinking and its head slowly tilting as it focused on the man running away. With a guttural rumble, its neck swooped low along the ground to follow after Beady Eyes, but without hesitation, Fitzgerald gripped both handles of his .50 caliber machine gun and fired.

The monster recoiled for a few seconds as bullets ricocheted off its thick plates. But once it realized it was unharmed, it viciously growled and lunged forward on all fours, shaking the ground.

"Now you've just made it mad," Alexander grimaced.

Fitzgerald laid another volley into it. "Come on, man! Hurry it up!" he boomed to Beady Eyes, who was almost to the Jeep.

He then turned to Alexander, "Now, Jim! Now!"

The professor shifted the vehicle into gear and swung it around onto the jungle path as Fitzgerald fired some more.

"What are you doing?" shrieked Beady Eyes, looking back over his shoulder at the beast that was beginning to move forward in spite of the bullets that were bouncing off its body. "You can't let me die out here!" He sprinted even faster, reaching out for the back of the Jeep but coming up short.

Drew's heart raced with adrenaline as he watched. "Uncle James, he's not gonna make it! I've *got* to help him!"

Before Alexander could say a word, Drew was climbing over his seat, crawling past the machine gun that loudly barked over his head. Hot empty casings hit him in the back before clattering onto the metal bed, but he gritted his teeth and paid no attention to the sharp pain. The jeep lurched and bounced down the trail over the potholes and rocks in the uneven ground, but he steadied himself by wrapping a secured cargo strap around one hand while he leaned out dangerously far to extend his other.

"Grab hold of me! I'll help you!" he yelled.

For the first time he saw Beady Eyes' dark and brooding face fill with life. The man could hear the thudding of the approaching beast behind him as it moved faster and faster, and he was about to turn his head when Drew ordered, "Don't look behind you! Just focus on me!"

Their fingers could almost touch. Just a little more... a little more. With one last burst of energy, the man leapt forward as far as he could, expecting to crash face first into the ground and become the creature's next snack. Somehow, he instead found himself caught by the young man's grasp.

Fitzgerald stopped shooting for a moment to help Drew pull the man up into the vehicle. Once safe, Beady Eyes collapsed in relief, but the momentum sent Drew and Fitzgerald down onto their backs. The beast charged closer and closer now; its tail whipped back and forth, showing great annoyance toward the elusive vehicle.

"This is going to be a close one, Jim!" Fitzgerald howled, trying to climb to his feet. "Here he comes!"

Alexander punched the gas, but the jeep only rocked more violently, almost to the point of being uncontrollable. He steadied the vehicle and clenched his jaw, "Speed won't get us anywhere!"

They could feel the hot breath of the beast as its head hovered almost above them. It savagely roared and snapped its jaws over and over again with a loud crack, but Alexander expertly weaved back and forth to avoid them. Fitzgerald pulled himself up by grabbing the handles of the big, mounted machine gun. With its yellow eyes enflamed with rage, the beast opened its mouth wide and sprang forward, coming right on top of them; but in the nick of time, Fitzgerald fired multiple rounds down its throat with a roar of his own.

The giant creature instantly shrieked and tumbled over itself. It breathed heavily and darted back into the woods, howling and whining as it crashed through the rainforest up the hill and over the ridge.

"Thank God we're safe!" Drew exclaimed. Fitzgerald rolled his eyes and was about to say something when Drew cut him off.

"And don't you *dare* say otherwise!" he pointed his finger at the man. "Give God the glory. You know it as well as I do — there's *no way* we should have survived that!"

He slumped backward, resting against the side of the jeep, and began to laugh and cry uncontrollably. The others joined in; they had no control over their emotions as the adrenaline broke down in their bodies. They were just glad to be alive and free from the terror of the jungle.

Beady Eyes held out his hand toward the young man for a firm shake. "Kid, I owe you my life. Thank you."

Alexander smiled and wiped the tears from his eyes. He didn't slow down, nor did he look back. The rest of them did their best to stay on high alert until they were able to join the rest of the convoy and get as far away from *Pachawañu* as possible.

Kaci gripped the edge of her seat in the back of the jeep as another loud rumble of thunder rolled through the jungle. The storm had started late that afternoon, and the roads quickly became impassible. The only thing they could do was huddle inside their vehicles and either wait for night to fall or the weather to clear.

The rain poured intensely. This was the one obstacle that Adrian Fitzgerald did not anticipate and couldn't control, and it greatly frustrated him because they were so close to reaching *"the forked tongue"* of the riverhead. What he'd hoped would only take them three days *did* turn into five long ones as Alexander had surmised. At least a half-dozen times, the convoy was brought to a standstill because of the torrential downpour. As much as he wanted to press on, no one was able to see the cart path they traversed and flash flooding was a very real threat.

"You should try to get some rest," Drew told his sister.

"How can I with this going on?"

"Yeah, I guess you're right." Lightning flashed just beyond the parked vehicles, and Drew tensed.

"What's wrong?" Kaci asked.

"Nothing," he murmured.

"Did you see something?" Jada sat in the jeep with them, along with Girly. The storm didn't seem to bother him as he snored loudly. Jada rolled her eyes at him, then turned her attention back to Drew. "Well?"

"It was nothing," he sighed. "The lightning's making weird shadows. Ever since we ran into that beast, I've been a little jumpy."

"Understandable. Must've been quite the sight."

"You have no idea. It's one of those things where you had to be there. I doubt anybody back home will believe us, and since we don't have any evidence of encountering it, my uncle said it would be best if we keep it to ourselves."

Kaci sighed and looked out the window.

"What? Did I say something wrong?"

"Not at all," she smiled. "You mentioned 'home.' I miss my

room, my bed, and our Christian school. I miss our friends in the youth group, and our sweet church." She wiped the tear that trickled slowly down her freckled cheek. "I miss Mom... *so much.*"

Drew put his arm around her shoulder and gave her a gentle squeeze.

"I miss them, too. A lot. But I'm sure everybody's praying for us."

"Touching. But it sounds like you guys don't get out much. Christian school? Youth group? Church? People *praying* for you?" Jada chuckled sarcastically. "What are you a part of? Some sort of cult?"

"No, it's an independent Baptist church."

Jada looked at her in bewilderment, and it dawned on Kaci that the girl probably had no clue what she was talking about.

Kaci smiled, "Have you ever been to church before?"

"No, not really. Well, I guess if you count Mom's funeral at the Catholic church. And I remember times when I was really young when dad would go and talk to a priest after he came back from a long 'business' trip, as he called them. When I got older, I figured he probably killed somebody or did something really bad and was trying to find peace in his soul. Not that it helped him at all...." her voice trailed off and she shrugged, her eyes glossing over as she stared off into nothingness.

Kaci and Drew exchanged subtle glances. *So Mr. Fitzgerald is somewhat of a religious man,* Drew thought to himself. *I wonder if he really believes in God deep down inside but has become very cold toward Him?*

"I would sit there on a wooden pew all by myself," Jada's soft voice broke the silence, "and look all around at the cathedral's high ceilings and gothic architecture. I watched as people came in to light candles and lay small pictures of their loved ones at the feet of statues. I guess they were saints or something. These people would pray and quietly weep, and I would think to myself, '*Why are you wasting your time? They can't hear you. They're all just hunks of carved marble!*'" She shook her head. "It really creeped me out."

"Well, I don't know how to say this…." Kaci gently began.

"Then just come out and say it!" Jada scolded. "You don't have to pull any punches with me."

"Okay. What you've experienced is not a real church. I mean, sure, it's religion, but it's an empty one. The Catholic church is not a Bible-believing church."

Jada frowned but leaned forward in curiosity, "What do you mean?"

"We don't believe that a person needs to pray through a priest or another human being to get atonement for his sins or to connect with God. The Bible teaches us that every person has direct access to Jesus. We can pray to Him at any time, and He hears us."

"Hmmm. Interesting. You know, I *have* seen you guys pray a lot and you just close your eyes and start talking to Him."

"And another thing," Drew spoke up, realizing that this was a God-given opportunity like he and his sister had been daily praying for. "The Catholic Church teaches that a person has to be baptized or be good enough in order to go to Heaven. But that's not what the Bible says." He looked at his sister, "Do you have our Bible?"

Kaci nodded and quickly pulled it from her backpack. They expected Jada to roll her eyes, mutter something sarcastic again, and try to change the subject; but she just sat there intrigued as Drew flipped open the Bible. Before she had any time to change her mind, he jumped back in.

"Here in Ephesians 2:8-9 the Bible tells us, *'For by grace are ye saved through faith; and that not of yourselves: it is the gift of God: Not of works, lest any man should boast.'* Salvation is a gift. It's something free that God lovingly wants to give to every single person, and it can only be accepted by faith. There's no amount of good deeds that a person could do to 'outweigh' their bad and get them into Heaven. Look over here at Romans 3:23. This verse tells us why we can't work our way to Heaven. It says, *'For all have sinned and come short of the glory of God.'* Sin is the bad things we do. No matter how hard we try, we'll never be perfect like God, and we'll never be able to get to Heaven on our own."

Jada placed her chin in the palms of her hands and listened intently.

"Because we've sinned, there's a consequence, and it's a serious penalty. The Bible says in Romans 6:23, *'For the wages of sin is death.'* Romans 5:12 teaches us that death has come *'by sin'* and death has *'passed upon all men, for that all have sinned.'* This death is not merely physical death, but an eternal spiritual death. It's separation from God forever in Hell. God's Word is clear in the book of Revelation."

He quickly flipped to the end of the New Testament and, as he did with the other verses, he used his finger to underscore what he read from the Bible. *'...the fearful, and unbelieving, and the abominable, and murderers, and whoremongers, and sorcerers, and idolaters, and all liars, shall have their part in the lake which burneth with fire and brimstone.'* And notice over here, *'...whosoever was not found written in the book of life was cast into the lake of fire.'*"

Jada's mouth fell open and she leaned back slightly, "Written in the book of life? You mean to tell me that according to your Bible, if a person dies in their sin, they'll go straight to Hell?"

"That's right. Pretty serious stuff, isn't it?" the young man hesitated and then ventured a guess. "Maybe you're thinking, *How could a God of love do this?* The truth is, He doesn't want to, but He has to. No sin can be allowed into Heaven; God is holy and perfect. It's our *own* sins that separate us from Him and cast us into that awful place."

"Well, it can't be that bad though, right?" She snickered. "I've always heard a lot of my Dad's men joke about going to Hell. How they're gonna party and live it up down there with Satan. Like, there'll be endless heavy metal concerts and people can do all sorts of bad stuff."

Kaci's eyes narrowed and locked with Jada's while she firmly yet sweetly declared, "I don't know where they got all that from, but none of it is found in the Bible."

"Yeah," Drew explained, "Hell is a place of horrific pain and endless suffering where people burn alive with no relief. There isn't *one thing* there that will be fun or enjoyable. It's the most gruesome place of torment in the Universe where there's weeping and gnashing of teeth, darkness, chaos, and torment."

Jada just blinked for a moment, then shuddered. "Wow. I never knew it was that bad. You're serious?"

Both siblings nodded and Drew continued, "It's a real place, and I believe that God in His love wrote about Hell to make us to stop and see what will happen to us if we die in our sins. He doesn't want anyone to go there; He wants us to be with *Him*... in Heaven. I love what Jesus says in the first couple verses in John 14: *'Let not your heart be troubled: ye believe in God, believe also in me. In my Father's house are many mansions: if it were not so, I would have told you. I go to prepare a place for you.'"*

"Fascinating. Who exactly is this Jesus?" Jada asked

Drew and Kaci glanced at each other, genuinely surprised. "You've never heard about Jesus?" Kaci asked.

"Well, yeah, kinda. Isn't He like God's Son or something?" she shrugged again. "I don't know. When the men get angry, they do yell His name a lot..."

"And I think the Devil finds great joy in that; but it breaks the heart of God," Kaci hung her head in sadness, "He certainly doesn't want anyone blaspheming the name of Christ."

"Because Jesus is the perfect Son of God," Drew explained. "He fulfilled more than 300 things that were prophesied about his life in the Bible hundreds and even thousands of years before He was born. He willingly came to earth to die on the Cross for our sins. The most famous Bible verse of all time is John 3:16, *'For God so loved the world, that he gave his only begotten Son, that whosoever believeth in him should not perish, but have everlasting life.'"*

"Yeah, I remember you quoting that the last time we talked."

Kaci rested her hand on Jada's forearm, "Jesus came for you. He came because He loves you."

A sharp knocking on the passenger window of their vehicle startled them. Girly jumped awake with a yelp, instinctively reaching for his holstered handgun.

"What are you all doing?" Fitzgerald shouted through the window, eyeing the Bible in Drew's hand.

"Why? What? It's nothing," Jada blew him off.

"Things are clearing up, and we've still got some daylight." Fitzgerald told them. "We leave in 5!"

The thunder was distant, and they hadn't even noticed that the rain had stopped.

"You think the roads will be okay?" Kaci asked Jada, worried.

"Honestly, I have no idea. Probably not. But I know we're so close to our next location, and Dad is driven to get there without any more delays." Jada rolled her eyes. "This should be fun," she added sarcastically under her breath.

Once the convoy began moving its way down the narrow jungle path canopied by rainforest, Jada looked in the rear-view mirror and quietly said only two words. But they were said with a glow in her eyes. They were two words that meant the world to Drew and Kaci.

"Thank you."

They knew God was working on her heart; it was evident. Kaci looked out the window and smiled. *Thank You, Lord.*

CHAPTER XVII

L ight rain came and went as they pushed forward late into the night, but most of the sky remained clear and bright. Fitzgerald's vehicle had been outfitted with a powerful lightbar on the front grill, so he and Alexander could properly see everything in their path to safely lead the convoy. As they crested the next hill, a valley filled with a vast rainforest sprawled before them, illuminated by the moon and stars above. An Amazon tributary lazily weaved through the jungle, splitting into two smaller rivers. On the shore of where the waters parted, large scraggly rocks jutted out along a gently rising slope that ascended to the base of a giant Kapok tree high above. Its thick bare trunk rose over a hundred feet into the night sky with its wide arching limbs forming an umbrella-shaped canopy over the stony terrain.

"My, my," Fitzgerald commented. "Would you look at that! *'Near forked tongue great life has sprung.'*"

"Yes," Alexander scratched at his scruffy jaw. "This certainly fits the description of our last clue perfectly. My guess is that our next guide is located somewhere among the rocks of that ravine. *'A soul that lies amidst the tree watches o'er all who breathe.'*"

It was extremely difficult to convince Fitzgerald to stop for the night and begin the scouting at daybreak, but Alexander's persistence paid off as he helped the man realize that nothing could be accomplished in the darkness.

The procession of vehicles came to an abrupt halt along the

road. As Drew and Kaci wondered what was going on, Jada's radio on the dashboard crackled with her father's voice, "Men, we've finally arrived at the location where we believe we'll find our next guide! As you're well aware, the ground is too soft for us to set up camp, so stay put in your vehicles for the rest of the night. I know the sacrifice is great, and the journey is long. But we are Bloodfists; each of you were made for this! Together we go onward to Paititi!"

"Guess we're still stuck in here," Jada remarked, then turned to Girly. "Keep your shoes on; this Jeep smells bad enough already! Can't open the windows because of the mosquitoes."

The big man grunted and reclined his seat, practically landing on Drew's lap. The young man shifted without complaining, trying to make himself more comfortable, and with their rucksack in the middle acting as a pillow, he and Kaci tried their best to sleep.

The following morning came quickly. Fitzgerald's "wakeup call" via radio squawked just before the sun spilled over the horizon.

"Rise and shine, sleeping beauties! Get some coffee and grub from the supply truck and gear up," he ordered. "Fairchild, meet me by my vehicle."

Kaci climbed out behind Drew, grimacing when she landed in mud up to her ankles. Both of them stood stiff as a board from their cramped positions over the past few hours and stretched to work out the kinks. After grabbing a few MREs, they walked over to where their uncle and Fitzgerald stood along the ridge with Fairchild; the three men were deep in conversation.

"It would be best for us to leave a majority of the crew here and a small team of us head over to the fork via the Zodiac rafts," Fitzgerald stated with his hands on his hips.

"Agreed," Alexander nodded.

"Fairchild, I want four other squads of five. The good professor here, Drew, Kaci, myself, and Jada will be the fifth squad. Have a group follow us down to the river to help us set up the inflatables. Then take the rest of the men and re-route the convoy to a better position along this ridge and set up camp."

"You got it," the man replied and slinked down the trail, calling out orders to the men.

"This is going to be exhilarating, Jim! It's our first time out on the water," Fitzgerald lightly jabbed him on the shoulder. He turned to Drew and Kaci, "Are you ready for our little adventure?"

Drew gave the man a thumbs up and teased, "As long as it doesn't include putting our lives unnecessarily in danger again, sure, I'm good with it!"

Fitzgerald bellowed, "Glad you woke up on the right side of the bed this morning!"

Alexander grinned, "Be sure you two grab whatever you need before we leave; I don't know how long this will take us, but I'm pretty sure we won't be back to camp until we find the guide."

"And hopefully, that will be by nightfall!" Fitzgerald interjected.

"True, but it's always good to be prepared just in case," their uncle gently reasoned.

As soon as the team had everything assembled, they drove as far as they could, "off-roading" it down to the riverbank. They made it most of the way there without getting stuck, but the last quarter mile had to be on foot. The men groaned as they helped each other unload the folded Zodiacs and their heavy engines. Drew noticed that Girly, Beady Eyes, and Goatee had joined them; he nodded at them since they were the only three in the group he had ever gotten to know. Uncle James and Beady Eyes pulled one of the 150-pound boat engines from the back bed of a Jeep and together with Drew's help carried it, while Girly smirked at them and effortlessly heaved one up onto his shoulders.

"Show off," Beady Eyes grunted.

A few of the mercenaries went before the group with machetes, hacking their way through the constant wall of interwoven vines and jungle overgrowth. Spider monkeys swung along on the moss-covered branches high above, and colorful birds squawked at them impatiently for disturbing their rest. At one point, a dark brown boa constrictor covered in tan patches slowly moved across their path. Without hesitation, Fitzgerald shot a hole through its raised head and spat, "Such nasty vermin."

At the sound of his revolver, the jungle instantly paused its constant buzzing and chirping, then slowly resumed. Once they reached the riverbank, everyone collapsed for a moment to catch their breath.

"All right, men!" Fitzgerald snapped his fingers. "We've got a guide to find!" Kaci marveled at how each black rubber commando-styled boat inflated in less than forty seconds. They were lined with bulletproof material and had a 55-horsepower two-stroke engine with pump-jet propulsion mounted on the back end. Since the team hadn't packed much gear, within ten minutes they were on their way across the river.

The rafts skimmed over the surface of the water, and Kaci grinned from ear to ear as she felt the thrill of the ride and the wind blowing in her face. It was a welcome relief after trudging through the humid dense rainforest where there was no breeze. She shielded her eyes with her hand and stared at the giant Kapok tree that loomed higher and higher overhead the closer they got to shore.

As they approached the bank on the point where the river forked, a few of the men jumped out into the shallow water to gently pull the rafts up onto the rocks.

"Let's get a move on!" Fitzgerald ordered once the five engines had cut off. "I need two of you to stay here and guard the boats. The rest of us, spread out in a sweeping formation. Let's find that guide!"

"We don't exactly know what we're looking for," Alexander instructed the group. "The guide could be out in the open or it could in some obscure location like it was in *Pachawañu*. Pay attention to detail and look for anything that might appear hewn or carved. We cannot afford to overlook anything! If you have any questions, call me over. And be sure to wear your gloves; you don't want to accidentally get bitten by something poisonous that we don't have an antidote for."

They took their time weaving through the large boulders and low-lying ferns as they climbed up the gradual slope, being wary of any snakes or jaguars that often liked to keep themselves cool in the shade. The work was tedious and mentally exhausting under the hot brutal sun. On a handful of occasions, a couple of the mercenaries thought they stumbled across something of significance, but it just turned out to be unique formations caused by the elements wearing away the rocks over the centuries.

They stopped for a brief lunch before finishing their assent to the top of the ravine. The last part was the steepest as the ground sharply sloped toward the base of the giant Kapok. Alexander sat down next to his niece and nephew who were perched away from the others on a large semi-flat stone, and together they prayed over their meal of MREs.

The team hadn't paid much attention to how high they'd climbed. Now, noticing the entire region lying before them, they sat in silence as they ate and enjoyed the breathtaking view. Gentle plumes of smoke rose in scattered places along the horizon, marking the locations of tribal villages. Fishing vessels, canoes, and the occasional supply barge dotted the sprawling rivers that coiled their way through the jungle.

"Beautiful, isn't it?" Alexander commented between bites to Drew and Kaci, who nodded with bright smiles. "When I see places like this I'm reminded of a couple of different passages in Scripture. Job 12 asks, *'Who knoweth not in all these that the hand of the LORD hath wrought this? In whose hand is the soul of every living thing, and the breath of all mankind.'* Everything around us has been made by the Lord; and being here, with the ability to see so much, fills me with great awe toward our omnipotent God!"

He paused his eating to quote reverently from Psalm 95, *"For the LORD is a great God, and a great King above all gods. In his hand are the deep places of the earth: the strength of the hills is his also. The sea is his, and he made it: and his hands formed the dry land. O come, let us worship and bow down: let us kneel before the LORD our maker."*

"He is worthy of our worship," Kaci smiled.

"Yes," Alexander's eyes moistened. "And the older I get, the more I fall in love with Him. The God of the Universe is my very best Friend. What a great joy it is to abide in His holy presence and be anointed with His Heavenly power every day. It is a privilege to worship Him and magnify Him. He is worthy of it not only from our lips, but also through our lives. I Corinthians 6:20 teaches us to *'glorify God in your body, and in your spirit, which are God's.'* I heard a wise preacher put it this way once," the professor began to count each point on his fingers as he listed them. "This should affect our mouths or what we say; our minds — how we think; our means — what we do; our motives — why we do what we do; our methods — how we live and structure our life; and our movies and music or what we allow to influence us. He is most certainly worthy of our obedience in every area of our lives!"

The young people stared off into the distance deep in thought. Drew broke the silence, "It reminds me of that verse, *'Whether therefore ye eat, or drink, or whatsoever ye do, do all to the glory of God.'*"

"Absolutely. Everything we do should bring Him honor, glory, and praise."

"You mean, even when we're in the middle of something really difficult and painful like a trial?" Kaci wondered with searching eyes.

"*Especially* during those seasons of life," Alexander added with a soft smile. "There are so many verses throughout Scripture that comfort us, reminding us that God is always in control. Since we're on this subject, I wanted to share with you a couple of verses." He pulled his worn Bible from the leather holster on his hip and began flipping through the pages. "I've had this on my heart the past few days. The first one is I Thessalonians 5:18, a very familiar verse." As he began to read it, the two teenagers quoted it along with him.

"*'In every thing give thanks: for this is the will of God in Christ Jesus concerning you.'*" The professor took off his glasses. "God wrote every word in the Bible on purpose, and the key here is to recognize that He specifically said *'In every thing'* and not *'For every thing.'* There's a big difference. Let's use, for example, someone who just found out they have cancer. *'For every thing'* would imply that God is saying, 'Praise Me for your cancer!'" Alexander shook his head, putting his glasses back on. "That's not what God intended; He is not a sadist. He's not sitting up in Heaven rubbing His hands together trying to figure out how to make life difficult for His children. Yes, tough times, trials, even tragedies come; but, He *always* allows things to happen for a reason."

Kaci tucked her golden hair behind her left ear, "For our good and His glory."

"Exactly," he pointed to the underlined verse in his Bible. "God wrote *'In every thing.'* In other words, not 'Praise me for your cancer.' But, 'Praise me as you go through your cancer.'"

"Wow, I never thought of it that way!" she replied.

Alexander turned over to I Peter 4, "Now look at this in verses 12 and 13, *'Beloved, think it not strange concerning the fiery trial which is to try you, as though some strange thing happened unto you: But rejoice, inasmuch as ye are partakers of Christ's sufferings; that, when his glory shall be revealed, ye may be glad also with exceeding joy.'*"

"That goes along with what we were talking about earlier this week!" Drew interjected. "How our lives can be a visible testimony for Christ!"

"Yes, and it's oftentimes through suffering that the Lord can shine the brightest through us to those around us."

"More preaching, eh, Jim?" Fitzgerald ribbed as he sauntered up from behind.

"Absolutely!" the professor turned with a grin. "It's a Biblical principle found in Deuteronomy 6:6-7, *'And these words, which I command thee this day, shall be in thine heart: And thou shalt teach them diligently unto thy children, and shalt talk of them when thou sittest in thine house, and when thou walkest by the way, and when thou liest down, and when thou risest up.'*" He pointed his Bible up in the man's incredulous face and added nonchalantly, "I enjoy taking any opportunity I can to talk about the Bible. Would you like to join us?"

The big man was slightly taken aback by the directness of

Alexander's offer, then broke out into a boisterous laugh as he pushed away Alexander's hand. "Well, you are certainly consistent, old chum — trying to convert me and get me to talk about Jesus — HA! You can believe in your Bible all you want, but it doesn't mean that I have to." He clapped the man on the shoulder. "At least you're not some flash-in-the-pan hypocrite like most in the church. I'll give you that."

"Why, thank you," Alexander grinned again. "Are you trying to give me... *a compliment?*"

Fitzgerald's radio clipped onto his khaki vest interrupted them, "Fairchild here. Just reporting in. Base location confirmed two clicks east of drop zone. Keep us apprised of your status and how we may assist. Over."

"I see them down there!" Kaci pointed across the river. The Bloodfists had lined up their vehicles on the path along the ridge and were carrying supplies to their campsite below on a flat grassy strip of land.

Fitzgerald clicked his walkie-talkie, "Update received. Target unknown, but possibly closing in. Keep the lights on for our return!"

"10-4."

"I think we're close, Adrian," Alexander explained while putting away his Bible and getting back into the mindset of their mission. "The clue specifically stated that the guide *'watches o'er all who breathe.'* It didn't quite make sense until we got up here. Look at this view! I believe we'll find it somewhere closer to the top!" His brow furrowed with concern as he looked out into the distance.

"I don't like what I'm seeing though," he commented pointing to the horizon. In a matter of minutes, the sky off in the distance had turned eerily dark. Lightning strobed in thick swirling clouds now billowing in their direction. "That could be upon us before we know it. The weather changes so quickly here. We don't want to get caught in that storm!"

"Then we'd better hurry," Fitzgerald recommended. He spun on his heels and motioned to his men, "Let's move out!"

Everyone was a bit sore from the constant climbing over the

past few hours, but they pushed on as they now faced the most arduous part. They scaled the sharp rise, hiking with their feet sideways and using their gloved hands when necessary to hold onto small tree saplings and ferns, trying not to lose their momentum and accidentally tumble down the hill.

When they reached the edge of the slope, the ground plateaued to a small clearing before spreading out into more jungle. The mighty Kapok tree, now larger than ever, stood atop a cliff-like outcropping, with its thick moss-covered roots webbing down the rocky surface, hanging like vines at the base before disappearing into the ground. There, carved into the stone amidst the vines about thirty-five feet above the ground was another face staring down at them.

"The guide!" Fitzgerald exclaimed, dashing forward.

"Ah! I get it now," Alexander chuckled. "'*Where a soul that lies amidst the tree.*' I didn't think it would be that obvious!"

Drew smiled, "But how would we have ever known?"

"Right!" he heartily patted the young man's back. "Let's just be thankful we don't have a collapsing ceiling to deal with!"

As the group surrounded the base of the small cliff and looked up at the magnificent tree and the statue, Kaci decided to speak aloud what everyone was thinking, "So how are we supposed to get to it?"

"Somebody's gonna have to climb," Fitzgerald muttered with his hands on his hips.

Jada stepped forward, "And that somebody is me."

"No," her father snapped. "Absolutely not."

She crossed her arms, annoyed, "Um, yes, I'm doing it."

Fitzgerald was about to protest when she interrupted him, "Dad, I'm the best free-soloing rock climber here! Don't deny it." She gestured to Drew and Kaci. "You've made everybody else hazard themselves and now it's my turn. Let me do this!"

The man had nothing to say in response because he knew she was right. Without waiting for permission, Jada took off her black vest and tossed it to the ground, then made sure she didn't have anything else that would snag on the jagged rock while climbing.

She held out her hand, "Camera, please?"

Reluctantly, Fitzgerald smacked it down into her hand with a steely look, "Be careful."

"That's the plan," she secured the camera strap to one of her belt loops.

Kaci wasn't sure how the girl was going to get up the cliff, but she watched in surprise as Jada grabbed hold of a tree root nearby and nimbly pulled herself to a vaunted position overhead. Carefully maneuvering from foothold to foothold among the roots, she found small fissures in the rock to help her ascend the cliff face.

Thunder rumbled and Kaci frowned, turning to glance behind her. Dark clouds were quickly blocking out the afternoon sun, and the wind suddenly whipped and rustled through the jungle trees.

"You've got this, Jada! You can do it!" she softly cheered to the girl, now fifteen feet above them.

Raindrops began pattering the leaves and then turned into a light drizzle as lightning split the sky in the distance. *You've got to be kidding me,* Jada chuckled to herself as rain dripped down her face. *Nothing is ever easy.* As she worked her way around the roots to find her next secure position in the rock, she felt how slippery the mossy bark had become. She tried holding on to the crevice but the palms of her gloves got covered in slick green slime. *Not good.*

Kaci glanced over at Fitzgerald and thought she must be seeing things. For the first time since meeting the man, he actually looked concerned, scared even.

"Jada, I'm still not too sure of this; it's getting too slippery. Come back down," he ordered.

"No, I can do this! It'll only get worse the longer we wait."

The man's eyes blazed a little, and he forced a smile to hide his rising anger, "She has a lot of her mother in her. No way to stop her when her mind is made up."

"Reminds me of someone else I know," Alexander grinned as Fitzgerald shot him a scowl. He then got down on one knee, "I'm concerned for her, too, Adrian. Let me pray for her."

"Uh, whatever; you do your thing."

Kaci held her breath, worried Jada might suddenly slip, but after a few more cautiously-placed steps in her ascent, the girl was able to pull herself up along the right side of the large stone face. Her feet were firmly planted in a small crevice and her arm looped around a tree root dangling off the rock wall to keep her securely in position.

Carefully removing the camera, she began taking as many pictures as she could. *Don't make any sudden movements; don't look down and you'll be fine,* she repeated to herself over and over again in her mind. *I've got to make sure I get everything! I don't want to have to climb this a second time.* She leaned out precariously far to make sure she captured all the Latin wording etched under the statue's chin.

"Which direction are the eyes pointing, my dear?" Fitzgerald called out.

"Pretty much straight north!" Jada replied, snapping another photo of them.

"Excellent! Be sure to —"

"Yeah, yeah!" Jada hollered back. "Remove them." She rolled her eyes, muttering under her breath, "You and your weird obsession."

She pulled out the knife sheathed in the small of her back and tediously worked the thin blade around each socket. *This is creepy. And exhausting.* Her arms and legs ached from being so rigidly poised in the same position for such a length of time. Her wet hair dangled in her face, and she tried to fling it out of the way, but it only made matters worse as the gentle rain intermingled with her sweat and mildly burned her eyes. She gritted her teeth and finished breaking the seal on the first gemstone. With a little prying, the bright blue jewel popped out and rolled down the face to the ground. Fitzgerald stood below among the ferns at the base of the rock wall eagerly waiting to catch it.

Jada's hand burned as she tried to gently coax the second from its socket. She scraped at the old mortar that held it into position. *Almost there, almost there... Got it!* The gem clattered against the rocks as it quickly descended.

The man laughed with joy as he held up both aquamarine stones for all to see, but he stopped short when he heard his daughter sharply cry out. Her knife had slipped from her hand while trying to reposition it and it spun wildly in the air! The big man instantly jumped back, and the blade stuck into the earth just inches from his feet.

"Jada!" he roared.

"I'm sorry! I can barely feel my fingers, and it's so wet up here!"

The wind began to blow with stronger gusts, and Jada did her best to hold on tightly. The rain very quickly had turned into a torrential downpour. Jada shivered while taking a moment to carefully pump her legs and flex life back into her hands. The reality of her situation was starting to set in. *And I thought the climb up was difficult! Getting back down is going to be much harder.* The broad canopy of the Kapok high overhead did nothing to shield her or those below as the rain came down almost sideways. *Just one step at a time. You can do this!* She gingerly felt for the next lower crevice with her foot. *There it is!*

Kaci squinted, struggling to see through the heavy drops filling her vision, and watched as Jada slowly descended.

"I'm really worried for her," she whispered to her brother above the howling wind.

"I know. We've got to pray like Uncle James," Drew said with a troubled look, pointing over to where the man was still on one knee with head bowed. Rain dripped off the rim of his glasses, and his lips moved silently as he interceded on behalf of the young lady.

A lightning strike abruptly flashed nearby, and thunder ripped through the air. Jada's heart jumped and her foot slipped off the ledge in a kneejerk reaction. She scrambled her arms to secure a hold but to no avail as her momentum began to send her backward in a terrifying fall to the jagged rocks below.

Fitzgerald rushed forward instinctively, "Jada!" he shouted.

In desperation, she snatched the other knife from her belt and slammed it into the stone in one final attempt to save herself. The blade dragged down the rock a couple feet until it sliced into a thick tree root and stuck firm. Her arm yanked and the hilt of the slender throwing knife dug deep into her fingers as she tightened her grasp, refusing to let go.

"Pray harder, Jim!" the man pleaded, distraught. "That's my little girl!"

Jada gritted her teeth and struggled to find a ledge or fissure — anything — to regain her position as her entire body remained suspended nearly thirty feet in the air, but everything was too slippery.

She closed her eyes, the rain streaming down her face, and breathed in deeply. *God, I really need you. I'm... I'm not making any promises, but I'll try to learn more about You if You'll let me get through this!* In that instant, she remembered the other throwing knife she always kept hidden in the side of her boot. *Yes!* She carefully brought her leg up to her free hand, the movement causing pain to sear through her body as all her weight pulled against the hilt of her only support. The blade was about to give way when she drove the other deep into the root next to her.

She sighed with relief. She wanted to laugh and cry at the same time; all sorts of emotions ran through her body while she trembled, holding on, trying to regain her composure from such a close call.

"I suppose I owe You a 'thank you'," she said aloud to the Lord.

"What's that, Jada? Are you okay?" her father hollered up.

"I'll be fine!" she replied with a strained voice.

Much calmer now, her feet found the crevices she had used before to scale up the wall. Retracing those steps from memory, she descended with ease until she came to the massive webbing of tree roots at the base of the cliff about ten feet from the ground.

All the moss had turned into a sort of thick green sludge. No matter how hard she tried, the tread of her boots couldn't find any solid footing.

"I don't know how I'm gonna do this!" she yelled over the storm. "Everything is so slippery, and it's too high to jump!"

Fitzgerald cupped his hands to his mouth, "Toss down the camera!"

"What?" she broke her concentration.

"The camera," he snapped. "Give it to me! I don't want it to get hurt!"

Jada felt cut to the heart. *What about me? Don't you care if I get hurt?* She shook her head, slowly retrieved the camera, then lobbed it down without warning, catching Fitzgerald by surprise. He caught it, but the momentum caused him to fall back into the mud.

"A little warning would have been nice!" he scowled.

"Yeah, well, a little 'please' or 'thank you' would've been nice, too."

His demeanor softened, and he picked himself up off the ground, "Do be careful as you come the rest of the way!"

Jada didn't respond, acting as if she didn't hear him. She deeply loved her father, but sometimes he treated her like the rest of the men. Most of the time it didn't bother her, but there were moments like this when she hated how calloused he could be. *He gets so consumed about what he wants, that he doesn't care —*

Before she could finish the thought, a harsh gust of wind and rain caught her off guard. Her boot missed the next foothold completely and her hands wrenched free from their grip in the rock. *Not again!* She managed to snag a vine-like root; it jerked her and sent shooting pain through her right arm.

Barely able to hold on, she slid, bumped, and scraped the rest of the way down, hitting the ground hard. Fitzgerald rushed to her side immediately.

"You did well, my dear. I'm proud of you!"

She winced a smile and sat up. Her arm remained limp next to her and with great pain she struggled to bring it onto her lap, "I think my arm's broken; I can't move it!"

"Oh no!" Kaci gasped.

Alexander strode over from where he had been kneeling, "Let me take a look!"

He gently rolled up her sleeve, then carefully felt and pressed despite Jada's uncomfortable moaning, "The good news is I don't believe you've fractured anything."

"And the bad news?"

"Your shoulder is out of joint." He placed a palm gently on her upper arm, his other holding her elbow. "What's your favorite color?"

She looked at him quizzically. "Uh — that's random. I like — *OUCH!!*"

Alexander made a quick jolt and snapped her arm back into place. Jada let out a bloodcurdling yell, doubling over in pain. She fell silent for a moment, then sat up with a smile on her face and began moving her arm again.

"Purple. My favorite color's purple," she chuckled. "I owe you one, Professor."

A lop-sided grin spread across his face, "No problem. I'm glad it was an easy fix."

"Oh, and I guess I should thank you for praying?"

"My pleasure, young lady, my pleasure." Alexander smiled, as Kaci began to clean the cuts on Jada's palm.

"Now that we've got what we came for, let's start making our way back," Fitzgerald interrupted over the rain and howling wind.

"Are you sure about that?" Alexander stood. "This storm is brutal. Let's give it a couple of hours, find some shelter, and then head back."

"Giving me orders now, are you?"

Alexander put his hands up defensively, "Not at all. Just trying to take a common-sense approach and avoid any more accidents —"

Without warning, loud cracking and popping erupted behind them from across the river. The two men's eyes widened. They whirled about and instantly ran to the edge of the plateau to discover that the ridge where Fitzgerald's convoy had parked was dangerously buckling. It had been raining so much for the past week and the ground was so saturated that now, under the pressure of such a massive amount of weight, the crest was beginning to collapse. The treeline rolled in fluid motion sending many of the trees askew as a huge mudslide formed and oozed down the steep hill toward the campsite below, gaining momentum.

"No!" the big man yelled and fired a couple of shots in the air from his revolver. His men, who were settled in their tents away from the raging storm, needed to know they were in danger. He frantically grabbed his talkie, "Fairchild? Come in. Anyone!" For a moment, there was nothing but static.

"Yeah, boss?" Fitzgerald's comms crackled.

"Get out! Get out! Get out!" he boomed, at a loss for words.

"There's a mudslide!" Alexander interjected.

They could hear Fairchild's sharp gasp and then silence.

The rest of the team now joined the two men and together watched helplessly as the vehicles tumbled chaotically, crunching into rocks and trees and creaking metallic groans as they fell onto the camp far below. The gas tankers exploded upon impact, erupting giant fireballs high into the sky, which turned into billows of black smoke as they intermingled with the heavy downpour.

As fast as it had begun, it ended. Kaci burst into tears and buried her face into her brother's shoulder. The smoke quickly dissipated, washed out of the atmosphere by the rain and wind. No one could speak after witnessing such a gut-wrenching catastrophe. From what they could tell, the clearing where their camp had stood was completely obliterated — now just a sea of mud, uprooted trees, and the crumpled hulls of Fitzgerald's convoy.

"Gone.... They're all — gone," he stuttered in disbelief; then after a moment, he flew into a rage, "This cannot be!"

"Adrian!" Alexander tried to put a hand on his old friend's shoulder, but he sharply pulled it away as he screamed wildly, kicking mud and loose stones everywhere. "It's over, Adrian!" he said with as much strength as he could, but his voice still quivered after what they had just witnessed. He tried to tug on Fitzgerald's arm. "Come on; let's find some shelter. There's nothing we can do now."

Fitzgerald growled like a beast and thrust his revolver squarely between the professor's eyes, "You have opposed me since day one!"

As fast as he had drawn his weapon, Alexander deftly knocked it out of his hand, clattering it down onto the ground.

"Get that thing out of my face. Enough!"

"How dare you!" Fitzgerald exploded and swung a roundhouse punch that Alexander blocked.

"Stop it, Adrian! What are you doing? This is madness!"

"I will never quit!" He swung again and again in blind rage. "Nothing will stand in my way!"

Alexander ducked and sidestepped Fitzgerald's aggressive assault with poise, then saw his opening and slapped him hard across the face with open palm, "Snap out of it, man! You've just lost your convoy and most of your men. There's no way we can go on!"

Fitzgerald recoiled for a moment, clutching his cheek in pain. For a moment, Alexander thought this had knocked some sense into him, but the man's face turned dark and his eyes yellow as he let his anger become fully unleashed.

"We're going to Paititi!!" he roared and lunged toward Alexander, tackling him and sending them both to the ground.

With all his strength, Alexander did his best to defend himself as they wrestled in the mud — one on top of the other, rolling as each tried to gain the upper hand in various holds.

"You've always thought yourself to be better than me!" Fitzgerald grunted.

"Not true!" Alexander yelled in his face as their hands were interlocked. "You were always one to skirt the rules, and it finally caught up with you!"

"Rules are meant to be broken —"

"No, they're not, Adrian." They tugged and pulled on each other, their clothes covered in mud. The rain was still coming down in thick sheets and thunder echoed off the rock wall where the eye-less face of the guide stared down at them. "It's your *own* fault you got banned from the Archaeological Society, and I wasn't going to let you drag me down with you!"

"You abandoned me!" Fitzgerald exploded. "You were my friend, Jim! And I'm who I am today because you never tried to help restore me!"

Alexander suddenly stopped and looked at his old friend. He could see pain deep within his eyes.

"Adrian, I didn't realize —"

Fitzgerald's blows stung as they glanced off his head, but Alexander instinctively responded by landing a series of rapid-fire punches to the man's rib cage, sending him flying backwards to the ground gasping for breath. The professor slowly rose to his feet, exhausted, and held out his hand.

"Adrian, I'm so sorry! You disappeared, and I thought that you didn't want any help, so I never went after you. But I'm here now. I'm here to help you now with God's help. You can get on the right path!"

Fitzgerald reluctantly grabbed the man's hand and their eyes locked sincerely for a moment, then he flashed a diabolical smile and yanked Alexander down to his knees. Before Alexander could recover himself, Fitzgerald had already leapt behind him and placed him in a chokehold.

"It's too late, old chum," he breathed harshly into his ear, squeezing tighter and tighter. Alexander struggled to loosen the man's grip, but it held firm. "I've already made a deal with the devil, and there's no going back."

"I-its...never...t-too late...." he gasped. Alexander's vision was beginning to blur, and he saw Drew about to leap forward to come to his aid. He shook his head "No" the best he could, imagining what Fitzgerald would do to the boy while he was in this rabid state.

Suddenly, a gunshot rang out into the air from directly behind them. Fitzgerald jumped, slightly loosening his grip, giving Alexander the split second he needed to pry himself free. Drew and Kaci rushed to his side as he knelt on all fours in the mud, coughing and trying to catch his breath.

Fitzgerald turned around slowly to see Jada standing there with his revolver in her hand. Smoke curled up from the barrel of the gun and for a moment, silence prevailed among them. The two teenagers gently helped their uncle to his feet and led him over to stand behind

Jada, who pointed the gun directly at her father.

"Dad, I'm only gonna say this once," she uttered firmly with narrowed eyes. "Stop it. This... this is foolishness!" The gun wavered in her hand slightly as she saw her father's nostrils flare and his features turn cold. She had no idea how he was going to respond and wasn't sure she even had it in her to pull the trigger.

"None of this should matter anymore. Everything's gone! We're stranded in the middle of the jungle." She glanced over her shoulder at Drew and Kaci and sighed when she looked back at her dad. "I can't believe I'm saying this, but... we need to go back!"

A smirk slowly spread across the man's mud-covered face. The rain was beginning to lighten up.

"You too, eh?" he muttered condescendingly, "These *children* have made you SOFT!"

"No, they haven't!" She widened her stance and regripped the big revolver with both of her hands to straighten her aim. "Don't talk about my friends like that. They're some of the bravest people I've ever met!"

Drew and Kaci exchanged glances while Fitzgerald rolled his eyes and grunted, "It is no matter; we are going to need 'all hands on deck' for what lies ahead of us."

"Dad, you don't get it! There is no going forward!"

He straightened his shoulders and looked around at the entire group.

"This has gone on long enough!" he bellowed and snapped his fingers.

Instantly, his mercenaries flanked him, their guns lowered at the ground, but the gleam in their eyes saying they were more than ready to point them somewhere else if told to.

"What?" Jada looked bewildered. "What are you doing? I thought you men would be with *me* on this one!"

Beady Eyes stepped forward next to his boss, "We are Bloodfists."

Jada shook her head. "You're all... you're all CRAZY!! My father is gonna get us killed!"

"Then it will be a worthy death," Beady Eyes calmly replied without blinking. "We don't think twice about what we do. We just do." He paused for a moment as he glanced at the others and lifted his voice. "We are *Bloodfists!*"

"Bloodfists!" the men shouted in unison, flexing their forearms bearing the grungy red tattoo.

Fitzgerald chuckled and stepped forward to take his revolver from her trembling hands.

"You thought you had me? NEVER. These men are loyal only to me, my dear. And the next time you challenge me, I *will* hurt you."

He backhanded her across the face with such force that it knocked her sprawling into the mud. She just lay there, her nose bleeding and her will broken.

Fitzgerald spun on his feet to address the men he had left. "We will take the sensible approach and follow the tributaries north by boat as the guide suggests. You all know that it was soon going to be impossible to traverse any deeper into the jungle by vehicle anyway. So when this storm passes, we will head back down and over to our base to see if there are any survivors or anything salvageable we can take with us from the wreckage."

He turned to Alexander with a warm smile, "Now that we've got our issues behind us, what do you say we continue forward, old chum?"

"Do I have a choice?"

"No!" Fitzgerald laughed amiably. "Let's find some shelter, as you advised, and take a look at the photos Jada got for us to see what our next step is!"

As he walked off, Kaci whispered to her uncle and Drew, "That man is crazy. He's like a schizophrenic or something. One minute he's nice and then the next he's gone mad!"

"Let me handle Fitzgerald. The two of you just focus on staying alive and working with Jada," Alexander instructed, nodding over to where the girl perched on a rock under a small tree by the plateau's edge away from the others.

"This has been a wild journey, and I've a feeling the next phase of it is going to be harder than ever." He weakly smiled, "But by God's grace, we'll make it through!" He patted them both on the shoulder, saying before he walked over to join Fitzgerald, "Pray for me; I'm really going to need it."

Drew and Kaci hugged each other.

"Why don't you go over and talk with Jada?" Drew suggested. "She really needs a friend right now."

"Can you believe she called us that?" Kaci smiled, then slowly walked over to where Jada sat.

"You okay?" Kaci asked as she sat down next to her.

"I'll live."

"Here," Kaci took a handkerchief out of her backpack and handed it to her.

"Thanks," Jada replied and wiped the blood from her face.

"Thank *you* — for trying to talk some sense into your dad."

Jada shrugged. "It didn't help; it just gave me a bloody nose."

"But you stood up for us again, and you called us your friends." Kaci smiled and put her arm around the girl's shoulder for a moment. "Thank you."

"Well, you both are pretty cool. I've kinda grown to like you. You've got guts."

"I... I honestly don't know what to say."

"It's okay," Jada smiled. "You don't have to say anything."

Kaci did the only thing she could think of. She took Jada's hand in hers and squeezed it. The girl squeezed it right back as they sat there in companionable silence watching the rain pour down upon the valley.

CHAPTER XVIII

For another hour, the storm raged. Alexander and Fitzgerald crouched side-by-side under the cover of two large boulders that leaned against each other, forming a small overhang that sheltered them from the elements, and carefully studied all of the pictures Jada had taken. Part of the way through, Drew joined them, and over the next several minutes, they pieced together their next clues etched on the ancient guide.

"This one here in Latin is pretty obvious," Fitzgerald looked at Drew and chuckled, "Well, that is if you can *read* Latin. It says, "*As Amaru lives, take your breath.*" He shrugged, "Obviously this is of some significance, but who knows what it's supposed to mean. Like the very first guide, it appears to have two sets of very different clues. One for our journey and another for something else which we have not been able to figure out as of yet."

Drew's features lit up, "Hey, maybe it's something we need to keep in mind when we find Paititi?"

"Yes!" Fitzgerald thumped him on the back and laughed. "That's the spirit! Did you hear the boy, Jim? He said *when* we find Paititi! Not *if* like you do all the time!"

"Right, right," Alexander nodded, not paying attention to the conversation, absorbed in translating the other clue.

"Okay, whatever," the big man sighed. "What have you found out from the Incan?"

The professor stroked his chin with furrowed brow as he

scribbled on his notepad, "Well, sometimes certain symbols could have a twofold meaning. After trying out all the variations, the one that makes the most sense to me is: 'A gaping mouth at river's end provides the light as you descend.'"

"Huh," Drew thought aloud. "Sounds like we need to find some sort of giant hole in the ground or something."

"True. Why make it complicated? From our past experiences with the other guides, we should take the clue at face value." Alexander unfolded their map, which was now getting quite worn, and spread it out, carefully shielding it from the drizzling rain. "We know we have to follow the river north, but it appears to go on for quite a long way." He traced his finger along the thin blue line that wove like a snake through the jungle, then tapped on the map. "But it looks like it leads us all the way to the base of this mountain area where the river fractures into a webbing of much smaller tributaries. Fascinating. This could be the place that our clue is referencing with the phrase 'at river's end'."

"Yes!" Fitzgerald lit up. "That's *got* to be it! This makes sense because it correlates with our other map. Take it out, old chum!"

Alexander carefully pulled it from the sealed leather tube he always had slung over his back. Shielding the animal-skinned document from any drizzle, the three of them peered down at it.

"See here?" Fitzgerald pointed to the words *'magna fractionis'*. "This means a great breaking or separating apart. It's trying to tell us that the river ends here and fractions into other tributaries. All things seem to be falling into place! Excellent!" He heartily slapped Alexander on the back, "We are getting so close, I can feel it."

"But we still need to find two more guides," Drew pointed out.

"What?" Fitzgerald tilted his head, puzzled, "How do you figure?"

"Maybe I'm totally wrong about this, but so far, we've only discovered four guides with four sets of clues, right? Well, look here," he motioned around the border of the map. "I think we should ask ourselves, why would there be a total of six faces?"

Fitzgerald's eyes flickered to Alexander, "Hmmm. The boy might be on to something."

Alexander nodded in agreement. "And look at what we still have ahead of us," he gestured to the drawings of a waterfall and a mountain resembling a skull of Incan design surrounded by a lake with a giant green serpent coiled at the bottom of it. For a moment, they sat there in silence, taking in the old artifact.

"Wherever we're going," the professor concluded, returning the document to its safe haven, "It appears that Paititi might be located somewhere in the mountain range ahead of us."

Fitzgerald squinted at their current atlas, judging the distance for the stretch of river they still needed to navigate. "What is that — approximately 300 miles?"

Alexander nodded.

"Yikes!" Drew exclaimed.

"It won't be easy," his uncle replied, then peered up at Fitzgerald, "And we're going to go through a lot of fuel."

"We'll be fine!" Fitzgerald stood to his feet and flashed a smile. "The river gives life, Jim. Where there's water, there will be people. Where there are people, there will be resources and fuel. And they will be *more* than happy to help us after they see what *I* can offer them."

"Why do I not like the sound of that?"

"Oh, don't you worry, old chum," Fitzgerald scolded and waved his hands to ease the rising alarm in Alexander's tone. "I'm a man of the people! Remember how we helped Tenoch and his village?" He laughed. "I'm merely referring to the 'emergency funds' I've got saved up for a crisis just like this! Money speaks a far more powerful language than anything else on this earth!" His smile instantly disappeared as he turned and barked to the rest of the group to gather their things and move out.

"Don't believe a word of that," Alexander whispered to Drew. "Money is *not* everything. *'A good name is rather to be chosen than great riches, and loving favour rather than silver and gold.'*"

Drew smiled and nodded, "Amen."

The rain had finally stopped, and the sun broke through the clouds, turning the dark overcast afternoon into a bright, sweltering hot one. Everyone hiked in silence as they carefully made their way back down the boulder-strewn ridge to the inflatables. At times, each of them slipped precariously in the mud but caught themselves by holding on to a tree sapling or a rock to keep from tumbling headlong down the hill. Once they'd returned to their boats, they proceeded as quickly as they could; Fitzgerald and his men were antsy to return to the camp and hunt for any survivors and salvage as much equipment as possible from the wreckage. Their grim features, however, showed they didn't expect to find much of anything after such a horrific catastrophe.

As they slowed their motorboat engines and gently approached the bank across the river, Alexander cleared his throat and kindly asked Fitzgerald if Drew and Kaci could watch the boats so that they could be spared from witnessing any carnage, to which the man agreed.

He turned to his daughter, who avoided his gaze. "I want you to stay with them, too, my dear. There's nothing here that you need to see."

The clearing where the camp was located lay not far from the shore, but it was surrounded by trees which shielded the young people. After a while, though, they couldn't help but noticed some of the men carrying bodies, digging makeshift graves, and burying the remains of what colleagues they could find in the debris and giant mudslide. The three of them sat in silence and just watched, until Kaci shivered and began to weep.

"Brings such a soberness. All of these men…we, we just saw them this morning! I can't believe they're gone…" Her voice trailed off.

Drew put his arm around his sister, "Brings a whole new meaning to Proverbs 27:1, doesn't it?"

She nodded. "*Boast not thyself of to morrow; for thou knowest not what a day may bring forth.*"

"Huh. I remember that from when you said it before," Jada

interjected. "Something about how nobody is guaranteed tomorrow." She shook her head. "It's crazy how things can change in a matter of moments. I honestly don't know what's gonna happen to us now."

"That's why we keep telling you about Jesus," Kaci mentioned tenderly, wiping the tears from her cheeks. "So you can be at peace with God. There is nothing more important in life."

"I'm..." Jada thought back to her promise to God she'd prayed earlier that day when she seemed only moments from her own death, "I'm just not ready yet." She abruptly stood and went from inflatable to inflatable to busy herself, checking the gear and engines to make sure everything was in order. She wasn't being rude, but it was clear that she didn't want to talk about it anymore.

Fitzgerald, Alexander, and the remaining mercenaries emerged from the jungle carrying a few black plastic crates among them.

"This is it," the big man muttered, motioning his men to load the boats carefully. "Be sure to distribute the weight evenly!"

"What exactly did you find?" Jada asked with her arms crossed.

"A few extra weapons, ammunition, and MREs. There are still a few others coming with a couple of small barrels of fuel we managed to siphon from the jeeps that didn't explode on their descent. And luckily, we salvaged some bedrolls from the tents."

Jada starred at him in disbelief, "How..." Fitzgerald held up his hand, stopping her before she said another word.

"I don't want to hear it! The dead have no need of them! Everything else — everyone else... is gone, and we will use whatever's necessary to continue our journey!"

As the men finished loading the last of the salvaged supplies, Girly approached with a barrel on his shoulder and with two men behind him struggling to carry another. They gently set them down into the inflatables as Fitzgerald directed them, and within the next few minutes, the remaining 25 members of the Paititi expedition headed out onto the river, uncertain of how they would manage in the heart of the Amazon.

※ ※ ※

Over the next couple of hours, they proceeded with caution, not wanting to push their engines as they worked their way forward with such a heavy load. Fitzgerald planned go as far as time would allow before the sun was completely down. As it crested the horizon, Alexander scanned both banks in deep concentration.

"What are you looking for, Uncle James?" Drew shouted over the loud engine.

"A certain kind of tree!" he replied, without taking his eyes off the shoreline.

It was almost dark when the man pointed with excitement toward a small clearing under an enclave of trees that stretched out over the water.

"There! Thank you, Lord! It's the perfect spot, exactly what we need."

"But we can go a bit further!"

"No, Adrian, we need to stop now; trust me!"

Grumbling, the man obliged, seeing the professor's earnestness. They headed toward the bank and gently pulled ashore. Large evergreen bushes were interspersed among the trees, and Alexander stood by one of them with a broad grin.

"*Humiria balsamifera,*" he declared to the group.

"What? This isn't some botany field trip, Jim!"

"No, but this bush is necessary for us to continue on yours," he shot back with a look of humor on his face. A few of the men chuckled, causing Fitzgerald to glare at them out of the corner of his eye.

"They produce a natural mosquito repellent that God made for the rainforest. The Lord knows we're going to need it without our gear! If He hadn't led us to this place, we'd all probably get malaria or yellow fever on our first night."

Fitzgerald was unsure how to respond, so he just awkwardly walked away, muttering to himself. While his men secured the boats and supplies, he collected an armful of the driest wood he could find to start a couple of fires. The three teenagers volunteered to distribute the bed rolls, and Alexander proceeded to gather handfuls of berries from the shrubs, placing them in a small rucksack.

They were all so hungry, but they knew they had to be careful and ration out what little they had before stocking up at the next village. After eating in silence, Alexander gave everyone the berries he'd harvested.

"Smash them, and wipe the pulpy sap on your face, neck, hands, and arms." Some of the men coughed from the strong odor it produced, and they grimaced while proceeding to follow his instructions.

"It will initially sting, but it's absolutely safe. This is the only protection you have between you and the jungle." He then grinned, "And don't forget to do your ears — just like your mother taught you when you were a child."

"Apply this every night!" Fitzgerald ordered. "And you will be responsible for gathering your *own* sack of berries before we leave in the morning so you have enough to last for at least a week!"

Darkness fell quickly and the night came to life with the chirping sounds of crickets and frogs blended into the background noise of the gurgling river that lazily flowed past. Occasionally, a curious call from a nocturnal animal rang out in the distance. Countless fireflies illuminated the jungle with their emerald green glow, and the bright stars above revealed the occasional bat swooping through the air catching mosquitos and other small insects.

The team kept the fires low. Drew poked at theirs, softly sending sparks up into the clear night sky. He and Kaci, sitting alone with their uncle, looked up in surprise when Jada walked up with a weary smile.

"Mind if I join you?"

"Of course! Anytime," Kaci perked up.

Almost everyone else had already fallen asleep, sprawled out on their thin bed rolls in utter exhaustion. Even Fitzgerald, who sat by a fire next to them, had his eyes closed with his back leaning against the stump of a tree.

"How are you holding up, young lady? How's your arm?"

"I'm doing okay; still a bit sore," Jada collapsed to the ground in fatigue and looked at Drew and Kaci. "I know that all of this is crazy, but Dad and I have actually been in worse situations, believe it or not. If we need supplies, he can get them to us by helicopter. He has the resources; it's just one call away on his SAT phone. But knowing him, he won't want to waste the time, because it would take a week to mobilize the manpower to get it done."

"I know," Alexander poked at the fire gently. "When your father sets his mind to something, he cannot be swayed, nor does he like to wait for help to get the job done."

Jada hesitated, listening to the thick ambiance of the rainforest, "What was he like back then? You know, when you both worked together."

Alexander's face softened. He set down his stick and stared into the fire, "He was a *good* man. Brilliant. Very resolved." He shook his head, chuckled, and continued quietly. "And very stubborn. Unfortunately, his passion for fame and glory got the best of him and corrupted his heart. He began cutting corners and pushing those around him too hard until he... got someone killed."

"So basically, he's never changed," she said sarcastically.

"It was an accident, of course, but it did send him down the wrong path."

"To where now he runs a criminal organization."

"True, but I still think there's hope for him."

"What? If he was caught, he'd be thrown in prison for life."

"That may be true, but no man is beyond redemption, Jada," Alexander replied softly.

"I don't know about that. He's a pretty bad man."

"God loves him. Jesus paid the penalty for all of the wicked things he's ever done on the Cross." His eyes shone. "I'm talking about eternal redemption, my dear. Your father will have to stand trial for the things he's done here on this earth, but before the Lord, there's still hope. I don't know if this means anything to you, but I pray for your father every single day — that God would save his soul before it's too late."

Jada's eyes moistened. She imagined what it'd be like to have a father who was a Christian like James Alexander. The man was always so kind and tender, yet still tough and charactered. A man's man. Her heart burned to know more about Jesus, but with her father sleeping within earshot, she decided to squelch the desire and change the conversation.

"Do you think we're going to make it, Professor?" she asked out of genuine curiosity.

He took off his glasses and cleaned the smudges around the rims with the handkerchief from his back pocket, "Honestly, hard to tell. We're following vague clues to the best of our ability in hopes of discovering a city that exists only in legend in an uncharted region of the Amazon Basin." He chuckled as he put his glasses back on, "I don't know how far we'll manage to get, but I'm thankful that no matter where we go, God is with us — even here deep in the jungle, far from modern civilization."

He waited for a moment to see how Jada would respond to him bringing up spiritual things again. When she instinctively leaned forward, he reached to retrieve his Bible. The golden cross emblazoned on the front of its leather cover glowed in the faint firelight.

"I want to share with you — with all three of you — a marvelous passage of Scripture that I believe will bring great comfort to your soul." He peered up over his glasses. "The promises of God are applicable to all seasons of life, not just when everything is going grand. But they are especially precious during the dark times of life because they illuminate our pathway."

"'Thy word is a lamp unto my feet, and a light unto my path,'" Drew quoted.

"Exactly. And lamps are most effective and appreciated in the darkness." He finished flipping through his Bible and placed his finger upon the verses he wished to read. "The Bible urges us in Psalm 37, 'Trust in the LORD, and do good; so shalt thou dwell in the land, and *verily thou shalt be fed. Delight thyself also in the LORD; and he shall give thee the desires of thine heart. Commit thy way unto the LORD; trust also in him; and he shall bring it to pass.'* What is the emphasis here?"

"To wait on God and glorify Him," Kaci answered, "And as we give things over to Him, we will experience His blessing upon our lives."

"Yes! And how wonderful this is! But it doesn't mean that life will be void of hardship and suffering. Regardless of what we face, God wants us to depend upon Him for every step we take. He may lead us to go beyond what is comfortable and enter a season like we're in right now that contains physical, mental, and emotional challenges. But He will never direct us to a place where He cannot protect us, provide for us, or empower us."

He flipped over a few pages to Psalm 23. Kaci watched Jada from the corner of her eye as her uncle quietly read the entire passage. The girl sat motionless, enthralled.

"Wow, that...that was so beautiful. I've never heard anything like that before."

Alexander was stunned by this, but Kaci and Drew exchanged knowing glances. They were aware, from talking with her before, of how little Jada actually knew about God and the Bible.

"I'm so thankful that we can share it with you," he gently responded. "I admire your awe for God's Word."

It was in this moment that Drew felt deep conviction.

How many times have I read this chapter or heard it in church before? He thought to himself. *Probably hundreds. And here's a girl that's not even saved finding greater joy in it than I ever have.* He turned his face away from the others for a moment so no one could see him fight back the tears welling up in his eyes. *God forgive me!*

"Several things are certain according to this passage, regardless of what is happening around us," Alexander continued. He used his fingers to count out the points. "God is going to take care of me in life or in death. He will lead me in the way that is best for me and supply all my needs. There's nothing that can separate me from Him, and He is closer than ever when I'm in danger. God's Word will stabilize me and strengthen me to remain consistent. God will refresh me amid even the hardest crisis, if I let Him. The Lord will fill me with joy and strength even in the presence of my adversaries —"

"Whoa, whoa, whoa, wait a second," Jada interrupted. "So you're telling me this is how you're able to keep such a level head when you're around my father?"

Alexander laughed, "Well, it's certainly been difficult, and there have been plenty of times along the way that frustration has gotten the best of me — but yes. In spite of how a person treats you, a child of God can always be happy in Christ. Why? Because our joy doesn't come from without, it comes from above. The Bible says in a different passage that *'the joy of the Lord is your strength.'*"

Jada turned to Drew and Kaci, "That's what you both told me a long time ago. Something about Jesus filling you with joy. I thought you were crazy, but I guess you were right. And I've seen it so much in all three of you. You're legit."

"We're far from perfect, but we try to be real," Kaci shyly smiled and tucked her hair behind her ears.

"Unfortunately, there *are* a lot of hypocrites in Christianity today," Alexander admitted. "And there's nothing that brings the Name of Christ greater shame than this. But I don't think a child of God would ever live hypocritically if they genuinely loved Him and allowed Biblical principles to be at the center of all they do — this keeps things God-centered and not man-centered." He paused for a moment then gestured with his Bible. "This Book, Jada, is the greatest treasure on earth. And in this Book, God shares with the world the greatest story ever told. It's the story of His love for us and how we can know with 100% certainty that when our life comes to an end we will go to Heaven and live with Him for all of eternity —"

"Yeah, if you believe in that stuff," a voice sarcastically chuckled in the darkness. Most of the campfires had reduced to smoldering piles of hot embers, but the glow from Fitzgerald's was just bright enough for the four to see the wild look in his eyes and the leering grin on his face. His hand rested on the butt of his holstered revolver.

"Trying to convert my daughter, eh? You —"

"Stop it, Dad," Jada cut in. "I was the one who brought it up. We were just making conversation."

The man ignored her. "You might need your Good Book, Jim, but keep your bloody religion to yourself!" His hand didn't move, his tone now threatening, "Go to bed — all of you. I don't want to hear another word!"

Although every muscle ached and exhaustion lay heavy on her eyelids, sleep did not come easily for Jada that night. Amidst the sounds of the jungle insects surrounding her, she tossed and turned as thoughts battled in her mind. All that Alexander had shared with her made sense, but she just wasn't convinced this Bible stuff was really worth giving her heart and life over to. Finally, after the doubts and worries had played ping-pong inside her mind for over an hour, sleep came.

⊗ ⊗ ⊗

Morning light dawned early, and everyone woke up stiff and sore from sleeping on the hard ground. Fitzgerald paced like a caged tiger, keeping a close eye on Alexander and the three young people as they ate their breakfast rations together. Once the team had refueled the boats and packed what meager belongings they had, they all made their way out onto the water and pushed further upriver.

The next couple of days passed by in a blur of monotonous water travel. Once in a while, the group was able to stop at small villages along the way to purchase gasoline, barter with the locals for dried fruits and jerked meats and learn what they could about the territory beyond. Their journey had now brought them so deep into the Amazon Basin that their map only showed an overview of the area with no markings of roads or settlements.

One afternoon, while the team enjoyed a fresh meal of steamed rice and flame-broiled fish at an open-air market, Fitzgerald approached a group of local fishermen and offered them large Brazilian bills in exchange for information. They happily obliged, congregating around the map Alexander spread out over a roughly-hewn table. Flies and mosquitoes buzzed around the natives' matted heads, at times even landing on their ears or nose, but this never phased them. They intently observed the map and were quickly able to show where the rest of the villages were located on their visitors' trek northward. Alexander carefully marked those spots and noted any other instructions they had for him about the terrain of the river and good locations for the team to make camp. As the conversation wound down, he noticed that the last marked village, Panjabi, was at least 40 miles from where the river fractured into other tributaries at the base of the mountain range. Furthermore, the men appeared to want to avoid talking about that entire region altogether.

Alexander decided to specifically circle it with his finger, "What's up here at the end of the river? Any settlements?"

The men exchanged glances, and no one spoke.

"Come on now, something's got to be up there. Our journey leads us through this region."

One of them hesitantly cleared his throat, "Those are dangerous waters, sir." He straightened his shoulders, as if summoning the courage to say, "Only fools go there. You will find nothing but pain!"

Alexander furrowed his brow deeply, confused. "What do you mean by that?" He motioned for Jada to show them a picture of the stone guide on the camera and asked if any of them had ever heard of a giant hole in the ground toward the river's end.

The men murmured among themselves, then snatched the money they were offered out of Fitzgerald's hand and began backing away nervously, "We do not wish to speak of this matter any further. If you must go, it is of your own choosing! But you have been warned."

They hastily disbanded and headed back to their dugout canoes, avoiding eye contact with any members of the team.

"That seemed odd," Alexander mentioned apprehensively as he

carefully studied the map. "They're definitely spooked about whatever lies before us."

Drew, Kaci, and Jada looked at each other with great concern.

Fitzgerald crossed his arms and smiled hungrily, "There's nothing more exhilarating than the thrill of the unknown!"

Alexander shook his head, wishing his old friend had at least a portion of common sense left in his insane mind. "Adrian, maybe we should take their caution seriously," he tried to reason.

Fitzgerald turned sharply, "You expect me to turn tail and run after all the progress we've made just because of a couple of superstitious natives?" He belted out a laugh that startled everyone walking past them.

"But they're familiar with the region and obviously know *something* that we don't!"

Like the flip of a switch, the man's mood changed. "Enough," he growled menacingly. "If you say *one more word* about turning back, I swear I will punch you in the mouth right where you stand!"

"Easy, Adrian," Alexander put up his hands. "I'm not trying to stop you. I'm just trying to help you see that we could be up against something very dangerous if we're not careful."

"It can't be worse than anything we've already faced."

Alexander knew there would be no reasoning with this man who was deliriously fixated on achieving his goal, no matter the cost. He quickly began folding up the map, nodding to the young people to pack up their few possessions and be ready to move.

As the team climbed back into their inflatables tethered to the crude wooden dock, Fitzgerald cranked the two-stroke engine on his boat. His eyes glowed with glee and sweat poured down his face, creased in a sinister smile. "Let fate throw its worst at us!" he bellowed to any and all who were listening. "Nothing and no one will stand in our way of finding Paititi!"

CHAPTER XIX

The sun spilled over the horizon just barely above the tree line and reflected its golden rays off the shimmering water. Pink river dolphins jumped playfully alongside the black commando rafts, clicking and splashing water to Kaci's delight as the team worked their way up the river. Jada smiled. She welcomed Kaci's joy in the little things; it was a refreshing deviation from the grueling monotony of their expedition. Little by little, their entourage made its way north, and now they could see a vast mountain range looming hazily off in the distance. The river seemed narrower now, the water thick and muddy. Jada slapped a mosquito who'd landed on her arm. Her dark clothing stuck to her skin as sweat continued its constant drip all over. She surreptitiously leaned down to sniff her shirt. *What I wouldn't give for a fresh pair of clothes right now,* she thought. *And a cold refreshing fruit smoothie. And...* she shook her head and sat up straighter, resisting the urge to slouch in despair. Wishing for things she knew she couldn't have was just a waste of time. She had to stay focused on the mission.

Kaci looked away from the dolphins and smiled at Jada, "At least *they're* happy to see us."

"What do you mean?" Drew turned to his sister.

"The natives in the last two villages have been anything but happy to see us. They almost seemed scared. Did you notice those little kids hiding behind their mothers, staring at us?" Kaci's expression was sad, wishing she could have stayed longer and befriended the sweet children. If she'd had some candy or gifts to share with them, that might have helped. But their rations were so low now, they had to conserve all they could if they had any hope of finishing their journey. They were able to restock some supplies and get more fuel in these villages, but they found no further leads surrounding the mystery of what lay before them at the end of the river.

Drew grinned, "They would love you, sis, if they could get to know you. You've got to remember, these villages are so far off the beaten path, they've probably never even seen a white person before."

Jada nodded, "Did you notice how sparse and small these villages are compared to the ones down south where we started our journey? No electricity or running water — such a simple way of living," she sighed. "I can't imagine living like that for my whole life."

Drew shrugged, "But it's all they've ever known. I don't think it bothers them like it would us."

He looked over at his uncle who sat next to Fitzgerald in the lead vessel and noticed the furrowed brow of concern etched across his face. He knew Uncle James had found it increasingly disturbing when everyone they spoke with the last two days looked at them strangely when they discovered where the team was headed. Anyone who saw a picture of the guide or was asked about the region quickly excused themselves and scurried away. Drew began to feel dread welling up in his stomach. With each passing hour, they moved ever closer to an unknown danger. He didn't mind danger as much when he knew what it was. But not knowing — that is what worried him the most. And seeing the raw apprehension in his uncle's eyes told him that whatever they were about to face might be something they would not survive.

Night would be upon them soon, and there was only one final village between them and the vast unknown. Thankfully, around the next long bend in the river, they saw a cluster of canoes lining the shore and the small fishing village of Panjabi coming into view. Fitzgerald let out a cheer and waved for his men to follow him as he began making his way to the dock. Curious onlookers ducked out of their huts and slowly gathered on the shoreline, but as soon as they saw the weapons that hung from the mercenaries' shoulders, they backed away nervously.

"I don't think they're excited to see us," Alexander commented under his breath.

"I don't care; we need answers, Jim. This is it!" the Fitzgerald muttered as he unzipped one of the pockets in his cargo vest. He pulled out a few valuable Peruvian and Brazilian bills and thrust them into the professor's hand.

"What am I supposed to do with this?" Alexander asked incredulously.

"Go work your magic, old chum!"

Alexander quickly folded the bills and placed them in his front shirt pocket, "I'm not comfortable with bribing people."

"Then don't think of it that way. Look at it as a bit of... *incentive* to get them to talk." Fitzgerald's dark eyes twinkled.

A small, broad-shouldered man with dark sun-weathered skin pushed his way through the crowd and gingerly walked toward them as they came up the dock and onto the marshy bank. The beads of his ceremonial necklace glittered in the last few rays of the evening sun, and his yellowed eyes matched the color of what few teeth he had remaining in his mouth. He glared from Alexander to Fitzgerald and then to Jada, Drew, and Kaci. When he spoke, he used the Quichuan tongue.

"I am Chief Huemac. Who are you? What brings you to our village? And why do you tread in these waters?" There were no pleasantries or warm greetings, just cold, rapid-fire questions with a bit of uncertainty.

"We are grateful to visit you and your people." Alexander kindly replied with a slight bow. "We have travelled a great distance to get here. My name is Professor James Alexander —"

"What do you want with us?"

"Good sir," he warmly smiled, "We are only looking for a place to eat and sleep for the night; and we also greatly need your guidance."

"Hmmm," the chieftain grunted, unphased by the professor's friendly manner.

"Give him the money, Jim! Give him the money!" Fitzgerald whispered out of the corner of his mouth.

Alexander hesitantly reached for the bills and held them up for all to see. "My friend here would like to generously compensate you for your time and any information you can give."

Huemac didn't move, showing no reaction to seeing the large amount of cash in Alexander's hand.

"What do you seek?"

"We are on an expedition toward the river's end and the regions beyond, and —"

"Then you are fools," the native spat.

Alexander tilted his head, "You're not the first person to tell us this."

"And you still have not listened? You must turn back now if you wish to keep your lives!"

"I'm afraid we cannot do this," he uneasily pressed on, nervously glancing to Fitzgerald out of the corner of his eye. "You see, we are in search of a stone face — a guide of sorts — to help us on our quest."

He then pointed over to Jada who stepped forward holding the camera for Huemac and those close enough to see the image on the large LED viewfinder.

Everyone immediately gasped and shrank backward, whispering the word *"Ch'utiy"* over and over in fear. Huemac spoke to his people in their local dialect, a language Alexander was completely unfamiliar with, making him feel lost for a moment.

"What does *'Ch'utiy'* mean? Is this the name you've given for this statue? You have seen it?"

Huemac barred his teeth, "Take your filthy money and go! You seek death, James Alexander, and we will have no part in it! Anyone who speaks of the *'Ch'utiy'* is mysteriously plagued by sickness or tragedy."

"I see what's going on here," Fitzgerald calmly walked forward and then suddenly screamed in a rage, "ENOUGH!" Everyone jumped. Children began to cry in fear, and the adults instinctively retreated from the man who seethed before them. "What is the matter with you people? Enough with the superstition trash! What are you hiding from me?"

"Adrian, stand down!" Alexander pulled him back by the arms. "They can't understand you, and you're only scaring everyone!"

"I don't care — I want answers! NOW!" he shoved the professor to the ground with a surge of extraordinary strength.

A few men from the back of the crowd stepped forward clutching machetes. Fitzgerald's men instantly leveled their AK-47s and pointed them at the people, threatening them in English not to move.

"Drop it! Drop it!" Beady Eyes ordered. Realizing their weapons did not stand a chance against the automatic firearms, the natives reluctantly let them fall to the ground and put their hands up.

"You must think carefully, Adrian," Alexander reasoned as he stood and laid his hand calmly on Fitzgerald's shoulder. "Are you really going to massacre these innocent people for information?"

"I'm done playing games, Jim," the man snarled, jerking himself away, his eyes and features dark and twisted. "You have no idea what I'm capable of or to what lengths I'll go to get what I want." He lifted his hand to signal his men to action.

"Dad, you've gone too far!" Jada lunged forward, doubling her fists and smashing them down repeatedly into her father's chest. "I'm done playing your games. You make me sick!"

"Traitor!" Fitzgerald snarled.

Before she could get out another word or land another blow, he grabbed her by the wrists and threw her back in his fury. She quickly crouched to her feet, knives drawn, ready to attack again when she heard a sliding bolt load behind her.

"Don't do it, Jada. I'll have to shoot." Girly gripped his machine gun, trying to steady himself. It was evident the big man was doing something he wished he didn't have to.

"How could you?" she snarled, her eyes blazing.

"I like ya, kid. But orders are orders. Bloodfists first, remember?"

"Bloodfists forever!" Goatee leered, stepping forward, training his gun on Alexander who now stood between Drew and Kaci.

"You've grown soft, my dear," her father declared. "Remember nothing and *no one* will stand in my way. Not even you!"

Fitzgerald slowly pulled out his revolver and paced back and forth, "By tomorrow, we will be at the end of this river, and we still have *no clue* what we're looking for! These people know about the guide; it's obvious by the way they reacted. I'm NOT leaving until we know *everything*. Somebody better start talking, Jim, or I'm going to start shooting people!" He leveled his handgun into the face of a young woman who hysterically whimpered, her eyes wide with fear, but dared not move.

He glared at Huemac. "NOW TALK!"

The chieftain dropped to his knees, pleading for mercy, and Alexander translated, "Please do not bring the curse of the *'Ch'utiy'* upon us!"

Fitzgerald fired a round from his revolver just past the woman's head and the bullet slammed into the wooden hut behind her. She fell to the ground in pure terror.

"No more lies! The next one *will not* miss!"

"You want to know? I will tell you. Please do not hurt my people!" Huemac stammered, breathing heavily. "The *Ch'utiy* are a large, savage tribe of man eaters who dwell in the mountains. They sacrifice people to your statue — that stone face of death! Very few have gone to the river's end and returned. Everyone who enters their waters dies!"

"That wasn't so hard, was it?" Fitzgerald grinned wickedly. He lowered his weapon, but his men did not. "So cannibals, eh? No problem — they will be no match for our weapons!"

Alexander confronted the delusional man, "*No problem? Did*

you hear what Huemac said? NO ONE comes out of there alive! We absolutely *cannot* proceed any further, Adrian. This is madness — it's a suicide mission!"

"Not really. It's sounds like it's either us or them. I choose us, don't you? So, we will kill these cannibals — kill them all if we must."

"I won't go along with this. You cannot just murder people!"

"It may not come to that, old chum." He patted the professor on the cheek and sneered, "Why don't you pray to your God that it doesn't? Besides," he pointed his revolver at Drew and Kaci, and Drew bravely stepped in front of his sister.

"Ah, how cute!" the man laughed. "Besides, you have no choice in the matter. Remember what happens if you don't comply?"

"Fine! Enough!"

"Now be a good chap and ask where we might be able to find these people in the mountains? Maybe the chief has heard of something? We find them, we find our next guide."

Alexander reluctantly obeyed, opening up their map and spreading it out on the ground. He profusely apologized to the chieftain for everything that had transpired, explaining how his hands were tied. He begged for any information about the tribe's whereabouts, but Huemac did not know any precise location. The fearful man hurriedly explained the layout of the region, wanting the men to leave his village as soon as possible. He circled a spot on the map with his finger as the best guess of where he assumed the tribe might be, from what he had heard rumored over the years.

"Good. Very good," Fitzgerald smiled. He motioned for his team to stand down, and as soon as he did, the villagers scattered away from the dock to the safety of their huts.

"It appears we have overstayed our welcome," he chuckled, sneering down at the chieftain still kneeling on the ground. "It is no matter; we have what we came for! Let us continue our journey just a bit further, shall we?"

Fitzgerald pushed the team hard that night, going much further than normal. The full moon shone brightly in the clear night sky, and he thought it best to take advantage of the extra visibility, traveling ever closer to the river's end. When he finally called for a stop, it was well past midnight. They had made it to the base of the low-lying mountains with their jungle-encrusted ridges and vine-covered trees.

As everyone stiffly crawled out of the inflatables, no one talked; they conserved what energy they had to set up camp. Besides their exhaustion, there was an awkwardness that hung thick among them after what Fitzgerald had done back at the village. Jada couldn't believe that her own father had ordered his men to keep her at bay. She shook her head, *I guess I'm a force to be reckoned with.* She was genuinely concerned, though, about her father's state of mind. She was no stranger to his brutality, but something was different about his personality now. Something about it was darker, brooding, and ominous. His life's pursuit was in reach, and his barbaric lust to get what he so desperately sought seemed to compel him to more dangerous things. Reckless things. Murderous things. He had even threated to have her killed, which she still could not wrap her mind around.

The team barely managed to build a couple of small fires before collapsing on the ground in utter exhaustion. Some of the men could care less if they were on their bed rolls or not.

"We're still miles away from the savages," Fitzgerald declared, looking at the map with his flashlight, "But I refuse to take any risks. I want three two-men teams guarding the boats and the camp at all times through the night. Break up into shifts, take turns, and get what sleep you can. I need you sharp to face whatever is before us tomorrow. We leave at 0800."

The men who received guard duty first groaned and slowly rose to their feet. Fumbling through his gear, Goatee grabbed supplies to put on a pot of coffee. As it warmed up, he stared blankly into the fire, more asleep than awake.

"I don't know if I can fall asleep with all those cannibals so close to us," Kaci shuddered from fatigue and dread. She snuggled deeper under her blanket, more for a feeling of safety than warmth.

"You need to rest, Kac," Drew mumbled with his eyes half shut. "We'll be fine. God will keep us safe." Within seconds, he was breathing heavily, sound asleep.

Alexander grinned wearily and rubbed his eyes. *"'The horse is prepared against the day of battle: but safety is of the LORD.'* It doesn't matter how prepared we are to face danger, at the end of the day, it's up to God to see us through." He yawned and rolled over on his mat. "Good night, my little monsters."

As he began to doze, the now familiar sounds of the vast jungle surrounding him, Alexander thought he heard something that didn't fit in with the rest of the cacophony. He roused ever so slightly from the brink of deep sleep. His ears tried to single out the sound, almost like a distant, faint beating of drums. But just as quickly as the sound had begun, it faded away again, and the jungle insects and breeze flowing through the tall trees quickly lulled him into a deep slumber.

Every time Kaci nodded off, she had startled herself awake imagining she heard something rustling beyond their small clearing in the overgrowth. Her heart beat fast and her eyes nervously bolted from left to right straining to see who or what was making the noise. Moments later, she would be dozing again.

This time, however, was different. She froze as she heard an unmistakable series of muffled cries and soft thuds. Then everything fell quiet — too quiet.

"W-w-who's there?" Kaci hoarsely whispered, shaking Drew's arm in an attempt to wake him up. To her dismay, he was deep in sleep and too groggy to respond.

Fitzgerald jerked awake with a gasp, instinctively reaching for his revolver. He looked over at her greatly annoyed.

"I thought I heard something, Mr. Fitzgerald! Something

terrible!" Her eyes were wide with dark circles of exhaustion sagging beneath them.

He sat still and listened carefully, noticing that certain portions of the jungle ambiance stopped for a brief moment and then resumed again. The hair on the back of his neck stood up. He smacked himself across the face to knock the grogginess out of his system and quietly radioed his men to check in. After a few moments of no one responding, his eyes narrowed with fear and he quickly jumped to his feet.

"Men, get up! We're under attack!"

He blasted his revolver blindly into the trees, and the gunshots made them all jump awake. Alexander bolted upright from his bed roll, grabbing his glasses as his heart raced at an electrifying speed. The others responded intuitively by cocking their automatic weapons and closing their ranks in a semi-circle arc with some kneeling and others standing.

Raindrops began pattering the ground around them, making it difficult to hear what was happening out in the jungle beyond.

The overgrowth rustled in random locations, causing Fitzgerald and his men to move their guns wildly back and forth. Some of the men shot fearfully into the dark, erupting the night into chaotic gunfire.

"HOLD!" Fitzgerald bellowed. "Don't waste any more ammunition until we see what we're dealing with!"

The drizzle turned into a downpour, and the team heard tribal war cries ring out into the night all around them, accompanied by drums.

Alexander knew they were in trouble. He backed toward Kaci and Drew, then put his arms around them.

A few natives darted out of the rainforest, weapons raised, with a blood-curdling war cry. Easily, Fitzgerald and his men raised their guns and mowed down each man as he came. This excited Drew and Kaci and for a moment, their hearts felt just a glimmer of hope.

"They're getting them, Uncle James!" Kaci breathed in nervous excitement.

Drew kept his eyes on the drama unfolding all around him. "We might just have a chance! I mean, how can spears beat out automatic weapons?" He raised his hand in a fist, silently cheering on Fitzgerald's men who were holding off the enemy as they trickled out of the brush a few at a time.

Jada drew her knives and took a poised fighter's stance. "Automatic weapons are only good if you have..."

Alexander woefully finished her thought, "...ammunition."

Just then, instead of the battering noise of gunshots, all was quiet. Cutting through the thickness of the sudden silence, there was the click of an empty chamber, followed by another, and another. One by one, the men realized in horror that they were out of rounds. The natives had planned for this all along, Alexander realized. They sacrificed just enough of their men to use up the last of the travelers' gunfire.

Fitzgerald called to his men, "We're out, boys! The rest of our rounds are back on the boats." He flipped his weapon upside down, gripping the barrel with his muscular hands. His eyes gleamed and he appeared excited by the fact that the odds were against him. "Fighting stances now! Find anything you can use in defense and hold your ground! We haven't come this far to go down without a fight!"

Suddenly, the silence of the forest was broken by the unified beating of tribal drums.

Jada's eyes were laser focused on the tree line and the enemy that gathered beyond. Her knuckles turned white as she gripped the handles of her knives. "Uh-oh. This is not good."

"Uncle James," Drew asked quietly, "what do we do?"

"We do the only thing we can do. We pray." Alexander sank to his knees in the dirt, the other two following his lead. He bowed his head and began praying softly.

"Really, Jim?" Fitzgerald mocked behind him. "Now? You think your God is going to swoop down and save us?" He laughed freakishly.

Alexander ignored him and focused all his energy on seeking

the Lord fervently and audibly. His praying became louder as his boldness grew. He gripped his niece and nephew and poured all his passion and faith into each word he spoke to his Father in Heaven. The war cries and drums grew closer. Fitzgerald growled instruction to his men, and Alexander sensed him, Jada, and the men left closing ranks. The truth was inevitable now. The natives were going to attack and kill them all, of that Alexander had no doubt. How had it come to this? Surely God did not lead them all this way just to be killed by a tribe of savages. He scrunched his eyes shut, willing them to stay closed.

"The battle is Yours, O Lord. We place our lives in Your omnipotent hands." His heart swelled with faith as the seconds ticked by and the drums continued to beat louder and faster. Any second now, the natives would attack. Any second...

"What in the world?" Fitzgerald exclaimed.

Alexander chanced a look and jumped. Emerging out of the brush, over 40 natives surrounded them. He noticed their spears rise in an even more threatening stance, as their menacing gaze pierced the night. Sweat shone off their muscled arms and legs. War paint eerily decorated their faces, with the darkest paint around their eyes, causing the whites to almost glow in the darkness.

Alexander bowed his head once again and whispered, "Oh God, please protect us."

He felt Drew and Kaci scrunched next to him, holding their breath, as he was. The silence was deafening. The attack was imminent. What were they waiting for? Suddenly, from all around them, gasps, whispered cries, and indistinguishable murmuring broke through the stillness. Alexander looked up, expecting to see a spear head in his face.

But he didn't.

Instead, he saw the natives backing slowly away, their eyes wide as they stared in awe and terror, not at Alexander or Fitzgerald and his men, but at something else. Alexander frowned, following their stunned gazes to the place beside him. There was nothing there but air. The natives let out a collective yell, some even hastily dropping their spears, and retreated into the jungle in pure fright. When the underbrush stopped rustling and the only thing they could hear was the steady stream of rain, Alexander climbed up from his knees, mystified.

Fitzgerald slowly holstered his gun at a loss of words, until he finally stated, "Well, that was unexpected."

"Yes, it was," Alexander agreed. What had the cannibals seen? He helped Drew and Kaci to their feet, ensuring they were okay. He hugged them both tightly and breathed a prayer of thanks to God. Were they out of danger? Probably not. But they were alive, for now. And for that, he was grateful.

CHAPTER XX

No one moved until the sounds of the night slowly returned to normal. Only then did they allow themselves to break formation and breathe a sigh of relief. Just as instantly as the rain had come, it stopped. The clouds slightly parted, allowing the moonlight to filter down and cast a glow on the jungle floor. Fitzgerald silently ordered Beady Eyes to take a couple of men and check on their boats and supplies.

"And bring back some ammo while you're at it," he hoarsely whispered after them, "So we'll be ready for those savages if they decide to return!"

"What about the others that are still out there?" Jada asked her father, sheathing her knives.

The man shrugged. "They're either dead or were taken. It's too dangerous to attempt a search until morning."

"You are ruthless," she replied coldly.

"They knew what they signed up for," he stated flatly, then straightened his shoulders and lifted his voice, "Isn't that right, men?"

They all nodded but avoided making eye contact with each other or Fitzgerald, just thankful they weren't the ones on patrol when the headhunters attacked.

After a few minutes, they'd stoked up a fire in the center of the camp to brightly illuminate the heavy undergrowth around them. There was no point in trying to keep a low profile anymore, since the natives knew they were here.

"Everything's still in one piece," Beady Eyes announced to the group, as he and his men returned with a couple of cases of ammunition. He then held up a crude feathered dart. "But the two who'd been guarding the supplies didn't make it. These were stuck into their necks."

"Poison," Alexander muttered as he carefully took the dart from the man and eyed it in the glow of the campfire. "The way these are crafted, they probably can be launched from at least 20 yards or more."

Drew looked around furtively and Kaci instinctively put her hand up to her neck, gulping hard.

Their uncle turned to Fitzgerald, "We'd better be on the lookout. If they do come back, they might take a quieter approach. We need to put our fire out so we're not sitting targets."

"You heard the man!" Fitzgerald bellowed. "Out with it until morning!"

Behind them, distant painful moans erupted from the jungle, startling everyone who was still on edge from their near-death experience just moments before. Something — or someone — crashed through the undergrowth, coming ever closer to the group huddled around the smoldering firepit. Fitzgerald drew his revolver to ready himself for whatever was about to appear, but he lowered it in shock when he saw in the moonlight one of his men from patrol stumble into camp and collapse to his knees.

It was Girly.

A broken-off spear stuck out of his chest. "I made it!" he rasped with a smile, revealing bloodied teeth. There were numerous lacerations on his arms and face and one eye was swollen shut.

Kaci buried her head into her brother's shoulder, and he protectively embraced her as he watched their uncle, Fitzgerald, and Jada rush forward to help the injured mercenary. Each man put their shoulder under one of Girly's arms and helped him get as comfortable as possible, leaning against a tree. The other members of the team slowly backed away, nodding in respect toward the big man as they reloaded the magazines of their AK-47s, wanting to give their friend space. They knew he didn't have long to live.

"They got the others, but they couldn't get me," Girly coughed harshly, spitting up more blood. "I fought them off. I fought them off the best I could, Fitz, and a couple of them stuck me to a tree with this spear. I... I must have passed out. When I woke up, I was all alone so I pulled myself off. I wasn't gonna be somebody's next meal!"

"If we pull this spear out of you now, old boy, you'll bleed out instantly," Fitzgerald stated softly.

The big man's eyes were wide with fear and distress, "I know. But I just wanted to see you all one last time, you know?" He lifted his voice the best he could, even though it was painful, "You all are...the only real family I got."

He put a hand on Jada's shoulder and smiled weakly, "You're a good kid. Take care of yourself and do good with your life. Not this stuff," his eyes weakly turned to glance at the group of mercenaries loading their weapons.

Fitzgerald stiffened and pursed his lips, biting his tongue to keep from spewing out the rebuke that rose within him. Instead he muttered, "You've always been one of my best. I'm going to miss you."

"Thank you, sir." Girly flickered his gaze over to Alexander, "I... did want to talk to you, Professor."

Gasping for each breath, he looked sharply at Jada and Fitzgerald.

"Alone."

For a few minutes, the two men spoke together in hushed tones; no one could hear their conversation above the incessant cricketing of the jungle. The glow from the moon and the stars above barely illuminated them, but as Drew watched, he saw his uncle put his hand on the big man's shoulder and they both bowed their heads. When the professor lifted his, Girly didn't move. He was gone.

Alexander slowly rose to his feet and approached the team.

Fitzgerald glanced up, "Dead?"

Alexander nodded, losing his fight against the tears that streamed down his cheeks.

"What was that all about?" the man pressed, somewhat annoyed.

"Nothing that you would understand, I'm sad to say. I do hope that someday you will."

Fitzgerald grunted and folded his arms. He commanded a few men to begin digging. "We'll bury him at first light," he announced.

No one slept the rest of the night and when the first streaks of sunlight appeared in the sky, Alexander pushed himself stiffly to his feet. He made his way to the graveside among the trees close to the riverbank, holding tightly to Drew and Kaci, who watched the ceremony with red-rimmed eyes. It was a quick, simple affair, over almost as fast as it had begun. A few of the men grabbed the shovels that stood off to the side and slowly began to fill in the unmarked hole. Their work was done in silence out of respect for their fallen comrade.

As the professor and the children walked back to camp, Kaci whispered, "First the landslide, now this... I can't stop thinking of how short life really is and how suddenly it can be over."

"For what is your life," Drew softly quoted from the Bible. *"It is even a vapour, that appeareth for a little time, and then vanisheth away."*

Alexander squeezed her a little tighter, "What matters most is what you do with the vapor that God has given to you."

Fitzgerald approached them just then, "We need to make plans to move on from here, old chum," he stated with his hands on his hips.

Alexander shook his head, a sad grin on his face, "Always thinking of yourself and furthering your agenda." He sighed, "One of your main men is not even buried yet, but let's do it. Let's press on for the cause," he punched the air sarcastically.

Fitzgerald opened his mouth to angrily reply, but before he could speak a word, he froze, his eyes gazing at something behind Alexander. Quickly, he drew his revolver.

The professor whirled around. Three natives stood at the edge of their camp looking quite different than they had the night before. Their faces had been washed clean and they held no weapons in their hands. The tall man in front with a broad chest looked Alexander in the eye, holding out his hands in a seemingly peaceful gesture. He said something, but Alexander wasn't sure of the dialect.

Fitzgerald growled menacingly as he stepped forward and leveled his gun at the three men, causing them to instinctively jump back in fear. Just as he was about to pull the trigger, Alexander gripped the barrel and forcefully lowered it to the ground.

"What are you doing, Jim!? Let go!" he exclaimed while trying to pry the weapon free.

"Stop! I think they come in peace!" He turned to the men and spoke in Quechuan, "Do you understand this tongue?"

"Little," the native stuttered with a thick accent. "No fight! Our chief want you come!" he gestured.

"How do we know you won't *eat* us?" Alexander asked slowly, enunciating his words and acting out the motions as if he was chomping meat off a bone.

The man laughed, "We no eat!" He pointed at them, "Men from Heavens. We die if we eat." The others nodded adamantly in agreement.

"See?" Alexander turned to Fitzgerald. "We'll be fine," he said with a lop-sided grin as he translated the men's words.

Fitzgerald hesitantly holstered his handgun, "I don't know about this, Jim. It could be a trap!"

"Possibly, but I believe they're sincere. Look! They didn't even bring any weapons. They're putting themselves at our mercy — a universal sign of good faith."

"Good faith," Fitzgerald spat. "I should kill them right where they stand after what they did to my men!"

"No," Alexander stated flatly. "No, you won't. Or you'd bring the whole village down on us, and then we'd *most certainly* be dead. They make sacrifices to our guide, remember? This village is the key to our next clue." He waved for Drew and Kaci to join him, and together they quickly followed the natives into the dense overgrowth.

Fitzgerald exhaled in frustration and ordered half of his men to stay put.

"Be on high alert! Two clicks from the radio means 'come in hot and shoot anything that moves,' understood?"

"Yes sir!" several men responded and vigorously crossed their fists in front of them in loyalty to their leader.

Fitzgerald turned to his daughter, "You will stay here."

She crossed her arms and was about to protest when he firmly put up his hand.

"Don't argue with me! My mind is made up. I know we have our differences, but if we need help, there is *no one* I trust more than you, my dear." He momentarily caressed her cheek with his hand. "You'll know how to find me in case I need you."

Without another word he spun on his heels and led the rest of his men forward after Alexander and the others, leaving her dumbfounded.

"Thanks for the... compliment?" she called out after him, bewildered. He didn't respond. *He's never this nice to me.* Shivering involuntarily, she wondered if that was some sort of attempt at saying goodbye.

Along the way, Fitzgerald carefully broke small twigs about eye level —leaving a trail just as he'd taught Jada when she was a little girl. His heart pounded as he tramped through the jungle. He'd gone up against his fair share of impossible odds — hired killers, factions of the military, drug cartels. But never before had he faced an entire village of cannibals, people that actually wanted him dead for food. He felt the hair rising on the back of his neck. *How could Jim and his 'little monsters' be so calm while facing such an adversary? How are we even still alive?* He regretted now his decision to be so headstrong, leading his team into this dangerous territory by night. But he just couldn't help it. His heart burned to find his beloved city. Whenever he closed his eyes, he could imagine it. Whenever he slept, he dreamed about it.

He knew he had his reckless moments, but everyone was absolutely worth it. They were so close now, he could feel it.

He hastened his steps forward through the thick vegetation, swatting at pesky flies that buzzed around his face. He could hear the growing sound of tribal drums and looked over his shoulder at his men. Their eyes were wide with apprehension and exhilaration.

"Steady on, boys. Remember, we have the firepower! For Paititi!"

"Paititi!" they replied in scattered unison.

Once they caught up with the others, they noticed the narrow trail wove further inland toward the mountain. It finally gave way to a wider grassy lane surrounded by mossy vines webbing down from tall jungle trees on either side. Thick wooden spikes also lined the pathway every few yards with human skulls atop them. Very little daylight penetrated the thick rainforest, but there was just enough to give a dull overcast glow that matched the somberness of the group. Ahead was a stone archway that stood two stories tall. This served as the only entrance or exit to the headhunters' village nestled in a high rocky gorge that dead-ended at the base of the mountain.

Kaci squeezed her brother's arm extra tight as the empty skull eye sockets seemed to stare right through her.

"This place gives me the creeps!" she shuddered.

"You can undoubtedly feel the spiritual darkness. Be careful not to make any sudden movements, team," Alexander warned as they passed through the archway.

The village now sprawled before them among low-lying ferns on a slightly uphill incline. Dilapidated huts circled out from what appeared to be a temple roughly hewn into the mountain's stone wall. Crude carvings resembling that of the guide were apparent on various smaller rock outcroppings that naturally jutted up throughout the settlement.

The broad-chested native who had led them gestured, "Our chief come!" Then he bid them to follow him a bit further into the village.

A crowd of painted warriors strode before them two-by-two with their large spears gripped in both hands centered before their chests. Their faces were creased with menacing glares and all of them growled a low hum. Behind them were a dozen shamans loudly beating in unison on animal-skinned bongos strapped to their sides. Bringing up the rear of the entourage were four muscular men, each bearing a wooden pole protruding from one of the corners of what appeared to be a throne of some sort. The carriage-like structure was veiled on all sides by hanging strings of colorful beads that jingled incessantly with the movement of the walking men.

"Must be the village chief," Alexander whispered, wishing he could see who was hidden behind the wall of beads.

"I don't like this, Jim!" Fitzgerald hooked his thumb on his belt close to his gun. "Look behind us!"

Alexander glanced over his shoulder and noticed other warriors had emerged from the jungle, surrounding them in a wide arc with their spears lowered, cutting off any chance of escape.

Keeping his right hand on his gun, Fitzgerald grabbed Alexander's arm with the other. "If this thing goes sideways, I *will* shoot every last one of them! You hear me?"

"I don't believe it will come to that. Be patient," the professor replied coolly, removing his arm from the man's grasp. "And whatever you do — no sudden moves of aggression. And please keep your hand off your revolver!"

One of the lead shamans in the procession let out a high-pitched yell, causing the natives to part in cadence, turn face and halt. They slammed their spears into the ground and leaned them forward with a guttural shout. As soon as the chief's throne was reverently placed on the ground, the drumming ceased. Only the spine-chilling growls emanating from the warriors continued. The chief's withered hand parted the beads and he slowly rose, causing the shamans and escorts around him to immediately kneel with their heads bowed.

He was a small, hunched-over old man with piercing dark eyes that were almost black. He was clothed with ceremonial robes and a beaded necklace with a small stone pendant on the end shaped like the guide. Thin strands of scraggly white hair hung from his balding head. He pointed a bony finger from Alexander to Fitzgerald and motioned for them to approach him.

"Follow my lead," Alexander whispered out of the corner of his mouth.

Carefully walking down the flanked row of guards, they humbly approached the chieftain and took turns bowing, introducing themselves.

"I am Amuta, chief of the Ch'utiy. So, you are the men who travel with the beings of light?" his raspy voice croaked in perfect Quechuan.

"Beings of light?" Alexander blinked and gave him a confused glance. "I'm not sure I understand."

"This is what my men speak of, James Alexander. Last night in the darkness they saw bright and strong warriors floating among you and standing around you. They held flaming swords and wore armor that gleamed as the noonday sun."

"Angels," Alexander said in awe. "They saw angels?"

"Is that what you call them?"

"We have read about the messengers and warriors of God before, in His Holy Word, the Bible. I have mine right here," Alexander calmly proceeded to withdraw his worn Bible from the leather pouch at his hip.

Fitzgerald fumed. "What is the meaning of this?" he hissed. "What are you doing with that Book?"

Alexander firmly turned to him, "You may not believe this — but last night, it seems God supernaturally answered our prayers."

Fitzgerald continued to seethe, clearly wanting to move on to talk of the guide and not spiritual matters.

Alexander, ignoring the man's impatience, turned back to the chieftain. "This Book is filled with the words of the God Who made the sky, the sun, the moon, the stars, and the earth. He has made everything you see. I can't summon His angels at will. It is only by His mercy that we have experienced such Divine protection. This has happened to others throughout history, and these Heavenly beings have been described by those who saw them in the same way you did."

Amuta seemed to accept his answer, looking in awe at the small book in Alexander's hands. He then bowed deeply before looking reverently up into the professor's eyes. "If your God has sent His mighty warriors to protect you, we will not harm you. We seek no battle with Him or His army. You and your team are safe in our midst."

His blackened eyes twinkled with a dark energy and he muttered, "Though you all would make a fine feast."

Alexander shuddered at the thought, realizing the man was serious.

"But if we tried to kill you, I fear your God would destroy us all with His 'angels,' as you call them."

He then turned to his men and spoke commands to them in their tribal tongue. They nodded and bowed. The aged leader turned again to Alexander with arms outstretched. "Whatever you desire, we will do, because you are chosen men. We place ourselves in your service."

Alexander proceeded to holster his Bible, then shared with him the vague details of their expedition and how the clues they'd followed brought them here. The chief was visibly shocked when he discovered there were other stone guides throughout the vast jungle like their own. Alexander carefully asked about their temple, sharing his desire to be allowed to see inside. He held his breath, knowing what a risk he took making such an invasive request. To his relief, Amuta nodded and bowed again.

"Our temple is sacred to us, James Alexander. Very few of our people are even allowed to enter, and never outsiders. But I will gladly show you what you wish to see if it keeps your God and His shining warriors happy."

The elderly man hobbled back to his portable throne and sat down heavily, then quietly clapped his hands together. Immediately, the throne bearers resumed their positions, lifting their leader once again high into the air. In unison, the entire procession began to make their way to the temple.

The warriors that had gathered around the village entrance lowered their spears in a non-threatening pose and marched forward, constraining the others to join up with Alexander and Fitzgerald.

As the team walked together, they huddled around the professor and became spellbound as they listened to him share what he'd discovered.

"Angels!" Drew grinned from ear to ear and pumped his fists in excitement.

"I can't wait to tell Jada all about this!" Kaci squealed with delight, clapping her hands together.

Fitzgerald was at a loss for words, and Beady Eyes rubbed his jaw, deep in thought. The rest clenched their AK-47s not knowing how to respond, the chief's testimony of a Divine miracle clearly making a profound impact on them.

Alexander straightened his shoulders and declared boldly, "Many of you have laughed at us and thought we were fools for believing in God and praying often, but it's only because of His great mercy that we're not all dead right now. I hope that what we've experienced will change your life and change your perspective about the Lord. He is real, and His Word is true. If any of you have any questions about God, and how He wants to have a personal relationship with you, I would be more than happy to talk with you about it."

"All right," Fitzgerald raised his hands and cut him off. "Enough! You've proven your point. But why couldn't *we* see the angels?"

The professor shook his head, "I don't know if I really have an answer for you, Adrian. The Bible calls them *'angels unawares,'* which implies the people surrounded by Heavenly beings are unaware that they are there."

He glanced around at the procession of cannibals, humming

their chants in unison and beating their drums to the same steady cadence. Many of the villagers now stood in the doorways of their huts and lined the streets. Several of them had bone piercings through their noses and ears with streaks of paint across their faces.

"The demonic oppression here, I fear, is so very heavy. The veil between the earthly and spiritual, satanic even, could be very thin. So thin, that for a short moment, these natives could actually glimpse through the veil and see some of the spiritual warfare raging last night. I have heard stories of these sightings, though they are rare. And every description of angels in cases like this throughout history has been the same."

Kaci's eyes lit up, "Which means they couldn't *possibly* be lying or making it up, right?"

Drew smiled, "Yeah, it's not like these people have the internet or old books to read to collaborate their story."

Alexander chuckled. "Exactly right," he declared. "I believe God allowed that veil to be lifted and those angels to be visible. He protected us, and for that, we should forever be thankful."

The young people nodded while Fitzgerald obnoxiously rolled his eyes with a grunt. The procession was now coming to a halt just a few yards from the door to the temple, crudely carved into the side of the mountain with Incan petroglyphs all around its border. The chief's throne was lowered, and the old man slowly disembarked. He began to walk toward the opening, then turned, looked at Alexander, and beckoned him to join.

Hastily stepping to the chief's side, the professor asked, "Could my niece and nephew also come with me, kind sir?" With Fitzgerald's erratic, violent tendencies, Alexander vowed he would never again leave Drew and Kaci out of his sight if he could help it.

Amuta faced forward with a furrowed brow. "No, James Alexander. Only you. This is not a place for young ones or those who may not respect our ways."

Alexander's shoulders slumped, but he knew better than to argue with a cannibal who was feeling merciful at the moment. One wrong move and they could all be dinner. He turned and gestured that the team had to stay behind. Drew and Kaci looked at him with worried expressions, not liking the idea of standing around with murderers, thieves and cannibals while their protector disappeared into the mouth of a mountain, but they knew they had no choice. They held each other's hand, trusting in the Lord.

Fitzgerald took a few angry steps forward, pushing through his men, and huffed, "What is the meaning of this, Jim? Are you telling me even *I* cannot join you in the temple? Does this man not realize who I am?"

Alexander held out his hand and tried to signal with his eyes that now was *not* the time to be stubborn. "He only trusts me, Adrian. I will go in, get the information we need, and be back out in no time. Please calm down, or you might ruin our chances of me seeing the guide at all!"

Fitzgerald growled but nodded and stepped back to join his men.

"Centuries ago, my people built our village around this," the chief explained to Alexander, as they walked through the doorway, "Believing it was the resting place for the face of the earth. As nature gave us life, we sacrificed some of our own to sustain this balance."

The inside of the temple was simple, being one large room with its ceiling vaulting high overhead into a smooth dome. A couple natives went ahead of them to light torches that lined the walls. In the flickering torchlight, Alexander noticed that the floor sloped downward from all directions toward the center of the room. Various Incan engravings adorned the walls and three symmetrically-placed rock slabs served as altars. He suppressed a wave of nausea that instantly hit him as he saw copious amounts of blood stains saturating the stone and even running down onto the floor he walked on. *These people are loved by God,* he reminded himself. *Created in His image. Jesus died for them, no matter how barbaric they are. Lord, help me see them as You do, with compassion and love.* Feeling the queasiness subside, he took a deep breath in and a brave step forward.

CHAPTER XXI

Alexander followed Amuta down the sloping floor of the temple, toward a gaping hole in the ground in the middle of the circular room. As he approached the edge and looked inside, he realized it was a cylindrical pit, about 30 feet deep, hewn out of the rock a very long time ago.

Chief Amuta spoke reverently, pointing down, "That, James Alexander, is our god."

Alexander peered into the darkness. There, gleaming up at him from the shadows were two aqua-colored eyes.

"The next guide," he whispered to himself. "Just like the clue described: a gaping mouth at river's end."

The chief eyed the professor, "You say there are others like this?"

"Many others," Alexander nodded adamantly, praying that God could use him somehow to pull these people out of spiritual darkness. Perhaps the knowledge of the other guides would prove that their "god" was not really a god after all. "The statues were established by the remnants of an old empire hundreds of years ago to point travelers toward a forgotten city. Do you mind if I get a better view?"

Amuta beckoned one of his men to bring a torch. "We have come this far; I will allow you to descend."

Alexander bowed in gratitude, accepted the light, and carefully began to make his way down the narrow steps carved out of the side of the rock. The torch flickered onto the floor of the pit, revealing hundreds of crushed and fragmented human bones strewn everywhere. Was it just his imagination, or was it colder down here? He could almost sense a dark, evil presence surrounding him in the air moving about. He shuddered, quoting Scripture and praying for faith and strength, and then kept going. When he reached the bottom, he warily made his way over to the guide, trying his best to ignore the crunching sound under his feet. He set his torch in a holder on the stone pedestal next to the statue.

Realizing he had never even thought to grab the camera before they came all this way, he pulled out the small notebook from his pocket and began taking careful notes.

First, he took notice of the aqua-colored stones. *Eyes point east,* he wrote. He saw a carved depiction of a waterfall on the statue's forehead. *Fascinating! This image is similar to what is on our ancient map!* He quickly sketched it out and then let his eyes scan further as he walked around the guide. *Aha. The Incan symbols.* He copied all of them for translation later. Under the giant face's chin was the final clue, again carved in Latin. He wrote each word in his notebook. Hastily scanning the surface one last time to make sure he hadn't missed anything, Alexander withdrew his torch and hurried back up the steps, eager to escape the suffocating spiritual darkness of this place.

"Did you find what you were looking for?" Amuta asked with genuine curiosity.

"Yes. I thank you for allowing me a closer look. What I found will greatly help us on our journey!" Alexander nodded, as he passed along his light to one of the natives who stood beside their leader.

"I've always wondered what those symbols meant," the old man scratched his chin. "Maybe our god is just a face of stone after all. Nothing more," he quietly muttered to himself, following the professor out into the light of day.

Alexander paused, taking a beautiful breath of fresh jungle air, then made his way over to Fitzgerald and the team while the chief spoke to his men in their tribal dialect.

"You're back!" Kaci exclaimed and gave him a hug, relief showing on her face.

"Mission accomplished," he said with a lop-sided grin and two thumbs up.

Fitzgerald slapped him heartily on the back, "Glad to see you still in one piece, old chum! Did you retrieve the eyes?"

"What? No. There was absolutely *no way* that I could do that and risk all of our lives," he pulled out his small notebook, "As it is I didn't have the camera so I had to sketch and jot everything down."

From behind, Chief Amuta gently grabbed hold of Alexander's sleeve and interrupted. "I have many questions for you, James Alexander. Might I convince you and your people to join my village for dinner? We have prepared a feast for you in hopes to please your God and his shining warriors."

Alexander paused, and, noticing the apprehension in his eyes, the chief snapped his finger and uttered a guttural command to his warriors. The men looked at him confused, and he spoke to them again more firmly with his old gravelly voice. They hesitated but then one by one they began to walk up to Alexander and Fitzgerald and drop their spears to the ground at their feet.

"Please, James Alexander, we mean you no harm," Amuta pleaded gently.

The team stood in awe, shocked by the change in these tribal people — one day about to stab them with spears and the next eager to show them kind hospitality.

"What is the meaning of this?" Fitzgerald demanded.

Alexander put his notebook away and placed his arms around Drew and Kaci's shoulders as they watched the long procession slowly walk past them.

"You're witnessing another miracle of God," He warmly reflected and then proceeded to explain the situation.

"So they want to feed us, eh?" Fitzgerald stroked his scraggly beard. "They're probably just fattening us up for the kill. Such is the way of cannibals, Jim."

"Some cannibals, perhaps," the professor agreed. "But I believe what we're beholding here is genuine. Chief Amuta is quite shaken by what he's discovered through us and desires to know more. This could be a turning point for Ch'utiy, Adrian, and we need to help these people while we can. Think of it!" his eyes glistened with excitement. "We could be instrumental in saving this entire region from cannibalism and terror!"

"I couldn't care less about that," Fitzgerald snapped. "As long as *we're* not the ones being eaten, of course. But I'm tired of constantly stalling with your grandiose plans of humanitarianism. Let's get on with it. You have our next clue! We should leave *now*."

Alexander put his hands on his hips. "And go where, pray tell? Sure, I have the clues from the guide, but I have no idea what our next step is. Let's catch our breath this afternoon and get a good night of sleep. We all need it."

The mercenaries around them fidgeted and mumbled in agreement.

"You're siding with *him* now?" Fitzgerald glared.

Beady Eyes cleared his throat and stepped forward, "We could really use the rest, boss, and a nice hot meal."

"Besides," Drew interjected, "Maybe the chief could give my uncle some insight of the area and help us know best how to go forward."

"Be quiet, boy," the big man spat, his eyes ablaze. "Nobody asked for your opinion." He then heavily sighed and put up his hands in resignation, "All right, fine, but we leave at first light!"

He turned to Beady Eyes, "Radio Jada and the others to join us. She'll know how to find us."

As the team, surrounded by natives, now slowly followed Chief Amuta's carriage back to the village, Fitzgerald muttered, "Keep your guard up, men. No matter what the professor thinks, I don't trust these people for an instant."

Discreetly clicking off the safeties on their AK-47s, the men gently laid their weapons next to them as they sat down on giant Taro leaves spread out evenly in the wide clearing at the heart of the village.

Over the next hour, the tribe performed numerous rituals and entertained their audience with special stunts and competitions. Chief Amuta, who now sat on a wooden throne up on a small platform under a thatched roof awning, clapped with delight as he watched his people. Kaci especially enjoyed the children's relay races, and Drew found dart blowing the most fascinating as men vied to see who could hit the bullseye on a crude wooden target from several yards away.

In the midst of these activities, Jada and her men were escorted into the village square by four guards. She sat down next to Kaci in complete surprise at how friendly this hostile tribe had become.

"Wow, what did I miss?"

With giddy excitement, Kaci told her everything, and Jada shook her head in utter amazement. *Angels?* She thought to herself. *Angels are real?*

As the ceremony came to an end, ladies in ornate garb, with multi-colored beads strung about their necks and feathers in their hair, passed out large wooden bowls filled with steaming hot vegetable goat stew, served with candied plantains on the side.

"How delicious!" Fitzgerald exclaimed, then flashed a smile. "But are we sure this is goat?"

Alexander shook his head at Adrian's poor choice of humor and pulled out his notebook to go over what he'd discovered in the mountain temple.

"Incan symbols and Latin just like all the other guides before?" Drew asked, looking over his uncle's shoulder.

The professor nodded, deep in thought. "The Latin here is pretty easy. *'Inter iuga post velum requiescit anima tacita.'*"

"*'Take heed to join through what in strength abides,'*" Fitzgerald translated, then shrugged. "Again, not sure what that refers to. But it must serve some significance to our quest nonetheless."

"Right," Alexander agreed. He pointed out the Incan symbols he'd drawn in subsequent order like he had found them on the statue. "A rough translation would be, *'Behind the veil amid the peaks rests the silent soul.'"*

"Is that a sketch of a waterfall, Uncle James?" Kaci gestured.

"Yes. I found it fascinating that on the forehead of the statue was a carving of a waterfall similar to what is on our ancient map!"

"Huh!" Jada interjected. *"'Behind the veil'*...like as in a waterfall? Maybe our next guide is in the rock behind it!"

"I bet you're right," Kaci smiled.

"And *'amid the peaks,'*" Drew nodded and stated matter-of-factly, "It's gotta mean that the waterfall is tucked away in the middle of the mountains."

Alexander chuckled, "You all are brilliant! That is exactly what I was thinking!"

"So with the eyes pointing east," Fitzgerald scratched his jaw, "we must head out at once!"

Alexander slowly stood. "Let me speak with Chief Amatu first. He might know something that could help us on our journey." He turned to Drew and Kaci, "I need your prayers!"

Fitzgerald grunted and folded his arms as Alexander made his way over to Amatu, who was being fed his meal by servants. He bowed after being warmly greeted by the chieftain, then sat Indian style in front of the man's throne.

The two of them communed together for over half an hour. No one paid attention to Fitzgerald loudly yawning, sighing, and clearing his throat with impatience. Drew and Kaci watched carefully in a spirit of prayer, asking God to give their uncle wisdom as he interacted with the cannibal leader and answered his numerous questions. A couple of times, Alexander pulled out his Bible and held it reverently to emphasis a spiritual truth in his response. The chief, meanwhile, rubbed his jaw as he mulled over everything he heard. Incredibly, the darkness on his countenance and in his eyes seemed to dissipate the more Alexander emphasized the truths of God's Word.

"You've got to be kidding me," Fitzgerald muttered under his breath.

"What's the problem?" Drew confronted him quietly, but he

had an idea of what was bothering the man.

Fitzgerald sharply glanced at him and mocked quietly, "Your uncle and his righteous crusade, of course. Why is he *always* doing this?"

"If you mean, why is he always looking for an opportunity to tell people about Jesus," Drew boldly replied in a whisper, "it's because he loves people like God does and wants to give them hope. The world needs Jesus, Mr. Fitzgerald, and you need Him, too." He looked around at the others of the team that were huddled close to him. "All of you do."

For a moment, Drew thought he was going to get smacked across the side of the head as the big man stared at him, sitting motionless, his right eye twitching. But after a few seconds, he merely let out a loud, irritated sigh and mumbled something to himself, uneasily fidgeting with his medallion.

Kaci grabbed hold of Drew's arm and pointed, "Look!"

Alexander was now on his knees, humbly bowing before the chief as Amuta tenderly removed the woven beaded necklace with a small carved totem of the stone guide on the end of it from around his neck. He held it out to the professor, and as Alexander respectfully reached for it, the chief kept it firmly in his grasp, both men holding on to it together for a moment. Their eyes locked, and the chief solemnly uttered something that moved Alexander to tears. The professor nodded adamantly and bowed again.

He returned to the others with a look of joy beaming on his face.

Drew's face lit up. "You told him about Jesus, didn't you?"

Alexander chuckled. "I did. I couldn't just leave this village without trying to share the truth of the Gospel with these blinded people." He fingered the colorful beads as he slowly placed them inside his waist pouch.

"Why did he give you his necklace, Uncle James?" Kaci asked, bewildered.

Alexander smiled and wiped a tear from his cheek. "The chief has so many questions, too many for me to answer in our short time here. He asked if someone could come back someday and tell them more about God and His Word." He set his hand on the pouch. "Amuta gave me this necklace and told me to give it to the one I chose to return to their village. When they see this, they'll know the man can be trusted because he came from me."

"I'm so glad he was open to the truth you shared with him," Kaci said.

Fitzgerald, who had walked over to talk with his men, approached Alexander's side. "I see you've returned," he commented impatiently. "I hope you've gotten actual answers and haven't wasted our time with more religious nonsense."

Alexander gave him a hard look, then took off his glasses and wiped his eyes. He paused for a moment, pulling out his handkerchief and clearing the moisture that had gathered on the rims from his tears.

"Well?"

"He shared that our next destination is indeed eastward."

"Very good! How long will it take? Did he say?"

"Five days or so."

Fitzgerald pursed his lips, "But that's by canoe. We could make it in two or three at the most!" He clapped his hands together in glee. "We're so close, I can *feel* it!"

Alexander put his glasses back on and shoved his handkerchief away into his pocket. "But we must be careful. He *did* warn us."

Jada rolled her eyes and crossed her arms, "Of course he did. Everything about this journey has been one ominous warning after another."

A lop-sided grin spread across the professor's face, "True. He said it was a place of — get this — dark metal birds that fly across the region and spit fire upon anyone who dares enter."

Drew furrowed his brow, "That sounds very strange."

"You mean that sounds very *ridiculous!*" Fitzgerald laughed.

"Maybe he's talking about airplanes," Jada thought aloud.

"But this far out into the jungle?" Kaci speculated. "There's *no way* that could be possible, is there?"

When the professor didn't respond, everyone turned to look at him.

"Uncle James?"

"Hmmm? Sorry," he blinked his way out of deep concentration. "I was thinking of an old hunch I've had for quite some time."

"Out with it, man!" Fitzgerald blurted, but Alexander waved him off and shook his head.

"It is highly unlikely. However, I would advise that we do heed the chief's warning and proceed with caution."

CHAPTER XXII

As the morning sun began to spill its first rays through the jungle trees, coffee boiled in a metal teapot suspended over a low-lying fire and filled the air with its delicious aroma. Drew and Kaci threw off their thin blankets and sat up on their bed rolls to find that the men were already milling about, packing their gear and supplies.

"Rise and shine, sleepy heads," Jada playfully teased, sitting close by, munching on a piece of dried mango and sharpening her knives. She chuckled. "If I had the camera right now, I would so take your picture."

Kaci covered her freckled face with both her hands, still groggily trying to wake up.

Drew stretched for a moment, then darted his eyes mischievously toward his sister, "She's right. Your hair — yikes!"

Kaci tossed her small, flattened pillow at his face and he laughed when he caught it and gently lobbed it back to her. She smiled and yawned, "For that, you get to put away my bed roll."

Drew grinned broadly, "Fair enough, little sis."

She took out the hairbrush from her backpack and began the attempt at smoothing out her long, flowing brown hair that now held streaks of blonde from the summer sun. She turned to Jada, "Do you think we're almost there?"

"Your uncle and my father believe so," she muttered and then shrugged. "But who really knows?"

Drew tightened one of the strings around the rolled-up canvas-covered foam mat, "I think there's a reason that only six stone guides are sketched on the map. It has to be a clue."

"I hope so," Jada sighed. "I want to be done with this whole thing."

"You and me both," Kaci agreed as she continued to comb through the tangled mess she had somehow created from her long night of much-needed sleep. She finally gave up and threw her hair up in a top knot. *What I wouldn't give for a hot shower and some shampoo and conditioner!*

Drew finished gathering their bed rolls and with one in each hand, he stood. "I'll be back. I'm gonna see if Uncle James needs anything!"

After dropping their belongings in the boat, Drew made his way to the make-shift table Alexander was bent over as he studied the maps intently. Drew hugged him with one arm around his shoulders, "Good morning, Uncle James. How's it looking? Do you know where we're headed from here?"

The professor removed his glasses and rubbed his bleary eyes. "I know the general direction, yes, but with so many tributaries this far into the jungle, I'm worried we could make a wrong turn and get ourselves really lost."

"Lost? Ha!" Fitzgerald sauntered up to them, a toothpick between his teeth. "How does your little Book say it? '*O ye of little faith*'?" He clapped the man over the shoulders and gave a squeeze. Alexander remained bent over the table, and Drew saw him grimace, holding back words he wished he could say to Fitzgerald's slander of God's Word.

The Scotsman continued, "Can you not see? We have been chosen by the Universe, Jim! We've made it this far. The odds are in our favor! All the forces of the earth are guiding us, pushing us, calling us to finish our quest. I am absolutely convinced that they will lead us to Paititi!"

Before Alexander could respond, Fitzgerald turned to answer a call on his walkie. After barking orders to the man on the other end, he signed off and clipped it back onto his belt. As he spun back around to face Drew and Alexander, the professor stood upright and looked into the eyes of his old friend.

"Unlike you, Adrian, I have chosen to place my faith in the God Who rules over nature, the earth, the skies, the seas, even over your beloved Paititi. We have made it this far by *His* leading, protecting hand and nothing more. If you cannot see that by now, you are even more blind than I thought." He began to roll up the maps and looked over to Drew. "We'll be leaving soon. Let's go see if there's anything we can do to help load the last few things into the boats."

With his arm over the boy's shoulder, they walked down to the shore together, leaving Fitzgerald standing there shaking his head and chuckling to himself. *I'll show them. I'll show all of them when I finally reach Paititi and become the richest man in the world. And I'll be immortal to enjoy my riches forever. They'll see that I was right all along!* He picked up the medallion hanging around his neck and kissed it reverently before heading off to find Jada and finalize the preparations for departure.

As Alexander and Drew approached the bank where Adrian's men scurried about, they spotted a half dozen *Ch'utiy* warriors paddling toward them from around the small bend in the river.

"Look!" Drew pointed into the distance.

To their surprise, the natives came ashore and pulled out from their dugout canoes small wooden crates filled with fresh fruit, vegetables, plantains, and cassavas — a type of flatbread tortilla made from yucca roots. Fitzgerald's men happily received the provisions and securely stowed them in the inflatables.

The leading warrior walked up to Alexander carrying in his arms several short wooden staves whittled to a sharp point on the ends. He respectfully bowed and spoke in Quechuan, "These will bring you aid on your journey." His fellow warriors began to distribute them, one to each mercenary.

"What in the world?" Fitzgerald asked uneasily as he

approached.

"They're fishing spears," Alexander translated to the team. Then he chuckled. "So we can hunt for our food the old-fashioned way! We won't have the luxury of bartering with villages anymore. This is pretty much the end of civilization, gentlemen."

The warrior bowed again, "Chief Amuta hopes to see you again someday. He believes your God will protect you."

Alexander bowed in return, "Please tell him thank you for everything. We are grateful for your gifts."

The man smiled and nodded, "We will now lead you to the river you seek."

The professor beamed as he translated the good news they'd just received.

"They're going to show us the way, Uncle James?" Drew asked, excitement in his voice.

"I — I guess so!" Alexander watched the natives getting back into their canoes and motioning for the foreigners to follow them. "Yet again, God provides guidance." He shook his head, wiping a tear from the corner of his eye. "I should never have doubted."

ⓘ ⓘ ⓘ

They followed the natives' canoes down the river for a couple hours, reaching the point where the tributaries split off. The whole time Fitzgerald stewed with impatience since they had to keep themselves at a very slow speed behind these men paddling in methodical synchronization, but Alexander saw this as yet another blessing. Now that they had nowhere to procure gas, keeping their inflatables throttled back would help conserve fuel and let them go farther before having to proceed on foot.

He thanked the Lord that instead of having to make an educated guess on which river to follow, they were being guided by Amuta's men to the precise one that led to the waterfall. When the group reached the tributary, the warriors waved farewell and turned around to head home.

The next couple of days were spent in their boats pressing deeper into the heart of the Amazon. The brown, murky river wove around one bend after another and meandered through the mountains.

No one did much talking. The air was thick and hot with no discernable breeze, and a haze hung along the banks of the river and permeated into the trees and sprawling jungle.

They were all tired and ready for the trip to be over. Even Fitzgerald had become quiet, but for different reasons. He spent the hours on the water dreaming of what his life was about to become. In the evenings, the group would come ashore wherever they could find a break in the impenetrable vegetation and make camp. Alexander and some of the men used the fishing spears from the *Ch'utiy* tribe to catch dinner; however, they quickly realized it was easier said than done. It was a good time, though, to relieve the stress that had consumed them as of late. They laughed at each other as they would comically lose their balance trying to snag ever-elusive fish that would curiously hover close to their legs and then dart away at the last second. Beady Eyes got so angry at one point that he snapped his spear in half with his knee and threw it into the water in a rage. This caused the men to roar with teasing delight, Fitzgerald the loudest of all. After he realized what he'd done, Beady Eyes shrugged and loafed out of the water.

Alexander wiped perspiration from his forehead, "Boy, what I wouldn't give for a fishing rod right about now!"

"What? And deny us this privilege of seeing you 'flounder'?" Fitzgerald chortled at his pun.

"Very funny," the professor quipped back. "I thought you were incapable of humor."

Everyone was in good spirits. Those on shore were captivated, watching those in the water as if it was an intense sport. When one of the men happened to be successful, the whole group would explode with cheers, scaring away the chances of anyone else getting a fish for the next few minutes.

"Looks like we need to get used to having veggie tacos for dinner," Kaci giggled as she, Drew, and Jada came back to camp with an armful of brush for a few campfires. In the end, though, the men did get the knack of how to use their spears and caught enough for everyone to have a few bites of freshly roasted fish with their vegetables that night.

Several of the men sprawled out and fell asleep almost as soon as the sun had gone down. The strenuous emotional ride they'd been on for the past week had sapped them all of energy and now having a few days between them and the cannibals, they felt as if this was the first moment they could truly relax.

The jungle reverberated with its nighttime ambiance, an occasional pop or crackle from their small campfires, and the low random rumble of men snoring. Drew and Kaci lay on their backs looking up into the night sky through the clearing in the trees above them; Alexander sat on the other side of their small campfire reading his Bible.

"I'm so happy, Uncle James," Kaci softly cut through the silence.

The man glanced up and smiled, "And why is that, my dear?"

"Because God has been so good to us. We've experienced *so much,* and He's kept us safe all this time."

"It really has been miraculous," Drew added.

The man chuckled, "Listen to what I just read a couple of chapters ago in Luke 12." He shuffled back through the worn pages in His Bible. "Jesus is speaking to His disciples, and He's trying to get them to understand how important each person is to God." He skimmed his finger down the columns to find the right verse. "Here it is — *'Are not five sparrows sold for two farthings, and not one of them is forgotten before God? But even the very hairs of your head are all numbered. Fear not therefore: ye are of more value than many sparrows.'"*

He grinned as he sat up straighter and gestured widely above him. "Our great God in Heaven loves us, and we are precious to Him. He is so familiar with our lives that He even knows the exact number of hairs we have on our head! Job testifies that God counts our steps. Psalm 139 teaches us that God even knows every single moment when we stand up or when we sit down. God knows exactly where we are and what we are facing. He will never leave us or forsake us."

Drew and Kaci propped themselves up on one elbow with riveted attention on their uncle. The professor could see their eagerness to hear more, so he continued. Placing one of his Bible's ribbons in Luke 12, he flipped back to the Old Testament. "Tucked away in Isaiah 43 we find a set of beautiful promises. It's something that I've recited to myself often whenever I find myself in the middle of some crazy escapade God allowed me to be a part of." He adjusted his glasses and read slowly so the two young people could soak up the words, *"'Thus saith the LORD that created thee, ...I have called thee by thy name; thou art mine. When thou passest through the waters, I will be with thee; and through the rivers, they shall not overflow thee: when thou walkest through the fire, thou shalt not be burned; neither shall the flame kindle upon thee. Since thou wast precious in my sight, ...I have loved thee: ...Fear not: for I am with thee:'"*

He quietly laughed in pure joy with a big heart-warming smile, "Haven't we seen God keep these promises time and again on our journey?" The two young people glanced at each other and nodded in agreement.

He softly exhaled, then folded his Bible up into his arms and hugged it close to his chest, "But what gets me every time is the glorious fact that God knows me by name, and I am *precious* in His sight."

He paused and intently looked from his niece to his nephew as he set his Bible down. "And so are both of you. God really does care about you. He knows exactly who you are, and He loves you. Do you believe this?"

"Oh yes!" Kaci blurted out, causing a temporary silence in the snoring that rose up from around them. Her eyes grew wide, and she sat up Indian-style, putting her hands over her mouth. But within seconds, the noisy breathing continued to reverberate across the camp. She visibly sighed and quietly continued, "And this has become so much more evident to me through our adventures here in the Amazon. I'm amazed at how God has led us. And through it all — He's drawn my heart closer to Him."

"Amen, my dear. I am so happy for this! He cherishes having a personal relationship with you. As you walk with Him, God will always guide you right. *'The steps of a good man are ordered by the LORD: and he delighteth in his way.'* He wants what's best for you, but the only way you can enjoy the fullness of His blessings is to remain ever-sensitive and surrendered to His leading."

"I really want to experience that, Uncle James," Kaci beamed, "I don't know if I told you this, but last year at youth camp I fully surrendered my life to Him. It was the best day ever, other than when I got saved as a little girl. I felt so happy and warm inside — like I'd been set free!"

Then she hung her head timidly and confessed, "But I'm ashamed to say that before we got kidnapped, my life was becoming wrapped up in school, friends, the possibility of getting a summer job and making money. I was even thinking about becoming a lawyer like Mom — I hadn't told her yet, but I was planning it in my heart. What's crazy is that I hadn't even prayed about it! I mean — I loved Jesus, but I wasn't surrendered like I once was."

She ran her fingers through her hair and looked up into the stars. "I feel like God had to bring me all the way down to the Amazon to get a hold of my life — like *really* get a hold of me. He's changed me, and now there's no turning back." She flashed a bright smile, "I can't wait to get home — not so things can go back to the way they were, but so that I can live for Jesus more! I don't care what I do. I just want to be in God's will!"

"Praise God!" Alexander softly chuckled at the intensity of how Kaci poured her heart out without holding anything back. "Please don't ever lose your sincerity. I'm so very happy for you! There is nothing more wonderful than surrendering your all to Jesus. But once a person makes that decision, they must *daily* remain yielded to Him in order to stay in a perpetual state of surrender — that's what many people fail to recognize. The key is found in Romans 12:1 which says, '...*Present your bodies a living sacrifice, holy, acceptable unto God, which is your reasonable service.*' Every morning I pray, '*God, here I am. Do with me today as you wish. I want your will, not my own.*' Paul shared that he had to '*die daily.*' As we yield ourselves to Christ, He will help us to not go astray."

Alexander's eyes flickered over to Drew who had remained unusually quiet, and noticed that he was staring blankly into the smoldering campfire. The struggle that had been raging in his heart off-and-on for quite some time had re-surfaced again, and it could be seen written all over his face. *Help me to break through, O God!* Alexander prayed and then decided to press a bit further.

"You both have *so much* potential in Christ. He created your lives on purpose for a purpose. You're special to Him, and He makes no mistakes. What's beautiful about being young is that you have your entire future ahead of you — but you must choose what you will do with it. God knows what's best for you, but you must decide to live this surrendered life in order to experience the fullness of what He has in store for you. The question you need to ask yourselves is: *What will I choose to live for?*

"There are many things you could pursue — money, pleasure, sin, power, worldly living, materialistic goods, your own will, and so on." He grabbed his Bible again and turned to I John. "But listen to what God has to say — you've probably heard preaching from these verses. '*Love not the world, neither the things that are in the world. ...For all that is in the world, the lust of the flesh, and the lust of the eyes, and the pride of life, is not of the Father, but is of the world. And the world passeth away, and the lust thereof: but he that doeth the will of God abideth for ever.*'

He looked up over his glasses, "The Bible is pretty clear, isn't it? God tells us this because He loves us and wants to help us choose what is right."

Drew cleared his throat and bit his bottom lip as he sat up,

"Uncle James, what was it like for you? You know… when did you surrender your life to the Lord?"

Alexander wanted to cry in that moment, hearing the quivering tenderness in his nephew's voice. "Well, let's see. It was during a youth service at Metropolitan Tabernacle in London, when I was 14 years old. There weren't very many young people there that night, and several didn't pay attention to the missionary speaking. He was an older man from Ireland who had given his entire life to reaching people in the mountains of Nepal. I still remember his big white beard and how it obscured his lips." He smiled while appearing in distant thought for a moment. "And he wore golden spectacles that wrapped around his ears and pressed up against eyes that always squinted. The young people snickered among themselves because of his strange look and accent. His preaching was not dynamic; he didn't tell any funny stories or use any engaging illustrations. But as I sat there, I couldn't escape the way God captured my heart during his message. He humbly spoke from Isaiah 48:17-18." Alexander wiped a tear from the corner of his eye and reverently quoted the verses, "'*Thus saith the Lord, thy Redeemer, the Holy One of Israel; I am the Lord thy God which teacheth thee to profit, which leadeth thee by the way that thou shouldest go. O that thou hadst hearkened to my commandments! then had thy peace been as a river, and thy righteousness as the waves of the sea.*'

"He preached that following God's will was life's greatest accomplishment and ignoring God's will was life's greatest tragedy. God struck a chord within me. Oh, how He *burned* in my heart! I uh — I uh…." His voice trailed off as he felt his throat tighten. He softly chuckled, then looked up into the starry sky and whispered to himself, "God is good!" He glanced back and forth at the two young people. Tears trickled down Kaci's cheeks, and Drew sat motionless, his features somber and gaunt with conviction.

"The invitation that night was short. I believe that God was working on several hearts, but no one moved or went down to the altar. My friends acted indifferent; it was a popular thing to be 'cool' and living for Jesus to them was not 'cool.' I could feel God burning in my own heart, but I was embarrassed to step out. What would my friends think? After the service was over, all of the young people filed out quickly to go eat and play in the church's small rec center. I couldn't move. I hung my head in shame and began to weep bitterly. I looked down at God's Word that I still held open in my hands. Had I missed my opportunity? Would there ever be another chance to surrender my life to Christ?

"I saw a shadow come across my Bible. I looked up, and there that missionary stood, smiling. His face radiated with Heaven's joy. He began to gently ask me what God was doing in my heart, and in that moment, my spirit broke. It was such a sweet experience that I'll never forget. Together, we went to the altar, and I gave my life to Jesus.

"As I grew older, I remained yielded to God's will for my life. He never called me into a full-time ministry capacity like a pastor or an evangelist — and that's okay. I just wanted to do whatever it was that God had for me. I understood that if I *did* go into full-time ministry and it wasn't the will of God, I would be absolutely miserable and would miss out on the work the Lord had truly created me for. I determined to remain completely surrendered and stayed faithfully engaged as a full-time Christian serving the Lord and being an active witness for Christ. After all — that is exactly how *every* child of God should be!

"Over time, He began opening doors, and I give Him all the glory — He's the One Who led me into the archaeological linguist field. But I don't look at my occupation as the 'purpose' of my life. I have a higher, nobler calling. My job is merely a means to an end — so I can fulfill God's calling upon my life to spread the Gospel and be a testimony for Christ in a darkened world. I get to meet thousands of people every year in the professional field that may never get another chance to meet a Bible-believing Christian like me. Most of them, sadly, are surrounded by Catholics, agnostics, or atheists. It is a privilege to be an 'ambassador for Christ.' I strive to be outspoken about my faith; I'm not obnoxious about it, but I want them to be able to see Jesus in me."

He shifted his position, pulling one knee up and resting an arm on top of it.

"Through my job, God has blessed me financially. I am able to support many church plants, Gospel-centered non-profit organizations, and missionary endeavors around the world. Our Lord is pretty clear —" Alexander flipped in his Bible to Matthew 6, straightened his glasses, and read verses 19-21: "*Lay not up for yourselves treasures upon earth, where moth and rust doth corrupt, and where thieves break through and steal: But lay up for yourselves treasures in heaven, where neither moth nor rust doth corrupt, and where thieves do not break through nor steal: For where your treasure is, there will your heart be also.*"

"I'm very careful to make sure money, possessions, or my career doesn't come between me and God. Those things are temporal and they're *not* what life is all about." He grabbed hold of the ribbon that he had placed in Luke 12 and let his Bible open back up to that passage. "Jesus says very, very clearly, '*Take heed, and beware of covetousness:*'. Now what is coveteousness? Well, it's a discontentment and lustful craving for more money and material possessions. This sin has consumed so many Christians and derailed them from being able to fulfill their potential in the Lord! Jesus says to watch out for this. Why does He warn us? Because He knows that we can easily fall prey to it if we are not careful. '*Take heed, and beware of covetousness: for a man's life consisteth not in the abundance of the things which he possesseth. ... But rather seek ye the kingdom of God; and all these things shall be added unto you.*'"

He glanced over at Fitzgerald who sat across their makeshift camp asleep with his back against a tree trunk. "Some people spend their whole lives seeking earthly riches, fame, immortality," at this, Alexander shook his head sadly. "They work their entire lives to make their own kingdom in this world. But I hope you two will always remember that the greatest thing you could ever do in life is to build the *truly* immortal kingdom. The kingdom of God. There is nothing more important in life than serving the Lord, impacting eternity, and leading other people to Christ.

"One man who has been a great motivation to me is a missionary by the name of C. T. Studd. Have you ever heard of him?"

Drew and Kaci shook their heads.

"Oh my! Then you need to read a biography about his life when you get back home. I have multiple copies in my library I will make sure to get to you.

"Studd was a daring missionary that God greatly used from 1885 to around 1930 in China, India, and the heart of Africa. He was the 'Michael Jordan' of his day, the most world-renowned cricket player at that time. But after he got saved, he turned his back on fame and fortune, realizing that there was nothing greater than the call of God and going all out for Jesus Christ. I have a few of his statements pasted onto the back flyleaf of my Bible. Listen to this — he said, '*How could I spend the best years of my life in working for myself and the honors and pleasures of this world, while thousands and thousands of souls are perishing every day without having heard of Christ?*' He also said, '*Only one life 'twill soon be past, only what's done for Christ will last.*' How true and how convicting!"

He closed his Bible, placed it back in his leather holster, then folded his hands and rested them on his knees. "There isn't *one thing* this world could offer you — money, position, power, or sin — that is more appealing than what the Lord has for you. There certainly is a pull, a draw on your flesh to give in to the world and turn your back on the Lord. You heart will try to deceive you, saying you're going to miss out on something." He flashed a small smile, "And you will."

Drew and Kaci looked at each other, momentarily confused.

"You will miss out — on the regret, bondage, suffering, scars, pain, and emptiness that living for sin and self brings."

He took his glasses off and rubbed his bleary eyes. While still holding the spectacles, he crossed his arms and sat back. "I've had the joy of meeting many people in my life, but I've never met anyone who lived for Jesus Christ and regretted it. However, those who have lived for something else besides the will of God wish they could go back and reclaim their wasted years."

He put his glasses back on and leaned forward, speaking quietly. "I once knew a Christian businessman who gave himself entirely over to his career. He was a well-meaning man, trying to make a difference in his field of industry, but it so consumed him that he ultimately lost his marriage and his children. A couple of years ago, he contracted pneumonia that only got worse and worse until it put him in the hospital on a ventilator. As he struggled to simply breathe, he realized that his days on this earth were numbered. It was told to me by his doctor — an old friend of mine from my college days — that one day he went in to check on this man, only to find him silently and uncontrollably weeping. Alarmed, he called for the nurses and rushed over to his bedside to see what was wrong. Between the man's gasps for air, the doctor could make out these words, *'I'm ashamed to die! I'm ashamed to die! I've done nothing with my life!'* They tried to calm him down, but to no avail. His lungs couldn't keep up with the frenzy his body was already in. He coded blue and then died."

He paused for a moment and looked at his niece and nephew tenderly, "Please live for Jesus; you will *never* regret it." He stretched his hands upward while looking into the stars and quoted Psalm 16:11, *"'Thou wilt shew me the path of life: in thy presence is fulness of joy; at thy right hand there are pleasures for evermore.'"*

Drew could feel a lump swell in his throat and a wave of emotion rush over him. He tried his best to hold back the tears, but he realized there was no use fighting it any longer. He began to weep uncontrollably. Alexander moved over beside him and wrapped his arm around the boy's heaving shoulders. He remained quiet and patient, knowing the boy would speak when he was ready. After a couple minutes, Drew wiped his eyes and began speaking, his words garbled and broken.

"Uncle James, I…I can't take it any longer. I need to tell you something," he sniffed and gave a small smile to his uncle as he accepted the handkerchief offered to him.

"Well, you probably already know, but I've been *really*

struggling with what God wants me to do with my life. On this journey, I feel like my eyes have been opened…just…seeing your passion for souls and how many people here have never even heard the name of Jesus… There is *so much* need — and *no one* is answering the call. For some time now, I know God's been trying to get a hold of me, but… I've been ignoring him. I can't resist Him anymore; I know He didn't call you into full-time ministry, but it *is* what He wants me to do —not football, scholarships, or anything else. I've got to surrender my life to Him right now!"

Drew immediately got onto his knees with his hands tightly clasped together.

"God…." he whispered between the tears.

Moments passed as he silently wept. Alexander remained next to him and gently squeezed his shoulder, encouraging him on. Kaci tenderly snuggled next to her brother and rested her head on his other shoulder.

"God, I give you my heart, my life, and everything about me. I don't want to mess up my future. I place myself in Your hands, and I trust You to direct me, no matter where it leads… because I know You will never make a mistake. I surrender myself to You completely. Please take my life and use it for Your glory and Your eternal kingdom. I answer your call upon my life… to preach."

Instantly, the turmoil that had been raging in his heart ceased. A sweet peace washed over him, and his tears of brokenness turned into tears of joy and laughter. Drew found himself enveloped into a giant hug that included both Uncle James and Kaci, and in that moment, he knew. No matter what came next, he would be okay. His heart was finally right with God. He was free.

CHAPTER XXIII

R AT-TAT-TAT-TAT-TAT!
The sound of machine gun fire jolted everyone awake from deep sleep in an instant. Kaci covered her ears from the piercing noise, and Fitzgerald's men scrambled out of their bedrolls in a complete daze, frantically grabbing for their AK-47s that lay somewhere next to them.

"What now?" Jada growled as she instinctively sprang from the sleeping bag into a ninja pose with her knives drawn, looking out into the complete darkness.

"Show yourselves!" bellowed Fitzgerald, pointing his revolver in random spots at the tree line.

Suddenly, harsh light poured over them from all around, causing the small band to automatically shrink back with hands raised to shield their eyes from the piercing brightness. Fitzgerald yelled in rage and fired a few shots blindly into the trees. It took Alexander a moment for his eyes to adjust, but he didn't need to see the enemy to have a hunch as to who they were. He had wondered how long it would take to finally meet them, but he wasn't sure how deep into the South American jungle they'd gone.

Slowly, in unison, dozens of uniformed men surrounded the campsite, each standing in the shade of the LED spotlights with MG42 machine guns at their hips. They wore gray long-sleeved coats with a red and white symbol stitched into the shoulder.

"Uncle James?" Kaci whispered nervously and moved behind

her brother. "Are those… are those *swastikas* on their uniforms?"

Alexander somberly nodded but kept silent.

"What is the meaning of this!" Fitgerald's voice reverberated across the stillness of the jungle as he glared at each of his men's faces. "How did this happen? Who was on watch?"

No one spoke.

A familiar voice called out in German from behind the uniformed men, causing them to immediately raise their weapons and unflinchingly advance on the campsite. With at least two machine guns trained on each individual, they unceremoniously yanked the guns away from Fitzgerald's men and began handcuffing them. Jada had already sheathed her blades and put her hands up in the air.

Alexander saw the men headed toward a defenseless Drew and Kaci. "Please! Don't hurt them! They are but children!" he spoke loudly in German. Drew stood tall in front of his sister to protect her, but the men grabbed him and slapped cuffs on him, too, while ignoring the girl.

When they turned to Fitzgerald, he pointed his revolver in their faces and dared them to try to take it away from him.

"It's not worth it, Adrian!" Alexander carefully reasoned with him.

"Shut up, Jim! I will be no man's prisoner!" he spat on the ground and shot the professor an ugly look. "And why do you look so unsurprised? Were you *expecting* Nazis?"

Before he could respond, a tall thin man in an officer's uniform slid from the shadows behind Fitzgerald and hit him in the back of the head with the butt of his Luger pistol. The big man temporarily crumpled to the ground, still conscious, and a couple of soldiers quickly scooped up his revolver and tightly cuffed his hands behind his back.

"Yes, Professor," the officer spoke with a thick German accent. "Please enlighten us. I am eager to know myself." The soldiers around him stiffened to attention as he lifted his face to the light and revealed his identity.

"Fairchild? What? How are you alive?" Fitzgerald gasped, staggering to his feet. His look of confusion contorted into rage as he attempted to lunge forward, but two soldiers gruffly held him back.

"When your convoy was destroyed, I realized it was the perfect opportunity for me to slip away and gather my forces while you all gallivanted through the jungle and found the rest of the clues. You have done all the hard work for me," he grinned wickedly.

"You traitor!" Fitzgerald spat into the man's pale face.

"Always with the dramatics," Fairchild muttered as he calmly wiped his cheek, then quickly landed two hard punches into Fitzgerald's ribs, causing him to double over in pain.

After a moment of wheezing, the big man looked up, grinning with wild eyes, "Is that the best you've got?"

Fairchild ignored his old boss and turned to Alexander. "You were about to say…?"

Alexander awkwardly cleared his throat. "I've been following clues regarding the Nazis for years, but it was your binoculars that gave it away. German-made. That serial number: HM88; 88 was the secret call sign of the SS, and HM are initials, aren't they?" Alexander looked into Fairchild's eyes.

"They are, my dear professor. My grandfather's."

"Your name isn't Fairchild, is it?"

"Hans Mueller, grandchild of the great Heinrich Mueller, Chief of the Gestapo." He put out his hand in an offer to shake.

"Ahhh. Your grandfather vanished after the collapse of Berlin. One of the few leaders that historians said disappeared off the face of the earth." Alexander ignored the man's friendly gesture. "This is where he went then?" Hans lowered his hand awkwardly and clasped both hands behind his back.

"De Fuhrer went mad in the final moments of the war. My grandfather was with him till the end, always at his side. Never questioning. Never doubting the cause." Hans slowly strolled over to Kaci and put a hand on top of her head then down the side of her face as he stroked her cheek. She shuddered and squirmed in disgust. Drew struggled with his cuffs and growled at the man to keep his hands off her, but quickly relented as a machine gun was shoved into his chest.

"But De Fuhrer had lost his way," Hans continued, "And it was better to put a bullet in his head and burn his body in the man's own bunker than to help him escape and attempt to reform what he had lost. My grandfather understood this… and killed him. Eventually the rest of the true Germans needed someone to guide them — someone to bring them to greatness after the failures of De Fuhrer. My grandfather took up the charge and led them secretly out of Berlin and the Fatherland. He lost many soldiers along the way, but eventually made it to the America's with our secret intact."

"He killed them all, didn't he?" Alexander bowed his head. "The soldiers who refused to follow him? The ones who finally had enough of the war."

"It was a necessary sacrifice. The Fourth Reich would not stand for weakness. But now, we are about to obtain something that will render us invincible!"

He waltzed over to Alexander and patted him on the upper arm, gently slipping off the cylindrical leather map case that was slung around his shoulder. "I don't believe you will be needing this anymore."

"Don't give it to him, Jim!" Fitzgerald hoarsely whispered.

"Shut up!" Hans snapped, and a couple of soldiers pummeled the burly man with the butt of their rifles. He turned back to Alexander and stretched out his hand. "And give me your notebook also."

"You know I can't do that."

Hans stepped right in front of the professor's face, "Do you wish to test me? I will not hesitate to put a bullet through your niece's or nephew's head," he uttered calmly yet coldly. "Hand it over, *now!*"

Reluctantly, Alexander dug the book out of his back pocket and handed it to the man. He smiled broadly and flipped through it with excitement, glancing momentarily at various notes the professor had jotted down along their journey.

"Good! See? That wasn't so bad, was it? Continue to cooperate, and I *might* let you live." His face went from being pleasant to wickedly sour, and he looked to his men. "Load them up! *Schnell!*"

Surrounded by soldiers, they were shoved forward. A few of the men stumbled as they tried to find their footing in the jungle overgrowth, and the Nazis barked at them in broken English to get up before they were shot to death on the spot. Drew and Kaci were pushed alongside their uncle, and as Kaci peered around her in the darkness, she locked eyes with Jada. For the first time, fear was visible on the young woman's face.

"How in the world did they find us, Uncle James?" Drew whispered.

"I imagine through some sort of tracking device among our things. Something probably no bigger than a grain of rice."

"Quiet!" the soldier behind them gruffly commanded and pushed them along the way.

They walked for another ten minutes until they came to a narrow dirt road carved out of the jungle. A Nazi convoy was waiting for them.

"Put those five —" Hans gestured toward Alexander, Drew, Kaci, Fitzgerald, and Jada, "in my truck and keep a close eye on the professor and his 'little monsters.' They're smarter than they look."

They were pushed up into the bed of an antiquated troop carrier, a tattered green tarp hanging over top of them. Spotlights streamed through holes and speckled the floor with a glow. Kaci, Drew, and Alexander were shoved in first with Fitzgerald and Jada following them. A soldier yelled out in German.

"He says to put out your hands, Adrian."

"What?" Fitzgerald's eyes were glossed over, and he sat down heavily onto the wooden bench in the back of the vehicle. Alexander noticed that the back of his head was bleeding. *He must have a concussion.*

Alexander gently grabbed his cuffs and pulled them forward. "I'm sorry, friend. Try to stay with us."

Two soldiers grabbed a long metal chain and hooked each pair of cuffs to one another, then sat down out of arm's reach with their guns trained on the group.

Hans suddenly appeared at the flap at the end of the truck, chuckling to himself.

"You…" Fitzgerald mumbled. They stared at each other for a moment. "What are you laughing at?" His weak voice coughed and sputtered. "You'll regret this…" The big man curled over, spitting out blood.

Hans snickered, "No, I won't, but *you* will if you don't cooperate."

He hastily lowered the flap, barking out orders in German for his men to prepare to leave. As he entered the passenger side of the truck, it revved to life and everyone in the back began to shake from the heavy vibrations of the vehicle's old motor. The convoy moved slowly through the jungle, causing the prisoners' chains to rattle incessantly in the pitch-black night.

Alexander bowed his head and decided to pass the time by silently praying. There was nothing else that could be done until he knew where they were going. If he were to take an educated guess, it would be to the waterfall. He smiled to himself, *What else would look like a dark metal bird other than an old Nazi Stuka?*

"Uncle James?" Kaci whispered after a long silence.

His eyes slowly fluttered open, "Yes, my dear?"

"What are Nazis doing in South America? I thought all of them had been captured and put on trial at Nuremberg for their crimes?" She had learned about the Holocaust in her History class near the end of her spring semester.

"Not quite. The Allies did their best to round up as many as they could. But some successfully fled during the chaos and hid away in countries around the world. Most of them renounced their Nazism and lived in the shadows. A few governments knew of their whereabouts but left them alone as long as they remained an asset to their military and technological advancements. Obviously, others such as Heinrich Mueller held to the old ways and waited for the perfect moment to resurrect the Reich. I've been following clues over the years that subtly proved Nazis were still active — and they always seemed to point me to the Amazon. I'm curious as to why they are interested in Paititi. Of course, it shouldn't surprise me that they are, as Hitler was quite obsessed with the mystic realm and immortality."

"Sounds like someone else we know," Drew commented dryly, gesturing over with his chin to the man sitting across from him.

Fitzgerald bobbled back and forth with the jostling of the vehicle. His eyes were thin slits, and Jada leaned heavily on her father to keep him as still as possible.

"Dad. Please. You've got to stay awake!" Jada's eyes sparkled with tears until she saw one of the soldiers looking at her. Her face went red with embarrassment and then quickly turned red with rage. She wiped her face.

"Jada," Alexander looked at her with sorrowful eyes, "your father is going to be okay. He has survived much worse." He turned his attention to Fitzgerald. "Adrian!"

"Huh?" the man stirred.

"Tell them of the time you and I discovered Bloodfist's lair!"

This immediately perked the man up as he straightened his eyes and beamed with pride at the thought of where their adventures all began.

As Fitzgerald incoherently babbled the tale, Kaci looked over at Jada. Her head was bowed and her eyes didn't move. Kaci thought of the day she and Drew had found out about their own father. Something in Jada's eyes just then gave Kaci a flashback of herself in those moments. She prayed for Jada to find the strength as Kaci had long ago. Fitzgerald wasn't physically gone, but Kaci was sure that's how Jada saw it - lost in his greed and desires. Lost from God.

A couple hours later, the truck came to a grinding halt. Roaring water could be heard outside, and the morning rays of sunlight were peeking through the canvas. None of them had slept.

"I think we're here," Alexander spoke groggily.

The soldiers jumped from the bed of the truck and flanked the opening in the canvas, quickly saluting as Hans approached with a few more soldiers.

"Gutentag, my friends. It is time to finish our little journey by boat." He waved his Luger, motioning for the prisoners to step out. The soldiers yanked on their chains, causing them to almost stumble over each other as they crawled out of the back of the truck.

"Stop pulling so hard!" Jada hissed. "We get it, okay? Just chill!"

Hans laughed. "You are wasting your breath. They have no idea what you are saying. Just do as you are told, and I might not kill you slowly."

Kaci shivered at the thought of torture. Her uncle gave her a look that everything would be fine, and even though they were all still handcuffed and powerless, she felt comfort in that moment that somehow God would help them through this.

As they began following Hans, they walked over bright ankle-length grass toward a rushing river. Fitzgerald's men, including Beady-Eyes and Goatee, were all chained up as well, being loaded into a collection of small boats. Kaci's eyes went from the muddy riverbank to what loomed over them high above. A mountain, lush with green vines and overgrowth, speckled with gray walls of stone, rose in front of them. Flowing from the top of the mountain was a wide stream of water, white with a foaming spray. It eventually came cascading down into the river, eliciting a mighty roar that went out across the jungle.

"How beautiful," Alexander murmured to himself.

"It's the waterfall from the map!" Drew exclaimed in awe.

The three of them stepped into the boat, accompanied by a single soldier. Fitzgerald and Jada had gotten in a different boat with Hans as they all shoved off the bank and went straight toward the waterfall.

Drew scooted close to his uncle, "Do think they're taking us to the guide?"

Alexander shrugged, "I don't know, but keep your eyes out for it. My gut tells me that they know more than we think they do; it's almost as if they were *waiting* for us." He smiled encouragingly, "I'm sure we'll find out soon enough."

The boats sped up as they got closer to the waterfall, the current pushing them back slightly. As they approached, the mist from above fell on their heads. Kaci and Drew both held open their mouths as small streams of water fell into the boat. They began to laugh uncontrollably at the realization that this was the first "shower" they'd had in weeks. Alexander smiled.

"Open the gates!" Hans screamed in German into a walkie-talkie.

Suddenly, whirling sounds of heavy machinery and moving pistons came to life over the crashing noise of the water, and the mammoth torrent began to be diverted to either side of the river. Slowly, a pathway through the falls opened before them.

"Professor!" Hans called out above the din as their boats drifted next to each other. He stood and motioned grandly with outstretched arms. "Welcome to the Fourth Reich!"

As they floated into the entrance, the view that extended out in front of them was striking. A short concrete tunnel adorned with Nazi propaganda banners hanging from the ceiling brought them to a smooth underground lake. The interior of the mountain was hollowed out into a tall cylindrical fortress, illuminated entirely with bright LED lights from ceilings hundreds of feet above. Caged elevator lifts led to different floors built into the rock along the walls of the mountain. Doors, halls, stairs and passages went in every direction and soldiers bustled about with their daily duties. But the most impressive sight lay before them at the far end of the lake. A massive Swastika flag accented with colored lighting draped down the wall. And in front of it, sitting atop a roughly hewn pedestal on a natural stone landing, the ominous face of their next stone guide stared at them with aquamarine eyes glowing from the spotlights that shone down on its face.

As the boats glided into a concrete set of docks where soldiers awaited their arrival, the mechanical sound of the doors closing behind them filled the cavern. Hans jumped off his boat and chuckled. "Quite impressive, isn't it? And this is just the beginning. We have an entire system of farms and training facilities throughout the Amazon where we are raising the Master Race. What you see here before you is just our headquarters." He gestured widely. "The Incan Empire had excavated most of this to make a home for their sixth and final guide to Paititi."

Alexander frowned, still taking everything in. "Wait. How do *you* know for certain there are only six guides?"

"All in good time, my dear professor," the Nazi grinned darkly.

The soldiers pulled on their chains, and everyone began to disembark. Their small band was split into two with Fitzgerald's men taken immediately to cells while Alexander, Fitzgerald, and the three teenagers were made to follow Hans. They traversed down winding corridors lined with portraits and placards of various Nazi officials from the Third Reich as he gave them a tour of the facility, trying to impress them.

Alexander noted that every soldier that Hans passed momentarily stood at attention with the click of his boot heels. *Okay, clearly, he's the top dog here. There's obviously a reason why he's keeping us alive.* Alexander prayed, *Lord, I need Your wisdom to somehow keep it that way!*

"Our base was built here during the zenith of our former glory as a black ops site to exploit the power of Paititi. During the second World War, my grandfather's agents had discovered within the Vatican the secret of its location from the writings of Andres Lopez."

"I knew his writings had been tampered with!" Fitzgerald interjected.

Hans smiled without acknowledging the man.

Alexander was stunned. "You mean to tell me — you've known where the lost city was this entire time?" Drew, Kaci, and Jada exchanged incredulous looks with one another.

"That is correct."

"Then what was the point of this whole ridiculous trip?" Jada exploded. A guard stepped close to keep her contained and she snarled at him to back off. Hans waved his hand to dismiss the soldier, not considering her a threat.

"It has been extremely important, my dear. As our ancestors came to find out, there is no use in knowing where the city is located unless you have the keys to unlock the secrets and gain access within."

"You're speaking in riddles, man," Fitzgerald muttered angrily.

"Do NOT interrupt me again," Hans sneered, "unless you desire a bullet between your eyes. I no longer have need of you, 'Boss,' and you should be thanking me for every minute I continue to let you live."

Fitzgerald's face turned dark. He wanted to respond but bit his tongue and kept quiet.

Hans stopped abruptly in the middle of the small atrium they'd just entered. The dome-like room was lined with columns, Nazi decorations, and tall mirrors encased in ornate gilded frames and had several corridors branching from it. He faced the group and ignored the soldiers and other uniformed officers who briskly walked past them.

"My grandfather and his people discovered the location of Paititi on an island high in the mountains."

"Let me guess," Drew cut in. "There's a giant skull carved out of the rock in the middle of the city?"

"Precisely. Just like your ancient map shows," Hans continued. "The city surrounding it is impressive but contains nothing of value — except for dishes, vessels, and crude tableware of gold and silver. This was quite upsetting to my grandfather. They were led to believe by Lopez's writings that the city would be overabundant with gold and precious jewels and even contain one of the greatest secrets of the ancient world —" the German sighed in frustration and gestured with disgust, "but to no avail. The key was to gain entrance into the skull; they gathered that beyond it lay an inner sanctum that contained all its preciousness. Unfortunately, nothing — not even blast charges — could open its impenetrable doors."

Hans paced back and forth with his hands behind his back in the crisp, methodical cadence of an officer. "They soon came to realize that the stone face in our fortress here had great significance because of the Incan and Latin clues engraved on it. They believed there *had* to be more like it. But how were they to know where to locate other stone guides in the Amazon? And how many were there? They sent countless expeditions into the jungle but always failed. Nevertheless, they refused to give up hope, deciding rather to simply bide their time and continue building themselves into a mighty army. They waited patiently until the time was right to emerge from the shadows."

He turned about-face in front of Alexander and Fitzgerald and smiled as he stared at the medallion that dangled around Fitzgerald's neck. "It was not until the two of you discovered Captain Bloodfist and his connection with Paititi, Carlos Mendina, and Aapo that we knew our future could be secured. We thought it quite ironic that the place where we had obtained the location of Paititi to begin with had held the answer to what we needed all this time. Of course, the Vatican archive is vast and how were we to know? But Aapo's letter to the Pope was the starting point necessary to find all of the stone guides."

Alexander and Fitzgerald looked at each other. "Fascinating," they muttered almost in unison.

Hans held up Alexander's cylindrical map case and notepad. "Now with the information you have assimilated on your journey, combined with the clues of our own guide, I believe at last we have everything we need to obtain Paititi's power!"

"What-what do you mean... power?" Kaci timidly inquired.

The Nazi grinned wickedly with a wild look in his eyes, "Why, immortality, of course. We will become invincible and conquer the world!" He spun on his heels and headed down one of the corridors. "Come along, Professor." He quickly uttered a command in German, and almost instantly a soldier grappled Alexander into his arms, unlatched his chain, and led him behind Hans, leaving the others to be taken to their cell. "I have some further questions for you. And if you do not comply — I will not hesitate to discard your bodies like the vile filth you all are.

CHAPTER XXIV

Alexander was led through several corridors and eventually pulled inside a dark room with walls, floor, and ceiling lined with a muted green tile. A single light shone down onto a complex metal chair in the middle of the room with thick leather strappings for the head, arms, and legs.

"Tie him," Hans growled and disappeared into another part of the room. A soldier lifted his machine gun and pointed it in Alexander's face, forcing him to sit while another tightly secured him down. Hans reemerged wearing a white lab coat over his clothes and a daunting leather toolkit filled with all sorts of scalpels and pliers. Both guards grinned from ear to ear, imagining what was about to take place.

Alexander cleared his throat, "Is there something broken, doctor? I feel like I'm still in working order." His hands twitched but he tried to keep calm. It had been a long time since he was last tortured, he wasn't ready for it again.

"Leave us," Hans curtly ordered in German while ignoring the professor and laying open his case on a stainless-steel table. The disappointed soldiers filed out slowly and locked the door behind them.

"Always the optimist, Herr Professor," the Nazi rolled the table close to the chair with a wild look in his eyes. "But you will not be so happy when I am done with you, I assure you."

Alexander looked bewildered at the oddly-shaped tool the man drew from his arsenal. "I've never seen one of those before."

"Ah, yes, it's one of my favorites!" Hans' pale skin and bleached blonde hair seemed to glow under the harsh LED light above him as he took another step closer to Alexander and let him have a closer look. "It is able to dislocate fingers quite easily and then pop them back into place. It does not cause permanent damage physically once the swelling goes down, but it leaves an indelible scar mentally from the pain." His eyes flashed a dark sense of delight at the thought.

"One that your grandfather crafted, I presume?"

"Crafted and perfected. Now stop trying to distract me, and let's get to work, shall we?"

"I'd rather talk to you, calmly and respectfully."

"But how do I know you will tell me the truth?" Hans slipped the special pliers over Alexander's ring finger and applied a slight bit of pressure, but he didn't flinch.

"Because pain is not the answer — it's only the means to break a man's will so he will talk. You can torture someone all you want, but it never guarantees you'll get the truth. A person will say just about anything to stop the pain." The professor looked from Hans' tool to his eyes. "I prefer to be sensible and take the civilized route."

The two men stared at each other. Alexander could feel a bit more pressure on his finger and was anticipating for it to break swiftly at any moment. He prayed for strength and grace to handle the pain, but the snap never came. The Nazi slowly withdrew the tool and placed it on the table, "Fine, I will try it your way — if you're willing to turn on your friend."

"He's not my friend."

Hans snickered, "That is true! I don't know how you have put up with him for so long. He threatened to kill Kaci if he didn't get what he wanted!"

"I am aware of that," Alexander paused for a moment and wondered what would happen when he finished his statement. "But it's because he's a lost, deranged man who's in desperate need of Jesus Christ… as are you."

Hans stiffened and his eyes blazed, "Don't you dare start preaching at me! I will not stand for it! Your Bible is a book of abomination to the Nazi creed. History did a service by killing that filthy Jew you call Messiah."

"No one killed Him," Alexander corrected him plainly. "Jesus willingly gave up His life as a sacrifice for the sins of the world. *'Hereby perceive we the love of God, because he laid down his life for us —'*"

"ENOUGH!" Hans slapped him so hard across the face with the back of his gloved hand, it left the professor reeling in agony. The room spun for a moment, his ears rang and pain pulsed over his cheek.

He managed to smile softly, "No matter how severely you may try to hurt me, I will not hate you. I will love you as Jesus loves you. He teaches me to love my enemies, bless them that curse me, do good to them that hate me, and pray for them —"

The German let out a blood-chilling scream and snatched his metal device off the table again in a flurry. He shoved it hard onto Alexander's pointer finger this time and got directly into his face, "You say one more word about your religion, and I will slowly break every part of you! You are a *fool* to believe such fables!"

"No, I'm not — it is the truth, and it will set you free if you'll let it," Alexander replied firmly. "Furthermore, *you* are the fool here — not me — because you insist on believing in the fabled Fountain of Youth. There is no such thing as earthly immortality — only eternal life in Heaven."

Their eyes locked in an epic stare down. Alexander's boldness surprised Hans — that he was willing to suffer for what he believed in. After a long moment, the man stepped back and withdrew his torture device. "I have never met a man who was willing to take a stand like you have." He slammed the oddly-shaped pliers down on the table. "I respect you for this. Obviously, we differ in our views on the topics of religion and Paititi. Believe what you will," he waved his hand with disgust. "It makes no difference to me. But now, I will only give you one chance to explain to me your findings and the notes you've taken along the way." He produced the professor's notepad from one of the pockets on his lab coat. "Tell me how I can enter the skull of Paititi. If you do not, I will torture you like you have never experienced before."

Alexander looked deeply into his eyes. He could see that same desire that was behind Fitzgerald's eyes, that same selfish greed, like an infection. In that moment, a thought came to his mind which he prayed about instantly. He sighed and decided to follow through.

"Okay. But on *one* condition…"

⊛ ⊛ ⊛

Kaci shivered as she sat quietly next to her brother. She tried her best to keep her mind off all the terrible things that might be happening to Uncle James. They'd already faced so much on their journey; she hadn't thought it could get any worse. But Nazis? She sighed and Drew squeezed her arm in comfort. They leaned their heads together and quietly did the only thing they could do now: they prayed.

Rough cobblestone surrounded them on three sides with thick wrought-iron bars sealing them into their uncomfortable cell. Adrian Fitzgerald was sprawled on the ground in front of them still dazed from his concussion, and Jada let his head rest in her lap as she leaned against the adjacent wall. The room was dark and damp, and what little light they had faintly shone from down the hall. The rest of Fitzgerald's men were crammed into the cell next to theirs and sat quietly together wondering what the next move would be.

Beady Eyes stared into blank space and then muttered, "I can't wait to get my hands around that traitor's scrawny little neck…."

Fitzgerald attempted to lift himself from the laying position but curled back in pain.

"Dad, you need to rest as much as you can," Jada spoke calmly to her father.

"I'll be fine. I can feel myself getting better already."

"Yeah, right," she rolled her eyes. A look of concern, however, was etched deep into her face as she looked from her father to Drew and Kaci.

"We're praying for you, Mr. Fitzgerald," said Drew quietly. "God can heal you."

The man chuckled to himself. "Your God would never help someone like me even if you wanted Him to."

"Be quiet, Dad. Rest!" Jada scolded her father as she lovingly stroked his head and rubbed his temples to alleviate the throbbing pain. She glanced back at Drew with a weary smile. "Thank you. He can use all the help that he can get."

A silence came over the group again as they huddled together for some time until they heard multiple footsteps coming down the hall. Drew and Kaci shot up and looked to find their uncle being escorted back in handcuffs by a group of armed guards, seemingly unharmed.

"Uncle James!" Kaci screeched. "Are you okay?"

Hans followed closely behind Alexander. "Your uncle was very brave."

"What did you do to him?" Drew boldly put his face between the bars.

"Nothing, Drew. He did nothing," Alexander spoke, but his voice cracked. "I'm fine."

One of the soldiers uncuffed the professor as Hans opened the cell door and shoved him through. He hugged his niece and nephew as quickly as he could, fighting back the tears.

"It has been an amazing journey, my little monsters, but this is the end of the line for you."

Drew stepped back in concern, but when his uncle gave him a slow knowing nod, he instantly understood what had been done, the sacrifice that was made for them to survive. Alexander would stay and help the Nazis gain entrance into Paititi if he could guarantee Drew and Kaci's safety.

Drew tenderly placed a hand on his sister's shoulder. "Come on, Kac. We're going home."

"What?" Kaci looked up in confusion. "I don't understand..."

Alexander smiled and tucked her golden-brown hair behind her ear. "You'll be flown to Manaus, Brazil, where you'll be given tickets to return to the U.S. and to your mother. It's going to be okay."

"No… this can't be! What about you?"

"Don't worry about me; I'll be fine. I may not see you again in this life, but we will never part on that Other Shore!"

"No… No!" she sobbed, wrapping her arms around him tightly.

Alexander began to cry as he felt her tears fall upon his shirt, but then gently pushed her away. "This had to be done, my dear. I have lived a very full life, but you have your entire future ahead of you. You don't deserve to die here."

"Enough," Hans spat impatiently, resting his hand on his holstered Luger and motioning to his men. "Take the children!"

He looked to Jada. "Come on, lovely, you, too."

Her eyes widened and then hardened. "I can't leave. I *won't* leave."

"You have no choice in the matter. It has already been arranged by the professor. A deal is a deal."

"NO! Don't touch me!" She struggled against a couple of soldiers who grabbed her and tore her away from her father.

"Uncle James? Uncle James!" Kaci frantically called as the three of them were pulled away from the cell and pushed down the hall. "I love you! I love you!" Drew kept his hand firmly on her shoulder to keep her moving forward.

"I love you, too," Alexander called. "Now go and live for Jesus!"

"Get them out of here!" roared Hans.

"Jim, what is the meaning of this?" Fitzgerald staggered to his feet, his mind clearing and his eyes glowing with rage. "What have you done? I *demand* an explanation!"

"It was the only way, Adrian," Alexander explained calmly. "It was the only way to keep those we care about safe!"

"You betrayed me? How could you? Paititi is MINE!" Fitzgerald lunged at Alexander. The professor flinched and put his arm up to block the sudden attack. Soldiers quickly sprang into the cell to keep the growling man at bay and threw him back against the wall.

"Stop it!" Jada screamed.

Beady Eyes lunged forward, slamming his body against the metal bars and tried to reach through as far as he could to grab hold of Hans, "Keep your hands off our boss!"

Other men in the cell also stood with him and began to threaten. The Nazi merely laughed sinisterly as his men punched the big man repeatedly until he sank to the floor in submission, and then trained their guns on him to make sure he stayed down.

Fitzgerald chuckled as he remained on all fours and put up his hand to put the room at ease. "It's all right! Stand down, men!"

He then slowly looked up at Alexander with a softened face — it was the first time the professor had ever seen him look that way — and uttered, "I understand why you did it. Forgive me, old friend. I might have done the same thing if I were you." His face twisted into darkness as he shifted his gaze toward Hans, "But I will kill you! I will kill you!"

Hans dashed into the cell, kicking him in the gut as hard as he could. Fitzgerald grimaced and doubled over in pain, gasping for breath.

"Bring this hunk of filth to my interrogation chamber. I must break his will to live!"

Hans put his hand on Alexander's shoulder as the soldiers pulled the man up and out of the cell. "Do not worry; I will make him pay. He deserves everything what will be done unto him!"

"No, you're wrong. Jesus says, *'Avenge not yourselves.'* Remember — *'love your enemies'*?"

The Nazi leader snickered and patted him on the cheek, "You are relentless, Herr Professor. But you will not succeed in pulling me into another one of your Bible talks." He then spun on his heels and walked out without saying another word.

Alexander faintly smiled and as his gaze followed the man, he locked eyes for a moment with Fitzgerald, who winked at him with a quick smile. He had seen that look before, back in their college days.

As soon as Alexander was by himself, a lop-sided grin spread across his face and he shook his head; the whole thing had been a ruse to get Fitzgerald out of the cell. *What does he have up his sleeve?* Alexander wondered. He got down on his knees and began praying for another miracle.

☒ ☒ ☒

Drew, Kaci, and Jada walked along in silence as they were led through a maze of stairs and winding corridors back to the central atrium of the underground fortress. The soldier in front strode briskly, beckoning for them to keep up, and the two behind them hovered at a distance as they nonchalantly conversed in German while keeping a wary eye on the three young people.

Ahead of them, the hallway opened broadly into a grated metal platform that wrapped around the side of the mountain, and down a flight of stairs. Close by sat one of the caged elevators on a smaller recessed platform littered with large crates and supplies. The young people took in again the massive display before them of the lit-up Nazi flag, the stone guide on its pedestal, and the vast networking of stairs, gangways, and levels that spiraled upward. LED spotlights illuminated portions of the blue-green lake and docks below, swiveling in a slow, automated search pattern.

Drew noticed that the boats were still there, but other than that the docks were void of people. He peered up and saw a couple of guards on the balconies above but noticed none were watching them. *I wonder how much time has passed by since we've been here,* he thought to himself. *This place is a ghost town. Maybe this is the midnight shift. Perfect!*

"Where is the plane?" Jada loudly asked the soldier in front.

"Up at top level. We go now!" He bounded down toward the elevator. Drew put out his arm and temporarily halted Kaci and Jada at the top of the stairs.

"Are you thinking what I'm thinking?"

"Yeah," Jada replied. "We aren't leaving *anyone* behind."

"You no talk!" one of the German soldiers snarled from behind. She ignored him, "But you gotta follow my lead, okay?"

"Hey! No talk!" the other soldier harshly jabbed her with the barrel of his machine gun.

Jada let the movement cause her to stumble over her own feet and tumble hard down the metal stairs to the landing below.

"Ow!" she grimaced in pain, grabbing her knee and rolling around in agony.

Drew and Kaci glanced at each other. *Is she faking it or is she for real?* Kaci wondered to herself with grave concern as they descended the stairs carefully, the guards pushing them from behind.

"Up!" the Nazi at the bottom pulled out his pistol and pointed it at Jada.

"I can't. I think I broke it..." She held out her hand, "You've gotta help me up."

The three guards look at each other, unsure of what she said since their understanding of English was so limited.

"Up!" He gruffly urged again, grabbing her by the arm and attempting to yank her to her feet. But as soon as his clasp came down on her, Jada grabbed him instead. The Nazi flipped over her shoulder and sprawled on his back, knocked out by an elbow blow to his temple.

A second soldier jumped in surprise at what was happening and tried to snatch Kaci, who was ducking out of the way so Drew could tackle him. The two went tumbling across the small platform, but Drew was able to get him in a sleeper hold, squeezing firmly until the man went limp, unconscious. The third guard stood completely shocked by what the teenagers had pulled off so quickly, that by the time he snapped out of it and tried to bring up his machine gun, Jada was already aiming the first guard's pistol directly at him.

"You talk, you die," she uttered calmly. The man slowly placed his machine gun on the ground and kicked it over to her.

"Watch out!" Drew rasped in alarm. The guard tried to pull his sidearm out as he stood, but Kaci kicked him in the chin more out of reaction than on purpose. The man tumbled backward, out cold.

"Way to go, sis!" her brother grinned.

"Nobody lays a hand on me if I can help it. Especially not a Nazi!" She looked at the gun in Jada's hand, "What now?"

"Oh," she pocketed the handgun and moved about the recessed platform quickly, "we stack these crates in the corner to cover up those guys so nobody can find them."

As they quickly proceeded to do so, she commented, "My father would want me to kill them — don't leave a trail, you know?"

Kaci gulped, but Jada shook her head and smiled, "Don't worry; you guys have rubbed off on me. I'll do the right thing. Let's just hope that they don't wake up before we can rescue your uncle, my father, and his men."

"I memorized all of our turns," Kaci remarked while she helped her brother drag the soldiers into position.

"Impressive — I did, too," Jada winked. "So, between the two of us, we should be able to retrace our steps to the cell."

"Let's do it!" Drew declared, "But first, we need to get to that guide," he pointed down across the lake. "If we don't do it now, we may never get another opportunity, and we *need* those clues to finish our journey!"

CHAPTER XXV

The three teenagers stealthily climbed down the zig-zagging flights of stairs to the landing platform by the docks and followed a series of narrow gangplanks wrapping around the edge of the underground lake. Before long, they'd arrived at the base of the final guide to Paititi. They crouched in the shadows nearby and looked up at the face. It sat high on a pedestal, its hewn features distinct and gaunt like all the others they'd encountered along the way.

"This is the last one!" Kaci whispered excitedly.

"Finally," Jada grumbled. "But how are we gonna remember what this thing says? We don't have the camera, and none of us can read Latin or Incan!"

"True," Drew grinned, "But we don't need it." He held up a clipboard with cargo manifests in one hand and a small yellow pencil in the other. "I swiped it when we passed by the docks."

Jada crossed her arms, "And what is that supposed to do?"

"I saw this in a movie once," he winked. "Let's see if it actually works!"

After looking around to see if there were any guards on patrol, he gingerly walked up the steps of the pedestal and laid the back of the paper over the stone. Slowly, he started to gently shade in the page.

Symbols began to appear as he shaded over the raised images underneath.

"Whoa!" Kaci quietly exclaimed.

"Nice thinking." Jada shot him a kind look.

She turned to Kaci, "You stay here with your brother."

"Where are you going?"

Jada pointed to a metal access hatch not too far from where they were. "When we arrived and were taken to our cell, I noticed a few men carry our supplies this direction. Maybe they took our stuff in there! I'm going to do some looking around. Give me five minutes!"

"Okay," Kaci squeezed her hand, "Be careful!"

Like a ninja, Jada darted from shadow to shadow in a blur to the door that led back into the base. After cracking the door open and finding no one down the hall, she slipped in and disappeared.

Oh God, please be with her. Don't let her get caught! Kaci prayed.

"Psst, Kac!" Drew called out in a hushed tone. "I could use your help. This symbol's too big to get on one piece." He lifted another sheet of paper, "Hold this one for me so I can try to get it onto both."

The two of them worked together and as Drew filled the sheets with symbol after symbol, he handed them to his sister who then filed them in order at the back of the stack on the clipboard.

"Almost there...." Drew said aloud to himself. "Just got this Latin phrase on the base." He scrunched down on all fours when suddenly a long and loud wail went throughout the compound and reverberated off the walls.

An alarm.

Drew and Kaci looked at each other with a mixture of dread and concern.

"Not good!" the young man uttered, as he frantically went back to work scribbling faster, yet carefully enough not to rip the paper.

"We gotta go!" Jada yelled out, bounding through the metal hatch. She slammed it closed and spun the large wheel in the center to seal it.

"That won't keep them locked in for long!" she ran up to them, her shoulders weighed down with a few of the Bloodfists' AK-47s, Kaci's backpack, and two duffle bags. "Please tell me that you're done!"

"Almost...." Drew held the page containing the Latin text up to the light and exclaimed, "Got it!"

"Awesome! So I hit the jackpot, but I might have stirred up a hornet's nest," she grinned. "Some of the barracks were back in there! But, I did find my knives, Dad's gun belt, the SAT phone, and your backpack —" she tossed both the phone and backpack to an eager Kaci, who quickly threw the device inside and zipped the bag shut.

"And guess what? I stumbled across a huge munitions' room while playing 'hide-and-seek' with some of the guards." She slipped off one of the duffle bags and opened it partway to reveal multiple C4 charges. Drew and Kaci's eyes grew wide, and Jada laughed. "Yeah, so I may have hidden a whole bunch of these on my way out here. We've got less than 45 minutes before this whole place goes 'kaboom'!"

Suddenly, a distant voice screamed from far above, "Stop zem!"

A spotlight hastily fixed itself on their position.

"Oh no!" Kaci shrieked. "They've spotted us!"

Gunfire rang out and ricocheted sporadically around them. They ducked for cover behind the stone guide, and Jada fired back with one of the AK-47s. Loud banging commenced on the sealed hatch.

"They're gonna knock the pins out of those hinges! Let's go!" ordered Jada.

She was about to run to the metal gangway when Drew held her back. She whirled around and glared at him.

"Not yet!" he pleaded. "The eyes! We need to know where they're pointing!"

"You've got to be kidding me," Jada grimaced. "Okay, fine. And here." She handed him one of her knives. "You probably should grab them too, or *Dad* will wind up killing us instead of these Nazis. Go on my mark."

Drew chuckled at her sarcasm and then gritted his teeth. He looked to Jada for the signal.

"NOW!" she began shooting up to where more soldiers were gathering on the platforms above.

God, help me! Drew prayed as he scurried around the face. His feet found a narrow crack in its mouth so he could pull himself up to be level with the sparkling blue eyes. *They're looking up and to the right... Northeast!* He quickly ran the sharp blade around the sockets of the stone guide. His body stiffened every time he heard gunfire, anticipating the feeling of hot bullets searing through his back and legs at any moment. *No, I believe you will protect me, Lord!*

"Drew! Hurry!" Kaci screamed out.

"Done!" he jumped down and pocketed the stones.

"Then let's go!" said Jada. "Things are gonna get crowded real fast!"

They sprinted toward the walkway and found that it was just beyond the reach of the spotlights since it was along the very edge of the lake and nestled close to the sides of the mountain. Soldiers began to scramble down the multiple flights of stairs.

Drew and Kaci darted out in front to lead the way, but Jada found it hard to keep up with them because of all the things she was carrying.

"Let us help you!" Kaci grabbed one of the duffle bags and slung it around her head and shoulder.

"Thanks," Jada smiled, out of breath.

"And I'll take these," Drew snatched the other bag and one of the AK-47s.

"Do you know how to use that thing?" Jada looked at him warily.

"Absolutely," Drew nodded while racking the bolt. "I'm actually one of the best marksmen in my county."

"Huh! And why have I never heard about this before?"

"Because we've never talked about it," Drew laughed. "And I don't think your dad would trust me with a gun anyway. We're your prisoners, remember?"

Jada hung her head with embarrassment, "Yeah, I guess so." *But you're more like a brother and sister to me now,* she finished in her mind.

Bullets sprayed into the water next to them, propelling the young people to run forward.

"You focus on keeping us alive!" Drew shouted over the siren and the gunfire, then pointed to the docks, "I've got an idea!"

The soldiers were still slowly working their way down to the landing platform, and Jada kept them busy by shooting in their direction.

"Kaci, figure out how to open those entrance doors!"

"Okay!" She scampered up into the control booth just a few yards away and began pressing buttons. She smiled to herself. *It would help if I could read German! But, it's probably this one. Big red buttons always say, 'Press me'!*

She was right. The mechanical sound of the doors opening filled the cavern.

Drew set down his duffle bag and clicked his weapon from automatic to single shot. He carefully aimed at the spotlights bearing down on them and took them out one at a time. The waterfront was now encased in darkness. He swiftly set down his machine gun and unhooked the tether from one of the boats. He jumped inside and started it, shifted it into gear, and jammed the accelerator. As the engine foamed to life and began pulling away, he dove off and landed hard on the pier. Jada, catching on to his plan, stopped shooting as the boat sped out over the lake and headed straight toward the massive metal doors. It soared through the entryway, scraping along the wall as it made its way out to the river. A few of the men near the bottom of the stairs pointed at the boat and yelled orders to shoot.

Drew swiftly picked up his gear and silently ran to where Kaci and Jada were crouching behind a couple stacked crates.

"That should distract them!" Drew whispered.

Jada gritted her teeth and pulled out her knives, "I hope so. If not, get ready to shoot, or we're dead."

The siren spread throughout the halls and past the doors of the interrogation room. Hans had just slipped his hands into a pair of gloves when it began ringing.

"What is that?" he demanded of the two soldiers who were cinching up Fitzgerald's harnesses.

The guard who was working on Fitzgerald's left wrist ran out the door, leaving Hans, Fitzgerald, and another soldier in the room. There was silence for a moment before the man returned in a panic.

"It's the children, sir!"

"What about them?"

"They've escaped."

"So? They're children! Round them up and cuff them more tightly next time!" Hans fiddled with his torture instruments on the stainless-steel table.

"That's just it, sir. They're in a boat. They escaped out the main doors."

"What?" Hans asked incredulously. "Who let them out? You can only open the doors from the dock!"

"I don't know, sir, but they're gone. Should we —" The soldier was quickly cut off.

"Don't just stand there!" Hans flailed his arms in anger. "Get out there, you two! I can handle this." The two soldiers disappeared instantly, the sound of their boots hitting the marble floor reverberating back into the room.

"Sounds like there's a real problem." Fitzgerald finally spoke. He didn't understand a word of the conversation in German but could hear Hans's anger.

"Be quiet," Hans snarled in English. He picked up a tool in one hand and turned from the shadowed table, revealing his face.

"Wouldn't be the kids giving you trouble, would it?" Fitzgerald mocked.

"QUIET!" Hans raised his hand and brought it down over Fitzgerald's cheek. His head shot to one side and hung off the chair. As he opened his eyes, he noticed that the strap on his left wrist was not fully tightened. He smiled and quickly righted himself.

He looked at Hans with a devilish grin. *If I can distract him....*

"What?" the Nazi spit angrily.

"Oh nothing," Fitzgerald leered. "Next time, just hit me like you mean it!"

"*Schnell! Schnell! Herr Müeller will sie lebend!*" one of Hans' personal guards screamed down into the cavern below pointing to the remaining boats. Out of breath, the two men hastily joined the others and sped away from the docks.

Drew silently pumped his fist and the three teenagers grinned at each other. As soon as the boats had disappeared through the doorway, they carefully peered around their crates to see if anyone had stayed behind. Just one lone soldier remained standing guard. He waltzed over to the control panel and pressed a sequence of buttons to turn off the alarm.

Jada tightened the grip around her knives, but Kaci placed a hand on her arm. The two of them locked eyes for a moment — Jada's stare was cold, and Kaci's implored her not to kill him. Jada sighed and sheathed the blades. When the guard turned to begin pacing back and forth, she dashed out and locked him into a sleeper hold with one hand over his mouth to keep him from shouting out.

Once he was unconscious, Jada dropped him to the floor and waved for the others to come out. Drew grinned from ear to ear as he went over to the control panel and closed the doors.

"Imagine the look on their faces when they find out they've been had!" Kaci giggled.

"Don't start celebrating yet!" Jada pointed across the lake. The soldiers from the barracks had finally broken through, and the metal hatch slammed hard onto the ground as it was pushed open off its hinges. One pointed straight at them and yelled out angrily in German.

The siren resumed its painful ringing throughout the complex.

"Not again!" Kaci sighed.

Jada glanced at the timer on her wristwatch, "We've got less than thirty minutes! Let's move!"

The three teenagers bounded up the stairs two at a time. Once they reached the metal platform, they could hear the soldiers below clamoring up after them. The grinding sound of the big waterfall doors filled the cavern again as one of the men reopened them. Drew briefly paused with Jada and Kaci at the railing and peered down. One of Hans' guards who'd led the men on the boat chase stood on his vessel's bow as it sailed back into the lake. He screamed furiously when he spotted the three young people high above. Before the boats could be secured to the dock, the men leapt from the water onto the concrete.

"They're madder than a hornet's nest!" Jada nervously stated over the siren, then looked at Drew and Kaci. "You go and get my father and your uncle." She nodded toward the elevator lift. "I need to stay here and guard our exit!"

She opened the duffle bags filled with armed explosives and grabbed one for herself. "I'm going to take out a few flights of stairs with this thing so these guys can't get up here. Make sure you throw the rest of these everywhere you can, got it? We're gonna bury this place for good!"

She stood and began firing sporadically, "Go!"

Drew and Kaci sprinted back down the hallway toward the prison cells, Kaci leading the way. She prayed for wisdom to remember every turn as they retraced their steps. They opened random doors to storage rooms and unoccupied offices along the way, tossing in the explosives as fast as they could.

Suddenly, the corridor shook around them, causing them to stumble over their feet. They steadied themselves against the wall as pebbles bounced down onto them from the ceiling. They looked at each other and grinned.

Jada.

They swerved left and saw the familiar faces of several Nazi figurehead paintings.

"Almost there!" Drew exclaimed. "I recognize this!"

Kaci ran her hand along the wall as they went, tipping the paintings off their hooks without care.

"Tssk. Tssk," Drew playfully scolded his sister.

"So much for the Fourth Reich!" she giggled. "Foiled with the help of a couple of teenagers!"

The young man grinned, then put his fingers to his lips as they entered the next corridor. Down at the end of the hall was the entrance to the prison block. They could easily approach since the siren still blared over the loudspeakers. Drew peered around the corner. Only one guard stood in the doorway, and on his belt hung the keys. But the man was twice his size.

Drew slipped off his AK-47 and now empty duffle bag. He demonstrated with his hands to Kaci what he was about to do and mouthed, *You take his machine gun!*

He took a few steps back and dashed around the corner, catching the Nazi by complete surprise. Before he could lift his gun, Drew wrapped himself tightly around the soldier's body and slammed him into the wall. The machine gun clattered to the ground. Alexander and Fitzgerald's men stood at the bars, straining to look down the hallway at what was happening, but they were too far away to know for certain.

The Nazi and Drew fiercely wrestled back and forth, but as soon as the guard turned his back to where Kaci was poised, she lunged out, scooped up the weapon, and wacked him over the head with the stock of the gun as hard as she could. The large man stumbled backward looking confused, then crumpled to the floor unconscious.

"Whew!" Drew wiped the sweat off his brow, "Thanks, sis!" He grabbed his AK-47 and snatched the key ring off the guard's belt.

When Drew and Kaci ran up to the prison cell, each of them holding a firearm, the professor looked at them in shock and then laughed, "Why am I surprised? I should've known this had something to do with my little monsters!" he said with a big grin. "Thank the Lord you're safe!"

"We've got to get out of here!" Drew exclaimed, as he fumbled with the keys in the lock. "We don't have much time!"

Alexander immediately frowned, sensing the worry in his nephew's voice. "Bring us up to speed."

Kaci briefly told them everything that had transpired since they'd left the cell, while Drew unlocked both doors.

Beady Eyes scratched his jaw, "I'm impressed!"

Kaci smiled and kindly handed him the German machine gun while Drew yielded his weapon over to Goatee.

"Let's get out of here and find Adrian!" Alexander ordered and led the group hastily through the empty corridors to Hans' interrogation room.

Suddenly, they stopped dead in their tracks as the thunderous sound of a shotgun echoed down the hallway. Then another and another. They were controlled and steady, like someone highly trained. Alexander placed his arms around his niece and nephew, bringing them in the middle of Fitzgerald's men. Beady Eyes and Goatee stood warily on either side of the group with weapons ready.

More shots. Then heavy footsteps came.

"Gib dich jetzt hin!" Alexander warned loudly to whoever was approaching. *"Wir werden Sie erschießen!"*

"Jim?" From down the hall came Fitzgerald's voice. "Is that you?" The big man turned the corner and instantly lowered his vintage tactical shotgun. He grinned from ear to ear, revealing bloody teeth and a battered face. "I'd recognize your voice in any language!"

"What took you so long?" Alexander joked. "I expected you in half the time."

Fitzgerald chuckled, "I got detained by Fairch--I mean *Hans*, that rat, and some of his men along the way." His eyes locked with Alexander's. "But he won't be a problem for us anymore."

"Heh!" Beady Eyes grunted. "Good riddance!"

"I brought you something, old chum!" Fitzgerald handed Alexander his cylindrical leather map case and notebook. "I found them in Hans' office next to that little torture chamber of his. And I also retrieved this —" He held up the waterproof camera that had documented their journey and tossed it to Drew for safekeeping.

"Awesome!" Drew exclaimed, slinging it sideways around his arm and neck.

But the man's face suddenly turned into a dark scowl. His eyes darted back and forth over the group. "Where's my daughter?"

Kaci stepped forward and blurted, "She's waiting for us and keeping our exit clear! We really need to get moving. We only have a few minutes before this whole place blows. Come on!"

As the group hastily followed her down the corridors, Drew filled a confused Fitzgerald in on the details and showed him the clipboard that contained the final clues.

The man grinned, "You all did that? Incredible! I knew there was great worth in keeping you two around!"

Drew rolled his eyes.

As they approached the platform, Jada glared at them between bursts from her machine gun, "It's about time! We've only got about five minutes!"

Fitzgerald drained the remaining shells of his shotgun into the group of guards that materialized in the hallway behind them.

"That's probably not the last of them! Things are going to heat up fast!"

He discarded his empty weapon, and Jada tossed him his revolver belt.

The Nazis below were cut off by a gaping hole in the zig-zagging stairways, but this didn't stop them from yelling viciously in German and firing an incessant volley that whizzed around the escaping group as they ran to the caged elevator.

They barely squeezed inside, and Alexander slammed the gate shut, then scanned the German-labeled controls. The gears creaked to life as the elevator slowly ascended to the top level marked *Hanger*.

"We're sitting ducks in here!" Fitzgerald muttered as bullets sparked and ricocheted around them. Some of the soldiers had gotten back into boats to get a better vantage point out on the water and they fired at will at the moving target.

"God, we ask for mercy!" Drew prayed aloud, putting his hand in the air. "You've spared us before, and I believe that You can do it again! Please help each of these men to know that You are God. Put a shield of protection around us, and we beg of You to let us escape! If this is not Your will, I am ready to die; I know I will be with You in Heaven. Please help these men around me to trust in You as their personal Saviour before it's too late, so they don't have to go to Hell!"

"Amen!" Alexander beamed, unable to hold back the joy he had for his nephew's unconventional boldness in such a daunting moment.

The elevator shuttered to a sluggish halt, and the gate clicked open.

"We made it!" Kaci squealed.

Jada glanced at her wristwatch, "But we've only got three minutes!"

They sprinted down the wide arched tunnel, paved and well-illuminated, and reached a set of metals doors at the end with the word *Hanger* stenciled across in German.

"Open them up!" Fitzgerald said in a huff.

The team took either side, pulling open the huge doors. What awaited them on the other side was extraordinary. The roof arched high overhead and was colored a dull brown with the sun filtering through. The floor was cement and on either side of the large room were two more huge doors.

Drew whistled, "This place is a museum!"

"They must have some sort of elaborate tunnel system to get everything out of here," Alexander mused.

The warehouse was brimming full of machines, each looking worn and like they had not been used in a very long time. Tanks and huge trucks were lined up in rows, and Messerschmitt warplanes sat dusty on the opposite side.

The men tried to open one of the doors, but it wouldn't budge.

"Locked!" Jada panicked. "We've got less than two minutes!"

"Over there!" Alexander shouted, pointing to various red

ladders along the wall which led to hatches in the ceiling. "They're marked as emergency exits!"

"GO!" bellowed Fitzgerald. "Every man for himself!"

On the surface, the sun was brightly shining in the narrow man-made clearing that led to the nearby river. The air was thick and hot; the water was crystal clear and sparkled as it flowed serenely over the rocks, but far downstream it turned into rapids as it swept over the cliff and became the mountain's mighty waterfall. In the water sat a silver floatplane moored to a dock that also contained a couple of speedboats and other small cargo vessels covered in camouflage. Birds squawked and flew overhead in droves. Jungle insects briefly paused from their incessant buzzing when numerous metal access points flew open and the team randomly spilled out into the tall grass.

Then the ground began to shake. Everything was falling, moving in sporadic motions up and down like a massive earthquake.

The shockwave rang out and came up from underneath them. Its force flew through the hatches and out into the air in a giant explosion, throwing everyone into the air. The roof of the hanger caved in and the front portion of the mountain that had made up most of the Nazi base and the waterfall crumbled into the earth, leaving a gaping hole.

Drew lay near the bank of the river, barely able to hear the flow of the water, his head ringing with the force of the explosion.

Jada fell backward, flying several feet from the hatch opening and falling hard in the grass.

Alexander was sprawled out looking up at the sky, squinting his eyes in the harsh sun. He had tried to help Fitzgerald to the surface and in his attempt went flying himself. Fitzgerald lay next to him.

"Jim? Jim, are you all right?"

He felt the man's hand on his leg and gave him a thumbs up without moving. His body was so sore.

"Jim, thank you. I could've died," the Scotsman rasped hoarsely.

"Don't just thank me, Adrian. Thank God. It's a miracle that any of us are still alive." Alexander's voice was weak, but he spoke confidently.

"Is everyone okay?" Beady Eyes stood, scanning the rest of the scattered group that struggled to get up. He walked over to Drew and helped the young man to his feet.

"I'm good," Jada said from across the field, trying to gain her equilibrium and carefully avoiding the edge of the caved-in hanger.

"I don't think all of us made it," Goatee said soberly.

Drew's eyes narrowed, and terror seized his throat.

Where was Kaci?

"Kaci? Kaci?" he frantically called out when he couldn't find her among the others. Alexander was on his feet now, feeling a pit of dread in his stomach.

"Do not worry. She's still alive… for now," a hauntingly familiar face emerged from the tree line.

"What?" Alexander blinked heavily to clear the fog away from his brain and rubbed his eyes. "How is this possible?"

Hans, his face blackened and his eyes wild, held Kaci in his left arm and his Luger in the other hand. She was barely conscious, having been flung into the jungle by the blast. Hans switched the gun back and forth, pointing it at each of them in turn and then back to Kaci, laughing sinisterly.

"I killed you!" exclaimed Fitzgerald.

"So you thought," the blonde-haired German smirked. "But you failed."

"How did you escape?"

"There are other ways outside of this base besides the route you chose," he sneered sarcastically. His face then twisted with a lust for power, and he wobbled back and forth excitedly with a madman's glee. "Now I will be immortal! I have proven to the gods that I am worthy!"

He pressed the barrel of his pistol hard into Kaci's temple, causing her to whimper in pain. "If you do not help me, Herr Professor — say goodbye to one of your little monsters."

"Let me put an end to this here and now!" Fitzgerald raised his revolver.

"You kill me — she dies too!" Hans pulled Kaci's body up closer in front of him.

"Really?" Fitzgerald grinned as he tilted his head. He thought for a moment, then cocked his gun to fire.

"Dad — No!" Jada screamed out.

"Adrian, please!" Alexander walked in front of his gun. "Put that thing away."

"You WILL NOT help him!!"

"And you will not shoot my niece," Alexander replied firmly with a wink unseen by Hans. "Gun down, NOW!"

Fitzgerald hesitated, then understood that his old friend was up to something. He lowered his chrome-covered pistol.

"Good, very good," Hans smirked and brandished his Luger around. "Now nobody moves except for the Professor here. And move very slowly."

Hans carefully walked backwards toward the edge of the river, stepping down into the water. Drew stood helpless like the rest of them, watching Alexander advance in cadence with the Nazi's retreat toward the long silver pontoon plane.

They were knee deep into the river when Hans ordered, "Untether the plane from the dock, then put these on!" He tossed Alexander a pair of handcuffs. The professor did as he was told.

"Now go sit in the cockpit! No funny business!"

Hans shoved Kaci away from him into the water and fired blindly toward the team, who dove into the tall grass as bullets whizzed overhead.

"Haha! You have lost, and I have won!" he yelled as he jumped onto the plane and lobbed a potato grenade from his back pocket toward the shore. The explosion violently rocked the plane and shot a large plume of dirt into the air, but it was just enough of a distraction to start the engine and begin heading upriver.

"Paititi is only a few hours from here by plane, Herr Professor, two days at most by boat," Hans bragged as set his pistol down on the dashboard to adjust the controls. "Are you ready for our little adventure?"

"No!" Alexander declared bluntly and brought down his cuffed fists hard onto Hans' neck. "I will *never* help the likes of you!"

The German flew forward into the yoke, causing the plane to slowly spin in the water. He grabbed for his Luger but Alexander firmly clamped onto his wrist and the two locked eyes.

"You never planned on helping me, did you?" Hans snarled angrily.

Alexander shrugged, "I needed to get my niece and nephew out of harm's way."

The Nazi launched himself at the professor like a rabid animal. The two wrestled around in the cockpit, and Alexander could feel the plane picking up speed.

One of us must have accidentally hit the throttle!

His movements were limited since his hands weren't free, but he'd learned enough self-defense to keep Hans' attacks at bay. The German grabbed his Luger but when he tried to bring it around, Alexander hit him in the stomach with his knee, and the pistol fell to the floor. The professor kicked it toward the back of the plane.

⊗ ⊗ ⊗

As Drew helped his sister out of the water, he noticed the craft jostling back and forth from the commotion of the two men fighting.

"Look!" He pointed, as the rest of the team gathered along the shore. "Uncle James is trying to escape!"

"But the plane is drifting downstream too quickly," Fitzgerald gritted his teeth, eyeing the waterfall. "I don't know if he'll make it!"

"We've got to do something!"

"Don't be foolish, my boy. There's nothing —"

"You're wrong," Drew cut him off. "Some things are impossible with men, but not with God. I *won't* stand idly by and watch my uncle plunge to his death!"

He spun on his heels and ran to the pier. He ripped off the

camouflage mesh on one of the speedboats as fast as he could, untied it from the dock, and jumped down behind the wheel.

Lord, please help figure out how to operate this thing, he prayed.

"Here, move over!" Jada appeared next to him. "For these you gotta punch it!"

She slammed on the ignition and the throttle at the same time and Drew heard the boat come to life, roaring past the end of the docks and down the river after the drifting aircraft.

The young man put his hands together in a prayer position and gestured to her, "Thank you!"

She smiled and nodded, then asked over the winds, "What's your plan?"

Drew feverishly looked through the supplies. He found a sturdy rope and secured it to one of the cleats.

"Get me as close as you can to that plane! I'll figure something out!"

Alexander lowered his shoulder and smashed Hans back out of the cockpit. He grabbed the controls and pushed the yoke to the side in an attempt to ground the plane on the riverbank, but the German quickly scrambled to his feet and yanked the professor back with him. As the two men tumbled aft, they rolled around on the small floor, each trying to gain control over the other. Alexander felt his body hit one of the supply crates hard, knocking the wind of him.

"You will never escape!" the Nazi hissed.

In that moment, he saw his Luger close by. He reached for it, but Alexander kicked him, and Hans lurched sideways into the door. It flew open, to their surprise, almost sucking the man out. With a yelp he caught the edges of the frame and pulled himself back in.

Between the man's legs, Alexander spotted a speedboat quickly approaching their position with Drew frantically beckoning for him to come. With a rope tied around his waist, Drew dove into the water, trying to get closer to the craft while Jada did her best to keep the boat steady against the raging current.

Suddenly, the plane lurched to a halt with a scraping sound, sending Hans across the cabin and crashing him into the bulkhead. Alexander staggered to his feet and saw nothing but sky out of the cockpit. The roar of the mighty waterfall surrounded them. Every few seconds the craft shuddered as the sheer force of the rapids sought to pull it from the rocks it was snagged on and thrust it down to the watery depths.

They were at the edge.

Hans' Luger rested just inches from Alexander's boot. He quickly grabbed it as the man lay there in a daze, eyes wide, then stepped over the German, pointing the weapon directly at him.

"Enough! You've been beaten!"

"Ah, so the professor has won, has he?" his eyes flashed with a disturbing evil on his blackened face. "Go ahead, shoot me. COME ON! You know you have been longing for this moment ever since you discovered my true identity."

Streams of sweat dripped from Alexander's dirty forehead. *I could justify it as self-defense.* But he shook the thought out of his head. "No, Hans. God is the judge of mankind, not me. I would never choose to end a life if I didn't have to."

He lowered the weapon as he steadied himself from the plane's lurching and stretched out his hand. "We must get out of here!"

The Nazi looked at him, surprised by the act of kindness, then sinisterly kicked the professor in the chest back toward the door jam. "I will never surrender!"

The sudden movement jerked the plane loose, and it began to teeter over the edge of the falls. Alexander jumped free with all his might, landing hard on the slippery rocks. He franticly grabbed for anything he could hold on to with his cuffed hands. The silver aircraft disappeared over the edge of the cascading falls, the German's hysterical laughter echoing eerily as it faded away into the mist below.

"Uncle James! Uncle James!" Drew screamed between

mouthfuls of water as the rope stretched taut behind him. He now hovered within arm's reach. "Take my hand!"

Only one shot at this, Lord, Alexander prayed. He exhaled in faith and launched himself toward his nephew, feeling his body get sucked backwards down the falls.

"Gottcha!" Drew grabbed him with a tight squeeze, and the professor slowly pulled himself around to hold on to the young man's shoulders.

Jada grit her teeth; the engine was already roaring in a duel with the falls as she tried to keep it steady. The throttle was almost wide open against the pull of the current. She gradually gave it a bit more gas, but the boat didn't move.

She pushed harder with her arm, her knuckles turning white as she gripped the accelerator. *God, You can do the impossible. I believe it. Please...help us!*

Almost as if being pushed by an unseen hand, the boat edged free of the rapids, moving toward calmer waters. Jada slowed the engine and slumped back against the side of the boat, exhausted. She looked up into the sky with a relief like she had never felt before.

They were saved.

CHAPTER XXVI

The team slowly made their way upriver in one of cargo vessels from the docks above the destroyed base. It was a small tugboat that hadn't been used in years, but at least it had been stocked with water, canned rations, and other supplies. Black smoke spewed from its short smokestack as it chugged through the water with a loud vibrating hum. The air around them smelled like burnt oil, but no one complained. They were just thankful to be on their way again and, based on Alexander's intel and their ancient map, the journey should take them less than two days. Fitzgerald pushed the vessel as fast as he could; he was eager to find his beloved city.

But at what cost? Drew thought to himself. He, Jada, and Kaci leaned against the handrail that surrounded the bridge and overlooked the deck where the rest of the men, except for Alexander, were sprawled out trying to catch some rest under the hot sun. Drew shook his head. Fitzgerald's team had come a long way — from a couple hundred mercenaries with an impressive convoy of vehicles and supplies to what was now a rag-tag crew of a half-dozen men. Sadly, their leader didn't seem care. In his mind, they were merely pawns — a means to an end. He justified every casualty with a shrug, saying they knew what they'd signed up for.

So many lives ruined and wasted by one man's obsession, Drew muttered under his breath as he looked over his shoulder at the smug Scotsman holding his head high in the breeze as he gripped the helm. Then Drew smiled and chuckled to himself. Little did the man realize that since their near run-in with death at the Nazi base, a few of his last remaining mercenaries had come to either Drew or Alexander and spoken with them about their eternal destiny. As a result of seeing the immense faith of the professor and the two young people over the past several weeks — and especially after Drew's bold prayer in the elevator as they were escaping from the Nazis — each of them felt greatly burdened to know more about Jesus Christ and His desire to save their souls. Drew couldn't help but grin broadly as he remembered how one by one, each man had gotten the matter settled.

He rubbed his weary eyes and watched the passing shoreline as he began to pray for the lost soul of the young lady that stood between him and his sister. The trees hung low along the bank with swooping vines, and the thick forest rolled with the small hills that surrounded them. He also noticed the water wasn't like the rest of the rivers they'd traversed; it was crystal clear and sparkling. But the deeper they ventured, the narrower the river became, the steeper the terrain grew, and the louder the jungled buzzed. There were so many new sounds he hadn't heard before. Animals scurried through the underbrush, only seen in the shaking of the leaves, and far away a big cat yawned with a bellowing roar.

The three teenagers didn't say much to each other. They were tired — very tired — exhausted, and ready to be done. Finally, Drew cleared his throat and weakly grinned at the girls. "At least we got the last clue, right?"

Fitzgerald overheard him through the open doorway of the wheelhouse and beamed, "Such good work, my boy! If it wasn't for you three, we wouldn't be able to complete our journey!"

The teenagers glanced at each other.

"Kinda wish we *hadn't* done that," Jada muttered unapologetically, then rolled her eyes. "But you know my father. He never would've stopped until he found the city. At least now this whole thing will be over soon. Come on," she motioned and headed down the bridge ladder to the deck below.

They found the professor in the main cabin pouring over his

notes, both maps, and the clues they'd discovered along the way. He looked up over the rim of his glasses as they came through the door.

"Do you mind leaving that open?" he kindly asked Jada. "It's getting a little stuffy in here."

"So what have you found out, Uncle James?" Kaci rested her elbows on the large wooden crate that served as a table.

"Well, from the symbol sketches you made from the last guide, I've figured them out to mean '*Stay true on the path of the rising tides.*'"

The three young people stared at him blankly.

"What is that supposed to mean?" Jada frowned.

Alexander chuckled as he took off his glasses to let his eyes rest, "Your guess is as good as mine, but I'm sure it will make sense when the time comes. The Latin clue reads, '*The wisdom of the worthy will set you free on the land surrounded by the sea.*'"

"I can understand some of that," Jada nodded and tapped her finger on the top right fringe of the ancient map. "'*The land surrounded by the sea*' is referencing the lake and this island we're heading to."

"Yeah," Kaci pondered. "But what does '*the wisdom of the worthy*' refer to?"

"I believe '*the worthy*' are the ones who follow all of the guides' combined wisdom," Alexander explained, but the teenagers looked at him a bit confused. A slow smile spread across his face.

"Let's review!" He put his glasses back on, crossed his arms, and began wandering about the room as if he were lecturing back at Cambridge.

"At the beginning of this adventure, I remember Adrian telling me — and I read for myself — that Aapo warned only '*the worthy*' could find the city. He and his people would guard the secret of its location with their lives and take this knowledge to their graves. He knew that if *anyone* from the outside world was going to discover it, they would have to first re-unite his master's medallion and figure out the initial clue he left in his letter to the Pope."

"So that's why he left his portion of the medallion at the

Vatican!" Drew surmised.

"Presumably so," Alexander agreed. "His first clue led Fitzgerald to begin the expedition at Machu Picchu and retrieve this map," he gently held up the ancient artifact, "during the June Solstice. There was a warning to retrieve the pendent if they ever wanted to complete their journey," the professor glanced over to Jada and remarked, "Which your father impulsively did."

"Huh," Drew thought aloud. "So the medallion still has a part to play in all of this."

"Correct. Aapo and his people then plotted a course through the vast jungle that carefully involved a series of clues left behind on stone faces they called *'guides.'* These clues worked in correlation with the direction each of the statue's eyes pointed, as described here in Latin."

With his finger he underscored the phrase *'Anima eius viam monstrabit'* along the edge of the map which meant, *'Its soul will point the way.'* The teenagers studied the words and looked over the rest of the drawings intently. The open-mouthed skull on the island in the upper right corner seemed to stare back at them.

"However, this is where it gets intriguing. Every stone face contained an additional clue that didn't seem to make any sense and had nothing to do with our journey. We have six of them now. What is their purpose? I've asked myself this over and over again, and I believe the answer has to do with something that we are going to face once we get to Paititi. Obviously, they must bear some great significance, or Aapo would not have gone through the painstaking effort of leaving them for *'the worthy.'* I think it would be wise of us to put our clues together all in one place so we can read over them more easily."

He looked at Kaci with a lop-sided grin, "Would you be willing to write everything down for us? If I did, it would become another form of hieroglyphics."

Kaci giggled and pulled out her trusty notebook from her backpack. As she flipped through it toward the back to find a blank page, the others noticed the numerous sketches she'd penciled on their adventure — all sorts of flowers, trees, animals, and even people.

"You're really good at that," Jada complimented.

"Thanks," Kaci grew red and instinctively tucked a strand of her golden-brown hair behind her ear, then proceeded to write out what her uncle instructed of her:

GUIDE ONE *(bottom of lake)*:
- Clue for Paititi: *"Be watchful of the waters deep."*
- Hint to finding next guide: *"Follow the crooked path. Don't lose sight of your feet, or the mighty raging you will meet."*

GUIDE TWO *(swinging bridge)*:
- Clue for Paititi: *"Lest you wake the writhing from sleep."*
- Hint to finding next guide: *"Deep with the dead by tilted head, away from moon and sun lies the search the ancients have begun."*

GUIDE THREE *(Amaru Cliff)*:
- Clue for Paititi: *"Without the stones you face your death."*
- Hint to finding next guide: *"Near forked tongue great life has sprung; where a soul that lies amidst the tree watches o'er all who breathe."*

GUIDE FOUR *(old tree on ridge)*:
- Clue for Paititi: *"As Amaru lives, take your breath."*
- Hint to finding next guide: *"A gaping mouth at river's end, provides the light as you descend."*

GUIDE FIVE *(temple of cannibal village)*:
- Clue for Paititi: *"Take heed to join through what in strength abides."*
- Hint to finding next guide: *"Behind the veil amid the peaks rests the silent soul."*

GUIDE SIX *(waterfall inside mountain)*:
- Clue for Paititi: *"Stay true on the path of the rising tides."*
- Hint to finding the location of Paititi: *"The wisdom of the worthy will set you free on the land surrounded by the sea."*

"There!" Kaci smiled, carefully tearing the page out of her notebook and handing it to her uncle. "I think we've got it!"

"Very good," the professor patted her on the shoulder and began studying the clues.

"I believe these first two clues go together because of the way they're worded," he observed while scratching the thick stubble on his jaw. He then slowly pointed to the map at the coiled serpent image in the bottom of the lake where they were headed. "Could there be a connection?"

Kaci shuddered at the possibility of coming face-to-face with another monster. Deep in thought over this sobering prospect, they all jumped when Fitzgerald abruptly roared with excitement from the wheelhouse above them.

"JIM! Where are you?"

"Coming!" he yelled back as he folded the paper up and put it in the front of his holstered Bible.

The group rushed out onto the deck and looked up at the large man leaning over the handrail. His medallion dangled out in front of him, and his eyes blazed with exhilaration.

"THIS IS IT!" He shouted breathlessly, then gestured broadly, "BEHOLD!"

Standing tall on the riverbank next to them was a huge head reaching almost to the top of the trees, bearing a similar appearance to the guides that had led them on their journey. This statue was covered with sheets of moss and had weathered cracks running up its front and sides. The further upstream they looked, the more of these heads they saw dotting both sides of the shoreline every few hundred feet like a row of columns.

"Incredible!" Alexander exclaimed, stumbling to the front of the boat. The three teenagers and the half-dozen Bloodfists that remained gathered behind him and took in the exotic sight.

At the end of the line of faces, two even larger statues stood as mighty sentinels on either side of a small stream that trickled out of the mountains.

Clearly etched on the base of each statue was the now-familiar symbol of Paititi.

⊗ ⊗ ⊗

They landed the ship on the banks of the river, securing it with a couple of mooring lines around a sturdy, vine-covered tree. Beady Eyes made sure they didn't let any supplies in the boat go to waste. While scrounging around in the cargo hold below, he even found a few old MP 40 machine guns that he was able to equip his fellow mercenaries with. In his mind, after all they'd been through, they couldn't be too careful.

The trek from there was slow, slower than Fitzgerald wished. His demeanor portrayed that he wanted everyone to sprint the rest of the way as he took wide strides through the overgrowth. As much as he wished they could move faster however, he knew they must conserve energy for what was to come.

The hike was steep and difficult, but soon they came across a worn path weaving along the bank of the stream that guided them up the rest of the mountain. The air was thick, unbearably hot, and still. The incessant buzz of the jungle and constant babbling of the ever-narrowing stream enveloped them as they persistently tramped along.

"Make sure you drink plenty of water," the professor warned the group when they paused for a moment to catch their breath. "Or you'll die from heatstroke out here!"

As the others turned to continue trekking uphill at the impatient behest of Fitzgerald, Alexander thought he spotted something move ever so slightly out of the corner of his eye. Something black and white disguised with moss. With narrowed eyes, he quickly looked back into the rainforest, scanning each tree. Nothing. The sounds of the jungle still echoed in his ears. He slowly turned and followed the rest, bringing up the rear.

After a couple of hours, Fitzgerald, who was quite a distance ahead of them, shouted back over his shoulder, "Come on, you slow pokes! It looks like we're almost there; I can see where it levels off!"

"Adrian," Alexander caught up to him and heavily whispered. "It might be wise to keep our voices down. We don't know what lies ahead; let's not attract any unwanted attention."

"What do you mean? The jungle?" Fitzgerald looked down at Alexander with a raised eyebrow.

"The jungle... or anyone else we might encounter."

"What are you talking about?" Fitzgerald smiled devilishly and pulled the gun from his holster shooting it a couple times into the thick rainforest. Alexander winced as the sound rang out like an echo. Leaves rustled and vines shook but nothing came through the brush. Fitzgerald's men warily kept their fingers next to the triggers of their weapons just in case anything suddenly launched out of the trees.

"You're paranoid, Jim! I'd like to see the jungle try and get in my way." Fitzgerald turned on the spot, holstered his weapon, and kept walking.

When they reached the top of the incline, they found the source of the babbling brook. The lake was moss-green, murky and stretched out for about a mile, its surface untouched by wind or any other sort of ripple. The whole of it looked like a dark sheet of glass. The surrounding land was steeped in deep vegetation; the only portion not covered in total forest was the shoreline they were standing on.

An island stood in the middle of the lake and climbing up from its sandy shore was a set of rolling hills. A massive mountain in the center loomed over it all. After the elevation that the team had already conquered, it was no surprise to Kaci that the mountain was covered mostly in clouds.

"Could it… could it be?" She fought back the tears. "Have we finally made it?"

"I believe so, my dear," Alexander put his arm around her shoulder and tenderly pulled her close to his side.

Everyone stood in awe, taking in the eerie yet breathtaking sight.

"The most coveted treasure of the earth lies before us!" Fitzgerald reveled. "We are on the threshold of greatness. There is no time to waste!"

He darted forward to an old set of dug-out canoes that floated motionlessly in the murky water, tied to the shore by home-spun flax rope. The slimy brown wood smelled musty and was rotting at the ends.

"These belong to someone," Alexander observed. His mind went back to what he thought he'd seen in the trees. Were there natives here who served as protectors of Paititi? Descendants from the original inhabitants of the city?

"These must've belonged to the Nazis." Fitzgerald loaded his pack into one.

"No," Alexander declared. "The Nazis flew onto the island, remember? They wouldn't have any use for these. They were left here by someone else."

"Stop over-analyzing everything, Jim! Maybe they were just meant for us," Fitzgerald flashed a smile. "You know — like your God in His providence providing for our every need?" He laughed sarcastically. "Either way, it looks like this is the only way for us to get across," the big man declared as he stepped inside, rocking the canoe and sending gentle ripples across the surface of the unusually serene water.

"Well, don't just stand there; come on!" he angrily motioned to the group, still hesitant about the idea. His voice echoed across the lake, "NOW!!"

A flock of white birds rose from a nearby tree and flew away, startled. Jada and Beady Eyes hastily joined him while Drew, Kaci, and

Alexander stuck together. The other men split up and uneasily climbed into the two remaining canoes.

"Uncle James, I've got a bad feeling about this," Drew whispered as he carefully knelt in the wobbly vessel and grabbed a paddle.

"You and me both," the professor nodded. "Everyone!" He got their attention with a hushed tone while they were pushing off. "Paddle with much care. We need to be quiet going over this lake."

"What?" Fitzgerald blurted. "Don't be absurd!"

"Adrian, we can't be too careful. Do you remember the second set of clues we were given?" Alexander looked to Drew.

"You said the first two might go together. *'Be watchful of the waters deep, lest you wake the writhing from sleep,'*" the young man recited confidently.

"Oh!" The man scoffed with a laugh. "So, you believe in mythical creatures now? Come on, old chum, that's just a bunch of nonsense to keep people away!"

Jada frowned. "Come on, Dad; think about it… *'the waters deep'*. I can't see the bottom, and I've never seen water so perfectly still. Where are all the fish? This place gives me the creeps!"

As she spoke, Fitzgerald and his men looked into the opaque water and failed to find any movement darting beneath the surface. Some of them even put their paddles in deeper to stir about the thick moss-like texture of the lake, but nothing responded to their probing. The movement did, however, send an unwelcoming number of ripples cascading across the lake.

"Enough!" Alexander whispered harshly. "The clues have not led us astray thus far, so why should we ignore them now? A depiction of Amaru was sketched in this very lake, and I for one do not want to take any chance of finding out what that is supposed to mean!"

Fitzgerald grumbled in agreement, muttering under his breath, and the team proceeded by quietly floating across on the meager push of small strokes. Every time Drew softly dipped his paddle beneath the surface, he felt like his wooden oar was being swallowed by the dark green murkiness.

Once they were a quarter of the way across, after an excruciatingly long thirty minutes, Fitzgerald shook the image of something underneath the water from his mind. He gritted his teeth and his blood pumped hard as he began imagining all of the dazzling treasures yet to be claimed in the massive mountain ahead — and the possibility of immortality if the legends were true.

"No! Stop this madness! It's just a lake! We're getting nowhere like this, and Paititi is within my grasp!" His boat began rocking vigorously as he paddled harder in frustration.

"Dad, what are you doing?!" Both Jada and Beady Eyes looked at him in horror.

"Let's get on with it!" He held a hand in the air and his bright red tattoo glistened under the hot sun. "Bloodfists — ROW!"

The two canoes of men followed their leader while Alexander, Drew, and Kaci lagged behind at their original pace.

"See, Jim?" Fitzgerald stood up in the boat and called out once he'd reached the halfway point. "NOTHING!"

Jada furrowed her brow in genuine concern and stopped paddling. "Um, hold on. Where are all these waves coming from?"

"What are you talking about?" her father snapped, then felt the boat rock to one side. He faltered slightly.

"Yeah, that wasn't caused by any of us," she said coldly.

Fitzgerald looked out, and he saw Alexander frantically waving at him.

"Go! Go! Go!" the professor yelled from a distance. "It knows we're here!"

The water was moving. Large smooth waves swelled higher and higher as if something was circling them.

"Over there!" Beady Eyes shrieked, pointing to a form, as black-green as the water they were paddling through, which poked itself through the surface. It was long and thick, with skin smooth and slimy. Its orange shining eyes stared at them through narrow slits as it glided through the water at lightning speed.

Suddenly, a series of shots rang out from Fitzgerald's revolver toward the creature, and it gaped open its mouth with a wild hiss, then plunged beneath the surface.

"LOOK OUT!" Jada screamed as whatever-it-was darted straight toward them.

One of the other canoes, headed by Goatee, flipped over wildly as the beast crunched into it and whizzed past. The other canoes fiercely bobbed back and forth while their occupants struggled to stay afloat.

"Where did it go?" Fitzgerald exclaimed angrily, trying to look deep beneath the surface.

"Help, boss!" the men floundering in the water stretched out their arms.

Fitzgerald ignored them, dropping his paddle and focusing rather on reloading his pistol.

"Next time it passes around — shoot it!" he ordered. Beady Eyes and the other armed mercenaries stood up, poised with their machine guns at-the-ready while the men in the lake flailed back to their capsized canoe in an attempt to turn it right-side-up, but to no avail.

A dark shadow glided close, immediately triggering Fitzgerald and his men to fire incessantly into the water all around them. When the turbulent spray from the bullets had settled, one of the men nervously called out, "What-what happened to the others? They're just … GONE!"

The hair on the back of Fitzgerald's neck stood on end as he realized his men must've been snagged under the surface.

"There's no way we can kill this thing! Every man for himself!" he bellowed as he grabbed his oar, then looked to Beady Eyes. "You shoot while Jada and I paddle!"

The men in the other dugout canoe scrambled to follow suit, but the slithering creature resurfaced and reached them with a CRACK, sending the half-rotted log into splinters and flinging the mercenaries into the water.

"Don't look back!" Fitzgerald told his daughter over the loud clanging of Beady Eyes' machine gun. "Just row, my dear. ROW!"

CHAPTER XXVII

By the time the creature was done wreaking havoc on the men who had fallen to its mercy behind them, Fitzgerald, Jada, and Beady Eyes were in water shallow enough that the beast did not pursue them. It did, however, slither as close as it could to the bank, eager to find its next prey; but, after a couple of well-placed shots by Beady Eyes, the large snake finally retreated to the murky depths.

Once they hit the beach, Fitzgerald jumped out of the canoe and ran along the shore ecstatic that the long-awaited moment had finally come: they had made it to his beloved island.

"Paradise!" He exclaimed with his arms stretched out wide. "You can smell it in the air! Haha! We are almost there!" But the jungle tree line appeared impenetrable, and soon he was pacing back and forth like a caged tiger with eyes that undeniably glowed with greed.

"Jim!" he shouted at the top of his lungs. "Where to next, man?"

Alexander, Drew, and Kaci had just landed a bit further down the shoreline. During the commotion on the lake, they were able to quickly and quietly float past the giant creature without being spotted. The two teenagers stumbled into the sand and sank to their knees, thankful to be alive.

Kaci looked up at her uncle through tears, "But what about those other men?"

He shook his head soberly, "Unfortunately, Adrian's corruption for wealth and power has destroyed everyone and everything around him. I'm just thankful they found peace with God before it was too late. It is only by the Lord's mercies that we haven't been consumed yet; God has been faithful to us and kept us alive."

"JIM!"

"Yes, yes, I'm coming," the professor replied, then eyed Kaci's backpack that now rested on her lap. "Whatever you both do, keep that SAT phone safe. It's our *only* ticket out of here." His sense of urgency chilled the two young people as the gravity of their situation hit them hard. They were on an island in the middle of a lake guarded by a ferocious serpent in some unchartered region of the vast Amazon jungle.

Drew spoke for them both. "We promise, Uncle James."

Alexander nodded and winked at them with a lop-sided grin, "Now let's pray that we're able to finish this quickly!" He turned and jogged along the shore up to where Fitzgerald stood with his hands on his hips waiting.

"We should do that right now," Kaci suggested as she secured her backpack.

"Absolutely!" Drew bowed his head and clasped his hands together, "God, thank you for sparing our lives back there. We humbly ask that You'd continue to keep us safe. We desperately need Your protection as we go forward and face who knows what? But God, we're comforted to know that You already know." He paused for a moment, then prayed further. "I just want to thank you again for using this crazy trip to get a hold of my heart and to save the lives of many people that we've come in contact with. We know now that You've meant this experience not for our evil, but for our good. We love You, and we ask that You'd please give Uncle James clear direction about what we're supposed to do and where we're supposed to go. In Jesus' name, Amen."

"Amen," Kaci smiled at her brother, proud of the godly young man he was becoming.

As they slowly rose to their feet, they couldn't help but notice that Jada and Beady Eyes still remained in their dugout canoe resting on the sandy shore. They glanced at each other and decided to head over to them.

"Are you okay?" Kaci softly asked as she approached and placed a hand on the girl's shoulder.

Jada found herself trembling as she firmly gripped her old wooden oar with whitened knuckles. *I could've died,* she thought to herself. "I… uh… I'm still trying to process what happened. I can't believe they're all — gone. How are you so calm?"

Before Kaci could respond, Jada cut her off, "Let me guess. Jesus?"

She nodded tenderly.

"Of course," Jada grunted and sluffed off Kaci's hand; but deep down inside, her heart burned. She felt so convicted of being mean with her fake, tough exterior. She really wanted to know more about Jesus and how to find peace with God. Her mind often dwelt on their conversations in the past about eternity, but she never had the courage to bring it up because of her father. She wished she could snap her fingers and instantly be somewhere alone with Kaci so she could open up and truly share her heart. Yet in that moment, all her fear, pain and true feelings were clearly communicated through her eyes as the two girls looked at each other. Kaci breathed in sharply and warmly smiled.

"LET'S GO," an impatient Fitzgerald snapped, jarring them back to reality.

Jada glanced over at Beady Eyes who was still looking out aimlessly across the now-perfectly serene water and shaking from the adrenaline wearing off in his body. She followed his eyes to the capsized canoe and the other wooden fragments floating motionlessly in the middle of the lake.

She sighed with disgust and tossed her oar to the ground. "I can't wait for this whole thing to finally be over!"

"It's not over until Paititi has been found and its secrets discovered," Fitzgerald scowled at her with a steely gaze, his thumb hooked uncomfortably close to his revolver. "We've come this far, my dear; we will *not* quit now."

His personality abruptly changed liked the flip of a switch, and he flashed an adventurous smile. "Come along! The professor and I have found the way!"

The team followed him single file as he hastily disappeared into the thick wall of dense overgrowth and vines. A sandy path lay before them on the other side, weaving through the rainforest. The trees stood tall with thick bare trunks and an outspread leafy canopy high overhead that allowed the sun to speckle through and light their way. The jungle gradually thinned out the deeper they progressed into the island until it finally opened into an expansive clearing that only contained sporadic ferns nestled in a sprawling blanket of forest compost.

"My! My!" Fitzgerald commented as they came to a halt and looked with wonder at the sight that lay before them. A wide staircase carved out of the rock ascended hundreds of steps up the mountain and into the overcast sky above. Stone guides, mossy and cracked, flanked either side the entire way, and a massive, breathtaking arch layered with gold and ornate Incan engravings stood in front of it all. But what caught their attention most was the pronounced symbol of Paititi made out of aquamarine gemstones in the top center of the archway serving as the entrance into the legendary city.

The big man leapt forward with exhilaration and mounted the first few steps. He turned to the group, his eyes wide, "This is it! This is it!"

"Indeed!" Alexander couldn't help but join in the excitement, and heartily slapped his niece and nephew on the back.

"Something doesn't feel right," Jada looked around at the jungle behind them and the mountain looming before them. "Do you hear that?"

Alexander frowned as he realized what she meant.

"Exactly. You hear nothing. The forest is quiet. Too quiet." Her hands rested on her knives. "I don't like this."

"Pish-posh, my dear! Stop downing the moment," her father scolded. "We have *found* Paititi — Haha!" He turned and bounded up the stairs, compelling the others to hastily join him.

The team proceeded in silence. The higher they climbed, the foggier it became. Alexander wished they could slow down so he could study the stone guides surrounding them and the symbols on the stairs they mounted. There was no stopping Fitzgerald now, but he was thankful at least for the gentle breeze that refreshed them on their grueling climb.

"What was that?" Beady Eyes blurted out startling everyone. He impulsively fired his weapon at a nearby Incan head, sending a shower of stone chips over them.

"WHAT?" Fitzgerald bellowed incredulously. "Are you insane? What are you shooting at?"

Beady Eyes shakily waved his gun around in paranoia.

"I saw something! It…it looked like a demon!"

"I *told* you something felt off," Jada interjected with her knives drawn.

"A Demon?" Fitzgerald pulled the man up the stairs, ignoring his daughter. "Get it together, man! You're a Bloodfist! Not a baby. Just keep walking!"

"Hold on a minute, Adrian," Alexander stepped forward, addressing Beady Eyes with a low voice. "Was it black and white?"

The man nervously nodded.

"That's what I thought."

Fitzgerald pulled his revolver, extremely irritated. "What are you talking about?"

"I saw the same thing on the other side of the lake. It was a blur of black and white."

"It was probably just an animal. Come on, we're wasting time. I can see the top of the stairs!" the Scotsman turned to keep climbing.

"Adrian, I don't think you're quite getting it," Alexander reached for the man's arm and held him back. "I told you those canoes were not left there for us. Sure, they were old, but the twine that kept them secure to the bank was freshly made. I believe that someone still *lives* here."

Fitzgerald pulled his arm away and cocked his gun, "Enough. I will not hear another word of this!"

A flash of movement suddenly went up to the next head on the outside of the staircase. It was barely noticeable from the angle, but Kaci spotted it.

"Ummm, guys?" she said tensely, stumbling backwards.

"I saw it, too," Drew steadied her. Concern deeply etched itself upon his face, and he whispered. "We are not alone, Uncle James!"

A sick feeling washed over Alexander, and he turned pale. His eyes widened as he looked past Fitzgerald toward the top of the stairs. Quietly and authoritatively, he declared, "Do not make ANY sudden movements. Slowly put your weapons away. We do not want to appear to be a threat."

The beating of Fitzgerald's heart became faster. As much as he didn't want to give in to Alexander's orders, he knew exactly what his old friend's tone of voice meant.

Figures, holding out steadied spears, began to emerge from around the guides, as if appearing out of nowhere. Their bodies were painted from head to toe in black and white and wrapped with sashes in the same colors. The symbol of Paititi was written on their arms. Their heads were shaved and entirely covered in white paint. The figures advanced, closing in around them and forcing them without saying a word to climb the stone steps.

Through the fog, Alexander could barely make out a line of these warriors standing at attention atop the staircase with spears down by their sides. An impressively tall man stood in the center of them with an old, gnarly wooden staff. As they drew closer, the professor noticed that this man was painted with the same colors but was wrapped with red sashes instead. He wore a formidable-looking Incan mask that had accentuated eyes and teeth painted in red and white, with feathers dyed the same colors covering his bald painted head and running down his back as a part of an elaborate headdress.

This must be the chief, Alexander thought to himself. *God, please give us wisdom.*

At the top of the stairs, the fog thinned into patches of low-lying mist, and the ground leveled out into a spacious plateau with scattered groves of bamboo before it ran into the mountain that sharply climbed into the thick overcast sky. A smooth stone wall with a single ornately-carved and gem-studded entrance loomed before them a hundred yards away. It uniformly curved in a semi-circle around the plateau into the mountain, safely nestling impressive Incan structures that rose above it.

"Paititi!" Fitzgerald exclaimed, fighting back tears, and clutching the pendent around his neck. The natives didn't seem to like his sudden movements and outburst. They extended their spears in a threat and snarled at his elated laughter.

Awkward silence hung in the air until the chief turned without saying a word and walked swiftly to the city. His men immediately filed around the group and forced them to follow two-by-two.

Drew and Kaci exchanged nervous glances, wondering what was going to happen next.

"We must be careful, Adrian," Alexander whispered as he and Fitzgerald walked together. He held tightly onto the map cylinder that was slung diagonally across his chest. "They won't be able to understand you. I know you are excited, but you must remain calm."

"Don't worry; I am not a fool. I want to find out what secrets this place holds more than anyone else on earth. I will do whatever it takes to achieve that end." He flashed a smile. "Even if that means letting you do all the talking."

As the team climbed through the entryway, they beheld the ancient city with awe. Crumbling temples, multi-leveled stone buildings with zig-zagging staircases, weathered statues of Incan deities, and scores of tall pillars lined the sprawling main boulevard. Smaller structures, yet no less impressive, lined streets that ran perfectly perpendicular with the meticulously clean and groomed thoroughfare.

But at the forefront of it all was the main spectacle. A huge carved skull at the heart of the city protruded from the mountain, formidably complete with numerous icons and pictograms engraved into its mossy and bleached-white surface. Drooping vines webbed out from the top of its head, its empty sockets, and around its chiseled pointy teeth. On either side of it stood a row of ornate pillars that fanned out to form a spectacular entrance into its unusually wide mouth. A series of shorter posts appeared to hold it open and flanked a set of shadowed stone doors at the back of its throat that appeared blackened from heavy blasts.

Right at the center of the skull's forehead was a huge symbol of Paititi.

The chief whirled about and slammed his staff into the ground. His men instantly backed away in fluid motion and raised their spears in perfect synchronization. Their unblinking eyes were dark and expressionless as they proceeded to encircle both their leader and their captives.

"Alexander." The professor said, motioning to himself and then pointing at the chieftain.

"Ircantu."

Alexander bowed, and the chief remained stoically quiet and still for a moment, then made a broad gesture toward the skull behind him.

"Is this what you seek?" He said in a language Alexander was not expecting to hear.

"I don't believe it!" The professor couldn't hide his surprise. "You speak... *German?*"

"It is a tongue that I learned long ago."

Though Alexander couldn't see the man's face behind the mask, he could tell by the wrinkles on his painted arms and hands that he was quite old, yet still in prime shape.

"But how? I'm aware that others once came here —"

"Ah," the chief cut him off and leveled his staff into the professor's chest. "You know of the barbarians?"

Apprehension welled up in Alexander's throat as he realized that he might have just said the wrong thing. Ircantu let out a deep growl and slammed his staff back into the ground. His warriors moved forward, thrusting their spears dangerously close to the team, forcing them to stand back-to-back.

Kaci couldn't help but shudder at the intensity of the moment as she pressed her shoulder against her brother's, but she remained in a spirit of prayer to keep herself calm.

"What did you say, Jim? You're going to get us killed!" Fitzgerald hoarsely whispered. He hooked his thumb close to his revolver, and Beady Eyes, keeping his gun barrel down to the ground, silently clicked off the safety.

"They came to our city when I was a boy and stripped my people of anything gold or silver," the old man explained while Alexander quietly translated. "They then demanded that my father, the chief, give them entrance into the Great Skull, but he refused. The barbarians had neither the key nor the means to pass the test. Our people have guarded the Sacred Mountain with their lives for generations. Only the worthy are allowed within. The barbarians took me as their prisoner, hoping that it would change my father's mind. But when he did not give them what they wanted, they killed him and as many of my people as they could find, including women and children. They were animals. They kept me as their prisoner and forced me to learn this foul tongue. They hoped that I would one day share with them how to get inside, but a few years later I was able to flee with my life. They returned to Paititi once more, but I hid with what few of my people remained. The barbarians tried to get into the Great Skull with much fire, yet nothing prevailed. The Sacred Mountain did not let them pass. They were not worthy."

"I-I'm so sorry about all that you and your people have suffered at the hands of the Nazis," Alexander humbly bowed again. "But we mean you no harm."

"Show him the map, Jim; show him the map!" Fitzgerald pressed with a nudge on the elbow and a hard sideways glance.

Reluctantly, Alexander unsheathed the delicate artifact from out of its leather case and unrolled it gently for all to see.

"Ircantu, we come in peace following the path made plain by your ancestors."

The chief snatched the ancient parchment out of his hands and observed it with curiosity. Then he shrugged and snarled. "It is just another trick! You lie. Our scouts observed that you approached us with one of the barbarians' vessels. You bear their weapons," he gestured to Beady Eyes' machine gun. "When I rebuilt our tribe, I vowed that no outsider would ever enter our city and live!"

"Even if they are worthy?" the professor interjected, causing the chief to step back with slight hesitation. "We come bearing the wisdom of Aapo and the ancient guides. Please —"

"Aapo? You know of him?" the old chief was taken back for a moment, then shook his head and snarled, "It is no matter!"

He ripped the ancient map in half to the astonishment of the team. With pure rage, Fitzgerald wanted to launch forward and grab the man by the throat, but he knew it would mean instant death.

"You speak with barbaric tongue! You have their skin! You are one of them!" the masked man slammed his staff into the hard earth again. His warriors sprang into action, disarming Fitzgerald and Beady Eyes and taking Jada's knives from her belt. The three didn't put up a fight because of the razor-sharp spears mere inches from their face and chest.

"No, you have it all wrong!" Alexander pleaded as he and the others were dragged to the edge of the city where an enclave of bamboo cages sat in a clearing surrounded by pedestaled torches. "Do we bear any of their markings on our clothes? Speak to any of my colleagues here and see if they know German. You will be able to tell from their eyes if they understand you! I'm telling you, the barbarians are gone. We destroyed their base and used one of their boats, having lost our own, to continue our journey here!"

Ircantu ignored him; he watched in silence as the team was thrust into two different cages against their will — the teenagers in one and the three adult men in another further down. He turned and walked slowly over to a torch and lit the two portions of the map on fire.

"*NO!* How dare you?" Fitzgerald exploded at the sight and tried to break apart the thick bamboo bars with his bare hands. He watched helplessly as the map went up in flames.

The old chief tossed it unceremoniously to the ground in front of the cages; the bright flames danced in the dark, unblinking eyes of the natives and scattered their glow across the gloomy-grey setting.

"We built these cages on the very place my father and our tribe were brutally slain," Ircantu shared without emotion as Alexander quietly translated to the others. "A sacrifice must be given to the Sacred Mountain to avenge what has befallen my people. Only this will allow us to regain the full blessing of the Great Skull who watches over us and protects us."

The chief turned and began walking away. Without looking back, he declared, "Tomorrow, you will die."

Kaci and Jada involuntarily gasped. Fitzgerald threw himself against the bars before Alexander could stop him and rattled the cage. "ENOUGH! Who do you think you are? I have been chosen by the gods to find you! Paititi and what lies within your mountain is my destiny!"

The medallion that he'd carefully kept hidden away in his shirt shook loose and was now dangling in front of him. The warriors around the cage gasped and stepped back, whispering something excitedly among themselves that caught Ircantu's attention. The old man paused, then turned back and stepped forward warily.

"My eyes do fail me. Could it be?"

He took a long look then cocked his head to one side. "Perhaps you do speak the truth. I must think over this until the morning. If you do not pass the test, you all *will* die."

CHAPTER XXVIII

The dull overcast sky faded into night and the vast city with its few inhabitants lay eerily quiet with only a few torches burning around the prisoners. No one spoke a word; a pervasive somberness hung in the air as they gravely considered their fate. Fitzgerald paced back and forth in the narrow space; his shoulders heaved with seething as he muttered to himself and occasionally clutched his medallion. Beady Eyes remained huddled in a corner, absently staring off into the distance, while Alexander rested calmly, sitting Indian-style with his eyes closed and his head down. He was so tired. He prayed silently between moments of dozing off.

"Things do not bode well for us, Jim, and you just sit there and sleep!" Fitzgerald snarled and kicked him softly in the knee. "We must come up with a plan! I — *we* have not come this far just to be slaughtered at the very end!" The big man fidgeted with his rolled sleeves and involuntarily flexed his sweaty forearms. "I will fight my way through and kill every single last one of them if I have to!"

"I don't believe it will come to that," Alexander looked up with a small grin. "There is still a silver lining to all of this."

Fitzgerald raised an eyebrow, "Have you gone mad?"

"Not at all. I've been praying for wisdom, and I think the Lord has reminded me of something."

The Scotsman grunted and rolled his eyes.

"Obviously, your pendant bears some significance, correct? Do you remember back to the inscription left for us in the Temple of Inti?"

"But of course! It said we needed this piece to complete our journey."

"Exactly. And Ircantu said something earlier about a key and mentioned passing some sort of test… Intriguing, isn't it? Everything changed when the people here saw the medallion. Perhaps *that* is the key." He pulled out his Bible from the worn leather holster on his back hip.

"Don't you dare start preaching at me!" Fitzgerald rolled his eyes.

"Relax. I have the compiled list of our clues safely stowed right here." He showed him the piece of paper. "But I need to ask you something first, Adrian. Has it really been worth it?"

Fitzgerald stopped in his tracks and slowly turned, partially bristling at the question.

"Is *what* worth it?"

Alexander looked him squarely in the eyes, "Losing everything in the hopes of finding Paititi."

"I have lost nothing. Those who served under me —"

"Yes, I know, they knew what they were signing up for. You keep convincing yourself of that, but their blood is on your hands."

Fitzgerald snarled and stopped himself from lunging forward and grabbing his old friend by the throat. "Who do you think you are to judge me?"

"I'm not judging you; I'm telling the truth."

Fitzgerald shrugged, "That's your opinion. With great risk is great reward. Do you understand what this mountain holds?"

"Possibly, but not what you think it does."

Fitzgerald's eyes narrowed, "Talking about *that,* are you?" He didn't want to say it in front of Beady Eyes or within earshot of the teenagers. He knew Alexander was referring to his hope of discovering the Fountain of Youth. Ever since he first heard of the legend, Fitzgerald had become obsessed with finding this source of immortality. If it were true and he located it in this city, he could become a god and rule the world.

Alexander interrupted his thoughts, *"'For what shall it profit a man, if he shall gain the whole world, and lose his own soul? Or what shall a man give in exchange for his soul?'"*

"What is that? The Bible?"

Alexander nodded.

"Enough of that nonsense! Don't worry about my soul!"

"It's my job to worry," Alexander smiled. "I'm a Christian. I am praying for you, and I will not give up on you."

"Then you're a fool, Jim," Fitzgerald chuckled.

"You can think what you wish, but as I've told you before, it's never too late to walk the path of redemption. Even the thief on the cross was able to turn to Christ —"

Fitzgerald sighed loudly and growled, "Can we *please* move on?"

Alexander understood that it wouldn't be wise to continue. His old friend was still hardened toward the things of God, and he didn't want to push him away any further. He switched gears smoothly by putting away his Bible and gesturing again with the sheet of paper in his hand, reminding Fitzgerald of their findings.

Adrian rubbed his stubbled jaw as he paced. "So, you're telling me that the Latin clues inscribed on each guide could help us gain further entrance into Paititi?"

"I presume so, and our third clue is quiet fascinating," his eyes twinkled. "Perhaps it has something to do with passing this tribe's test. It reads: *'Without the stones you face your death.'*"

Fitzgerald muttered it to himself repeatedly as he resumed pacing. Suddenly, he stopped and whirled about, his eyes glowing. "That's it, old chum!"

The big man plopped down in front of Alexander mirroring his Indian-style sitting position. They continued to eagerly discuss the matter in hushed tones; Beady Eyes was now riveted to their conversation and hope seemed to grow across his features.

Meanwhile, Jada loosely held onto the poles of the cage that she, Drew, and Kaci were locked in and nestled her head between the bamboo where she stood.

"I wish I knew what they were talking about," she murmured.

"Yeah," Kaci agreed, sitting next to her brother. "Whatever it is, your father seems pretty excited about it."

Jada rolled her eyes. "He's always excited about whatever is going to benefit *him*. He honestly doesn't care about the rest of us as long as he gets what he wants."

Distant jungle sounds, the flickering of the torches nearby, and the low babbling of the two men conversing prevailed for the next few minutes.

Kaci hesitantly breathed in, her heart pounding, and decided to cut the silence, "I know it must be difficult for you to bring yourself to forgive him."

Jada stiffened and slowly turned around as she crossed her arms, "What did you say?"

"You secretly blame him for your mother's death, don't you? You wish you had a normal family life like everyone else instead of being stuck as his daughter. You hate him for training you as an assassin and grooming you to one day take over his organization."

"How dare you!" she snarled and lunged at Kaci, grabbing her by the throat.

Drew wrestled Jada's hands off his sister and the two struggled for a moment, before she surrendered and weakly melted into a crumpled form on the ground.

"I hate him! I absolutely hate him!" Jada sobbed. "He's ruined my life!"

"Sit with me." Kaci scooted to her right and patted the open spot between her and her brother. Jada slowly crawled over, and Kaci took her hand.

"Your father is a very lost man blinded by his obsession with greed and power. What he needs is Jesus. Jesus is the only One Who can open his eyes. We're praying that he'll get saved before it's too late." She squeezed Jada's hand lovingly. "And we're praying for you, too."

"You're crazy," the girl tried to wipe her tears, but they kept flowing.

"I know we are," Kaci smiled, and Jada found some sweet release in chuckling at her remark.

"We've been praying for you ever since we first met... the day you kidnapped us," Drew declared.

Jada hung her head in shame, causing her dirty, straight blonde hair to drop forward. "Ugghhh. I never told you this before, but I feel really bad about all the terrible things we did to you — that *I* did to you and... and for how rudely I've treated you."

"It's okay," Kaci said tenderly. "Actually, over the past few weeks, you've been rather kind."

"You know, Jada," Drew spoke softly, "whatever you and your father may have meant for our evil, God meant for our good. We're actually very thankful for this whole 'nightmare' we have experienced. It's brought us so much closer to God."

Kaci squeezed her hand again, "We truly do forgive you, Jada, and we love you."

She looked at them in disbelief, "I don't understand. How could you?"

"It's simple. The Bible says, *'Let all bitterness, and wrath, and anger, and clamour, and evil speaking, be put away from you, with all malice: And be ye kind one to another, tenderhearted, forgiving one another, even as God for Christ's sake hath forgiven you.'*"

"If God could forgive us for all the wrong things we've done against Him," Drew explained, "then we can certainly find it within ourselves, with His help, to forgive those who've wronged us."

Jada didn't bother trying to clear her face of tears anymore. "Wow. You guys are like — true Christians. I've never met anyone like you before."

"It's because of Jesus," Kaci sweetly replied.

The young lady repositioned herself to sit in front of them so she could see them both at the same time. She realized there was no point in holding back any longer. This was it. This was the moment she'd been waiting for — when she could finally open herself up to them privately.

"So, okay, you're right; I *am* bitter at my dad. It's eating me alive, but honestly, I don't know how to break free of it, you know? Is this something that Jesus can help me with?"

The siblings silently nodded.

"Good, because I've been wanting to talk to you guys about Jesus for a long time now. I always had the excuse of my dad being around before. I didn't want him to overhear and get even more angry with me. But he's not here now. So… I'm ready."

Kaci and Drew looked at each other, smiling, then looked back at Jada and nodded.

With tear-stained cheeks, the girl continued, "Jesus lives inside of you; it's obvious. We've faced danger after danger, and you're both so…happy. You have peace. Sure, you might feel some fear every once in a while — but who doesn't, right? You're always calm. At first, it drove me nuts; I thought it was some religious front. But the longer we've been together, the more I've seen how genuine your faith in Jesus is."

Her shoulders slumped, "I've been the one who's such a hypocrite, putting on a tough act against you guys. Deep down inside, I admire you. I feel so lonely, hollow, and empty. I *need* what you have. I want to feel that same love, joy, and peace. I guess what I'm trying to say is…I need *Jesus.*"

Jada began to shiver uncontrollably in the hot summer night. "More importantly, I need Him to *save* me. If we get killed in the morning like that Chief told us we might, I know I will go straight to Hell! I'm a sinner, and I can't stop picturing myself screaming in agony and being on fire forever."

She paused for a moment, looking them directly in the eyes, and pleaded with a whisper, "I'm scared to die. Please help me!"

Drew and Kaci glanced at each other, feeling overwhelmed. Now it was their turn to stop fighting back the tears.

"Jesus *can* and *will* save you, Jada," Kaci comforted her. "You can take care of this right now; there's nothing stopping you. He's standing in Heaven with His arms opened wide in love ready to receive you."

"Really? Please... please tell me what I have to do."

"You are ready," Drew grinned. "You understand that you're a sinner, that the penalty of sin is death in Hell, and that we cannot save ourselves — only Jesus can. Do you believe Jesus is the Son of God and that He died on the Cross for your sins and rose again from the grave?"

"Yes," Jada emphatically nodded, "Yes, I believe that!"

"Then the Bible promises in Romans 10:13, *'For whosoever shall call upon the name of the Lord shall be saved.'* It's as simple as praying and asking Him."

She hesitated then looked back and forth at them timidly. "Okay, but I don't really know what to say."

Kaci warmly smiled through her tears. "That's all right. Saying specific words in a prayer doesn't magically save you; it's about what takes place in your heart. Just sincerely call out to Jesus in faith; He's listening. It's as simple as asking Him."

Jada grabbed both of Kaci's hands, "Then let's do this."

She shivered no longer in fear but with excitement, and in brokenness she bowed her head and wept her way to Christ.

"Jesus? It's me, Jada. I... I'm sorry for the really awful things I've done in my life. I don't know how You could love someone like me," she sniffed and looked up quickly at Kaci, who nodded in affirmation. Jada gave a slight smile and bowed her head again, "Thank You for dying for me so that I could be saved. I know I deserve to pay for my sins in that horrible place called Hell, but... I don't want to go there. I would really like it if I could be forgiven and live with You in Heaven someday. I do believe that You died on the Cross and rose again for me. Please, Jesus, forgive my sins and save me. I know You're the only One Who can. Um, I know I've heard Drew and Kaci use this phrase a lot at the end of their prayers to You, so here goes... in Jesus' name, Amen."

Jada looked up at them as a warm feeling of peace and joy

bubbled up inside her, causing her lips to part in a smile bigger than they'd ever seen before.

"I'm saved! I just know it! I can feel a difference inside of me. There's no more weight of sin or guilt from all the wrongs of my past. I'm free!"

Jada lunged forward and embraced Kaci. She squeezed her tight and didn't want to let go, crying and rejoicing in her newfound Saviour.

"You know, we're sisters now!" Kaci grinned. "When someone trusts in Jesus, they become a part of the family of God."

The girls laughed together and hugged again. Drew held up his hands in praise as he looked beyond the bamboo poles of their cage. The clouds that had cast a gloominess over them had dissipated, and now a starry night sky could be seen twinkling with joy above.

❁ ❁ ❁

Weak sunlight tried to pierce the heavy mist surrounding the cages; the dull glow of the early morning cast somber shadows across the ground of the ancient structures of the city. Alexander was still sitting in the position he'd fallen asleep in sometime in the middle of the night after the torches had gone out. He groggily lifted his head and strained to see his niece and nephew. He grinned when he noticed all three teenagers sprawled out on their cell's dirt floor sound asleep.

Jada looked uncharacteristically peaceful. The dark circles under her eyes were almost gone, and her face wasn't creased with a grimace like it normally was when she slept. *It's amazing what Your peace can do to a person,* Alexander said silently to the Lord. *I can't wait to hear what happened!*

He'd purposedly kept Adrian busy the night before with conjecture regarding their next clue and other details of their expedition, when he noticed the three young people engaging in deep conversation. Of course, he couldn't tell exactly what was going on because he had to keep his attention focused on Fitzgerald, but he hoped and prayed that this was the moment Jada would finally turn to Christ.

He stretched his aching back and sore muscles that had conformed to the hard poles of bamboo.

"Wakey, wakey, sleeping beauty," Fitzgerald muttered as he anxiously paced from corner to corner of their cage.

"Did you get any sleep last night?"

"How could I? I'm on the verge of making the greatest discovery in the history of the world! Besides, someone had to be on the lookout in case we were ambushed by these savages. No one will kill me —"

He stopped and listened intently for a moment with wide eyes, his head cocked to the side.

"They're coming," he whispered harshly and kicked Beady Eyes on the foot, startling the man awake. "It's show time!"

Through the mist came Ircantu in his full regalia as chieftain. A half-dozen painted warriors wearing ceremonial feathers and garb flanked him on either side. The old chief stood in front of their cage for almost a full minute in absolute silence.

"Well?" Fitzgerald demanded impatiently. "Enough of this!"

His bluntness pierced the air and caused the teenagers across the clearing to stir from their deep sleep.

Ircantu slowly took off his mask to reveal a scarred face that had clearly suffered brutal torture from the Nazis so many years ago. A stern look caused the wrinkles and scars on his face to appear even more exaggerated.

"You have given me much conflict," he declared in German while Alexander translated. "I want to put you to death, but the law of the ancients forbids it!"

He turned to Fitzgerald, "You bear the key to the Sacred Mountain." He pulled out something from around his neck — an identical pendant to the one Fitzgerald wore. "I thought only I had this power. This has been handed down from generation to generation, but you come to our city bearing the same rite of passage. How is this possible?"

"Incredible! Thank the Lord!" Alexander rejoiced in English, his foreign words puzzling the chief. The professor grinned and proceeded to concisely share with him the exploits they'd accomplished to find Paititi.

"Ah," Ircantu stoically stroked his chin. "Quite the journey, led by the great ancients to give outsiders a chance to behold Paititi." He then hung his head, "I am ashamed. It pains my heart to have destroyed the map he crafted. I was blinded by rage and did not understand that you are not like the others." His eyes momentarily flickered to Fitzgerald. "At least most of you. Something disturbs me about this man. He may not be one of the barbarians, but he is still barbaric."

"Is he talking about me?" Fitzgerald tried to ask with a polite tone and fake smile.

"He means you no harm," Alexander quickly tried to reassure the chief, but inwardly he knew the lengths that Fitzgerald would go to if he didn't get his way. While he prayed it wouldn't come to that, Ircantu didn't seem convinced. "He is just rather... *eager* to discover what the Sacred Mountain holds."

"Only the worthy are allowed within!" The old man slammed his staff into the earth and turned to Alexander with a piercing gaze. "You might possess the key, but we have sworn an oath that no stranger is allowed to enter unless he bears a soul that will spare his own. Without it, you *will* die. Do you understand of what I speak?"

Alexander could feel his heart beating inside his chest. *This is it! This is the next test.*

He carefully translated what the chief said to Fitzgerald and the rest of the team.

Drew's eyes lit up, "...Bears a soul... I know this sounds crazy, but — could he be talking about the eyes from the stone guides?"

"The clue!" Kaci stammered. "The third clue! '*Without the stones you face your death.*'"

Alexander nodded vehemently, "Yes, yes! Exactly what we

thought! It's now or never. Show him, Adrian!"

Fitzgerald slowly pulled out a small leather pouch from one of the side pockets in his cargo pants and spilled its contents into his big hand. He spread out his palm to reveal the light blue stones they'd collected on their journey. The natives immediately gasped and stepped back in astonishment.

"I cannot speak," Ircantu fell down on one knee in reverence with his head bowed and the warriors that surrounded them followed suit, also laying their spears on the ground as a gesture of peace.

"*Now* are you convinced that we're worthy enough?" Fitzgerald laughed. He knew that the natives couldn't understand him, but it felt good to speak his mind.

He looked around at the team wildly, "And you all thought I was crazy to gather these stones!" He slapped Alexander heartily on the back and roared with delight, "I *knew* they would be of great significance!"

"No, you didn't," Alexander stated flatly. "You collected them out of greed, and you superstitiously thought the gems would give you some sort of power."

The big man shrewdly squinted his eyes and grinned, "Could it be that they are the only things that have sustained us?"

"Don't be a fool, Adrian. You must see by now it is the grace of God alone that has brought us this far."

"You may have your beliefs, Jim, but I have mine. And I believe that *ultimate* power lies inside that mountain!"

Ircantu rose to his feet and approached the bamboo bars with an outstretched hand and adamantly gestured to Fitzgerald.

"What? What do you want?" the Scotsman coldly stared at him.

"He wants the gemstones, Adrian. Give him one for each of us!"

Fitzgerald skeptically did so, half expecting the chief to renege on his word once he took what he wanted. But as soon as he received the sixth crystal, the old man snapped a curt order in an unknown tongue, and his unblinking warriors hastily unlocked the prison cells.

Fitzgerald was the first out of the cage; he stretched and

breathed in deeply. *Freedom*. Out of the corner of his eye he saw his daughter running straight at him as if she was going to tackle him. He braced himself, then felt her grip him with a bear hug and bury her face in his chest.

"I love you, Dad."

The big man was flabbergasted. *What sort of tom-foolery is this?* But he found her embrace irresistible. He wrapped his arms around her and tenderly patted her on the back.

"I... uh... thank you, my dear."

They held each other for a moment; it had been years since the last time she'd hugged him or shown him any affection.

Alexander put his arms around Drew and Kaci's shoulders as they approached, grinning from ear to ear.

"She got saved last night, Uncle James!" Kaci whispered.

"Ah! Praise the Lord! I was praying for you all."

"It's like she's a totally different person," commented Drew. "We talked late into the night about spiritual truths; she has such a hunger for God's Word."

Alexander nodded, "That is wonderful to hear. *'Therefore if any man be in Christ, he is a new creature: old things are passed away; behold, all things are become new.'* I am eager to see her grow in grace. God has a great future for her!"

Ircantu stepped forward. "You bear the key and the stones that permit your entrance. You will not die this day. At least, you will not die by *our* hands." He paused just long enough for the six to exchange wary glances. "Come. You must regain your strength in order to finish what you have started."

The team was led into one of the massive stone structures on the main thoroughfare close to the Great Skull. Its ceiling arched high above them, and torches lined the walls revealing ancient Incan murals from a by-gone era. A long stone slab lay in the center of the floor and Ircantu sat at the head of it. He broadly panned his hand, motioning for the six remaining expedition members to sit in similar fashion.

Porridge and stewed fish were brought before them — to their surprise in bowls and platters of pure gold.

Ircantu's eyes twinkled, "The barbarians did not steal *everything* from us; some of our women were able to safely hide a few of our ancestors' belongings. Now eat."

"Look at the silverware, Jim!" Fitzgerald whispered out of the corner of his mouth. "It's actual silver! If this is a sign of what's to come, we are rich men!"

It had been days since they'd gotten a decent meal, and even though the food was somewhat bland, it was hot and fresh and thus well-received — far better than the stale expired military rations they had found on the tugboat.

They ate in silence until Ircantu crossed his arms. "Are you prepared for what lies before you?"

"We are uncertain of what that entails," Alexander carefully replied. "But we do have a few clues left by the great Aapo that should help us."

The chief grunted. "We will see soon enough. You must proceed with caution. All things do not appear as they seem. We will give you water, that is all."

He snapped his finger and a couple of the servants laid two canteens crudely made out of animal skin next to Alexander.

"Tell him we want our weapons back, too," Fitzgerald demanded.

Alexander reluctantly translated this, and the chief flickered his eyes back and forth between the two men. "You will not need them for where you are going. If you come out alive, then I will return them to you." He grabbed his staff and stood to his feet.

"Up. We must be going!"

Ircantu led the way, while the team filed behind him two-by-two with the decorated warriors surrounding them. They held their spears in front of them with both hands and they marched in unison ceremoniously as the group made their way toward the Sacred Mountain. What few inhabitants there were in the city came out from hiding and lined the street, watching the procession and working together to pound on giant bombos while a handful of ladies played a mysterious tune on pan flutes.

As they walked into the gaping mouth of the skull, it felt like the mountain was swallowing them alive. Brightly colored parrots sat on old gnarly vines that sagged above them, squawking an ominous off-pitch call as if issuing a warning.

Drew and Kaci held each other's hands and gave a quick nervous glance at their uncle. Alexander smiled and whispered, "This is it! Be strong, my little monsters. And stay close."

They nodded and blinked a few times as their eyes adjusted to the dim lighting.

Ircantu pointed with his staff to a carved indentation in the rock next to the blackened stone doors at the back of the skull's throat.

"Your key. There."

Fitzgerald stepped forward and reverently took off his prized medallion. He clutched it for a moment wishing that he didn't have to part with it, then hurriedly gave it a kiss and placed the gold piece correctly into its resting place.

As soon as he gave it a gentle push, a soft click was heard coming from somewhere behind the rock. The mighty entryway before them heaved open with a shower of pebbles and wisps of dust to reveal a dark, foreboding tunnel leading into the Sacred Mountain of Paititi.

CHAPTER XXIX

Drew clutched his torch as the team slowly journeyed forward. They'd traveled so deep now that the dull light from the mouth of the skull had disappeared altogether. His heart beat rapidly with nervous exhilaration as he listened to their echoing footsteps mix with the hollow ambiance of the wide corridor and the distant echo of the deep drum that the Paititi natives had started beating when they'd entered. Kaci held onto his arm tightly. With every step they took, he could sense her apprehension by the way she squeezed, but they both knew there was no going back.

Jada put a hand on Kaci's shoulder and smiled. "Don't you worry," she whispered. "I won't let *anything* happen to you, sis!"

No one else spoke, but quietly took in everything they could as they strained their eyes in the faint orange glow of their flickering torches. The tunnel walls and its curved ceiling above had been carved with absolute precision. Every dozen meters, ornate pillars and archways were meticulously sculpted out of the rock.

Alexander held his own torch close to the walls and curiously studied the white painted symbols, now faded with age, covering the smooth surface.

"Fascinating! It appears that the entire history of the Incan Empire has been recorded here!"

"No one cares," Fitzgerald muttered impatiently and rolled his eyes. Alexander looked at him incredulously.

"Now is *not* the time, old chum; that's not why we're here! We must find what secrets this place holds. We're on the precipice of greatness; I can *feel* it!"

The big man darted ahead and approached a broad stone staircase that suddenly descended into darkness.

"Come along!" he looked over his shoulder, eyes gleaming with sheer delight and lust.

The steps led to a large cavern, complete with stalactites looming high overhead. The walls around them were a mixture of rough, naturally forming rock and hewn brick. Seeing a torch mounted nearby, Fitzgerald lit it with his own flame and to his surprise, a hidden channel of oil linked to the other torches lining the room kindled the rest in rapid succession.

As the team worked their way toward the middle of the chamber, they carefully walked over large cracks that ripped through the broken-up floor. Steam gently arose from its black depths as if the whole earth under their feet was boiling. More stone columns, adorned with hieroglyphs, icons, and symbols of Paititi surrounded them along the perimeter. But what captured their attention most were the three massive stone guides glaring down at them with aquamarine gemstone eyes that looked big enough to crush a man if they were taken out. Beneath them was a single set of solid gold doors.

Fitzgerald gave a deranged smile, "Yes! Destiny awaits!"

"We must proceed with caution," Alexander quickly warned, grabbing the man's elbow as he was about to lunge forward. "One wrong move could get us all killed, and I have *not* come this far with you for it all to end here."

Fitzgerald looked at him with annoyance and yanked his arm free. "Do you take me for a fool, Jim? Of course, we must be careful! But there's nothing wrong with being a wee bit *excited* about what we're on the verge of discovering! You—"

Drew cleared his throat to cut through the moment. "So, there are three guides, right? Maybe that's a heads up that we need to pay attention to the three clues we have left?"

The Scotsman shrewdly peered at him, opened his mouth to

scold him for interrupting, but then closed it, thinking to himself.

"Hmmmm," Alexander rubbed his stubbled jaw. "You're probably right."

He pulled out his Bible and read the next clue from the folded piece of paper Kaci had written them all on. "'*As Amaru lives, take your breath.*'"

"What's that supposed to mean?" Beady Eyes asked with a worried tone.

"I guess we'll find out," Fitzgerald grinned mischievously. "But we won't by just standing around here; come on!"

He warily made his way to the other side, demonstrating to the others where to safely cross the remaining fissures. The final one, however, was at least six feet across and had completely severed the main floor from the landing surrounding the golden doors. To their relief, it was still manageable with a short run and jump.

In a single file line, they followed his route. Jada went first and, like a ninja, she leapt from place to place with ease, allowing her momentum to carry her. Beady Eyes was next, then the professor. Drew and Kaci decided to go together, and thankfully so, because there were a couple of places where Kaci would've lost her balance without her brother there to steady her.

Drew had to leap across the last chasm by himself, since it was too wide for them to do together.

"Come on, Kaci." Alexander called as he and Drew held out their hands.

"All right...." She took a few steps back from the crevasse and got ready to run. She kicked off and jumped at the right time but the edge beneath her feet crumbled slightly. Her foot extended just beneath the other ledge, and she felt the vertical wall of the chasm skid against her toes. Her eyes instantly widened in horror as she began to fall helplessly toward the dark, steaming abyss. She watched their legs and feet flash in front of her, then the stone wall, but suddenly her forearms were clasped tightly by her uncle and brother, and she was pulled onto the edge safely.

"Th—Thank you!" Kaci stood up slowly and dusted herself off.

Fitzgerald chuckled, "That wasn't so hard, was it? Now that we're all here — gentlemen, give me a hand!"

"Don't let my dad's cold heart intimidate you," Jada whispered to Kaci while the men pushed and strained to open the heavy gold doors. "We've got this. God will help us, right?"

Kaci smiled weakly, still shaken from her near-death experience, and nodded. They put their arms around each other and intently gazed through the doors slowly opening before them. Light from the cavern's torches reflected off the gold and shimmered within, illuminating a room covered in stone tiles with the Paititi symbol etched into each one. Lining both sides of the wall were miniature versions of the stone guides sitting on short pedestals about two feet off the ground. Each of them looked as if they were grinning maliciously with small slits in their mouths. Kaci found this rather odd since all the other guides they'd encountered along the way had lips sealed with a stoic expression. On the opposite end of the room was a tunnel roughly hewn out of the rock leading to who-knows-where; it was so narrow that a person had to turn sideways to fit down its passageway.

When the doors were completely open, the team heard a soft click, which immediately caused Alexander to jerk his head up with alarm.

"What was that?"

Jada stepped forward and pointed at the floor, "You see that first big tile?"

"You mean the one that's unavoidable?" the professor gave a lop-sided grin.

"I think it's a pressure plate. I watched it slowly rise when you guys were pushing the doors open. My gut's telling me that when we step on it, the doors will close behind us!"

Alexander carefully felt around one of the doors to see if there was a knob or handle of any kind. He furrowed his brow with deep concern.

"It appears we will only have one shot at this. There's no way back out once the doors are closed!"

"And why is this a problem?" Fitzgerald stepped forward in his characteristically blunt manner, but Alexander put his arm out to block the doorway as he carefully took in the layout of the room.

"Steady now, Adrian. I've seen my fair share of booby-trapped rooms, and I fear this is definitely one of them. See those open mouths?" He pointed to the stone faces lining the room on both sides. "They probably shoot out poisonous darts — " He stopped himself mid-sentence and shook his head. "No, no, the clue said, '*As Amaru lives, take your breath.*'" His eyes widened. "They most likely release some sort of poisonous fumes."

"That's why there's a pressure plate!" Jada interjected. "To set off the gas and seal us inside at the same time."

"Exactly," the professor replied.

"But why did the clue specifically bring up Amaru?" Drew thought aloud.

Kaci suddenly gasped sharply, causing everything to look at her to see what was wrong.

"That's it! I've got it!" she exclaimed. "How does Amaru — or a snake — live?"

Jada smiled and nodded, "On its stomach!"

Kaci snapped her fingers, "Yes, and I know I just saw some dust swirling along the floor of the room — Look! There, it happened again!"

Both Fitzgerald and Alexander whirled around at the same time and lay prostrate on the ground to carefully watch for themselves.

"My, my," the big man commented wryly. "The room *does* have a draft; you can feel it down here. Way to spot that, my dear. I presume then that the clue is telling us that we need to crawl our way to the other side?"

"Yes!" Just as quickly as Alexander had dropped to the ground, he got up again and beamed, "Kaci, you're a genius!"

He then turned to Fitzgerald and held out his hand, "I need your vest."

"Huh? What for?" he retorted.

"To help save our lives."

Reluctantly, he took it off and gave it to the professor.

"Okay, we're not all geniuses," Drew joked. "So how does crawling help us?"

"It is likely that the gas the Incans used is lighter than air, and that's why the guides' mouths are so low," Alexander explained as he tore off pieces of the vest, to Fitzgerald's dismay. "The gas spreads and rises as soon as it is expelled. It cannot pass downward through the draft, making it safe to traverse the space as long as we stay low."

"Slither like a snake; got it," said Jada. "But that doesn't answer why you're ripping up my dad's old sweaty vest." The professor handed her and the others a piece the size of a napkin, doused with water from one of the animal-skin canteens.

"Everyone, hold this tightly over your nose and mouth. Though it might have a rather peculiar and — ahem — *strong* smell, it will, Lord-willing, keep you alive, filtering out the toxins."

They all gave grim looks at their pieces of cloth, except for Fitzgerald who smiled smugly.

"Now, I advise that we put out our torches, so we don't ignite the gas if it's flammable. Also, we should go in pairs. It will allow us to move across more quickly; we don't know how much gas will build up or how quickly."

"Jada — " Fitzgerald was quickly cut off.

"Adrian, you're with me. We'll go last." Alexander said.

"What? You can't be serious!"

"It's the right thing to do. Others before ourselves."

Fitzgerald rolled his eyes, then glared at them all. "Fine, but you better move as quickly as possible!"

"I'll go with Jada." Kaci placed her arm on Jada's shoulder. Drew looked at Beady Eyes.

"I guess it's you and me then," the mercenary muttered nervously, and Drew nodded with confidence to assure him that everything would be okay.

Alexander stepped into the foyer of the room, careful to stand clear of the pressure plate just a few feet beyond. *God, I hope we're right about this. Please protect us!*

The others filtered in behind him and Jada and Kaci got down on the floor.

The professor knelt down by his niece, "Remember, as soon as you go over that pressure plate, time is of the essence. Stay in the middle of the room as you crawl and stay as low to the ground as possible. Your life depends on it!"

Kaci and Jada covered their mouths with the damp cloths, fearful eyes looking at Alexander as he counted down, "Three — two — one — GO!"

The two girls darted forward with their elbows, and the doors behind all of them swung shut with a mighty force. A gruesome hissing sound like that of a dozen vipers came from the slits in the grinning statues and a yellow vapor began to fill the air.

"Quickly! QUICKLY!" Fitzgerald screamed as he clamped the cloth even more tightly over his face. For the first time, Alexander saw genuine fear in the man's eyes.

Beady Eyes and Drew went next, each with his unlit torch in hand. The girls had now reached the other end of the room and, seeing the professor adamantly pointing for them to keep going, they stood and worked their way down the narrow, jagged corridor away from the deadly mist.

Finally, it was the men's turn. The hissing sounded louder than ever, and Alexander tried not to focus on the ever-thickening cloud of gas hovering above them. He firmly held the fabric over his nose and mouth, clutched his torch, and kept his head along the floor where he could feel the cool current of fresh air wisping against his face.

It felt like an eternity journeying to the other side, but as soon as they did, Fitzgerald quickly scampered to his feet and squeezed himself down the corridor in pure panic.

When Alexander stood, his trained eye caught a glimpse of a

small panel made of smooth tile just inside the passageway on the roughly hewn wall. In the center of it was the symbol of Paititi. He instinctively pressed it, and then jumped back as a sheer rock slab fell from the ceiling, closing them off from the gas chamber.

The professor slumped against the wall, thankful to be alive. He prayed for renewed strength as he slipped sideways down the coarse tunnel, working his way carefully so he didn't rip his clothing or hit his head on the sharp outcroppings. He found the air hotter than normal with a tinge of sulfur that burned his nostrils.

"Somehow I don't think this mountain is just a mountain." Alexander quipped, wiping sweat from his brow with his handkerchief as he joined the others. They huddled in a small clearing that opened up in the middle of the passageway. Beady Eyes struggled to light his torch in the darkness because his hands shook so badly. Drew gently grabbed the lighter and got it burning for him, and then lit the three others. The flames danced along the walls and ceiling; more hewn brick and Incan carvings were patchworked into the rough stone surrounding them. Ahead, the cobblestone floor spiraled downward into another staircase.

"Is everyone okay?" Alexander voiced his concern.

"I think we're good," Drew took a long look at Beady Eyes who'd finally calmed down from the exhilaration of the moment. "I think it's just this heat that's getting to us. I feel like I can hardly breath."

"It's the thrill of adventure, my boy!" Fitzgerald grinned, back to his normal self, and slapped the young man heartily on the shoulder. "We are one step closer; only two clues left!" He waved his torch and pressed forward.

They made their way cautiously down the steps and through a series of jagged corridors, each ornamented with the symbol of Paititi and small etched carvings of the stone guides. They rounded the corner of a tight rock formation and climbed out onto a pebbled landing at the edge of a cliff in another enormous cavern filled with black emptiness. Fitzgerald warned the group to take it slow as they congregated together and stared out over the void. On the other side lay the continuation of their tunnel.

Fitzgerald kicked a few loose pebbles down into the darkness. At the bottom of the formidable chasm, barely visible by torch light, were wooden spikes dug into the ground and jutting haphazardly upwards. A few blanched skeletons lay scattered among them, having suffered their ill fate centuries ago, waiting to be joined now by the next victim.

"Hello? What's this?" Alexander gestured over to the side where three ropes were fastened to the rock. The four men lifted their torches as high as they could, following the ropes to the ceiling. Their combined light revealed numerous ropes suspended overhead, equally spaced apart. Next to each one was a small tile with what looked like a gold symbol on it. Nearly all the tiles were different.

"It looks to be some sort of puzzle," said Alexander solemnly.

Beady Eyes took a few steps toward the edge and looked down again. "With a very hefty price to pay for getting it wrong."

"This has to be where our next clue comes into play!" Drew declared.

"I presume so," the professor nodded and pulled out the paper that was now in his front pocket. "*Take heed to join through what in strength abides,*'" he read and looked up at the others.

Fitzgerald repeated it over and over in a mumble while scratching his jaw. "How utterly confounding! There *must* be a way for us to get across."

Alexander remained in deep concentration as he tilted his head, trying to read the symbols beside each rope. Then it dawned on him.

"All those markings represent different letters in the Incan alphabet!"

"Fascinating! So we need to spell something out then?" Fitzgerald speculated.

"It appears so, but the ropes here are attached to the Incan equivalents of 'I' 'P' and 'R'. There are so many different word combinations. I'm guessing there is only one that is correct." He started deciphering as many symbols as his straining eyes could see from where he was standing.

"AND?" Fitzgerald impatiently echoed into the vast darkness.

"First, I need to check a theory." The professor passed his torch to Drew and grabbed the rope that led to the letter "I." He yanked on it with all his might and the quick grinding of decayed stone filled the room. The rope and the rock it was attached to plummeted down into the spikes.

"What is the meaning of this?" Fitzgerald yelled.

Without saying a word, Alexander pulled on the next rope which met the same fate as the first one.

"JIM!"

With only one rope remaining, the professor gave it a hard tug, but nothing happened. He tried again more forcefully this time, and it stayed firm.

"My hunch was right! Only the correct letter stayed secure. This means there is a specific word that we must spell!"

Fitzgerald's eyes narrowed coldly, "Then you better choose wisely, or we will all face certain death."

"Not to worry!" A lop-sided grin slowly spread across Alexander's face, but inside, his heart and mind raced. Trying to keep the mood light, he turned to the three teenagers. "Can any of you guess which of the three letters still remains?"

"It has to be the 'P'," Jada declared without hesitation.

He was surprised by her confidence and correct answer.

"And why is that?"

"There's only one word that makes sense at this point."

Kaci's eyes lit up, "'P' for Paititi!"

"My thoughts exactly!" Alexander agreed. "Our clue said, '*Take heed to join through what in strength abides.*' I believe it is speaking of this place — a hidden citadel that has stood strong and remained impenetrable for all of these centuries. If I can get '*through*' to other side, perhaps something there will allow the rest of you to cross!"

"What if you're wrong?" Fitzgerald glared at him sharply.

Alexander smiled. "Have faith, Adrian, and pray. It's all we can do right now; and it would do you some good. Besides, why else would the clue use the word *join*? It could have said anything — why that, specifically?" His eyes twinkled. "I'm telling you, it bears great significance."

"Let's hope — I mean, pray — that you're right, old chum!"

The professor firmed his grip on the rope and ordered, "Concentrate your light on the ceiling for me!"

"Uncle James," Kaci pleaded, "Please be careful!"

He backed up as far as he could, closed his eyes for a moment in prayer, then jumped out over the chasm.

He spotted the next tile that was marked with an "A", and with a quick pump of his body and a desperate reach, he pulled himself toward the rope dangling from that spot and grabbed hold. He quickly scanned the next row of gold lettered tiles; his arms were growing sore as he held on with all his strength. He swung over to the 'I' and released his grasp from one rope to the other, feeling gravity pulling him down. He felt his body slowly slipping as he desperately scanned the ceiling, trying to locate the "T". Seconds felt like minutes. Then he saw it, farther away than he would've liked, but again he had no choice but to go for it. He caught the flax rope and felt his fingers burn raw against the coarse fibers.

The notebook in his back pocket felt like it was coming loose with every swing he took, but he couldn't worry about that. If he tried to reach back and secure it, he knew that he'd probably lose his grip and fall to his death. *We don't need it anymore,* he convinced himself. *All the clues have been consolidated and are secure in the Bible in my front pocket.*

"You're almost there, Uncle James!" Kaci's voice echoed from behind him. He gritted his teeth and prayed for Divine strength. Steeling himself, his eyes spotted the repetitious "I-T-I" among the symbols that would grant him safe passage. In rapid succession, he snatched one rope, then the next and the next, allowing his momentum to carry him. On the last rope, he swung back and forth twice and then jumped for it.

As the notebook fluttered from his pocket — to Fitzgerald's horror — and landed among the spikes below, Alexander fell to the dusty ledge on the other side. He rolled to a stop near the tunnel entrance, panting, sweating, and aching. The cheers of relief from the teenagers echoed across the ravine.

Thank you, Lord. He caught his breath for a moment and wiped off the fogged-up lenses of his glasses. His whole body was sore, his muscles screaming. He got up off the ground, slowly scanning the tunnel and the roughhewn walls around him.

"I hope we didn't need that!" Fitzgerald shouted, pointing down into the blackness where the book had fallen.

"I think we'll be okay!" Alexander wheezed back as loudly as he could.

"Is there anything there that will help us cross?"

The professor looked around again and spotted another small panel of smooth tile with the symbol of Paititi in the middle of it on the ground close to the edge of the cliff. He knelt and glanced up with a smile, "Ask, and ye shall receive!"

He held his breath and firmly pushed in the symbol. The ground rumbled beneath his feet, and the whole mountain seemed to shake. A thin stone bridge slowly emerged from the cliff face, joining to the other side.

"Haha! Another step closer!" Fitzgerald roared with glee and jumped down onto the narrow structure.

Drew was shocked that the man didn't even look down or watch his feet. Without losing stride, he swiftly crossed and leapt onto the ledge next to Alexander. The rest of them took their time. Kaci balanced herself carefully with her arms outstretched. As soon as she got close enough, her uncle grabbed her by the hand and help her up.

"There is only one clue left!" Fitzgerald declared. "No time to delay!" He took the lead again, raising his torch high for all to see. The team had to walk at a brisk pace to keep up with him, but the tunnel grew wider, making it easier for them to traverse. The walls were lined with more curious carvings and symbols and were supported by more stone archways. They followed it for what seemed like half an hour as they wound deeper into the mountain.

"I think we're almost there! I see something!" Fitzgerald pointed excitedly and bounded forward to be the first to discover what it was.

Alexander also noticed the deep glow of red reflecting off the curved walls ahead of them. When they rounded the corner, it was much brighter, emanating from where the tunnel suddenly ended. Alexander couldn't tell exactly what it was, but he knew it couldn't be man-made — no ancient civilization could achieve that bright a source of light and keep it going for centuries.

"It's getting *so* hot!" Kaci wiped her brow.

"Yeah," Jada fanned herself. "And we thought the jungle was bad!"

Fitzgerald stood framed in the doorway of the tunnel. Alexander saw him drop the torch he was holding in surprise. It rolled away into the room and a searing sound came moments later, as though the torch had melted away spontaneously.

"What is it, Adrian?" Alexander called up.

"Take a look for yourself." Fitzgerald stepped back slightly, letting the others pass.

Alexander's eyes widened, taking in the sight before him, "Well, that is unexpected."

"That's one way to describe it." The big man muttered.

They stood precariously atop a high platform at one end of a cavernous room. Suspended between the two sides was a maze of stone walkways, some supported by pillars of stone, some not, with pedestaled landings along the way. Beneath them flowed a sluggish river of bubbling molten lava covering every inch of the floor and lighting the massive open space with searing heat. A suffocating breeze wisped up through the shimmering air around the webbing of rock paths, creating a deadly ambiance that sounded other-worldly. Along the walls on both sides were etchings of Amaru with beady eyes, coiled in between large carvings of the ominous stone guides jutting out of the rock.

Alexander ran a handkerchief over his face and neck. Through the hazy air, he couldn't make out which path would lead them to safety. None of those paths looked safe to tread on.

He sighed in exhaustion, "Things keep getting more bizarre."

"How are we supposed to make it across?" Drew asked, sounding almost defeated.

Alexander smiled weakly and quoted, "'Stay true on the path of the rising tides.'"

"What?" Fitzgerald glanced up, snapping himself out of his disbelief of what lay before them.

"The third clue — 'Stay true on the path of the rising tides.'"

"Ah, 'the path'!" he squeezed the professor's shoulder. "This means there must, once again, be a correct route to take!"

"But what does it mean by 'rising'?" Kaci wondered nervously.

Alexander hastily crouched with one eye running along the ground and grimaced, "I'm afraid there's no way to avoid finding out."

He got up and directed their attention to the six-foot wide stone slab that lay before them; they had to walk across it in order to gain access to the first bridge.

"This slab appears slightly more elevated than the rest."

"Another pressure plate?" Jada groaned.

The professor nodded.

Drew furrowed his brow, "I've got a bad feeling about this."

"Then we better make this quick!" Fitzgerald ordered and jumped on the stone.

"Adrian! What are you doing?" Alexander shouted, dumbfounded.

His question was answered almost immediately. The rock sank a couple of inches, and the mouths of the stone guides on the walls opened with a painfully sharp grating sound. Fresh, bright yellow lava began to pour out into the river, sending sparks into the air upon impact, and splashing the hot liquid against the sides of the chamber. It streamed steadily, and every ounce that fell made Alexander's heart beat faster.

Kaci shuddered, "*Rising* tides. I get it now."

Fitzgerald's eyes widened then darkly glistened, and a sneer crept across his face. "There is no stopping it at this point! We must press onward! It's up to you, old chum, to guide us on the right path. I suggest that you move quickly!"

Alexander was speechless as he frantically looked about to see if there were any hints for their next move. Nothing.

"Don't just stand there; come on!" the big man bellowed with a wave of his hand.

Alexander closed his eyes to pray in the moment and then clenched his jaw. At least they didn't have to worry about anything until they got to the first junction. His eyes flickered open with resolve, and he stepped out onto the thin path that stretched across the lava.

Carefully looking through the steamy lenses of his glasses, he put one foot in front of the other. He could feel Fitzgerald's presence behind him uncomfortably pressing him forward, but he realized that truly, time was of the essence. Grabbing hold of the rock pillar on their first landing, he deftly worked his way around it, studying each side, but nothing was etched onto its rough crumbling surface. He looked out over the next two paths and wiped his glasses with his handkerchief. *Lord, which direction are we supposed to go now?*

Suddenly, he got an idea as he studied the entry stones of each path; the rock underneath them wasn't naturally black but was covered in thick soot. *I wonder...* Going down on one knee, he took his handkerchief and wiped the surfaces of each entry stone. Sure enough, the symbol of Paititi was carved into one of them.

"Logical and simple!" Fitzgerald rejoiced as he peered over the professor's shoulder.

Alexander tried his footing on the path with the symbol. It felt sturdy enough. "I suggest that we cross one at a time," he recommended to Fitzgerald.

The man agreed and then flashed a devilish grin. "Hold on; I want to see what would've happened if we'd gone the other direction!"

He yanked a sizable rock that had broken off the pedestaled column and lobbed it out onto the path. Instantly, the bridged wobbled and collapsed into the sea of lava, hissing as it melted into nothingness.

Alexander looked at Drew and Kaci grimly, understanding that his own life was not the only one at stake, then hastily crept along the next thin pathway to the second fork in the maze of bridges.

"Dust that one off!" Alexander shouted, tossing Fitzgerald a spare handkerchief once he'd crossed over. "We must hasten — the river is rising faster than I expected!"

In single file, they carefully focused on the winding paths that lay before them one after another. Drew brought up the rear and spent his time passionately praying for his uncle as he led them forward. Just one slip of a step on the sooty rock could send any of them to their doom. Despite the heat, chills ran up his spine at the thought of one of them dying, and he quickly shook the horrible vision from his mind.

"Hello!" Fitzgerald exclaimed ecstatically. "Do my eyes fail me or is that another set of gold doors far beyond?" As the group steadied themselves around another pedestaled landing, they strained to see for themselves through the steam and haze.

On the raised platform they were meticulously traveling to, the orange glow of the lava reflected off what looked like a gilded entryway. Above it was a large, sparkling, jewel-studded symbol of Paititi.

"Jim! We are on the very threshold of what we seek!"

The chamber had grown much hotter. Kaci noticed that their clothes were beginning to smolder as their profuse sweat evaporated through the fabric; and if they stood in one spot for too long, the bottom of their shoes began to melt. She looked down and saw that the sloshing magma had risen well over halfway up the wall.

"Guys, I really think we need to hurry!"

"On it!" Alexander agreed, wiping away at the soot. "Only a few more to go!"

The travelers felt themselves growing more and more weary with each arm of the bridge they crossed. At last, they found themselves at the final junction that spanned nearly thirty feet before bringing them to safety. Alexander tried to clump his handkerchief together the best he could, but it failed to insulate his fingers as he brushed the final stone clear of soot. With his hand practically raw from the heat, he finally felt the indentations of the chiseled-out symbol of Paititi.

Without uncovering the symbol entirely, he yelled by faith, "Here! It's over here!"

The skin on their faces was starting to become bright red and blistered. The temperature was now unbearably searing, and they leapt up onto the landing panting for breath with only moments to spare before the sheer heat would have killed them. They fell to the ground which was cold to the touch in comparison to the bridge they had just traversed. Drew, Kaci, and Jada had never felt more thankful for a cold, dusty floor in their lives.

A large pressure plate similar to the one where they'd started lay before them on the ground in the middle of the platform. Alexander crawled on top of it, his hands shaking from the burns he'd suffered. He felt it slowly lower and click into place. He sighed with relief as he saw the mouths of the stone guides close and the molten sea of lava subside from valves deep in the floor.

"Incredible!" Fitzgerald jumped to his feet and staggered forward to the tall and wide glistening doorway nestled into the rock, surrounded by beautiful craftsmanship. There were no handles on the doors and they didn't budge, much to the crazed man's frustration. Anger bubbled up within him like boiling lava. In rage he slammed his fists against the doors, demanding entrance. "I am worthy! I've passed your blasted trials. Let me in, I tell you!"

He leaned his sweltering forehead and palms on the cool smooth surface of the door, then closed his eyes while clenching his jaws and flexing his tattooed forearms. *I deserve this. I will have Paititi's wealth and find its source of immortal power. Nothing has stopped me on this quest, and nothing will stand in my way now.*

CHAPTER XXX

We need to get beyond these doors!"

"I'm not sure what to do, Adrian," Alexander answered while pouring some water over his hands. "We're all out of clues."

"What about this?" Drew called out from one side of the platform. He and Kaci were leaning over, curiously studying a cylindrical marble column that stood about waist high.

"Describe it to me," Alexander requested while he ripped the sleeves off his shirt and wrapped them around his hands as makeshift bandages.

Fixed in the center on top of the column was a miniature version of the guide carved entirely out of aquamarine gemstone. This rested on a polished brass plate that appeared to serve as a compass with all cardinal and ordinal positions inlaid on it. Drew was able to swivel the head with his hand and noticed that he could also lock up or down into one of the directions.

"There seems to be another one of these on the other side!" Jada dashed over to it. "Yes! I think it's the same!"

Alexander slowly moved back and forth between both and came to the same conclusion.

"And there's something here on the side, too," Jada mentioned.

The professor held his glasses while leaning down to read the Latin on the column out loud:

"One final test for all who dare
Enter the heart of the golden lair.
Recall the path that brought you here,
Of dangers faced and conquered fear.
The guides who led you are the key,
Timeless warriors placed in harmony."

"AHHH!" Fitzgerald threw his hands up into the air in pure frustration. "What sort of confounded nonsense is this? Haven't we done enough already?"

Alexander chuckled. "Aapo and the ancients wanted to make sure that we are who we say we are — that we truly did traverse through the jungles of the Amazon following each of the guides to get to this very spot where we stand here and now."

"So what are we supposed to do?" Kaci looked to her uncle.

Alexander examined the small sparkling head on top of the pedestal. "Well, the six guides we encountered along the way are the key. With the directions of the compass here, perhaps we need to remember all the different ways that the guides led us?"

"The eyes!" Jada nodded emphatically. "The direction of the eyes!"

"Yeah!" Kaci dug through her backpack, pulled out the digital camera, and flipped it on. "We've got the answers right here!"

"Except for the last one at the Nazi base," Drew reminded them. "But I know those eyes were pointing northeast."

"Excellent!" Alexander beamed.

Kaci began rapidly scrolling back through the photos, but before she could flip back to the beginning of the album, the camera suddenly went black.

"That's not good," she frowned. "I think the battery just died!"

She tried turning it on again, and it shut off almost immediately.

"No, no, NO!" Fitzgerald was beside himself and paced around the platform in utter rage. "This *can't* be happening! Not when we're so close!!" He spun on his heels and glared at Alexander while pointing his finger in the man's face. "I told you we needed that notebook!"

"It'll be okay, Adrian. We can do this —"

"You better hope so! If we do not open these doors, I will not hesitate to kill you right where you stand with my bare hands!"

"Enough with the threats," Alexander declared calmly but firmly. "We all must simply *think*. Focus on the events that influenced you the most surrounding one of the guides; I believe it will come back to us!"

"FORGET IT!" the big man shouted angrily. "How am I supposed to remember what happened *weeks* ago?" He slammed his fists repeatedly against the golden doors.

"Wait!" Drew interjected, closing his eyes and concentrating carefully. "I definitely recall the one where I crossed the swinging bridge."

Fitzgerald turned with eagerness, "And?"

"I'll never forget that day because I know God helped me. That's when I really started to understand that I can trust Him...with anything."

"That's beside the point!" he snarled with disgust. "The *eyes*, young man, what direction were the *eyes*?"

"They were looking north — I'm sure of it."

"Mine was in the cannibal village," Alexander spoke confidently as he looked into the distance. "We experienced real angels walking among us and God's protecting hand over us. The gemstones were pointing east."

Kaci closed her eyes and imagined herself being in the water again. She shivered uncontrollably for a moment when she saw flashes of the violent fish attacking her, but she scrunched her brow and forced her mind to work beyond that trauma to the moss-covered face she encountered.

"Northeast!" she blurted out, picturing it clearly now. "They were pointing up and to the right! It truly was a miracle of God that I made it out of those waters alive... My life is God's."

"Mine were looking north." Jada said. "You know — the one up in the old tree?" She smiled and looked from Alexander to Drew and Kaci. "I remember because it was the first time I felt what it was like to have friends. I have God to thank for that, because now I'm a Christian."

Fitzgerald's head jolted around and his eyes narrowed. "You are *what?*"

"Yeah, I got saved last night, Dad! Jesus is living in my heart," she bubbled joyfully. "And now I'm praying you'll get saved, too!"

"Saved? I — uh — what about the last clue?"

Beady Eyes lifted a hand. "The one under Amaru's cliff — that one's mine. I almost died there from whatever that beast was that we faced, but I got this young man to thank for saving my life." He squeezed Drew's shoulder softly, and the two shared a look of appreciation. "Through all we've experienced, I've come to believe that there is a God. I was never an atheist — just more of a skeptic. But I know now that He is real. I don't know why He's spared me, but I'm willing to find out more about Him if He'll let me live through this."

Fitzgerald threw his hands up in the air in exasperation and scoffed. "Unbelievable! What is this? A time of reckoning and spiritual confession?"

"Why not?" Alexander stepped forward and confronted him. "Tell us, what has God done in your heart on this journey?"

For a moment the room was silent except for the distant sound of foaming lava. No one moved. No one dared.

"Who cares about that? The only thing that matters is getting through these doors!" He glowered at Beady Eyes. "Out with it, man! What direction were the jewels?"

"They were pointing east."

"Ah! There you have it, Jim, all six directions! Now, can we *please* proceed?"

"I suppose," Alexander frowned and shook his head at how hard his old friend's heart was. *Lord, is there any hope for him?* He turned to look back at the columns. "So, I find it interesting that our clue here uses the phrases *'recall the path'* and *'placed in harmony.'* I believe this means that we must put these directions in the right sequence. And, since the columns are identical, I presume that we will need to turn and lock both heads on the compass at the same time."

Fitzgerald immediately walked over to the other pedestal and placed his hand on the carved aquamarine gemstone, "Ready!"

Alexander nodded and assumed a similar position. "The first direction is northeast. On my mark — three, two, one!"

For each direction, the two men loudly counted down together in cadence and pressed the head down into position with smooth synchronization. After the sixth and final direction, a long deep rumble filled the chamber, shaking the platform and sending a shower of dust from the ceiling. The columns disappeared into the floor, and the huge doors groaned open to reveal their next passageway.

Blue light flooded over them like a shimmering ocean wave, and Kaci's jaw dropped at the magical sight that lay before them as they slowly walked in. The tunnel was a massive geode with its walls and ceiling covered entirely with crystals of all different shapes and sizes. Thousands of bioluminescent worms dwelling among them softly glowed, and their combined sapphire radiance was beautifully refracted by the quartz. A perfectly formed trail made of black obsidian gravel lay in the midst, and the chamber felt alive as the team heard a faint hum resonating from the crystals, as if inviting them to journey deeper into the mountain.

Fitzgerald rushed forward, bathing himself in the cascading light and gentle ambiance, "We're standing in the midst of legend, Jim! Can't you feel the spiritual energy pulsing from this place?"

The man then laughed in such a way that both startled and alarmed Alexander as he mixed delightful bliss with pure evil to make a reverberating cacophonous roar. The harsh sound killed the tranquility that had remained undisturbed for hundreds of years, and an eerie silence settled upon them when his laughter faded. With a complete disregard for the beauty that surrounded them, he impatiently ran ahead, hollering at the rest of them to keep up.

Their feet crunched and echoed loudly as the path wove around scattered outcroppings of large geometric crystals. Drew noticed the glow worms didn't like this because they appeared to pulse faster and become more withdrawn into their hovels. The further they went, the more the passage grew as it gently curved back and forth. Thin veins of aquamarine gemstone could now be seen webbing out along the floor and up behind the clear quartz on the walls. As they entered the final bend of the tunnel, they could see its large mouth directly ahead give way to a voluminous cavern that seemed larger than life.

Fitzgerald slowed, fell to his knees, and crawled the last few feet up to the threshold, trembling at what he was about to see. The rest of the team gathered around him and beheld in speechless wonder what sprawled out before them.

A broad staircase crafted of polished granite descended at least one hundred meters into a cratered valley filled with an underground city made of gold. Solid gold. On the far side of the cavern flowed another river of molten lava that fractured into a multitude of tiny streams and sluggishly ran through the cobblestoned streets. The city sparkled with hues of yellow, orange, and deep red, revealing how well the buildings had been impeccably preserved. More colonies of glow worms far above lit up the expansive atrium like the night sky, and other bioluminescent insects flew in wisping droves throughout the cavern, adding a sparkling affect to the already breathtaking view.

What captured their attention the most, however, was the single ziggurat in the middle of the city towering several stories high. It rose close to the ceiling where it met a gentle waterfall pouring forth from a cluster of crystals into the center of a room on top of the pyramid.

"This... this is it," Alexander stammered, wiping a tear from his cheek, relieved the journey was finally over. Drew and Beady Eyes gave each other a high five and cheered, while the two girls smiled at each other happily and linked arms together.

Fitzgerald began to laugh hysterically, his eyes wide with exhilaration, and he scampered to his feet.

"We've found it, Jim!" he pulled his old friend into a bear hug. "Just imagine how *rich* we'll become!" He slapped him on the back, then hastily turned and descended the stairs with reckless abandon. When he reached the bottom, he shouted in triumph and rushed about taking in the grand opulence of the city.

The others hadn't moved yet, still stunned with the magnificent spectacle of their discovery. Jada noticed her father working his way deeper into the city as he carefully jumped over the small lava streams. He hurried from place to place looking in the open doorways and then disappearing into one.

"Wealth! Unimaginable wealth!" they heard him shout repeatedly with sounds of clattering and clanging. He emerged with a fist full of coins that he threw into the air with elation. In his other hand, he clutched a couple diamond gold necklaces and held them up for all to see.

"I will become the most powerful man in the world!" he bellowed and brought them down over his head to proudly wear.

"Wait for us, Dad!"

He gazed up with a crazed look. "No!" and then slowly pointed toward the ziggurat. "We all know what the temple holds... I *must* see it for myself!"

Alexander raised his hands and waved at him vigorously, "Adrian!" But it was too late — the man had already vanished among the buildings.

"Come on!" the professor ran down the stairs with urgency. "We've got to stop him before he does something foolish!"

"What do you mean?" Jada's voice wavered with deep concern as the team raced after him.

"We both know your father has been obsessed with the myth that Paititi holds the Fountain of Youth. It's not true! There is no such thing as immortality on earth!"

"But didn't he have some old writings that confirmed it?"

"Nothing of the sort! His entire belief has been based on what he *thinks* they said. Andres Lopez, who visited Paititi, wrote about the city's riches but was probably sworn to secrecy about their Sacred Mountain filled with gold. He simply indicated that there was something far greater lying within — which alludes to the mountain — *'where there is power and life to do that which is desired.'* Your father thinks this directly refers to immortality because he's listened to so many lies and fables. I believe it's just poetically speaking of all the billions of dollars in treasure we're surrounded with."

At the bottom of the staircase, the buildings loomed higher and larger than they realized. Intricately carved columns embedded with jade, emeralds, and other precious stones were scattered among the structures, and gold statues of Incan deities, especially of Amaru, sat on every corner. The amount of wealth that lay before them was astoundingly palpable.

They carefully yet quickly made their way through the streets, leaping over hot pockets and tendrils of lava as they journeyed toward the temple. Drew glanced into many of the doorways they passed and found each room uniquely filled with large clay pots that lined the walls. He finally came to the place where Fitzgerald had rifled through some of them and spilled their contents. Countless gold coins, vessels, cups, and piece of jewelry littered the floor. He suddenly felt himself strangely drawn to it as it glistened so brightly with the deep red glow of the magma that filled the cavern. *Maybe I could just take a couple things? I would be able to do so much with it!*

"Don't let greed set in!" Alexander warned, clamping a loving hand upon the young man's shoulder.

"I — I'm sorry, Uncle James," Drew shook himself out of his daze. "I don't know what came over me."

"It's okay," the professor declared in all seriousness. "I can feel the pull, too. Undoubtedly, if a man could claim all of these things for himself, he would be the richest man on the planet. But remember — *'a man's life consisteth not in the abundance of the things which he possesseth'*! The love of money is the root of all evil!"

The professor turned to the rest of the team. "We need to stick together. Any of us can get lost in here easily." He looked out in the distance toward the pyramid and saw Fitzgerald's lone figure climbing up its colossal staircase to the shadowy room above.

"We must hurry!!"

Kaci had never seen her uncle look more worried than he did in that moment. His face was pale and gaunt, with concern etched deep in his features. The burden of his friend's lost soul weighed heavy on him, and he genuinely worried for the man's life in his unstable condition. With a new burst of energy, the professor sprinted down the street, shouting out after Fitzgerald.

It took what felt like an eternity to reach the base of the temple. The craftsmanship was immaculate and perfectly square. Each golden brick had been precisely laid. Symmetrical pillars flanking the wide steps led up to the ceiling of the glowing cavern. Massive stone guides with the inscription of Paititi in their foreheads and eyes inlaid with light blue gems sat stoically like sentinels on either side of the entrance.

Though every muscle in his body burned with exhaustion, Alexander mounted the stairs two at a time without slowing down, his mind racing over every possible scenario of what Fitzgerald might be doing inside the temple. Jada ran right next to him, keeping up with his pace. She feared for her father's life. Tears trickled down her face, and she didn't do anything to hide them or wipe them away.

When they reached the top, Drew looked over his shoulder. The city was just as hauntingly beautiful from this vantage point as it was from the other side of the cavern. The cascading sound of the gentle waterfall now filled their ears, and Kaci pointed up to the shimmering liquid flowing from a crystal-studded mouth in the cavern ceiling. It glistened with the light blue aura of the glow worms and fell into a golden cistern on top of the enclosed chamber that lay before them. A fearsome depiction of Amaru wrapped in a tight coil surrounded the single entryway that led within. The creature's two heads met in the middle with their mouths wide, eager to devour the emerald Paititi symbol that rested in the center of the arch.

"That can't be a good sign," Drew muttered as he felt the hair on the back of his neck stand on end.

"Adrian?" the professor called out into the narrow foreboding hallway.

No answer.

"ADRIAN?" he repeated with increasing alarm, then disappeared into the darkness.

"Uh—" Beady Eyes said quietly, "it might be best for me to wait right here."

Drew looked at him with uncertainty.

"Fitzgerald may try to make me to do something that I don't want to do. I like you kids. But I'm a Bloodfist, remember? And I don't trust myself."

Drew nodded and shook his hand with respect. "Okay, we'll be back soon."

The three teenagers warily entered, feeling along the petroglyph-covered walls to keep themselves from stumbling. A moment later, they caught up to Alexander. The hallway jutted to the left and right like a maze until it ended at a room in the center, brightly lit by sheer opulence. Every surface was shiny and polished. The ceiling above where the cistern rested was made of gold so pure that it was almost translucent, and they could see the waterfall surging into a pool directly overhead. The soft hues of blue and red from the cavern danced across the room, shimmering through the water.

In the middle of the room, Fitzgerald knelt beside a small basin of beautifully clear water, made all the more inviting by the priceless gems inlaid into its bottom. His hands reverently gripped the edge, and he blankly stared down into it with a devilish grin as his diamond necklaces dangled in front of him. Around the sides of the basin was moss, growing out from the water and running along the floor. At each corner of the room, water delicately trickled down engraved channels from the ceiling feeding the basin from underneath the ground.

"Dad...." Jada ran past the others. "What are you doing?"

The man slowly lifted his wide, wild eyes. "I wanted you all to be here to witness this occasion."

"What? Don't do anything foolish! The Fountain of Youth is not real!"

Fitzgerald's eyes flickered darkly to Alexander. "So you have turned my own flesh and blood against me? It's *here*, Jim, like I always said!"

"You really believe this will give you eternal life?" Alexander walked up and glanced into the water, but he stopped in his tracks as Fitzgerald thrust out a sharp ceremonial dagger.

"Back off, Jim." Fitzgerald sat up on the edge of the basin. "I really don't want to hurt you, but I will if you try to stop me!"

Alexander raised his hands and slowly moved away, "Adrian, this water doesn't hold immortality. It's not what you think it is."

"Shut up! I don't want to hear it. There *must* be a reason why the Incans would build a temple around such a place as this!"

"I don't know why, but I can tell you —"

"Just. One. Drink." Fitzgerald spoke over Alexander, producing a small golden chalice that he'd swiped from the building he'd ransacked.

"Adrian, please!" The professor took an unnoticeable step forward. "If this water gave immortality, then why is no one here? The most beautiful city in the world, abandoned. The natives who lived centuries ago would still be alive!"

Fitzgerald ignored him, dipped the cup into the water, and brought it up overflowing. "They were not worthy like me! I deserve this! I will be a god!"

"STOP! Don't drink that!" Alexander lunged at Fitzgerald, knocking the vessel from his hand as it hovered close to his mouth. "The water is poisonous!"

"How DARE you!"

The two men wrestled together on the floor; Alexander grasped Fitzgerald's other hand holding the knife and tried to pry it away. Drew and Kaci remained frozen, unsure of what to do, while Jada dashed over and grabbed the chalice resting sideways on the floor.

"Stop this, Dad! Now!"

"You all are just trying to deceive me and keep me from what is rightfully mine!" Fitzgerald snarled.

"No, I'm trying to save your life!" Alexander slammed the man's fist into the ground, clattering the knife free.

"I...must...take...a drink!" Fitzgerald reached for the blade again, but Alexander swung his foot around and booted it to the other side of the room. The two men locked arms and grunted heavily as each of them tried to gain the upper hand over the other.

"You can't! Mercury has been mixing with the water for centuries, and who knows what other deadly minerals are floating around in there. It's completely toxic by now!"

Jada went to the edge of the basin and saw what Alexander was talking about. How could her father be so blind? A silvery bubble floated at the bottom blending in with the shining gems and then she noticed another and another as she looked throughout the water. The basin was full of it.

Her eyes widened in dread, "Dad... DAD!"

But Fitzgerald didn't hear her as he kicked Alexander in the stomach hard, making the professor gasp loudly and clatter back into the wall. He pressed his attack further by a series of rapid-fire painful blows to the man's chest and face.

Kaci covered her eyes, bursting into tears, and turned her head away.

"Enough!" Drew yelled at the top of his lungs and rushed forward to help his uncle.

"Stupid boy!" Fitzgerald backhanded him with all his might, sending the young man careening backward clutching his face. Alexander weakly slumped to the floor, clutching his sides, and Drew sank to the floor next to him in numbed shock.

Fitzgerald whirled about and snatched the chalice out of his daughter's hands in lightning speed.

"Dad, please stop!" Jada pleaded, trying to fight him. "Professor Alexander is right. Something is in there, I tell you!"

But she was no match for his raw strength. He shoved her away, and she stumbled onto the ground.

"You're wrong!" Fitzgerald sneered diabolically. "I'll show you! I'll show all of you!"

He filled the vessel again and chugged the water with loud gulps.

Jada ran to her father frantically, trying to pull the chalice from his lips but to no avail. He finished it and gave a long, loud sigh of satisfaction.

"See? There is nothing to worry about, my dear. Look at how clear and sparkling it is!" He grinned from ear to ear, but his voice rasped off-pitch with a metallic sound. After a few moments, his face became flushed, and he began gasping for air in short, curt breaths. He desperately scooped yet another cupful but found himself not able to hold it still in his hands. His whole body was now shaking. *Nothing is wrong with it,* he told himself. *It must be the power flowing through my body.*

"Dad?" Jada looked at her father in horror. "You don't look well!"

His eyes were turning glossy and yellow. "Jada. Please. Drink some. It's the Fountain. It has to be. It has to be!" He tried to take another drink, but collapsed to the ground, violently coughing. The cup of water spilled out onto the gold-covered floor and mixed with the blood that had begun to drip from his mouth.

He frowned, "That's... that's odd. What is happening? I thought...."

His body went limp, and he had just enough strength to lay on his back. He blinked a couple of times, confused, trying to clear his vision, but everything remained blurred. Jada crawled over and frantically managed to pick up his head and shoulders and hold him in her arms.

"Oh God," she cried out. "Please, no!"

Alexander wiped the blood from a cut on his cheekbone with his sleeve and went to kneel beside them. Tears of compassion welled up in his eyes and slowly rolled down his cheeks.

"You old fool," he whispered gently, softly squeezing the burly man's shoulder. "What have you done? Why did you have to drink it?"

"You... were... right," Fitzgerald gasped at every word. "Something... terrible... is happening. I...I c-c-can't feel m-my chest!"

Jada became distraught seeing her father in such a state; she felt helpless. "He's getting worse! Please do something, Mr. Alexander! ANYTHING!"

"I don't know what..." Suddenly he remembered. He turned and emphatically motioned to his niece, "Get the —"

But Kaci had already read his mind and was yanking off her backpack.

"— emergency kit!"

She dumped the contents on the ground, found the small silver case her uncle had given her at the beginning of their journey, and tossed it to him as quickly as possible.

Inside was a syringe with multicolored vials that contained different medicines and sedatives.

Alexander filled the needle with one of the substances and stuck it carefully into Fitzgerald's arm. Almost instantly, his convulsing slowed, and he started breathing more easily.

"Th-thank you, old chum."

Alexander hung his head regretfully. "It won't heal you; it's only morphine. But it will help with the pain. I'm afraid there's nothing else I can do; the poison is already in your bloodstream by now."

"How ironic," the man chuckled through bloody teeth, "The very thing that I thought would bring me immortality will instead bring me death." He began coughing uncontrollably until his daughter was able to help him settle back down. He was weak and so very tired.

Then reality hit him. He was *really* going to die.

In that moment, the man's hardness began to melt away. His eyes cleared and the old Adrian Fitzgerald that Alexander once knew came back. "James? What have I done? I've — I've made a foolish mistake! My lust for power consumed me. What... what was I thinking?"

He looked up at Jada and touched her grimy, tear-stained cheek. Genuine remorse was etched on his face. "I'm terribly sorry, my dear. I have failed you."

Jada swallowed hard. "Stop talking like that. I love you, Dad. I love you." She held him tightly.

"I... I love you, too."

This made Jada weep uncontrollably. The last time she'd heard him utter those words to her, she had been a little girl. It felt so good to hear them again.

"Dad, I beg of you. Please. I'm so scared for you right now. You can't die and go to Hell. I want — I saw the truth of it all last night. Drew and Kaci, my best friends, showed me how only Jesus can give eternal life — He is the living water, Dad! He is what you've been searching for."

Fitzgerald's nature wanted to bristle up against what she said, but deep down in his heart, he knew she was right.

"Please ask Jesus to save you," Jada pleaded. "Let Him take you up to Heaven."

"Is this possible?" Fitzgerald looked to Alexander, his eyes truly searching.

The professor nodded, and he lovingly held the man's hand.

"How can this be? I don't understand. I — I'm such an evil man; I've done *so many* wicked things." Fitzgerald stared blankly into space as he thought back over his past. He became disgusted with himself and tried to shake Alexander's hand free, "I'm not worth saving! Just let me die and go to Hell!"

But the professor refused to let him go.

"I can't let you do that, old friend. I've prayed for your salvation every day since our journey began; and in this moment, it's not too late. Though you may have turned your back on God, He has never turned His back on you!"

He pulled out his worn leather Bible, and it fell open to Psalm 86 where he had it bookmarked. "*'For thou, Lord,'*" he quoted, his voice quivering with emotion, "*'art ready to forgive; and plenteous in mercy unto all them that call upon Thee.'* God also promises in Romans 10:13, *'For whosoever shall call upon the name of the Lord shall be saved.'*"

Tears flooded down Fitzgerald's inflamed cheeks; the effect of the poison from the contaminated water was ramping up its effect on his body. It wouldn't be long now.

"Adrian, He can and will save you, if you'll let Him."

Fitzgerald understood. "Just like… the thief on the cross."

Tears welled up again in Alexander's eyes and slowly dripped from his face and landed on his open Bible. "Yes, my friend. Yes."

Fitzgerald looked up to the translucent ceiling above him and spoke softly, losing strength by the second. "God… I-I've been such a fool. I deserve it. I deserve death and Hell. I'm so wicked and cruel...and so...mean." Fitzgerald paused a moment, trying to catch his breath. "I'm sorry for my sins. I don't deserve Your love or this chance for mercy after all I've done. I don't understand why You would allow it so, but I am grateful. I don't…"

Fitzgerald gathered himself again, his voice fading to a whisper. "I see now. I believe! I truly believe. Please accept me. Please… Jesus…"

His bloodshot eyes remained motionless. The soft hint of a peaceful smile was on the corners of his mouth. Silence prevailed for a moment mixed with the ambiance of trickling water.

"Dad?" Jada tenderly shook him. "Dad?" She bent down to feel for any breath out of his mouth on her cheek.

He was gone.

Jada looked up at Alexander and wept. Alexander sobbed along with her as he helped her reverently lay her dad on the floor. Slowly and lovingly, he closed his friend's eyes with his hand. Jada wrapped her arms around her legs and allowed deep grief to pour out of her, while Kaci sat beside her, holding her and crying, too.

Drew placed a hand on his uncle's shoulder, and the man stood to tightly hug his nephew. The whole room filled with tears. Tears of sorrow. Tears of joy. Tears of relief.

Kaci's soft, soothing voice rose above them, and Drew and Alexander joined in the sacred melody.

"Amazing Grace… how sweet the sound… that saved a wretch like me. I once was lost, but now I'm found. Was blind but now I see…."

EPILOGUE

Drew and Kaci climbed in their comfy beds and slept for almost two days straight. It felt good to be home.

After Fitzgerald's death, the team found another way to exit the mountain. Thankfully, Jada had thought to grab her Dad's SAT phone before they escaped the Nazi base. Alexander called one of his military contacts in Brazil, and they were picked up the next morning on the beach of the island by a search-and-rescue chopper.

Alexander made sure that no one would ever find that place again. Enough lives had been lost because of greed and the lust for power. If they revealed its location to the world, he could only imagine the fighting and pandemonium that would ensue. Of course, it would be extremely difficult for someone to find, even the most skilled of archeologists. The eyes of the stone guides had been removed along the way, with even some of the guides themselves being destroyed. The ancient map drawn by Aapo was left in a charred pile of ash on the mountain, and Alexander's notebook still lay at the bottom of the chasm with wooden spikes. Alexander was thankful that Paititi would remain a legend in the pages of history.

Before Drew and Kaci got on a private jet in Manaus, Brazil, to head back home, Alexander reminded them that gold and earthly treasure was not the answer — these things could never satisfy an empty heart. Rather, what mattered most was living for God and for His truly immortal kingdom. He kissed and hugged them goodbye and promised he'd see them soon.

His parting challenge was for them to memorize II Corinthians 4:18. As soon as they were in their seats on the plane, the siblings poured over the Bible from Kaci's backpack and read the verse: *"While we look not at the things which are seen, but at the things which are not seen: for the things which are seen are temporal; but the things which are not seen are eternal."* Drew and Kaci smiled at each other and knew the work that God had done in their lives through this adventure would leave them forever changed.

Ten days later, Alexander stepped off of the plane in America, elated to be visiting his 'little monsters.' He definitely needed a break after all they had been through in South America. Thankfully, the university had no problem giving him 90 days of paid sabbatical — time for grieving as well as consolation over the whole ordeal. Now he was right where he wanted to be, among his family, tossing a football in the backyard with his nephew and spending time with his niece and his sister Susan.

"I really never understood the whole American football thing, but this is quite fun." Alexander laughed, as he tossed the ball back to Drew.

"Yeah... I *love* the game! But you know, Uncle James? It doesn't have a pull on me anymore. I'm going to go all out for God and use the rest of my days to further the Gospel." Drew threw the ball, and it shot like a laser into Alexander's hands.

He winced when he caught it, still sore from the burns he received in Paititi.

"I'm sorry if I threw it too hard! I guess I just got excited."

Alexander chuckled. "No worries at all, my boy!" He tossed it back. "I'm thankful you answered God's call upon your life. There is nothing more rewarding than fulfilling His will and being engaged in His work. God is going to use you in a wonderful way in the days ahead!"

Drew was about to throw the ball back, when Kaci and their mother emerged from the house with a platter filled with fruit and a pitcher of lemonade.

"Hey, boys!" Mrs. Howard called out. "Let's have a snack! It's so hot out here — you need to rest and have a drink."

Drew, Kaci, and Alexander exchanged knowing glances — this weather was *nothing* compared to what they'd lived in for weeks in the Amazon! They laughed and sat down together.

Alexander prayed over the food, and Kaci began to make everyone plates while Drew poured the drinks.

"I talked with Jada just a little while ago," Kaci mentioned.

"Oh?" Drew looked up. "How's she doing?"

"Really good! She said she's settling into her new college dorm and, though she's registered for the fall, she decided to fill her days by sitting in on summer classes! She's thrilled to be on the campus of a Christian college and can't soak up the Bible knowledge fast enough! She's very grateful for your help with that, Uncle James."

A joyful grin spread across the man's face. "It was easy enough. I'm glad her father set aside so much money for her schooling. Shows how much he really loved her. Did she say anything about going to the church I recommended?"

"Yes!" Kaci sat down to eat. "And she absolutely loves it. I'm shocked at how fast she's growing in the Lord!"

Drew took a drink from his lemonade. "Sorry to change the topic, but what will happen to the Bloodfists? Is she going to be safe?"

"Well, as far as I know — yes, she should be fine. Without Fitzgerald at the helm, the organization has crumbled apart. Jada — who was the heir apparent — wanted nothing to do with it and has decided to give away all of her father's wealth to charities, churches, and missionary work."

"That's awesome!" Drew smiled, his mouth full of fruit. Strawberry juice dripped down the side of his chin. Everyone giggled.

"Oh, and speaking of 'awesome' things," Alexander continued. "I spoke with a missions' agency earlier this week, and they agreed to ship a container of Bibles to the villages we visited! They're also going to send a team... and they want me to lead it!" Alexander reached in his pocket and pulled out the bead necklace that Chief Amuta had given to him. "I've decided to join them; we're leaving next week. I can't wait to share with you the churches that will be started as a result of this!"

The conversation quieted down for a moment, as the three of them reflected independently on various aspects of their journey. Mrs. Howard was just happy to have them all safely home, and she sat there, holding her children's hands and taking in the sight of them, finally back together again.

"One thing I keep asking myself," Kaci piped up, "is why *did* the Incans build a temple around that crystal waterfall?"

"Hmmm. I honestly don't know," Alexander replied transparently. "Maybe they believed that the water had healing properties? They certainly worshipped a number of false gods, including the sun and the moon. It would not surprise me if they built it to honor the life-giving qualities of water. After all, it is essential — nothing in the world lives without it and everything depends upon it for their survival."

His answer seemed to satisfy the children's query.

"What happened to Beady Eyes after we flew home, Uncle James?" Drew asked as he filled his now-empty glass with more lemonade.

"Ah, you mean Jacques?" Alexander smiled at the surprised response from the young people at hearing the man's real name for the first time. He chuckled, "With the Bloodfist organization gone, he had nowhere to go. And, truthfully, he had no desire to return to that life of underground crime anyway... so I offered him a job."

"You did?" Kaci squealed.

"I really believe he will be a great asset to my work, with a little training! At first, he feared he'd be arrested and charged with all his past crimes, but I assured him that just as God has pardoned our sins, I would overlook his. You see, in the eyes of the authorities, Jacques doesn't even exist, and his criminal record is buried so deeply in layers of clandestine operations, no court would be able to find any evidence pointing to him even if they wanted to."

Drew sighed, relieved. "So... Bead — I mean, Jacques is a free man. But, not completely, because he hasn't broken free of his spiritual chains yet, has he?"

Alexander leaned back in his chair and smiled. "Not yet, Drew. But we've already had a few conversations about salvation and he's close! Don't stop praying for him!"

Just then, his phone buzzed on the glass patio table.

"It's Simmons!" the professor grinned. "He's probably checking up on me."

Kaci silently clapped, "Ooh! Can we say hi?"

"Sure!"

After swiping the touchscreen to answer the call and placing it on speaker, he gave a silent count of three, and they all chimed in with a hearty "hello" to their family friend.

"Greetings to you, Professor. And greetings to you all! Lady Susan, it is a joy to hear your voice, as well." The tone of his voice changed. "I'm sorry to disturb you, sir, but this is a matter of utmost importance. You've received a call here at the mansion that I must patch through to your cell immediately."

Alexander's eyes narrowed. He scrambled to his feet and took the phone off speaker.

He waited for a moment and then said, "Hello, this is Professor Alexander. How may I be of service?"

He listened intently, his body growing rigid. Drew and Kaci exchanged glances, knowing something was off.

The professor hastily turned about and retreated into the backyard. Before he was out of earshot, they could hear him say, "But the very hairs of your head are all numbered."

"Huh? That's random," Kaci whispered. "What do you think it means?"

"I don't quite know," Drew replied. "Maybe it's some sort of code?"

"Your uncle has a lot of connections and is always working on several things at once," their mother smiled. "He must take precautions. I'm sure it's work-related."

They watched their uncle pace back and forth for several minutes and speak rather intently with whoever was on the other line. He finally walked back and stood by the patio table still on the phone.

"And you're sure of this?"

There was a brief pause.

"Thank you."

He hung up the call and sat back down, deep in thought.

"May I ask what that was about?" Drew respectfully inquired.

Alexander took off his glasses and wearily rubbed his eyes. He looked at his sister and then at his niece and nephew for a long moment, utterly at a loss for words. He muttered something to himself as he wiped the lenses with a napkin by his plate.

"That was an informant of mine who works undercover in Turkey." Alexander paused, "He's very deep in what he's involved with. It appears he's discovered something that's... well, rather astounding."

He put his glasses back on and rested his elbows on his knees as he leaned forward. "It's about your father... he's alive."

DIGGING
DEEPER

Below are thought-provoking questions we have prayerfully developed from the story for you to think over and answer. Our purpose in writing this novel was for the reader to be spiritually challenged, strengthened, and changed through the Scriptural truths discussed by the characters. If you are reading this book together as a family, youth group, or class, these questions would serve as great topics of conversation. — ***Caleb & Katie Garraway***

1. Do you believe God has a purpose for your life? Have you ever struggled about God's will like Drew did after his big football win? What can you learn from Proverbs 3:5-7 to help you as you seek God's will? *(Chapter 2, Pages 34-35)*

2. What was the only thing Drew and Kaci could do when they were kidnapped? Why is it really the most important thing any Christian can *ever* do? *(Chapter 4, Page 56)*

3. Alexander took a strong stand against alcohol when Fitzgerald jokingly offered him some. What are some of the arguments he made against strong drink? Do you agree with him? Why or why not? When Jesus Himself was given alcohol on the cross (see Matthew 27:34), he refused to drink it, showing by example that it is wrong. According to Proverbs 20:1, 23:29-35, 31:4-5 and I Thessalonians 5:22 how should *you* view drinking alcohol? *(Chapter 6, Pages 97-98)*

4. How did God help Drew when fearful thoughts about Fitzgerald washed over him? Whom or what do you turn to when you are afraid? What should a believer depend on in times of fear? *(Chapter 7, Page 112)*

5. Have you sometimes struggled to stay close to Christ consistently, like Drew and Kaci did? Like them, do you notice a connection between your time in the Word of God and the closeness of your walk with him? How can you improve that? *(Chapter 9, Pages 130-131)*

6. Alexander talked of God's omnipresence — how He is with you today and also already in your tomorrow. Do you believe this? How would this knowledge affect your response in a sudden trial? *(Chapter 9, Page 132)*

7. Alexander explained how peace in the world's eyes can come and go with the ups and downs of life, but the peace of God can rule in a Christian's heart no matter what they go through. When you face a difficult time, do you find your peace in the presence of God? Do you know of anyone who has faced trials and never lost their joy? How has their testimony of resting in God impacted you? *(Chapter 9, Page 133)*

8. Drew and Kaci felt like they were leaving a piece of their heart with Chief Tenoch and his village after their uncle had shared the Gospel with them for the first time and many were saved. Alexander assured the teenagers that the more they invested in missions, the bigger the heart God would give them. How about you? When a missions offering is taken in church, do you give? When a missions trip is planned, do you go? Have you ever experienced leaving a piece of your heart on a mission field (whether at home or abroad) and then God growing your heart for the souls of others because of it? *(Chapter 11, Page 154)*

9. The more Drew and Kaci lived like *"real-deal Christians,"* the more Jada was drawn to them. What do your unsaved friends and family see when they look at the way you live? Do they even know you're saved? Can they tell you are the *"real deal"*? *(Chapter 12, Page 156)*

10. What does the Bible mean when I Thessalonians 5:18 says, "*IN*

everything give thanks"? Can you think of a trial or difficult circumstance you have experienced when you wondered if God had made a mistake or wasn't in control? How could knowing the meaning behind the wording of this verse change your attitude during trials? *(Chapter 17, Pages 229-230)*

11. Fitzgerald believed money spoke *"a far more powerful language than anything else on this earth."* Alexander disagreed and quoted Proverbs 22:1, *"A good name is rather to be chosen than great riches, and loving favour rather than silver and gold."* Do you think God cares more about how much money you make or what kind of character your life exemplifies? How would this knowledge affect your major life decisions (college, career, service for God, future spouse, etc)? *(Chapter 18, Page 247)*

12. When many of the Bloodfists perished in the mudslide, Jada realized just how short life is. Drew and Kaci shared Proverbs 27:1 with her, *"Boast not thyself of to morrow; for thou knowest not what a day may bring forth."* If today was your last day on earth, what would you do differently? Would you spend more time with God? Would you be more soul-conscious? Would you get right with your parents or someone you've wronged? Do you think God would have you live this way every day? *(Chapter 18, Page 248)*

13. When Alexander read Psalm 23 to the three young people, Drew and Jada had opposite responses. Drew, a long-time Christian who had heard the passage many times before and probably had it memorized, was somewhat calloused to the power and beauty of the chapter. Jada, on the other hand, who'd never heard it before, found greater joy in it than Drew ever had. Has God's Word become boring, old or not as special to you the longer you've been saved? How did Drew deal with this realization? How should you deal with it, if you are living in the same spiritual apathy? *(Chapter 18, Page 254)*

14. Jada realized that Alexander, Drew and Kaci were authentic Christians. The professor shared that unfortunately, there are a lot of hypocrites in Christianity today. Do you see this to be true? When others get to know you, do they find you to be a hypocritical Christian or are you *"legit"*? How can a child of God avoid being a hypocrite? *(Chapter 18, Page 255)*

15. Alexander reminded Drew and Kaci that surrendering their life to God is not a one-time experience — they must daily remain yielded to Him in a perpetual state of surrender. Has there ever been a moment in your life that you have completely surrendered everything to God? If so, you've probably noticed times when you have taken yourself back off the altar. Is it difficult to stay yielded? Are you willing to *"die daily"* as the apostle Paul did? What are some of the distractions in your life that you know keep you from being fully surrendered to God? *(Chapter 22, Pages 301-302)*

16. Does being a *"full-time Christian"* always mean you will be a pastor, evangelist, or missionary? If not, what does it mean? What did it mean for James Alexander? *(Chapter 22, Page 304)*

17. Do you struggle with covetousness and a craving for more money or material possessions? According to Luke 12:15 & 31, what should you be seeking after instead? *(Chapter 22, Page 305)*

18. Like Drew, do you find yourself pulled to a life of fame (sports, music, climbing the career ladder to success, etc)? How would C.T. Studd's statement, *"Only one life 'twill soon be past, only what's done for Christ will last"* affect your decisions in the future and even your choices on a daily basis? Do you agree with Alexander, that there isn't one thing this world could offer you — money, position, power, or sin — that is more appealing than what the Lord has for you? Why or why not? *(Chapter 22, Page 306)*

19. The story Alexander told about his friend in the hospital ashamed to die is actually a true story. If you were on death's doorstep today, would you be ashamed of how you've lived your life or would you be at peace, ready to meet Jesus? Would you be confident that you lived every day He gave you in a way that pleased Him and built His kingdom? *(Chapter 22, Page 307)*

20. When Drew fully surrendered his life to the Lord (specifically to the call to preach), he felt *"free"*. From the world's perspective, it may seem he just put on chains of slavery to God. They would look at surrender in a negative light. What is your opinion? Do you believe surrender to God is enslaving or freeing? Have you come to a place of full surrender? Would you surrender your heart and life to Jesus

now? (If so, please see the next page.) *(Chapter 22, Page 308)*

21. Jada held a lot of bitterness and hatred in her heart toward her father for how she was raised. Drew and Kaci encouraged her to let go of that bitterness and forgive him. Ephesians 4:31-32 says, *"Let all bitterness, and wrath, and anger, and clamour, and evil speaking, be put away from you, with all malice: And be ye kind one to another, tenderhearted, forgiving one another, even as God for Christ's sake hath forgiven you."* They were able to easily forgive her for kidnapping them and treating them so badly, because they understood how much Christ had forgiven them. Is there a person in your life you are holding bitterness in your heart against? Have you wondered, as Jada did, how it could ever be possible to forgive? When you truly realize the amazing forgiveness of Christ toward you, does it make it easier to consider forgiving that person? If you haven't broken free and experienced this yet, what is holding you back? Will you choose to forgive? Why not do it today? *(Chapter 28, Page 377)*

22. Although he was physically strong, Fitzgerald was really just a weak man enslaved to his greed, anger, and lust for power. How did his rage against the sealed golden doors in Paititi show this? *(Chapter 29, Page 403)*

23. When Drew and Alexander saw the gold, jewels and vast wealth in Paititi, each felt pulled toward it for a brief moment. They could have given in and stolen riches for themselves, excusing it away saying they'd *"use it for God."* If you would have been there, do you think the treasure would have pulled at you too? Alexander reminded Drew of Luke 12:15. Do you think it would have been right for them to take those coins and jewels? Why or why not? *(Chapter 30, Page 411)*

24. Fitzgerald finally realized he needed a Savior and only Jesus Christ could save him from his sins and give him true eternal life. What about you? Have you accepted God's free gift of salvation? As Fitzgerald learned, no life is too far gone, no sin is too great that God can't and won't forgive. Can you remember a specific moment in your life when you prayed and put your faith in Christ? If you are not saved, what is keeping you from trusting Jesus as your personal Savior? Will you pray and accept Him now? *(Chapter 30, Pages 418-419)*

Through reading this book, I have decided to pray and trust Jesus Christ as my personal Saviour. I am now a child of God!

Signed: _____

Date: _____

Through reading this book, I have decided to fully surrender my life to God, holding nothing back, and become completely willing to do whatever He wants me to do with my future.

Signed: _____

Date: _____

If you have made either of these decisions, we would love to rejoice with you! Please email us the good news at our personal correspondence: **calebgarraway@gmail.com**

SCAN TO **WATCH/SHARE**

THE GOSPEL FILM

SCAN TO **GIVE ONLINE**

ABOUT THE
AUTHORS

Caleb and Katie Garraway travel in full-time evangelism a majority of each year with hearts that burn for Heaven-sent revival. Their ministry has reached millions globally with the Gospel through preaching, the printed word, and film. Their ministries offer many resources for the church, family, and home, and they would be delighted to hold revival services at your church.

Caleb and Katie have written a number of other books including: *A Biblical Approach to Music, All For Jesus, America: A Journey of Faith & Freedom, Baptists and the American Revolution, Echoes of Yesteryear (Volume 1-3), Found Fully Faithful, Her Knight in Shining Armor, Let God Write Your Love Story, Men on Fire, Modesty: An Issue of the Heart, Not I But Christ, Thriving As A Busy Mom,* and *Our Blessed Book* — a practical study on the inspiration, preservation, and translation of Scripture into the English language.

The Garraways have been blessed with four children, David, Jonathan, Alyssa, and Julianna. They make their home in Washington, Iowa, and are based out of Marion Avenue Baptist Church.